Elizabeth Elton Smith

The Three Eras of Woman's Life

SALZWASSER
VERLAG

Elizabeth Elton Smith

The Three Eras of Woman's Life

Reprint of the original, first published in 1859.

1st Edition 2022 | ISBN: 978-3-37513-047-3

Verlag (Publisher): Salzwasser Verlag GmbH, Zeilweg 44, 60439 Frankfurt, Deutschland
Vertretungsberechtigt (Authorized to represent): E. Roepke, Zeilweg 44, 60439 Frankfurt, Deutschland
Druck (Print): Books on Demand GmbH, In de Tarpen 42, 22848 Norderstedt, Deutschland

THE
THREE ERAS
OF
WOMAN'S LIFE.

A NOVEL.

BY

ELIZABETH ELTON SMITH.

BOSTON:
T. O. H. P. BURNHAM,
148 WASHINGTON STREET.
MDCCCLIX.

THE

THREE ERAS

OF

THE LIFE OF WOMAN.

CHAPTER I.

It was a glorious day in autumn. The sky of unsullied blue glowed like a sapphire. The universal air was filled with stillness. Not a breeze whispered,—not a bird flapped its wing. It was the triumph of repose,—when the undying energies of man slumbered for a moment,—when even the conflict of his passions was suspended. Beautiful, melancholy autumn! whose ruddy ripeness whispers of decay; whose richest teints mingle with "the sere and yellow leaf," as if the lusty year had toiled through youth and manhood for wealth which overflows, just when waning life indicates that the power of enjoyment is passing away.

A small grove of noble chestnuts threw its kindly shadow over a house of modest elegance. Sheltered from the fierce beams that darted from the south, the weary wayfarer gazed on it with a longing eye, as a nest of domestic comfort. And in that spot the dearest household charities had flourished; it was the home of a widow and her only child.

But now an awful visitant was there. Death had laid his hand on the beloved, the revered, parent. For *her*, time had sounded his last note, and she was whispering her dying counsels in the ear of the fair creature who knelt by her side. Pale as the young face was, which was turned upward, now to the dying mother, now to heaven, it was glorious in its rare beauty. Sorrow and watching had dimmed the brilliance of its colouring; but the eye of holy blue, the noble brow, the polished forehead, the glittering hair displaying its golden luxuriance as it hung neglected and unbound—were still there. It was the face of an angel in its beauty; but the feelings, the sufferings of a mortal were marring its brightness.

The last words,—the last blessing were spoken; the long, lingering, faint embrace given; the last prayer breathed;—and the spirit had departed.

Not a whisper broke the terrible stillness. The fair girl's head lay on the bosom of her mother in a sleep that seemed not less profound. The moment so long expected, but for which the loving are never prepared, had arrived, and she yielded to the overwhelming might of the stroke it inflicted.

It was many months before Catharine Vernon was again able to take a part in the business and cares of life,—longer still before she could comprehend the entire change that had taken place in the circumstances which surrounded her. She awakened at last, as from a long slumber that had been disturbed by painful dreams. Her acquiescence in all to which others had prompted her had been so perfect, that volition not only seemed, but was, actually suspended. Her being was absorbed in one intense consciousness; she knew that the mother beloved beyond all earthly things was gone for ever, and she cared not to look abroad upon a world, which, in the bitterness of her anguish, she felt must to her henceforth be a desert.

It was a sense of pain,—of privation,—of discomfort, of which she at first became sensible. Words of consolation, of advice, of reproof, reached her understanding, and came with a cold chill upon her heart. She missed the free breath of the country,—the shadowless sunbeam,—the song of the birds,—the accustomed perfume of flowers,—all the lovelinesses which had surrounded her own happy home. Her eye ached as it gazed on a line of tall houses rearing themselves opposite to her,—at once irregular and monotonous—as she strove to inhale the evening breeze at the open window. She was in that most unpicturesque of all possible situations,—a denizen in the principal street of a second-rate provincial town.

Hitherto she had wept little, but now her tears fell freely, as she came to comprehend, in all its details, the extent of the evil which had overtaken her. She became alive to the daily inconveniences resulting from it, and she began to recall the dying counsels of her mother, to reflect deeply on them, and to shape out for herself such a mode of existence as they had recommended. She felt that, although she might shrink from certain annoyances which would inevitably torment her during her residence in her present abode,—the house of Mr. Revely, her uncle, and the rector of the principal parish of Golding Magna,—it would be wise to remain there for the present, until indeed she could endure to return to the dear cottage, and find such a companion as her own youth rendered desirable. As her mind regained its composure, she began to delight in modelling all her actions according to what she knew to be her mother's principles and modes of judgment. She resumed her ordinary avocations as a duty,—irksome, indeed, at first, for the voice that had directed, encouraged, commended, was silent, and the bitter tears of regret frequently interrupted her progress. But as she persevered, she gained fortitude; she began to feel the gratification of bringing into practice precepts which had so often been inculcated, and which her reason acknowledged to be correct. No human mind is insensible of the value of a conquest over self, and gradually Catharine, if not cheerful, was as calm and as self-controlled as usual.

As she regained her composure, and as the death of Mrs. Vernon gradually became more remote, the family of Mr. Revely emerged from their strict seclusion, and returned to their ordinary habits. They began to receive those friendly visits which formed the limits of their social enjoyments, and to expect that Catharine should not avoid the presence of their guests. This was a grievous trial, but she resolved to endure it patiently; and repetition, if it did not render less irksome a thing which, in itself, possesses all the materials of ennui, at least made it less painful.

Catharine had that sort of respect for her relative which a conviction of perfect integrity must necessarily inspire, but which is compatible with disapprobation of every other component part of character and manner. She had the firmest confidence in the sincerity of his piety, but she condemned its demonstrations as mistaken and sectarian. There was in Mr. Revely a strong leaven of pride mingling with the austerities of his life, and trampling, like the cynic of old, on the pride of the world out of greater pride. The same desire of distinction, that in warriors and legislators resolves itself into ambition, had constituted him the head of a religious party, and inspired much of the zeal and industry which had obtained the reward he coveted,—the reputation of being the most popular preacher of the neighbourhood. His own disciples considered him *almost* inspired; but occasional hearers, whose observation was not obscured by the spirit of sect, accused him of considering the impression made by the *teacher* rather than the doctrines he inculcated; of intruding the *man* on the attention of his congregation, more than became the *minister* who was speaking of the great things that pertain to eternity. The very spirit of the peculiar doctrines he inculcated destroyed that charity which others deem the loveliest characteristic of Christianity,—universal love. He could not allow of salvation beyond *his* pale without inconsistency. If, as he maintained, faith in *his* doctrines was absolutely essential to salvation, it followed, that the vast multitudes who doubted were necessarily in a hopeless state. Arguing thus for ever in a circle, he had come to be persuaded that only what *he* preached was the great immutable truth of God; and the results of this belief were apparent in the contraction of his sympathies with his fellow-creatures. He loved to dwell on the mysteries of the Apocalypse, and to give a form and hue to the events of the unknown future. Of late, indeed, his discourses had been more abundant in mystic shadowings forth of things to come, and many thought that his mind indulged in reveries of this kind more than was compatible with its preserving a healthy state. Nor was he ignorant of the opinions that were abroad, but he compared his accusers to those who had also said to Paul, "Thou art beside thyself;" and he felt pride in exciting reproach, as being the necessary consequence of "the offence of the cross," and a manifest token of the truth of his doctrines,—an involuntary testimony of the enemy.

Mr. Revely was naturally a proud man. He had been distinguished at college, and this distinction had strengthened "his besetting sin." As he had gradually become the coryphæus of a party in a country town, where pre-eminence of any kind is particularly gratifying to a spirit *that would not be second at Rome*, because it is continually making itself felt, his manner assumed a more dictatorial tone, and his opinions were delivered with the dogmatism of one who, himself considering them infallible, expected that others should receive them with the meek acquiescence of disciples. The temper of his wife encouraged the arrogance of his own. She was one of those women who like to do nothing without direction; who feel it desirable to be able, in case of unfortunate results, to lay the onus of their actions on injudicious counsel. It is astonishing that a person so undeniably clever as Mr. Revely should feel pleasure in being constantly looked up to by his wife, for the intellectual stature of that man must have been very diminutive to whom Mrs. Revely would not, or ought not to have looked up. The enemies, at least the satirists, of Mr. Revely said, that the lady had three attractions which had captivated her husband: a very pretty face; a very easy temper; and an intellect, the size of which would allow him to consider his own colossal. Perhaps this was as nearly matter of fact as satire can be.

One daughter was the result of this well-appointed union; and the education of this child was the only point on which Mrs. Revely had ventured even to whisper an opinion that was not in perfect accordance with her husband's. She did not see the wisdom of his teaching the little Rachel so much Greek and Latin as he thought fit to do, and she absolutely essayed woman's final appeal—*tears*,—when she saw her poring over a mysterious-looking volume filled with diverse shapes and signs, which betokened something almost as dreadful as the black art, and which, in fact, was a volume of Euclid. Notwithstanding this violent opposition,—and, considering the usual position of the parties, it *was* violent,—Mr. Revely persevered in teaching, and the little girl in learning, with the concession of a moderate portion of time to Mrs. Revely, who employed it in impressing the mind of her gentle child with the importance of the recondite mysteries of needlework "in all its various branches." Neither parent had either the power or the inclination to instruct her in those accomplishments which are called *modern, par excellence.* Without knowing a note of music, she "warbled her native wood-notes wild" with a voice that might have charmed a very fastidious ear, coming as it did, especially, from a mouth that was perfectly beautiful. Luckily for Rachel, her mind was of the best natural *matériel;* and she passed through the ordeal of a most injudicious education without becoming either a fool or a pedant.

CHAPTER II.

Mr. Revely was not Miss Vernon's only near relative. Her father's sister, Lady Darley, was not only a person of rank, but one actually living in the very first monde,—a circumstance which may, perhaps, explain why so little intercourse had taken place between her and the family of Colonel Vernon. A woman of fashion has no particular predilection for cultivating the acquaintance of relatives who only come under the class of gentlemen by virtue of a commission, and who support the rank by the economical management of a moderate income.

Mr. Revely had, however, thought it a matter of duty to communicate to Lady Darley intelligence of the event which rendered her niece completely an orphan. He had addressed his letter to her house in town, but whether it had reached her was a point of considerable uncertainty;—she might be in the country,—she might be on the continent. The Morning Post never adorned his breakfast-table;—the whole fashionable press,—yea, the whole fashionable world, might have been swallowed up by an earthquake,—without exciting in him a single regret;—the first never amused,—the last never interested him. He considered the class so hopelessly and unredeemably reprobate, as to be beyond the reach either of reproof or counsel,—and in that conviction he would have deemed it a waste of mental anxiety to be concerned for any individual member of it. He thought it quite as probable that Lady Darley had read his letter and thrown it aside, as that she had not received it. It was quite in keeping for one of her caste to care for no earthly being who did not minister in some way to her comfort or consequence. Catharine Vernon was not in circumstances to do either; she was at a distance, and she was only just not poor. Notwithstanding Mr. Revely took all possible pains to impress the mind of Miss Vernon with sentiments such as his own, she clung to the hope that she should yet hear something from her aunt. Lady Darley had occasionally written to her mother,—had even sent some trifling tokens of regard, which, though "few and far between," implied her sense of the propriety of bestowing some sort of notice on the widow of her brother. Catharine's reasoning, therefore, was not very inaccurate, when she inferred that she would extend an equal degree of proper notice to her brother's orphan; and, just as her hopes were on the point of extinction, and Mr. Revely's suspicions had been confirmed into positive certainties, a letter arrived which very materially changed their relative states of mind.

"My dear Catharine,

"I have been for so many months at Paris, at Geneva, at Florence, at Naples, at Rome, that it is not surprising I only read Mr. Revely's letter yesterday; the wonder is, that my people should have preserved it so carefully. I need not express my concern at hearing of the dreadful loss you have sustained, nor weary you with commonplace condolence and consolation. Time, I hope, has done much for you; it always is the best comforter of the young. I assure you I feel for you, but expressions of sympathy are not my forte, and, knowing so little of you as I do, it is not likely that, if I made any, they would be adapted to your particular taste or sentiments.

"I thought a great deal of you last night, and had a thousand plans in my head for your benefit. I should like to have you with me for a short time, that we might see how we suit each other; but at present I really am not able to manage it. I have two nieces of poor Lord Darley's to bring out this next season, and they have been so badly cultivated that I shall have a world of trouble with them. I mean to keep them with me at Darley until April, in a kind of preparatory training, but you see you could be of no use in the world in such a case;—you would be in their way, and they in yours. I could not undertake to produce three girls at once. These two are heiresses, so I hope to have them off my hands shortly, and then I shall turn my thoughts to doing the best I can for you, who, after all, are my own nearest relation.

"At present, I think it would be advisable for you to remain with Mr. Revely. He is the rector of a large parish, and of course of some consequence where he is. This makes his house an eligible abode for you, and I should suppose it must be sufficiently cheerful—more so than your former home at the cottage. Clergymen in provincial towns generally see a good deal of society, such as it is.

"I shall be glad to hear from you at any time. Your letters, addressed to me at my house in Grosvenor Square, will always find me sooner or later. Tell me all about yourself. Are you thought to resemble your poor dear father? He was considered a very handsome man in his day;—your mother was a beauty in *hers*, so that you have hereditary claims to be well-looking. Are you a brunett or a blonde? What colour are your eyes and hair?—Are you tall?—Do you play,—or sing,—or draw?—What is your age?—I fancy you must be nearly nineteen. I was no older when I married poor Lord Darley. I suppose you have read a page in the romance of life: that is to be expected from a young lady living in the country. By-the-way, has Mr. Revely any sons?—I have known very little of him, and that through your mother's letters.

"Cherish youth of appearance as much as you can; consequently avoid fretting, which remedies no earthly evil. I hope to be useful to you at no distant period. Meanwhile, believe me Your affectionate

"PENELOPE DARLEY.

"P.S. Purchase with the enclosed any pretty little ornament you have longed for, and denied yourself on prudential motives. Say something proper from me to the Revelys."

Catharine read this letter more than once, and, when she had done so, she was as little able to determine whether she ought to be pleased or displeased with it, as at the commencement. She rather suspected that it was not very satisfactory, because she detected in herself an unwillingness to show it to Mr. Revely, a thing which she nevertheless felt ought to be done, for, although addressed to her, it was, in point of fact, a reply to *his* letter. The enclosure mentioned in the postscript was a bill for fifty pounds—a very considerable sum to Catharine, and one which, considering her near affinity to the donor, she thought she might accept with great propriety. Moreover, she was gratified by the delicacy with which the present was made, and she trusted that the generosity of Lady Darley would cover the multitude of sins which Mr. Revely might see or fancy in the letter itself.

Mr. Revely perused it very deliberately, refolded and opened it again with equal deliberation. Catharine had armed herself with patience to listen to his comments, but she had not calculated on having to endure one of the *silen-*

ces for which he was famous, and which, by assuming a certain expression of countenance, he contrived to render less tolerable than the keenest satire or the severest rebuke. At length, after a preparatory interjection, he addressed himself to speak.

"So!" he began. "My curiosity is gratified; I have read the letter of a very fine lady. I have had a glance into her mind. I have seen how *she* talks of death; what she thinks,—no, I wrong her,—what she does *not* think—of its tremendous consequences. Pray, Catharine, how old may Lady Darley be?"

"I never saw her since I was quite a child; I have not the least idea of her age."

"It would be charity to suppose her yet in her teens,—but that, I fear, is hardly possible. *You*, her niece, have nearly run through them; I do you the credit, Catharine, of believing that *you*—with all your errors, your defects of education—are incapable of writing such a letter under such circumstances. Lady Darley is your father's sister—his *only* sister; we will allow him the advantage of ten years' seniority, which is an ample allowance, and which—I believe my calculation is correct—will place her on the elderly side of forty: you have great cause for thankfulness that you are saved from the risk of association with her. Good springs from evil here as elsewhere. Her unfeelingness is your preservation."

"I think my aunt hints at some future opportunity of receiving me," said Catharine, with the inexplicable unwillingness to hear one of whom she herself hardly ventured to think favourably, but who still *belonged to her*, condemned by another.

"The life-time of Methuselah would not suffice to pay off the debts with which worldly people like Lady Darley load the future," returned Mr. Revely. "They silence the importunities of the thing they call conscience, by satisfying the debts due to the present with bills payable at an indefinite period. They console themselves for neglecting every possible duty, by the resolution of performing all with the most scrupulous exactness hereafter. Miserable self-deceivers! The human mind cannot conceive a delusion more fatal than this. At present Lady Darley has to take two wealthy relatives to Vanity Fair; when she has disposed of them, she will have some other equally laudable and indispensable occupation, which will furnish an excuse for declining to encumber herself with the poor orphan of her brother."

"But her offer was voluntary. I have understood from you that your letter did not even hint at an expectation, either on your part or my own, that she would receive me into her family."

"Granted: but her ladyship, you perceive, or ought to perceive, has herself to satisfy as well as us. People are troubled with certain feelings of the fitness of things, which sometimes disturb the repose of the most inveterate selfishness."

"At least she has sent me a substantial acknowledgment of our affinity," said Catharine, blushing deeply, partly from that feeling of degradation which all delicate minds experience in accepting a pecuniary obligation, and partly from being compelled to rest her defence of her relation on so ignoble a foundation.

"Ostentation!" said Mr. Revely, with a sneer.

"There was no ostentation in her manner of making the gift," said Catharine, who felt herself here on safe ground. "The most fastidious cannot accuse my aunt of displaying any indelicate desire of making me sensible of my poverty. There are many ways of doing the same thing, and, I confess, I am weak enough to like that elegance of manner which so much lightens the weight of obligation to the person on whom it is conferred."

"Yes," said Mr. Revely, with a deeper sneer; "elegance is a very specious thing; a showy varnish, which makes an execrable picture pass, among the vulgar, for a fine painting. Young ladies educated as you have been attach a high value to it, which, with your permission, I, in my poor judgment, shall continue to think factitious."

Catharine extended her hand for the letter without any reply, for she thought, whatever errors of feeling or principle could be contained in so few lines, had been visited by sufficiently severe criticism. Mr. Revely was not by any means weary of the subject. In *hunting down* a motive, an action, a person, that he disapproved or condemned, he boasted a perseverance which knew no weariness, a tenacity which clung to its victim until it was completely crushed. He did not quit the theme of Lady Darley's enormities because he thought he had expended enough vituperation on them, but because he suddenly recollected that he had a matter of importance to discuss with his niece.

"The cottage," said he, referring to her beloved home with an abruptness that shook Catharine's composure; "I have found a tenant for it."

"A tenant!" said Catharine, turning pale.

"Yes, an invalid, who will take it as it stands,—furniture,—every thing, for a year; perhaps longer. I will be answerable that the house will not be injured while in his possession. The garden, perhaps, may be converted to useful purposes instead of idle ornament. He has no relish for harmless follies, and thinks time too precious to be wasted on the culture of a parterre."

"I do not want a tenant," said Catharine, gathering courage as she felt the attack on the tastes of her mother. "I shall not let the cottage."

"Not let it!" said Mr. Revely, either feeling or affecting great amazement. "Is your income so large that you think yourself justified in relinquishing a fair opportunity of increasing it? Charities,—the holiest objects, the noblest ends of man's being, demand your assistance. *Gain that you may give.*"

"The cottage is my home," replied Catharine, firmly. "No other place can ever be so dear to me as that. I shall be a better, a wiser person there than elsewhere;—the whole house will breathe of my mother;—the very breeze will echo her lessons;—every tree, every flower, is associated with her precepts;—to *me* the place will be holy with blessed recollections. It is filled with my mother;" and she wept, but gently, like one beginning to feel "the joy of grief."

"This is, I conjecture, *sentiment*, about which I have, in the course of my life, heard much, but which is too sublime to be within the limits of my poor comprehension. If you will condescend to talk plain sense, or to favour me with opinions founded on reason, perhaps I may be able to reply to them; and, as this is a matter of business, it may be as well to make the trial."

"I will not trouble you with my reasons," said Catharine, recovering her calmness as she felt the irritating sarcasms of her uncle. "I believe I have the right of acting for myself, and I shall endeavour to do what I am convinced my mother would have approved. It was her wish that, as soon as I regained tranquillity, my home should be the cottage; as if she could still speak to me,—as if she could witness my obedience,—I shall obey her."

"That one so young should voluntarily relinquish the protection of her uncle to become the independent occupant of a house of her own, is likely, I should think, to provoke the censure of the most charitable," said Mr. Revely, with great asperity. "It never could have been my sister's desire that you should be the solitary inmate of the cottage."

"You are right. When declining strength warned her that the time of our separation approached, she obtained the promise of her dearest friend, Mrs. Warren, to reside with me; and, in some sort,—Oh, could it be!—to supply her place to me. At present Mrs. Warren's arrangements compel her to remain in London; but she is willing and anxious to redeem the pledge she gave to my dearest mother."

"I have not another word to say," replied Mr. Revely, evidently angry. "My sister's sentiments differed in many espects so widely from my own, that I ought to feel no surprise at her taking a step so evidently injudicious as this."

"*Not* injudicious," said Catharine, with dignity; for there were times when the haughty spirit of her father predominated over the sweet gentleness she inherited from her mother. "She was aware that, from my habits and education, my residence in your family would inflict on you a series of annoyances which you might find intolerable, or subject me to restraints which it would be impossible to endure. To avert this evil,—to prevent the almost necessary consequence of such dissensions as would imbitter the existence of all parties, she took the wise resolution of procuring for me the countenance of Mrs. Warren's protection in an independent abode. Surely it was not injudicious to desire, that the affection which ought to exist between her only brother and her only child should be maintained in all its integrity."

"If our habits and modes of thinking are so opposite that proximity will bring offence, one of us must be right and one of us wrong," said Mr. Revely, with less severity. "It is hardly too much to say, that from my years, my profession, the nature of my studies, my opportunities of judging, *you* are more likely to be in error than myself;—in error where error is fatal!"

"Errors of conduct may be fatal; but errors of opinions, examined with caution, received with humility, supported with meekness,—are these also fatal? Surely not;—or we should not find such diversity of judgment among men distinguished equally as the best benefactors of their species."

Mr. Revely was too angry to trust himself to reply, and he quitted the room.

Catharine, now that it was over, was glad she had had the opportunity of opening her future intentions to Mr. Revely. She had been sensible that he was considering her a permanent inmate in his family, when, in point of fact, she meant to be only a temporary guest, and she felt satisfied that nothing could have been better timed than this éclaircissement. Moreover, now that Lady Darley's letter had been condemned with a severity far greater than it deserved, she read it with increased gratification, detecting in it a vein of kindness which had escaped her, until Mr. Revely had insisted on the intense selfishness apparent throughout. Altogether, Catharine retired to rest this night with a lightened heart, and was actually indulging herself with believing that Lady Darley would find an opportunity of inviting her, and wondering when the invitation would be made, when she sunk into the profound slumber of youth, health, and innocence.

CHAPTER III.

A PROLONGED residence in Mr Revely's family did not render it a more agreeable sojourn to his niece. She endured, with more impatience than was consistent with her generally sweet temper, the prospect of being compelled still to remain there for an indefinite period. The business which kept Mrs. Warren in London was a suit in chancery, and that ominous name boded, to Catharine's apprehension, nothing but long and lingering delay. She endeavoured to be resigned to the inevitable evil; but resignation is a virtue not quite so easy in practice as it appears to be in theory, especially when the person called upon to exercise it has the assistance neither of sympathy nor occupation. Her present mode of life completely prevented the regular prosecution of her usual pursuits. Mr. Revely eschewed all music but sacred, and refused to admit a piano-forte into his house, on the plea of its being an interruption to his studies and a temptation to idleness. She had either too much ambition or too much humility to paint. She knew that the excellence which it costs men of genius a life-time of toil to attain, could never be within *her* reach; and she had learned to appreciate the beauties and glories of the wonderful productions of this art with too keen and accurate a taste to endure the feeble and abortive attempts of her own pencil. Mr. Revely's library was, as might be expected, composed of the works of authors of the gravest and gloomiest kind; and, though she did not dislike the occasional perusal of them, she found it impossible to make them her constant mental aliment without endangering that cheerfulness which she had been taught to believe a duty. She could contemplate with awe and delight the grandeur and the terror of a thunder-cloud, but she preferred, as the "ethereal canopy" that was to spread over her daily home, the calm and azure sky. At the time of her removal from the cottage she had had no thought of providing for her own future comfort, and she shrank from the prospect of visiting the small library there, unsupported by the presence of Mrs. Warren. Mr. Revely would not, probably, decline such a commission, but to *her* that spot was holy ground, and she could not endure that the selection of books made by the judgment of her parents should be condemned in terms so severe and unmeasured as, she was quite sure, her uncle would employ when he examined them.

At the house of Mr. Revely, as has been already said,

parties of his own immediate followers occasionally congregated. But these social meetings, far from being a refreshment to the mind of Catharine, either wearied or disgusted her. She shrank from hearing those mysteries of which she scarcely ventured to think but with breathless awe, discussed with the freedom of people admitted into the innermost recesses of the sanctuary,—mysteries which "the cherubim veil with their wings." It appeared to her irreverent to mingle these "deep things" with the tide of gossip that would occasionally flow. She disliked the invidious spirit which supported its condemnation of a man's avowed principles by prying into the privacy of his domestic life, to drag out the errors that had sullied his hearth-stone. She abhorred the uncharitable *sectarianism* which seemed to believe the strength of its own party increased, in proportion as it detected the weakness or failings of those who cherished different principles. Nay,—she perceived that even the links of that brotherhood of belief and prejudice which would seem to bind together the whole sect, were not strong enough to defend the members of it from the attacks of each other. The absent were the prey of the present. If they were indignant when their avowed adversaries assailed an individual of their party, and united to protect him, they felt no compunction in themselves becoming the assailants. Catharine suspected, that if the world had not elevated them into importance by its attacks, and confirmed their opinions by opposition, schism among themselves would rapidly have dissolved the confederacy. Nevertheless, the leading principles which distinguished them were common to all;—all united in abjuring every ordinary recreation, and in wearing an air of austerity and gloom, as if smiles were the livery of sin. The females affected the most rigorous plainness of dress; thereby indicating the humility they professed, even as they passed by one whom they believed, in their own phraseology, not "to be of them," with eyes superciliously cast down or averted, and an air of affected compassion, which seemed to say, "Stand by, for I am holier than thou!" The same ostentation of religion arrayed them in untrimmed bonnets and sober-coloured garments, that enlarged the phylacteries of the Pharisees of old. In their discourse they cultivated a "religious Patavinity," which, though sometimes found in unison with excellent principle, never coexists with good taste. But with them a peculiar style of expression was the Shibboleth that distinguished the "true Israelites;" and if they did not affect all the peculiarities of the Puritans, they still retained many of their phrases, and would, perhaps, have doubted the most self-evident truth itself, if conveyed in the ordinary language of modern times.

"Is this 'note of preparation' for one of your usual parties this evening?" said Catharine to her cousin Rachel, as she saw the maids busy in altering the arrangements of tables and chairs, and giving the room as uninhabited an appearance as possible.

"Yes," replied Rachel; and then in a few moments she added, with a slight blush, "it is something more than an ordinary meeting of our friends;—Mr. Fulton, papa's new curate, is expected to arrive to-day, and his old acquaintances are assembling here to meet him."

"These tea-drinkings are one of the miseries of human life in country towns," said Catharine, with a sigh, seeing nothing in the expected presence of Mr. Fulton that was likely to alleviate the accustomed dulness of the party. "I wish Mr. Revely, who insists, generally, on the improvement of every moment, would consider, as I do, visitations of this kind one of the idlest wastes of time that the imagination can conceive."

"Occasional recreation is necessary," said Rachel, mild ly; "these meetings are at least harmless.—sometimes useful and instructive."

"*Every thing that is received, is received according to the capacity of that which receives:—the sun melts wax, but hardens the earth,*" replied Catharine, translating the French aphorism. "Happy you who can find amusement or instruction where I experience only ennui or disgust. You are the bee who can extract honey from the meanest flower,—and I am the fastidious nightingale who sings only to the rose."

"You wrong yourself. I am not ignorant how much—how very much—there is among us to be lamented and condemned. To a stranger eye the evil must appear of formidable magnitude, but I am so used to it that I can be contented to avert my eyes from it, and to fix them resolutely on the vein of pure ore that does, despite the ruggedness of the surface, run through the mass. Besides, habit, you know, blunts the moral sense."

"It does, and I would rather that mine should *not* be blunted."

"But have not our meetings *some* good, even in your perception? Can it be mere waste of time to discuss and elucidate what is mysterious,—to ascertain what is doubtful,—to compare prophecy with fulfilment, and, from things that *have* been, to trace the analogy of the predictions concerning things to come? Is this useless?"

"To some minds, mischievous," replied Catharine; "I speak with reverence. Is the tone of dogmatism proper to man in speaking of divine things? Is it an humble or a trusting spirit which leads him to pry into mysteries into which the angels desire to look? To fix 'the times and the seasons which the Father hath put in His own power?' To fix the occurrence of mighty events in such a year or in such a century, to afford ground for the cavils of the infidel and the derision of mockers? No, dearest Rachel, this is *not* useless—it is worse."

"It is not charitable in you to awaken in my mind doubts, where to doubt is to be wretched."

"Not doubt of the truths of religion, dearest,—only doubt of the inspiration of false prophets: let none of us shrink from examining our opinions from the fear of detecting falsehood in them. Do not let us prefer darkness to light, only because we would not choose to be roused from the fond delusion that the path we are thridding is the one which must assuredly lead to truth. It is not, surely, consistent with *your* character, to prefer a feeling to a principle."

"Of late, my character appears to develop only inconsistencies," said Rachel, with a sigh. "Since I have enjoyed your society, you have awakened in me a world of thoughts and desires, which, if they had a previous existence, nevertheless slumbered so profoundly that, to me, they were as if they were not. You have opened to me a vision of something so beautiful in this lower world,—so beautiful both to the sight and the heart,—that I shrink from looking upon it, lest I should rest satisfied with its glories, and desire nothing brighter than they."

"And therein are the mischievous results of the restraints imposed on your most innocent tastes in childhood and youth. An accustomed eye appreciates these things at their proper value; it is only the novice who invests them with exaggerated and imaginary worth. Why should we, with the melancholy hallucination of Pascal, shut out from our view the loveliness of this fair earth,—that divine work, formed to minister at once to our necessities and to our most innocent enjoyments,—a sojourn meet for the good? Sinful!—What?—'to look through nature up to nature's God?'—To adore the Creator in his works?—To drink in delight and joy from the abundant glories so profusely spread around us?—To revel amid the songs of birds,—the gushing of fountains,—the music of the forest-trees,—the voice of the wind?—To feel gay and happy when a rainbow of flowers absolutely dazzles the eye that rejoices over its beauties?—Or to stand awed, but elevated, when the thick clouds hang heavily over us, and the thunder speaks the majesty of Him 'who tunes its awful roll?' It is an insult to our Maker to avert our eyes from that which he has created expressly for us, and which he himself has pronounced *good*. Our very joy in it is religious."

"It may partake of natural religion," said Rachel; "the belief of a Christian is faith in what is revealed."

"And if your faith be less alloyed than mine, it is not

greater,—more implicit," replied Catharine, earnestly. "My meaning is, that as natural religion is implanted in our minds by our Creator, and associated with our perceptions of the beautiful and the good in his creation as well as in his providence,—being, moreover, by no means contrary to what is revealed, but rather supporting and confirming it, *fitly* if not *necessarily*,—it is not blameable, but the contrary, to cherish the feelings derived from it."

"I remember Mr. Fulton once said something like that, but papa silenced him with a reproof," said Rachel, blushing intensely.

"Doubtless he must be a very sensible person, then," said Catharine, playfully. "And so he is expected this evening, is he? Is he older than Mr. Revely, or younger? Many clergymen have gray hairs who have not benefices."

"Mr. Fulton is quite young; he was papa's pupil before he went to Oxford;—once or twice, during the vacations, he spent a day at Golding Magna, and papa has given him a title to holy orders."

All this was commonplace enough; Mr. Fulton was doubtless just such a young man as the pupil and chosen curate of Mr. Revely might be expected to be; one who would add his quota to the ordinary discussions of the evening; from whom neither novelty nor entertainment was to be expected. Catharine considered every accession of acquaintances of this kind but as an additional grievance, and she prepared to meet *this* evil with the resignation due to what is inevitable.

Dinner had just finished when a post-chaise drew up to the door. Mr. Revely rose hastily;—"Fulton is arrived," said he, and he went out to welcome him. Mrs. Revely desired the servants to bring back the more dainty part of the meal, on a tray, and Rachel kept her seat in silence, by turns blushing to a teint of the deepest carnation, and anon, paler than the sickliest lily. Catharine, meanwhile, looked and felt precisely as she did before.

Presently Mr. Revely ushered in his guest, who shook hands with Mrs. Revely with an air of friendship, and with Rachel with something of *empressement*. When Miss Vernon was named to him he made a most unexceptionable bow, and Catharine perceived that the new curate had at least the advantage of as fine a person as the eye could desire to gaze upon. His manners were modest, and, if tainted with that academical rust which always hangs about a man who has just kept his terms, not awkward. Catharine's recollection of her father, one of the most elegant men of his day, was the standard by which she judged of all manly proprieties; and when she applied her infallible rule to Mr. Fulton, she suspected, and with truth, that the friction of society would presently smooth down all the little angularities that were at present objectionable.

CHAPTER IV.

The perfection of female education, in this our day, is supposed to consist in the acquisition of the greatest possible quantity of such accomplishments as may best serve the purpose of display. It is the fashion to play and sing, to speak two or three of the languages of Europe, and to dance with grace; and it *is* the fashion, because men of fashion choose their wives from the accomplished class. *Marriage* is the great end for which girls submit to a drudgery that might, if otherwise directed, have sufficed to attain the highest honours of learning; this is the mighty recompense by which mothers and governesses stimulate indolence and encourage talent. Marriage may, in a twofold sense, be called the *end* of all this toil; for it is not only its object, but its termination. The goal once reached, ambition becomes extinct. Acquirements gained by painful industry are relinquished as distasteful, or pursued as an occasional amusement. The dissipations of the world abundantly occupy time; and that vacancy of the mind and abundance of accomplishments coexist more frequently than is generally suspected, is a truth which the husband begins to find gradually dawning on his understanding when knowledge comes too late.

Catharine Vernon, though the inhabitant of a cottage, had not been a recluse. In the society of her mother she had visited France, Switzerland, and Italy, improving her knowledge, and enlarging her ideas. She possessed, in an eminent degree, that least cultivated of all accomplishments, the art of agreeable companionship. She conversed well, because she had within her the elements of conversation, ideas. People complain of the emptiness of "female talk;" they must search a little farther to arrive at the root of the matter, and then, peradventure, they may complain of the emptiness of female heads; well would it be if complaint produced remedy.

If half the pains that are expended on teaching girls to play well, sing well, and dance well, were employed in teaching them to talk well, men would have companions instead of playthings, and might learn to be domestic. As it is, they seek elsewhere for that mental recreation not to be found at their own firesides; and the wife, feeling herself deserted, becomes a warning, when, with happier training, she might have been an example.

Mr. Fulton was not long in discovering the superiority of Miss Vernon to the class by whom she was surrounded, and he manifested sufficient gratification in her society to make her a partner in his discovery. For her part, she was very well satisfied that he should think it worth his while to contribute to her amusement so much as he contrived to do. His lodgings were near, and he was always a welcome visiter to Mr. Revely, who, if he suspected him of a slight inclination to overvalue mere human learning, and to admire the frothy literature of the day, believed that his example, his admonitions, the influence of the party of which he was expected to be a leader, nay, even the mere lapse of time, would bring amendment. Mrs. Revely, secure of her husband's approbation, begged the young curate to look in on them whenever he had a leisure moment; and, if a slight blush and a gentle smile were symptomatic of gratification, he must have been quite satisfied that his presence was by no means distasteful to the fair daughter of his rector. He had the amplest assurance that his visits were agreeable to Miss Vernon, for she frankly assured him how sensible a relief they were to the generally unvarying monotony of their domestic circle; and she always accepted, with the most grateful thanks and the most gracious smiles, the loan of some of the best of the modern standard writers, who figured on the shelves of his small library. Nothing could have been a greater addition to her comfort than this unexpected supply of literature, when the want of it had been so severely felt. It was mid-winter, and the dulness of the long evenings would have been intolerable, but for the frequent presence of Mr. Fulton and his agreeable books. His manner seemed to diffuse an ease through the whole circle, that contrasted delightfully with its ordinary formality. The conversation still had too frequently a tinge of controversial divinity; for in Mr. Revely's society no man, whatever might be his wishes or his will, could possibly avoid polemics. Mr. Revely had no other idea of conversation than as being the vehicle of argument or exhortation. It was a great proof of Mr. Fulton's tact, that he had address enough to keep general topics so much in the foreground as he contrived to do.

In another point of view, Mr. Fulton was a very useful person. Although the season was severe, Catharine and her cousin were too confirmed pedestrians to relinquish their walks for any less cogent reason than "the pelting of the pitiless storm." Not having the fear of red noses before their eyes, they had no objection to face a cold north-easter and enjoy the sunshine of a clear frost. With Mr. Fulton as a cicisbeo, they penetrated into regions hitherto unexplored, quitting the suburbs of Golding Magna, and visiting the neighbouring villages. The influence of the fresh air, the feeling of escape from the long dismal streets of a smoky town, gave a brilliant animation to Catharine's manner, which, if it excited no envy in the pure heart of Rachel, nevertheless cost her keener pangs than her experience had ever yet proved. She would not have had Mr. Fulton admire Catharine less; she only wished that her own endowments had been less humble. And yet, even as she admitted that wish, she shrank from its impiety, and strove to tutor her spirit into that content which had hitherto been its blessed aspect. She listened to lively discussions between her companions on topics of which she was utterly ignorant, and sometimes she asked herself whether they perceived her silence. They did *not*. The calm and sustained cheerfulness of Rachel never rose into vivacity; her ordinary manner was so quiet, that two lively people engaged in interesting topics might be excused if they did not always remember her presence. Moreover, she possessed in so remarkable a degree that "most excellent thing in woman," a gentle voice, that it required perfect stillness around to hear its tones; and what with the rushing wind, the hum of human life that rose from the neighbouring town, and their own gay laugh, there appeared no space for the voice of another. Sometimes Rachel detected herself in condemning Mr. Fulton's gayety as exceeding the decorum incumbent on his profession, and in wondering what judgment her father would pass on him. Then again all her anger, if anger it was, was subdued by the sudden pause which indicated their remembrance of her, and which was made for the purpose of some kind inquiry after her feelings, of evincing some good-natured consideration for her feebler constitution, offering to walk more slowly, or to return, if she were sensible of fatigue. And when Fulton, looking on her pale cheek, persisted in attributing its paleness to weariness, and compelled her to accept the support of his arm, all her disapprobation—all her secret murmurs, were converted into such halcyon feelings of satisfaction, that her whole being seemed to bask in the sunlight of perfect happiness.

"Really," said Catharine, after one of these walks, "Mr. Fulton is a delightful companion; I allow that his agreeableness is the more striking from its contrast to the dulness to which we are generally exposed; nevertheless, he would be considered superior to the general run of young men anywhere."

"He is superior," replied Rachel, as quietly as usual.

"It is really wonderful, considering how much you and he have been thrown together,—how much attraction exists on both sides,—that he has escaped falling in love with you, as it is called."

Rachel smiled faintly, and blushed intensely, her consciousness of which increased her discomposure.

Catharine thought it by no means unnatural that any

young lady, more especially such a one as Rachel, should blush under so grave an accusation as having just missed a lover,—so she went on:—

"He appears to have a good deal of imagination, considering the sect—the party—to which he is said to belong. Perhaps you have not vivacity enough to please him?"

"Or, more probably, he has never thought of me at all," said Rachel, striving to smile.

"And yet," pursued Catharine, unmindful of the remark, "people are said to love from the force of contrast rather than from resemblance. Your composure and calmness would harmonize admirably with his vivacity. Your different tempers would diffuse the most agreeable light and shade over the domestic picture: I cannot conceive how so obvious a probability never came to occur."

Rachel recollected that she wanted something in her own apartment, and went away rather more rapidly than usual.

CHAPTER V.

"The church was quite crowded last night," said Catharine to Mr. Fulton, as, together with Rachel, they proceeded on one of their usual walks.

"Yes; it was a large congregation," said Mr. Fulton, endeavouring not to appear too much gratified.

"You are clearly in the way of becoming a popular preacher," continued Catharine.

"You jest,—or you flatter," said Mr. Fulton, who was too young to be aware of all the intellectual, all the moral degradation, that may consist with such popularity.

"I never jest on such topics," said Catharine, gravely, "and I flatter on none. In this instance you will at least acquit me, when I tell you, that the mere fact of a clergyman's pulpit-popularity would not inspire me with the slightest possible respect for his talent. Tolerable vehemence,—some gesticulation,—a pleasant voice,—and a little showy declamation, have sufficed to procure notoriety, and will achieve it still, if you are ambitious of the distinction."

"But the converse is not true; it does not follow that because a clergyman *is* popular, he either declaims or has no talent."

"A most unfair inference, to which I plead not guilty," said Catharine; "but—frankly—I could not help recalling a passage from Chalmers when we returned home last evening."

"It will be kind in you to give me the benefit of it," returned Fulton, rather discomposed.

"'If he, the preacher,'" Catharine gave the desired quotation—"'on the one hand, proudly conceiving the sufficiency to be in himself, enters with aspiring confidence into the field of argument, and thinks that he is to carry all before him by a series of invincible demonstrations; or, if his people, on the other hand, ever ready to be set in motion by the idle impulse of novelty, or to be seduced by the glare of human accomplishments, come in trooping multitudes around him, and hang on the eloquence of his lips, or the wisdom of his able and profound understanding, a more unchristian attitude cannot be conceived, nor shall we venture to compute the weekly accumulation of guilt which may come upon the parties when such a business as this is going on. Surely it were a sight to make angels weep, when a weak and vapouring mortal, surrounded by his fellow-sinners, and hastening to the grave and the judgment along with them, finds it a dearer object to his bosom to regale his hearers by the exhibition of himself, than to do in plain earnest the work of his master.'"

Mr. Fulton walked on in thoughtful silence for some minutes. Rachel at one moment was indignant with Catharine, and at another admired the frankness and the strength of mind which had enabled her to utter such wholesome truths, at the risk of offending a companion whose society she ac knowledged to be most acceptable.

"I feel the reproof," said Mr. Fulton, at length breaking the silence. "I see my danger; and you will allow it is a great virtue in me to kiss the rod when I am smarting from its effects."

"I gave you credit for so much candour," said Catharine. "I did not for a moment suspect that you would be displeased with truths which were uttered only from a desire to warn you that you might possibly sink far below yourself when you believed you were 'soaring into the empyrean.'"

Mr. Fulton's cheerfulness rose immediately above the temperate point. He exulted in the interest Catharine appeared to take in his real welfare, as the effect of sentiments similar to those of which he himself was conscious. He dwelt on the subject in the hope of hearing more of her opinions, to which he might pay the practical homage in his power. He quoted Cowper's description of the unworthy pastors of the flock, Jeremy Taylor, the "saintly Herbert," as he has been called, and others on the same subject. Catharine listened, smiled, and acquiesced; but, having no desire to try the effect of her eloquence or her beauty, left the quotation from Chalmers to make its own impression.

And it did make an impression, the effects of which were visible to Mr. Revely, who took occasion to warn his curate of the danger not only of being, but of seeming to be, lukewarm.

He advised him sedulously to cultivate the gift that was in him; assured him that while reasoning only addresses itself to the cultivated, the appeals of eloquence are the surest means of reaching the feelings of the ignorant. He admonished him that the present age, so miserably distinguished for infidelity, or, if not positive infidelity, laxity of religious belief, required to be roused by the Boanerges of the pulpit, as much as they who lived at the apostolic era. To all this Mr. Fulton agreed, but he said he was resolved to content himself with plainer discourses, lest the indulgence of an ornamented or impassioned style should prove a temptation to him. He acknowledged that he felt and dreaded his own weakness; shrank from the possibility of being more anxious about the garb in which his doctrines were clothed, than about the doctrines themselves. He had endeavoured to impress on his mind, as a guide and an admonition, the short description given by Julian Pomerius of the difference between a good and a bad preacher;—"The one seeks the glory of the Saviour by explaining doctrines in familiar discourse. The other uses the utmost strength of his eloquence to gain reputation. The latter handles trifles with elaborate language; the former elevates a plain discourse by the weight of his thoughts." He deprecated the idea of lukewarmness, but, at the same time, he thought it necessary to watch over himself, lest, by endeavouring to assume an appearance of extraordinary zeal, he might not only deceive others, but become at length the deceiver of himself.

Mr. Revely was by no means satisfied with this view of the matter. He knew perfectly well by what means his congregation was kept together, and he was quite sure that the calm and chastened discourses of his curate would not tend to preserve its integrity.

People who were used to stimulants were not likely to be satisfied with plain meats. Mr. Revely was too secure in his own pre-eminence to dread a rival; but he desired that his mantle should fall on a successor likely to keep his flock together, and many circumstances existed which seemed to point out the probability of Mr. Fulton's being that successor. He therefore proceeded with his exhortations, and enforced on his curate the absolute necessity of being, in this particular, "all things to all men." Mr. Fulton listened patiently, but said nothing, and—which Mr. Revely considered a very objectionable interpretation of his silence—he continued to preach in the same temperate strain as before.

The parishioners of St. Andrew's were very much of the opinion of their rector. They thought the manner of the young curate in the pulpit wanted that *divinus afflatus*, that unction, to which they were accustomed. Habituated to strong excitement of the feelings, they condemned appeals to the judgment as cold and tame. Probably they did not dislike the truth, but they required that it should be accompanied by pathos. Without being aware of it, they were liable to a charge from the slightest imputation of which they would have shrunk with dismay, that of requiring that the plain simplicity of the gospel should be exchanged for a certain dramatic effect which interested their imaginations. Moreover, they preferred a limited range of topics, and desired that the sublime consolation of the ATONEMENT should be insisted on to the exclusion of the *example*. They liked controversial points to be fully and vigorously asserted; they considered the enforcing of precepts which "they who run may read" as supererogatory. The curate was sinking in the estimation of his congregation; and his talents, which had formerly been at a premium, were now rapidly falling below par.

Mr. Fulton was sensible of his loss of popularity, and he felt it keenly. He began to suspect that Mr. Revely's view of the case was sounder than Miss Vernon's, and that people must be fed with that mental aliment which they prefer. He considered that as it is in the highest degree essential to impress truth on the human mind, that is a blameless, nay, a laudable art, which presents it in the form in which it is likely to prove acceptable. He suspected that he had allowed his attachment to Catharine to warp his judgment, and he condemned himself for permitting any less sacred sentiment to interfere with his paramount duty, or the faithful discharge of his ministry.

Mr. Fulton was young, and he had hardly yet attained the elements of that most mysterious knowledge, the knowledge of his own heart. He was sincere in his views, but he did not detect the fact that he was moved alternately by two antagonist principles, love and ambition; that, as the opinion of Miss Vernon had produced one effect, so the opinion of the multitude was now about to opérate in producing a contrary one.

To those who are moving in a more extended sphere,—whose mind is to affect the destiny of empires, whose voice is to resound in senates, whose name is to gild the page of history,—that must indeed appear hardly worthy of the name of ambition, "that last infirmity of noble minds," which covets the applause of the coteries of a country town, and sees distinction in the small fame of a provincial preacher. Nevertheless, Mr. Fulton had talent, but, like the mass of mankind, he was the creature of circumstance. He did not belong to the giant few who triumph over it. He had been educated for the church, nay, within yet narrower limits, for a sect in that church, and he had learned to consider it *an object* to be a leader of that sect. What we have long deemed desirable,—what we have exerted ourselves to obtain,—assumes an immense importance in our eyes; we view it through the magnifying medium by which we see every thing connected with self. As colour does not exist in things themselves, but in our perceptions of them, so the hue—the magnitude of our pursuits, is not inherent in *them*, but in *us*. No man sees the object of another in the same exaggerated proportions in which it appears to himself. In the view of an indifferent observer, the giant phantom so eagerly pursued shrinks into a dwarf of most unshapely form. Each throws his own pebble into the stream, and amuses himself with observing how circle after circle grows and enlarges round it, and dreams that he alone is troubling the waters, forgetting that his neighbour a little higher up the current is engaged in an occupation precisely similar, and is subject to the same delusion.

That Mr. Fulton loved Miss Vernon, had long ceased to be a matter of doubt to himself; but it was equally certain that he had no design of relinquishing that hope of distinction—after its kind,—which had animated his studies ever since he had been of an age to desire it. He flattered himself, moreover, that Catharine would pardon a deviation from her own opinion when she saw the results; for it was a point of belief with him that no woman is insensible o the distinction of her lover.

CHAPTER VI.

THE world of Golding Magna,—that is, the subjects of Mr. Revely's *imperium in imperio*,—were not generally admirers of Miss Vernon. They had the instinctive consciousness of being inferior to her, and they suspected that she was quite as sensible of the circumstance as themselves. They naturally disliked a person who, as they expressed it, was among them, but not of them; and, as naturally, they were anxious to detect something in her conduct or principles that should sanction such dislike.

It is expecting too much of human nature, considering its gregarious propensities, to believe that in a country town it can escape the infection of being scandalous. People live in so small a compass,—they revolve in so narrow an orbit,—that they cannot reasonably be supposed capable of moving without looking in at their neighbours' doors or windows. Moreover, activity is essential to some constitutions, and where a large space is not afforded for its exercise, it will travel repeatedly round a smaller one. It would have been strange if anybody at Golding Magna had been ignorant what everybody had for dinner; or if everybody were not as well acquainted with the contents of anybody's wardrobe as anybody himself. Anybody too was, or pretended to be, tolerably well acquainted with everybody's feelings, views, and principles; it was fair, therefore, that everybody should claim the prerogative of examining into, and reporting upon, anybody's actions.

In such a community it could hardly be expected that the frequent rambles of the new curate, made constantly in the society of Miss Vernon and Rachel Revely, should escape animadversion. All who listened to Mr. Fulton's sermons believed themselves so far invested with the character of patrons, as to be entitled to require that his proceedings should be shaped after their peculiar standard of propriety. It was quite self-evident that people would not gather together, as this trio did, for the mere purpose of walking about the country. Mr. Fulton was young,—youth was the season of divers temptations,—principally of that of falling in love. Rachel Revely, with her simplicity, was no match for such a person as *that* Miss Vernon, who seemed to fancy she had a right to supreme consideration; the foundations of which right it would puzzle a person of common sense to be able to discover. If Mr. Fulton were to fall into the snare, the church would lose a pillar. And this conclusion being decisive, it followed that all possible exertions should be made to prevent such a loss.

One of the most zealous of Mr. Revely's followers—a lady who, if she did not spend all her goods in feeding the poor, was at least so generous as to bestow the greater portion of her time in distributing tracts among them and most gratuitous advice—was the first to open his eyes to the melancholy probability of his curate's making a most unsuitable union, and ultimately degenerating into the foulest apostacy. Mr. Revely was slow to admit a supposition so contrary to his own private wishes—so destructive of certain airy castles, *chateaux d'Espagne*, which he had ventured to erect for the future. He assured his informer that Mr. Fulton was a young man of the soundest principles, and little likely to be insnared into being "unequally yoked" with one who, if not a decided unbeliever, was yet far below the standard of those "professing godliness." He admitted the weakness of human nature, and the strength of temptation, but he acknowledged that he had certain private reasons for supposing that, even in a worldly and human point of view, Mr. Fulton was better guarded than it was at present convenient to avow.

But though Mr. Revely thought fit to profess such a belief, he was very far from being in that comfortable state of certainty regarding the issue of the matter which he affected. He was sufficiently aware of the power of beauty to feel that his niece's attractions were considerable, and that those graces of manner which he, in his private judgment, condemned, were not likely to be particularly disagreeable to a young man, let his principles be as strict as they might. Mr. Revely felt that, if his curate should really yield to the potency of her attractions, the dearest earthly hope of his own heart would be wrecked; and it is justice to him to add, that he conscientiously believed that the union he dreaded would be pregnant with mischief of the most fatal kind to a young man of Fulton's prospects. He was convinced that neither the education, habits, nor opinions of Catharine, qualified her to be the wife of a clergyman professing those peculiar and ultra-Calvinistic tenets which Mr. Fulton was pledged to maintain and advocate. In his phraseology, instead of being a guide and a helpmate for him, she would be "a let and a hinderance." Indeed, so palpable did this appear to himself, that he believed Mr. Fulton must absolutely be ignorant of the real nature of Catharine's religious belief, if he could for an instant entertain the idea of uniting himself to her in the indissoluble bonds of matrimony. And he thought it prudent in him to terminate that ignorance immediately.

It was not difficult to lead Catharine to the avowal of her own opinions. She abhorred religious controversy, but she did not shrink from maintaining sentiments that had not been adopted without careful and serious examination. A mind trained to such habits of inquiry as hers, was not likely to adopt important opinions without endeavouring to acquaint herself with all their bearings and tendencies; and her integrity would not endure that any persons should give her credit for agreement with themselves, through her want of courage to avow wherein she disagreed. If Mr. Fulton and herself had not yet been at issue on the great questions which divide Christians, it was the result of his avoidance of sectarian points rather than hers. Having enjoyed the loveliness of the external world together, it was impossible that two minds, both imbued with sincere religion, could avoid recurring to Him "who made it all;" but *piety did not lead them to polemics*. Mr. Revely was quite correct in his suspicion, that Mr. Fulton was not aware of the extent of the disagreement between himself and Catharine on controversial points, but he was probably wrong in the inference he drew as to the effects of his being enlightened. Love achieves every day triumphs over obstacles much more invincible than this.

Mr. Revely soon found an opportunity of proving the degree in which his calculations were accurate. Mr. Fulton had joined their evening circle; he was reading a paper in the Quarterly, which excited much notice everywhere at the time of its publication, and excited it especially in the religious world. It was a very able, if not a very charitable attack, on the professors of the opinions of Calvin; and, as Mr. Fulton read, Mr. Revely animadverted. As the remarks of the writer became more severe, the animadversions of Mr. Revely became warmer, until at length warmth amounted to indignation, and indignation, exasperated to the highest point, displayed itself in an *anathema maranatha*, the intense rancour of which filled Catharine with horror.

Mr. Fulton laid aside the book, and began more temperately to disprove the assertions and invalidate the arguments of the writer. He agreed with Mr. Revely that it was lamentable so much talent should be displayed in the heinous attempt to overthrow the truth of the gospel.

"Does the writer make such an attempt?" said Catharine. "I have not so understood him. He is labouring rather, I apprehend, to build up Christianity than to pluck it down. I always supposed the Quarterly was peculiarly the review beloved by the high-church party."

"Your mind is darkened," said Mr. Revely, gloomily; "the writer of that article, whoever he may be,—peer, poet, or prelate,—seeks to pervert the truth, and to uphold a 'damnable heresy.'"

"But suppose," said Catharine, mildly, "as it is a question of *opinion*, that yours should be partly wrong and his not altogether right?"

"Far be from me such a supposition!" said Mr. Revely, with fervour. "*Opinion* is not the word to express the sol emn doctrines I hold and teach."

"But, after all, our private interpretation of every doctrine is but opinion," said Catharine, firmly, but with the modesty befitting her age; "thus at least I have been taught by her I most revered; and what mortal shall venture to say his opinion is infallible?"

"I do," said Mr. Revely, emphatically; "for mine is based on the immutable truth of revelation."

"But he who, on these particular points, arrives at conclusions directly opposite to yours, derives them from the same source; he believes, as you do, in the inspiration of the sacred volume, but his interpretation differs. And as this diversity is permitted, we have authority to infer that it answers wise and useful ends. While I see a person spending a life in works of love to mankind and reverence to God, can I venture to pronounce him an outcast from divine mercy because on certain points of belief, even such as to my apprehension are of immense importance, he differs from me? Much has been left in doubt, much in darkness. But the injunctions to universal love and charity, and the virtues of truth and meekness, which follow in their train are alike understood by all, and admit of no diversity of sentiment."

"I very much doubt, Catharine," said Mr. Revely, his gravity approaching to sternness, "whether you have read the Thirty-nine Articles."

"Yes, I have."

"Perhaps you do not receive the points contained in them as essential to salvation?"

"Undoubtedly not. I venerate a great number of dissenters, and believe them to be on the high road to heaven."

"And what, then, if I may presume to ask so very independent a young lady, are your points of faith?"

"Hope in the unbounded mercy of God; fear of his justice; conviction of imperfection and sin; thankful acceptance of the propitiation offered; in the quaint but expressive language of the Common Prayer-Book, 'newness of heart and life,'—and universal, active love to man."

"A very compendious creed," said Mr. Revely, with a sneer particularly unsuited to the topic.

Catharine did not reply. She had, on former occasions, been betrayed by the warmth of disputation into saying more than she meant;—into opposing opinions which were not perhaps quite incapable of assimilating with her own perceptions of truth. She had resolved—and she did not now swerve from that resolution—to avoid all extemporaneous polemical discussion. She found how much candour, consideration, forbearance, should be brought to the combat,—qualities which probably are incompatible with a controversy of the moment, begun of course by accident, and irritated by opposition;—what had been but dry leaves producing flame by friction. Her silence did not, however, terminate the subject. Mr. Revely was on a favourite topic, and he was quite as well pleased to harangue as to argue. In analyzing the article "under revision," as reviewers say, he had an opportunity of enlarging on the condition of the reprobate, which his gloomy imagination was capable of depicting in terms of terrific grandeur and energy. He loved to pause in the midst of moral storm and darkness. His weapons of persuasion were the terrors of the Creator, not his mercies;—his wrath, not his love. His eloquence was more than usually overwhelming on this evening, for he had been animated by the opposition of Catharine, gentle as it was. And as she listened to the sonorous periods his voice—*ore rotundo*—enunciated;—as she watched his glowing eye, his kindling cheek, his almost apostolic countenance, she felt wherein lay the power of his preaching, and paid him, in her heart, the homage due to a sincerity of belief in the faith he professed, that could not be surpassed. The bigoted Calvinist was at the same time the devout Christian, and Catharine thought he had never appeared more worthy of reverent regard than now, when, whatever might be the primary object exciting his eloquence, she at least was a secondary one.

But Mr. Revely's design in exhibiting Catharine to Mr. Fulton as the holder of opinions so opposed to his own, was not attained. Mr. Fulton was startled as much by the courage of the avowal, perhaps, as by the liberality of the opinions themselves; but he was not alarmed,—not deterred. He regarded woman as so much "the weaker vessel," that he considered it by no means an Herculean labour to bring over Catharine, gifted as she doubtless was, to the adoption of his own tenets. Without a tinge of coxcombry of any kind, Mr. Fulton had the consciousness of talent; and when he looked down on female intellect, from what he believed, *in relation to her*, the unapproachable height of his own, he was inspired neither by arrogance nor vanity, but operated on solely by habit and education. He could most conscientiously have said with Milton's Adam,

> ——"Well I understand in the prime end
> Of Nature her th' inferior, in the mind
> And inward faculties which most excel."—

And he hardly needed the counsel of the angel,

> ——"Be not diffident
> Of wisdom; she deserts thee not, if thou
> Dismiss not her, when most thou need'st her nigh,
> By attributing overmuch to things
> Less excellent, as thou thyself perceiv'st.
> . . . . Weigh her with thyself;
> Then value. Oft-times nothing profits more
> Than self-esteem grounded on just and right
> Well managed; of that skill the more thou know'st,
> The more she will acknowledge thee her head,
> And to realities yield all her shows."

There was one of the party,—pale, patient, silent,—not a looker-on, but sustaining the most painful character in the drama that was on the eve of evolvement, who penetrated more accurately into the real state of things than Mr. Revely had done. It was his timid, pious, beautiful child. She, with all a woman's power of endurance, preserved an appearance of tranquillity, while stretched on a rack of mental agony, the more intense because she felt that a single groan was forbidden. None suspected how the pulse throbbed beneath that serene brow;—with how martyr-like a resignation that placid smile was worn. She was now reaping the fruits of that power of self-control, the acquirement of which had been the great lesson of her life. She saw that the man of her own early choice—the love of her childhood, the vision of her youth—was lost to her for ever. She beheld the dissolving of her bright dream, and looked upon the dark desolation that was to succeed it. She felt the withdrawal of the sunbeam that had so cheered her dull existence. She estimated the extent of her father's disappointment; for, if her own hopes had not sprung into being at his command, they had at least been cherished by his avowed desire for their fulfilment. Rachel was not ignorant of one single figure in the aggregate of the torments that awaited her; but, in the strength of woman's fortitude, she endured, "and gave no sign."

CHAPTER VII.

Mr. Fulton enjoyed the blessing of independence. No worldly motives rendered the indulgence of his passion for Miss Vernon imprudent. Her competence, united to his, would, in his situation in society, be affluence. He saw nothing to make it imperative on him to undertake the painful task of subduing his attachment. Whatever might be the errors of Catharine's opinions, religion, at least, was the foundation, and it would be a delightful task to love to win her from those errors. That Mr. Fulton still delayed his proposals did not result from any doubt of his own sentiments, but from his uncertainty regarding hers. He was not so complete a novice as to believe that the pleasure she evidently and avowedly felt in his society, was necessarily the effect of such a preference as he wished to inspire. He trusted—he hoped—that there might be a deeper feeling for him than friendship, concealed beneath that suavity of manner to which an early initiation into various modes of society had given its polish. But he doubted,—and until he obtained some farther insight into her heart, he hesitated to take that decisive step which, he believed, would so materially influence his future destiny.

Catharine herself was susceptible of no desire so strong as that of quitting her uncle's house,—the wearisome monotony of its circle became less supportable daily. She loved her gentle cousin truly, but she knew there was no community of feeling between them. Rachel, with her limited views,—her abundant *learning* and little *knowledge*,—could not comprehend the requirements of a mind constituted as Catharine's was, and was incapable of appreciating the extent of the privations she was compelled to endure. She sympathized sincerely with trials which she was able to understand; but there were others, and those not the least severe, of the existence of which she had no idea. Catharine's thoughts began to dwell very much on her aunt, Lady Darley, on whose evident forgetfulness of her niece Mr. Revely never failed to insist, when enumerating the delinquencies of people of fashion. The more he indulged in vilifying or aspersing her father's sister, the more imperatively Catharine felt herself called on to defend her; until at length, by a natural mental process, she came to regard her aunt as an innocent, excellent, and unoffending person, whose chief offence against Mr. Revely consisted in being superior to him; and, having at length brought herself to this state of feeling, she found so much satisfaction in it as to be unwilling to relinquish it, even when days—weeks passed away, and she heard no more of Lady Darley, and felt that "hope deferred maketh the heart sick."

Spring was commencing,—a very early spring. It was "the ides of March," but the air was balmy, and a world of fragrance breathed from the hedges, beneath which violets and primroses were yielding their sweetness to the almost "desert air." Catharine had never yet felt so glad to witness the departure of winter, with its slate-coloured days, that harmonized too well with the sober grayness of Mr. Revely's family;—its long wearisome evenings adding deeper gloom to the gloomy discussions that were the incessant occupation of the hours. Youth can scarcely believe that dulness and sadness can linger through the joyous influence of the gayer seasons of the year,—the bright promise of spring,—the rich maturity of summer,—the golden harvest of autumn. She indulged herself with imagining that Mrs. Warren's interminable chancery-suit would almost immediately "die the death" of the chancellor's decision,—that she should return to the lovely home of her youth,—a return to which had, under the happiest auspices, and from the most glorious scenes, been always hailed with delight. In short, she trusted that the period of her deliverance from Mr. Revely's house approached; and in that belief she thought his religion less bigoted, his censures less severe, than they had formerly appeared to her. Even Mr. Fulton,—always an agreeable, always an acceptable companion—was invested with higher claims to her regard; and the unconscious softness of her manner added to the delusion under which he was labouring, and threatened to accelerate a crisis which must add considerably to the irksomeness of *her* position.

In the country, going to church is an event. To the followers of a popular preacher, it has an interest over and above that of being an act of solemn public worship. Their curiosity is excited to know in what new point of view he will exhibit their favourite doctrines;—whether he will give them a sermon worthy of his former reputation,—whether he will rise above or sink below his ordinary level. Then, descending from generals to particulars, they begin to indulge in sundry speculations on the probability of the lapse of some hitherto zealous follower having reached his ears, and of his gathering food for instruction and admonition to his flock from the fall of one member. They bethink them that certain families have been less regular in their attendance than heretofore, and they anticipate the merited rebuke that will probably be *insinuated*. In a word, few who have not been among them can even conjecture the variety of thoughts and expectations that mingle with higher, and purer, and holier impulses, in the congregation of a popular preacher in a country town, about to assemble for the ostensible purpose of divine worship.

Among such a congregation the presence of a stranger is always an event, that is, with the qualification of the stranger's being clothed "in goodly raiment, and wearing a gold ring." It was the second Sunday in March,—gilded with brighter sunshine than had yet shone on the spring,—that Mr. Revely, from the eminence of his pulpit, descried in his own family pew a stranger, whose port and bearing, having "no sign of profession" about them, were sufficiently indicative that he was "not mechanical." He was a very aristocratic-looking personage, apparently just verging on middle life, but not a day more advanced. Every thing in his appearance was in excellent keeping;—plain as the most fastidious exclusion of ornament could render him;—intent on the business to which the church-bells had summoned him, as a thinking man ought to be, who knew that it related to eternity. Rachel, with a heart too preoccupied by one sole dominant idea to have even an eye for aught of his sex besides, was scarcely conscious of the presence of a stranger; but Catharine, "whose bosom's lord sat lightly on its throne," saw, with a glance, that her new *vis-à-vis* was an inhabitant of a very different sphere from that in which *she* was moving. He breathed of another atmosphere, and she could not help being conscious that it was refreshing to look upon one who bore about him all the signs and tokens of belonging to a higher race of beings.

The stranger was reverently attentive to the whole service, which, to say the least of it, evinced good taste, if not right feeling. He remained in the pew after the rector's family had quitted it, although Mrs. Revely lingered to the latest possible moment; for she was vain enough of her husband to desire the unknown to understand the relation in which she stood to the powerful preacher to whom he had been so attentively listening. But, though "with reluctant step and slow," she at length felt it incumbent on her to depart, as she saw the stranger look towards Mr. Revely as if he did not intend to quit the church without obtaining the honour of his acquaintance.

Mr. Revely never invited guests on Sundays. He disapproved altogether of Sunday visiting; his family, therefore, were the more surprised, when they saw him return home accompanied by the object of so much speculation in the bosom of more than one of its members. Yet he did not appear to be particularly pleased with his companion. There was a cloud on his brow, sadly at variance with the smile which occasionally settled on his lips. He slightly named "Sir Greville Cleveland" to Mrs. Revely, and then, leading him to Catharine, said, "This, Sir Greville, is my niece, Miss Vernon;—Catharine, in Sir Greville Cleveland you see a friend of Lady Darley's."

Sir Greville made a bow of the most unequivocal good-breeding, and he followed up the favourable impression it was likely to produce by touching on innumerable particulars relative to Lady Darley, assuming that they must be more interesting to her niece than any other topic. He contrived to inform Catharine of every point on which she might be supposed desirous of information, without for a moment seeming to imagine that the correspondence between Lady Darley and her niece had left the latter ignorant of any thing. He rather alluded to circumstances and facts than related them, but his allusions were so full and explicit, that Catharine felt how much she was learning of her father's nearest relative that had never reached her ears. Sir Greville described Lady Darley as not only one of the most favoured votaries of fashion, but actually a leader in that circle beyond whose pale there is no refinement. But he spoke of her not only as a woman of fashion. He had too much tact—was too deeply read in that extensive volume, human nature—to place the chief attraction of the person whom he wished to represent in the most amiable colours, in precisely that point which he judged his attentive hearer least likely to estimate or comprehend. He had much to say of Lady Darley's graces,—her accomplishments,—her knowledge,—every thing likely to attract one who was a novice in the world, but had evidently understanding enough to appreciate the value of all those elegances with which he designed to kindle her imagination. Catharine had acquired manner in the best society of the continent; and the constant companion of a mother, intellectually endowed as hers had been, was not under the influence of *mauvaise honte*. Conscious, too, of her own superior talents, she had no other diffidence than was consistent with the charm of her youth. There was more courteousness in her manner than deference;—as if, while she evinced every possible consideration for her companion, she never forgot her self-respect. Sir Greville, with the readiness of a man of the world, adopted that tone which Catharine's dignity seemed to require. He threw aside the air approaching to patronage and condescension which had slightly marked, on his first entrance, his sense of being *only* in a parsonage, and in the society of its inmates. He listened with the profoundest attention to all Catharine's remarks;—gazed, not oppressively, but earnestly, on her beautiful countenance, as if he could read a history in her eyes; and on taking leave, offered to call on the morrow for any letter she might have to send to Lady Darley, whom, he said, he was quite sure to see on his way to town, for she was one of a party staying at the house of a friend, which he should join for a few days previous to the general migration to the metropolis.

Catharine accepted his offer, without exactly knowing why she should write to Lady Darley, who had vouchsafed no reply to her last letter, and yet pleased with the excuse for doing so afforded by her unexpected interview with one of her aunt's friends. However, Sir Greville received her acquiescence as a matter of course;—said he should quit Golding Magna at noon on the following day,—trusted he should not compel Miss Vernon to abridge her communications, by giving her so short a notice,—communications which he was sure his friend, Lady Darley, would receive with all the pleasure they were calculated to bestow;—he would call for the letter at the latest possible moment, *en passant*, on his way from the town;—made his adieux to Mrs. Revely and her daughter with the politeness of a gentleman whose claims were too well authenticated to render hauteur incumbent on him;—thanked Mr. Revely for having presented high and sacred ideas to his mind under a new point of view, and enabled him to feel that he had spent at least one hour of that day in a manner on which it would always be satisfactory to dwell,—and was gone.

"Plausible!" said Mr. Revely, who, however, not only looked, but was gratified by a compliment so delicate and judicious. "A visit of inspection, I conjecture. Sir Greville Cleveland does not sufficiently feel the imperative duty of making the sabbath a day of rest, to have submitted to the dulness of eight-and-forty hours at Golding Magna on that account."

"As the matter is doubtful, let us give him the benefit of a charitable interpretation," said Rachel, the very personation of the charity she inculcated.

"What motive could he have? It is not probable that he deemed us of sufficient importance to influence his movements," said Catharine, rather curious to learn the extent of Mr. Revely's knowledge on the subject.

"Lady Darley appears to be a person of weight with him; and such as he is," replied her uncle, with his usual cynicism, "he may have been commissioned to ascertain what pretensions her niece may have to be enrolled among the privileged to whom she extends her favour. He avowed that, knowing where Miss Vernon resided, he was desirous of paying his respects to her father's daughter; he had a recollection from his boyhood of Colonel Vernon, he said;—and he was not less anxious to make the acquaintance of his orphan, because she was the near kinswoman of his friend Lady Darley. Enough has been said; let us dismiss from our minds the visit of Sir Greville Cleveland, and turn them to topics more befitting this holy day."

And Catharine strove to obey this injunction, but she found the forbidden subject constantly recurring. She could not avoid indulging in conjectures of what might be its results;—she could not prevent the air, person, manner, voice of Sir Greville, from occupying her imagination so strongly, that she recalled every word, every look, of the interview with him. She had rarely seen a man so gifted with personal advantages,—so adorned with that perfect good-breeding which unites ease with dignity. She had never before understood so clearly what was that *air spirituel et noble* so much talked about, and so seldom existing. She felt that she had seen a realization of one of those visions which had haunted her solitary musings, and she enjoyed the same kind of mental delight as a lover of the picturesque may be supposed to experience, when some glorious landscape bursts on his eye, after having long gazed on arid sands and barren rocks.

She rose early the following morning to prepare her letter. Catharine hitherto had felt the luxury of "wielding the pen of a ready writer," but her ordinary powers availed her nothing now. She experienced the difficulty of addressing a person with whom she had no personal acquaintance,—who dwelt in a circle the precincts of which she had never entered,—who could not be expected to be interested in her particular feelings,—and with whom she had no sympathy except on one topic, and that not now to be dwelt on—her father. She shrank from enlarging on the unsuitableness of her present associates, because she felt it to be ungenerous to complain of those who, with all their peculiarities, were substantially kind to herself, and because she dreaded affording Lady Darley the slightest grounds for believing that she wished to be indebted to her compassion for the means of escaping *désagrémens* that were inseparable from a residence in Mr. Revely's family. It was easy to express her regret that she heard so seldom from the only sister of her father; to assure Lady Darley of her desire to show, by every possible means, her affectionate regard for so near a relation; and to say that she could not allow Sir Greville Cleveland to leave Golding Magna without the letter of which he had volunteered to be the bearer, and which he had kindly assured her would be acceptable to her aunt. Thus much was written, and, meager and brief as it was, Catharine felt that it must suffice, for she did not possess that feminine accomplishment of filling three sides of a sheet of letter-paper about nothing.

Punctually at the hour of noon Sir Greville Cleveland's carriage drew up at the door of Mr. Revely, and its master once more entered the chillingly neat parlour of the rectory. Courteous to all, his conversation, during the half hour he remained, was principally directed to Catharine, and she wondered, on reflection, how in so short a time he had contrived to touch on so many topics, and to draw from her so many opinions. He was rather more animated than on the previous day, and Catharine believed it was impossible to possess a countenance more resplendent with the light of intellect. All the favourable impression made by his first visit was abundantly confirmed—was more than confirmed—by his second. And when he departed, and all the excitement of his presence had passed away, Catharine could not conquer the feeling of desolation with which she turned to the dull realities—the gloomy commonplaces—that surrounded her, or cease to regret that she too was not "among the Athenians."

CHAPTER VIII.

NOT an hour after the departure of Sir Greville, Mr. Fulton called to fulfil an appointment made some days since to walk to a neighbouring site, whence the view was sufficiently beautiful to be esteemed a lion in the county. It was, moreover, the scene of innumerable pic-nic parties during the summer,—a species of gregarious amusement, proverbially begun in folly and ending in matrimony,—in such cases, probably, the greatest folly of all. The season at present was too early to render it probable that their ramble would be disturbed by meeting a group of this kind, and both Rachel and Mr. Fulton were anxious that Catharine should enjoy the scene with those indispensable accessories—quiet and leisure. The weather was beautiful,—balmy and clear, as an early spring always is, and they set forth on their ramble filled with feelings as full of hope as any prospect-fanciers could indulge.

Their walk to the appointed spot, the Park Hill, as it was called, was distinguished by nothing more remarkable than the silence of the parties. Yet this was not observed by any of them. Absorbed in their own reflections, they had not leisure to think of the taciturnity to which they were indebted for the uninterrupted indulgence of their reveries.

But, as soon as they had arrived at the goal they had proposed to themselves, the charm was broken ;—another spell was on them. The glories of the visible world triumphed over the selfish dreams which had been suffered to engross the unseen mind. The companions of Catharine gazed on her to watch the effect produced by the hitherto unknown splendour of the magnificent scene spread out before her while all *her* other senses seemed suspended to give additional poignancy to that of sight.

"And is it criminal to gaze with a glowing heart on glories such as these?" exclaimed Catharine, as her spirit drank in the beauties of the landscape. "Is it wrong that our pulses should beat highly as we contemplate 'the might —the majesty' of this world's loveliness? Surely, Rachel, —surely even *you*, with your disciplined feelings, are made to understand that there is something within us which, with a louder voice than a thousand dogmas, compels us to look abroad upon the creation and to rejoice."

"But to mingle tears with our rejoicings," returned Rachel; "and when we see a barren spot,—or a tree that has been blasted by lightning,—or a relic of the pomp and power of by-gone ages scathed by war, like yonder ruined fortress,—to remember that sin has shed its poison even into the bosom of nature."

Rachel spoke with more fervency than was usual, and Catharine gazed on her as she did so with a feeling of unconditional admiration. She was always pretty ;—*now* she was beautiful. Animation supplied the charm that had been absent,—the stamp of the immortal soul within. Constant self-restraint—unwearied watchfulness over her own thoughts—had impressed on her features a calmness,—a placidity which almost amounted to monotony, and taught the gazer that there might be some weariness even in looking on beauty. But now truth and feeling triumphed over form and rule, and Catharine, loving Rachel truly as her gentleness—her excellence deserved, felt that she had never appreciated her until this moment.

There was also another eye fixed on that unusually glowing countenance,—an eye lighted up with the surprise which a traveller might feel on finding a garden full of beauty where he had been taught to expect only a desert. Mr. Fulton had no conception of the depth of the stream of feeling within, from which this little rill had gushed forth; but he was startled even by what he saw, and a shade passed his brow, which one well versed in the mysteries of man's heart might have failed to interpret.

"You are right, Rachel," said he, after a pause of some duration; "but it is easier to admire than to reflect."

And Rachel, blushing beneath his earnest and approving

eye, looked so beautiful, that even the brilliant being by her side did not cast her modest loveliness into the shade.

Long before the eyes of Catharine had "drunk in their fill" of the beauty of the scene, the flight of time warned them to quit it, and with "reluctant steps and slow" they returned towards Golding Magna.

"I hope, Miss Vernon," said Fulton, as they descended the hill, abruptly breaking a silence of some duration, "your visiter brought you pleasant tidings of Lady Darley."

"Sir Greville Cleveland?—Yes,—very, so far as they went," returned Catharine, with a perfect composure that accorded rather with the hopes than the expectations of the questioner.

"Sir Greville is a relation, perhaps?"

"No,—I never heard of him before;—only a friend of Lady Darley's."

"It must be gratifying to see a person acquainted with your unknown relative."

"It was;—and not the less because Sir Greville himself happens to be one of the most elegant men I ever had the advantage of meeting."

Mr. Fulton coloured to the very temples. Catharine did not observe that evidence of secret emotion, but Rachel did,—as what change in him escaped her?—and her own cheek had more than its ordinary paleness.

"Ah, *nimium felix si sua bona norit!*" said Mr. Fulton, in a subdued voice.

"I hope that is complimentary," said Catharine, with a smile; "but, alas! you know it is 'heathen Greek' to me. Rachel, enlighten me, 'for thou canst.'"

But Rachel at that moment caught a glimpse of a violet on the bank by the roadside, and was so intent on securing her prize that she had a fair excuse for not appearing to hear the request of her cousin.

"Violets! the first violets!" said Catharine, when Rachel, after a long examination of the bank, rejoined her; "the flower of promise; dearer than the rose, because it is a herald of the approach of the 'garden queen,' while *she* reminds us that violets and the spring are gone."

"And yet violets are no fitting emblems of *you*," said Mr. Fulton, in a lower tone than usual; "they love the shade, and I imagine you would choose to bask in the sunshine."

"*C'est selon*," said Catharine; "I am not sure that you are right,—I cannot say that you are wrong. If Golding Magna constitutes the shade of which you are speaking, and violets have any *penchant* for it, they, as you say, are not fitting emblems of me."

"And yet 'the mind is its own place.'"

"We have authority to suppose *not*, when we reflect that our first parents were exiled from Eden as a punishment.

According to your theory, having lost that 'sweet peace which goodness bosoms ever,' they might have been as miserable there as in that terrific abode where the speech from which you have quoted is supposed to be made."

"Your casuistry is ingenious," said Fulton, with a smile; "all experience, however, teaches us that, fortunately for human nature, habit reconciles us to much which, at first view, we are ready to pronounce intolerable."

"It can be only at the expense of blunting one's finer perceptions,—of perverting one's taste,—or, perhaps, even of corrupting one's principles: either effect most undesirable. And, as we are supposing a case in which a choice of situations is offered, my reason would lead me to select that in which there was the least hazard of deadening those keen sensibilities to the true and the beautiful on which I pique myself."

Mr. Fulton sighed. "I fear Golding Magna is not to number you among its permanent residents."

"There is not the shadow of a probability—of a possibility," returned Catharine, decisively. "You are aware that I wait only the release of my friend Mrs. Warren from her tedious chancery-suit to return to my own dear home,—whose shade, by-the-way, violets love, and therefore I will hardly allow that they are not fitting emblems of myself."

"Would it consist with your happiness to reside for ever in the country?" inquired Fulton, anxiously.

"Where the revelry of the birds rings loudest,—where the wreaths of flowers are brightest,—where the air is balmiest,—where the evening is stillest,—where the morning is most cheerful? Yes, oh yes! The city for my visiting-place; the country for my home."

Mr. Fulton walked on in musing silence. "With my interest," he said at length, "it would not be difficult to procure a country living in exchange for the next presentation to St. Andrew's. If—" he looked doubtfully at Catharine, and Rachel, who saw the agitation of his countenance, felt that he was about to say what she could not—dared not—hear. She paused; and Catharine, turning to inquire whether she were fatigued, caught the glance of Fulton, and for the first time suspected the truth.

A moment's embarrassment, and she was at the side of Rachel, directing all her attention, apparently all her thoughts, to her cousin's weariness,—suggesting a few minutes' rest on the bank; and, when Rachel objected, giving the assistance of her own arm, and begging Mr. Fulton to offer his, that they might render the remainder of the walk as easy to her as possible.

Rachel tacitly accepted the kindness of both parties, but she felt that the attempt to speak would be accompanied with tears. Her cheek was so deadly pale that even Fulton, engrossed with the absorbing sentiment that had so nearly been revealed, was alarmed and anxious. He felt the hand that leaned upon his arm tremble violently, but his concern and compassion were so plainly expressed that Rachel had the relief of knowing her secret was not even suspected.

Their progress was slow and silent. None of them had a mind sufficiently at ease to discuss indifferent topics. Each was occupied with the other; but how truly is it said that "man walks in a shadow!" How all unknowing are we of what most concerns us! What treasures of affection for us lie buried in a heart where we do not take the trouble to look for it,—which we care not to unlock; what a world of anxiety and tenderness we lavish on an indifference which will never warm for *us!* The honest and true affection that yearns for us, we reject,—to be ourselves rejected when we in turn become "covetous of love."

Once awakened to a knowledge of the state of Mr. Fulton's feelings, Catharine, with the usual decision of her character, prepared to act. Her reflections shaped themselves thus;—"What am I doing? Do I love this young man? Is my preference of his society,—my approbation of his sentiments,—my estimation of his talents,—love? Could I make, for his sake, any sacrifices of taste or feeling? Should I grieve to see him the husband of another,—of Rachel, for instance? Far from it! How often have I thought that nothing could be more suitable than their union! But why needlessly put these questions to myself? Does love leave one the power of shaping such doubts?"—and she blushed with the prophetic instinct of woman's heart, as she imagined what *love must be.*

And, having arrived at a knowledge of her own feelings, all Catharine's embarrassment ceased. It was her object to spare Mr. Fulton the pain of a refusal, by preserving a calm friendliness of manner which no man could mistake who was not resolved on being deceived; or, if necessary, to relinquish entirely his society,—an act of self-denial which can be appreciated by none but those who have been condemned to the dulness of Golding Magna, *et hoc genus omne*, and know the value of an agreeable associate in such a position.

Mr. Fulton was invited to remain at the rectory for the day,—an invitation he was not slow to accept. Rachel explained her pale cheeks and heavy eyes, by pleading fatigue and headache, and gladly obeyed the prescription of her mother, which enjoined bed and chamomile tea.

Catharine saw what awaited her. In the evening, after dinner, Mr. Revely was always so engrossed, either by reading or writing, as to be beyond the reach of companionship; while his wife, absorbed in the mysteries of cutting out and stitching together, had neither sight nor sound to bestow on her associates. Precisely as the clock struck the appointed hour, she folded up her work,—the accustomed refreshment was brought in,—and with all due decorum she presided at the tea-table. *Steam* would have performed all the functions which denoted her to be a sentient being quite as accurately as she did, and would have been more agreeable, inasmuch as it would assuredly have been incapable of *hearing*—a faculty which Mrs. Revely's associates could never be certain was quite as dormant in *her* as those of sight and speech. Catharine perceived that her resolutions with regard to Mr. Fulton must be carried into effect from that moment, as they had the prospect of being, to all *conversational* intents and purposes, tête-à-tête for at least an hour or two during the evening; and, if Catharine *could* have offered any plausible pretext for quitting the ordinary sitting-room, and so avoiding what must necessarily ensue, she would hardly have been guilty of the weakness of postponing what was inevitable.

Precisely what was to be expected came to pass. Mr. Revely was buried in his book—Luther on the Will,—Mrs. Revely was intent on her work, making two frocks for two poor children out of an old, cast-off, faded gown of her own, —and Mr. Fulton thought that, if it were not quite safe to discuss *love* as to its particular bearing, he might venture to speak of it metaphysically in its generalities.

Catharine, for the sake of being employed, was netting a purse, of which Mr. Fulton admired the mixed colours—black and gray. Miss Vernon acknowledged it was too gloomy for her taste, but the purse was for Rachel, and with her lay either the fault or the credit of the choice. Mr. Fulton naturally fell into some commonplaces about *gages d'amitié* and *gages d'amour*,—sprinkled them with a few classical illustrations not altogether misapplied;—fortunately recollected the fatal centaur-died mantle sent by Dejanira to Hercules, and, by a series of logical sequences, found himself in the midst of a dissertation on the mighty evils which that mightiest of the passions had produced in the world.

Miss Vernon suggested that many other passions—ambition, for instance—had been quite as fruitful in misery to mankind, and objected to the omnipotence which Mr. Fulton seemed to assign to love. It was the dominant passion, she thought, only of particular natures;—an ambitious man, possessed by *his* peculiar demon, might be incapable of it. From all she had read, heard, and seen, she fancied love was very much misrepresented. She thought the exertion of a little common sense might prevent much of the misery supposed to attend it. She could imagine only *one* state of disappointment in which poets had not exaggerated the degree of suffering,—when two people, having loved long and intensely, one still loving had to bewail the faithlessness of the other. It was very much in a person's own power to prevent any other kind of disappointment.

"But," said Mr. Fulton, with great significance, "a man may love one of the brightest examples of female excellence, and be unable to obtain the affections of his object."

"There can be no love without hope, the experienced tell us," replied Catharine; "if a man will resolve not to be blinded by his wishes, he cannot be deceived in the nature of the sentiments with which a woman of integrity regards him."

"Without venturing to flatter himself that he is beloved," said Mr. Fulton, with a voice rather less clear than before, "he may indulge the hope that perseverance,—intimacy,—farther knowledge of him,—may kindle indifference, or ripen esteem, into a warmer sentiment."

"With some, perhaps," replied Catharine, with a smile of perfect frankness. "I have read that, if you would know the heart of others, it is only necessary to look into your own; but perhaps this rule does not hold good in this particular instance. Some women may be won by solicitation, or wearied by importunity, or gratified by incessant and protracted homage, until he who offers the incense becomes necessary to them. I can speak positively only of *my* personal feelings, and I fear I am so hard-hearted that perseverance would have no effect on me. I cannot understand how a woman can leisurely set herself about the task of learning to love any human being,—of endeavouring to see in her suiter such qualities as she wishes him to possess,—such tastes as are essential to her happiness,—which, at the very outset of her acquaintance with him, when neither self-interest nor prejudice warps her vision, she is quite sure he does not possess. A woman in that predicament seems to be about as rational as if she were to shut herself up in a panorama of her own painting, and resolve to believe that *that* was the world."

"Is not friendship an excellent foundation for love?" inquired Mr. Fulton, with a pleading countenance.

"I have seen how the tenderest friendship grew out of love in the case of *one* happy union," said Catharine, with a sigh to the memory of her parents. "Some might, perhaps, be able to answer your question in the affirmative; but, I should think, in the case you suppose, the transition must be imperceptible. What appears unintelligible to me is, that any woman could act on a resolution formally taken to heighten the one sentiment into the other."

"Seeing what you must see," began Mr. Fulton, lowering his voice,—"knowing what you must know—do you mean—"

"To spare you pain," returned Catharine, impressively. "I am sure you cannot misunderstand me. By my frankness I prove to you how much I value your friendship; and now that we are quite intelligible to each other, I shall wish you good night, and pass an hour with Rachel, if she be disposed for a companion." And Catharine, folding up the purse which had led to so important a declaration, retired.

CHAPTER IX.

Miss Vernon proceeded to the apartment of her cousin, who was still awake, and, in despite of the evidence of pale cheeks and heavy eyes, persisted in declaring herself better, and quite sure of being completely recruited by a night's rest.

Catharine sat by her bedside, resolving, notwithstanding Rachel's ill-concealed impatience of her presence, to remain, in the belief that she had that to impart which would prove of greater benefit to the sufferer than the whole contents of the pharmacopœia,—even than rest itself.

"Mr. Fulton is not yet gone," she began; "he has great reason to bewail your indisposition, Rachel, since it deprives him of the society of both of us. Poor man!—he is left to the mercies of Mr. Revely's book, and the frocks for John Brown's children."

"Pray go down again," said Rachel, earnestly; "it must be so uncomfortable for him!"

"Let us moderate our compassion, by reflecting that it is an evil which he has frequently experienced before, and to which he voluntarily subjects himself," replied Catharine. "Besides, it is but a slight penalty to pay for long walks taken with us, and all the cheerful and amusing nothings with which I—not to say we—entertain him."

"Not *we*," said Rachel, trying to smile. "My talent does not lie in being entertaining. I have neither wit nor imagination—"

"Nor sense,—nor acquirements,—nor self-command,—nor gentleness,—nor any other estimable or attractive quality," interrupted Catharine, playfully. "I give you credit for every possible deficiency which you are resolved to enumerate among your sins of omission. Hark! the door closes;—Mr. Fulton is gone. How pleasant the ease and freedom of his bachelor's apartment must be after the formality—forgive me—which is now and then to be found at the rectory!"

"I doubt whether he thinks so," said Rachel, attempting more vivacity than was natural to her, even in her best state.

"The rectory at present is the casket which holds the jewel *he* esteems most precious."

"My fair self, you mean?" said Catharine, composedly. 'Whatever value Mr. Fulton may attach to that inestimable treasure, rely on it, he does not dream of appropriating it."

Rachel shook her head incredulously.

"He knows he might as well 'woo some bright particular star, and think to wed it.' Give Mr. Fulton credit for great discretion. He is not weak enough to waste his sighs on that which is unattainable;" and, wishing Rachel "a fair good night," Miss Vernon left her in the certainty that she had "administered to a mind diseased."

As Catharine had anticipated, Rachel rose the next morning looking nearly as well as usual. She was a little nervous;—an occasional knock at the door startled her, and heightened her colour, and Catharine, who began to be observant of symptoms, saw that she became restless as the day drew to its close without bringing Mr. Fulton. His visits hitherto had been so regular, that an interval of twenty-four hours passed without seeing him seemed an extraordinary absence. Even Mrs. Revely made a remark on it,—a remark actually originating with herself, not an echo of her husband's.

But when two succeeding days elapsed, Mr. Revely began to be alarmed, and resolved on setting forth to look after his curate; declaring, with his ordinary and single attempt at facetiousness, that "if the mountain would not come to Mahomet, Mahomet must go to the mountain."

Mr. Revely remained some hours,—a weary length of time to his daughter, whose suspense was the more painful from her efforts to subdue every appearance of it. And, after all, how little success attended them! She could command her voice to utter an occasional remark,—she could affect to be occupied with her usual employments,—but she could not control the changing cheek—the wandering eye—the nervous start when an approaching footstep seemed to indicate the return of her father—or the sigh when her expectation was disappointed. Catharine saw quite enough to confirm her former suspicions, and to "make assurance doubly sure."

When Mr. Revely did at length return, his communication did not tend to diminish the sufferings of his daughter. He had found Mr. Fulton, he said, so unwell, as to require medical aid; his disorder seemed a severe cold, the effect, probably, of the imprudently long walk which had produced Rachel's indisposition. Quiet and confinement had been prescribed for him; and his illness was of that depressing kind which removed every fear of his disregarding the injunction; he seemed as little inclined, as able, to go abroad or to seek society.

"Ah, poor young man!" said Mrs. Revely, with a sympathizing sigh, "I have always had doubts of him. I don't like that little short cough which always hangs about him. And his complexion—there is a great deal of danger in a good complexion; it is a strong consumptive symptom."

Rachel was intensely pale. Her lips were parched and half open, and she evidently breathed with difficulty.

"I hope there is no danger in Mr. Fulton's present illness?" said Catharine, making the inquiry which she saw Rachel was unable to make. "Judging from his appearance, I should not have thought that he was of a delicate constitution, or likely to yield to a slight attack. Perhaps Mrs. Revely's friendship for him has rather exaggerated those consumptive appearances which, I confess, I never suspected."

"I do not consider Fulton constitutionally consumptive," said Mr. Revely. "A severe cold, attended with a decided cough,—pains in the chest,—headache, and so forth, has often, however, produced decline when one would least have expected it. Aggravated, too, by anxiety of mind,—I thought I knew all Fulton's circumstances and feelings," he continued, rather thinking aloud than addressing himself to any particular person; "I cannot conceive whence arises the distress which even his surgeon perceives. He *can* have no pecuniary wants;—with his income that is out of the question. Can he have any secret follies to bewail? —No,—quite impossible. He has been at Golding Magna these four months, and they would have been matter of public discussion long before this. Has he—Rachel, have you and Fulton quarrelled?"

"I?—Dear papa, no!" said Rachel, the deadly paleness of her cheek disappearing, and a flush of crimson mounting to her forehead. "Why should we quarrel? He has been always so uniformly kind and friendly to me, that—that"—and Rachel, notwithstanding her violent efforts to subdue the rising emotion, burst into a passion of tears so hysterical as to terrify even the stoical Mr. Revely, accustomed as he was to see in his daughter the same unruffled placidity, —the same unvarying sweetness, under almost every possible variety of circumstance and situation.

"Poor thing!" said Mrs. Revely; "these long walks are too much for her, as well as for Mr. Fulton. She is quite nervous, I declare. Don't you think, Mr. Revely, she had better lie down for a little? She wants rest."

"I think she does," replied the softened father. "Rachel, my dear, I advise you to keep yourself quiet, and to remember in whose hands we are. All of us must bear our appointed burdens; let us not forget that the same hand lays them on us that dispenses all the innumerable blessings of our lot. Go, my child, pray for resignation."

Rachel, still weeping, but less painfully, retired, supported by Catharine, whose hand clasped hers with a pressure that told her she was understood and pitied.

"Pity, if you can, without despising," she whispered, as she entered her chamber.

"Despise *you*, Rachel!" said Catharine, tenderly, seating herself by the side of her cousin. "What heart that knew you could resist loving one so gentle,—so excellent?—There is much in your feelings to be compassionated,—but nothing to be condemned. Under your circumstances, how could you avoid feeling for Mr. Fulton as you do feel for him?"

"I knew you suspected my weakness; and it is a blessing to feel that there is at length one to whom I may speak without the fear of being misunderstood," said Rachel, with greater composure. "Believe that I have striven,—oh, how mightily!—*of late*, against feelings which I saw were never to be returned. But the dream had continued long—so long, Catharine!—Even in the boyhood of Fulton I learned to love him. A union between his child and his pupil was almost the only earthly wish my poor father ever earnestly expressed. I have sometimes thought, that if Providence had given me a sister on whom to lavish the love which yearned to be bestowed, I should have been contented to know no other affection. I longed to be permitted to love something that would receive my attachment with gratitude; a bird—a spaniel—any living thing that would have been conscious of my caresses and have loved me for them. The more I strove to subdue this desire, the stronger it became; self-condemned, I acknowledged to my own conscience that I was indulging wishes that were criminal; that my affections ought to be set on heavenly things, whereas they were wandering among the fair and the beautiful of this unhappy world."

"Self-condemned! and wherefore?" said Catharine, warmly. "To check the charities that sweeten human existence is to blaspheme the goodness of the Creator. Can you show me an instance in which their lawful indulgence has led to evil? Is it thus with the passions, the formidable enemies of man, to yield to which is crime always, often despair? Examine the different issues of passions and affections, and see whether they be not as far apart as right from wrong. Did Heaven frown on the friendship of David and Jonathan, which 'passed the love of woman?' Was not Jacob's well-beloved son, Joseph, restored to bless his age? Did not that same Jacob love Rachel with an unreproved devotedness, which led him to endure for her so many years of toilsome service, that 'seemed to him but a day' for the love he bare her?"

"I have not been taught to consider things thus; what education,—what habit,—have made me, such I am; an unhappy creature, subject to perpetual conflicts between natural feelings and acquired principles," said Rachel, with a bitterness that seemed incompatible with the ordinary meekness of her nature. "And yet those feelings—that aptitude to love—*would* gladly have flowed in the prescribed channels, if sympathy could have been found there. My father was contented with being 'honoured;' he neither cultivated nor desired to awaken a warmer sentiment in his child. My mother, satisfied with doing what she conceived to be her duty, keeping me neatly dressed, curing my colds, attending to my health, and superintending my purely feminine occupations, had no idea that more was essential to my happiness. Could this satisfy the restless craving of my heart for that tenderness which is to be felt —sighed for—but not to be described? Imagine then the intensity of the love that was lavished on Fulton, when in him I believed I saw the object whom my father himself had selected as the companion of my life. And in *him* there was nothing which taught me that I might be cherishing a preference, the disappointment of which would be more intolerable than all the barrenness that had preceded it. He sought me as the confidante of all his griefs, the sympathizer with all his joys;—as a brother may love his only sister, even so he loved me; but I did not learn how different was *his* love from mine, until I was conscious of the mean—the unworthy jealousy, with which I would fain have depreciated *you* to myself. But the worthless effort was not successful, Catharine. I could hardly be angry that he preferred what seemed to me so exalted above myself; it was but a fitting homage to that which I myself regarded as most beautiful,—most excellent! I did not love you less because he loved you more. Should not that which he esteems so precious, be, so to speak, even sanctified to me?"

"Whatever may be the nature of the sentiments with which Mr. Fulton has regarded me, be assured he entertains them no longer," said Catharine. "Give him time, dear Rachel. The vanity inherent in human nature, which may possibly have received a wound, will lead him with joy and gratitude to seek for the balm of an affection so unshaken—so devoted as yours."

"He has then declared—told you;—you have, in short, refused him."

"No, my dear Rachel, no proposal has been made; but in truth and sincerity let me tell you, Mr. Fulton understands that no possible combination of circumstances could ever inspire me with a regard warmer for him than friendship. Some time or other he will be grateful to me," she continued, with more playfulness, "that, wearied as I am with Golding Magna, I did not resolve on encouraging his—

what shall I call it?—*fancy*, as a means of escaping from the weariness of its eternal monotony. In a few days he will be in his usual health, for 'men have died from time to time, and worms have eaten them, but not for love.' Meanwhile, dear Rachel, meditate on a lesson, the theory of whch has been impressed on me by her whose own conduct illustrated all her precepts; happily for me, I have not yet been called on to practise it; 'time alleviates all pain—softens all disappointment. It is the part of wisdom and virtue to anticipate time, and to redeem so much of existence from discontent and repining.' And now a fair good night, Rachel. In the morning I shall hope to see you cheerful."

Rachel returned the affectionate caress of her cousin, and her slumbers that night were sweet as those of innocence should be.

In as short a time as Miss Vernon had predicted, Mr. Fulton reappeared at the rectory. There was a slight agitation in his manner when he addressed Catharine, but the friendly and unreserved kindness of her inquiries rapidly removed his embarrassment, and he conversed with tolerable ease. Rachel was the least composed of the party, but her retiring habits were favourable to her now, for they rendered her silence less remarkable.

It was not vanity in Catharine, but the result of her knowledge of human nature, which led her to wish, for the sake both of Fulton and Rachel, that Mrs. Warren were at liberty to return to ——shire immediately, that she might establish herself at the cottage. She felt that her absence would greatly hasten Mr. Fulton's conquest of his attachment, and that, constantly in the society of Rachel, he could hardly avoid contrasting her loveliness, simplicity, gentleness, and good feeling, with the harsh, bigoted, and austere class who constituted the majority of his acquaintance at Golding Magna. Moreover, she suspected that he himself was convinced of the prudence of a cessation of intercourse between them for the present, and she dreaded that he would contrive some cause for quitting his curacy, a measure which threatened to be fatal to Rachel's interests. Mrs. Warren's letters afforded no prospect of a speedy termination to her vexatious suit, and Catharine began to enumerate in her mind the friends of her mother, and to think of inviting the most eligible as her temporary chaperone, when she was spared all farther difficulty by receiving the following welcome communication from her aunt, Lady Darley.

"My dear Catharine,

"I am very glad I thought of desiring my friend, Sir Greville Cleveland, to call on you. I hope you were delighted with him. He is the most *répandu* person in *our* world. I should have written to you ages ago, but I have been worried to death with a thousand troubles and vexations about those two girls, poor Lord Darley's nieces. Nothing can be more annoying, more replete with care, and often mortification, than the office of chaperone, and girls can never be too grateful to those who undertake it in their behalf. Sophia and Fanny Darley, on the contrary, thought that they were really conferring an obligation on me by coming out under my auspices: unfortunate creatures! this very fact may indicate how ignorant of all necessary knowledge they were. I dislike nothing more than having my house in the country filled with a parcel of people to whom one is obliged to play the part of 'lady hostess,' and for whom one is incessantly compelled to contrive amusement or occupation. Yet for their sakes I was contented to endure all this world of fatigue and annoyance. And how have I been repaid? Sophia, who was really pretty, had evidently made an impression on Sir John Oakley, a man whose pretensions were of the best possible kind; and, just as I had told her that there were reasonable grounds for expecting his proposals, she thought proper to elope with a man of the guards, who wanted her fortune to pay his debts, and has nothing on earth to offer her in exchange, besides bringing on me all the disagreeable notoriety of the thing. As to Fanny, it appears that she had formed a sentimental sort of *liaison* with some country parson, her governess's brother, I think, which she was resolute on fulfilling. I have wasted a great deal of time and argument on her, but she was beyond the reach of common sense; so, to avoid farther publicity, I agreed that the ceremony should take place at my house in the most private manner possible, just before I quitted it for the London season. Thus, you see, I have fairly got rid of these two girls, and have reason to congratulate myself that these *contretemps* occurred before I had produced them here.

"Sir Greville, the best of all possible judges, assures me that you are quite a different kind of person. He says you have the family countenance, no ordinary compliment, by-the-way, for our female ancestors form quite a gallery of beauties. Your manner, too,—but I remember your mother, in her younger days, was, as Napoleon said of Josephine, 'not graceful, but grace itself.' In short, for I have travelled nearly to the end of the third page, I wish you to come to me *immediately*. I will send my carriage for you with my own woman, who is one of the cleverest creatures in the world, and whom you will find useful in a thousand ways. I flatter myself you and I shall suit one another amazingly. Believe me, I have nothing more at heart than your welfare, and my great anxiety is that you should make your début on the theatre of life under the most auspicious circumstances. Write to me directly, and say when you will be ready, but do not think of any arrangements regarding your wardrobe until I have seen you. Of course you have nothing fit to wear at such a place as Golding Magna; but don't distress yourself about it; I shall see to all that. I cannot imagine any reason that should delay your leaving Mr. Revely's longer than two or three days after I get your answer. I hope you will say that my carriage may be sent off on Monday next, which will give you sufficient time to make the first stage of your journey on Tuesday evening.

"Give my compliments to the Revelys, who, I hear, are good enough kind of people in their way Of course you do not read my letter to them.

"Your affectionate,

"PENELOPE DARLEY."

Nothing could have happened more opportunely. To return to that dear cottage which was her home, would have afforded Catharine the keenest delight that could have resulted from mere change of abode. But, as that was unattainable, she could rejoice in the fact that she was about to quit Golding Magna, to escape from the ungraceful monotony of Mr. Revely's domestic circle, and to enter on scenes of more cultivated existence. Above all, she was delighted to remove from Mr. Fulton's sphere, as affording the best chance of his feeling the influence of Rachel's angelic temper, and her great personal attractions. The only pang of parting was her separation from Rachel herself, who clung to her, weeping, as if reluctant to be left to the desolation that awaited her. But—Lady Darley's carriage was at the door, assurances of affection and constant correspondence were exchanged, and Catharine entered on new scenes with the elasticity of spirit which expectation of novelty always imparts to the young.

CHAPTER X.

THE rapidity with which Catharine Vernon had passed from one mode of human existence to another that bore no moral resemblance to it, seemed to her as the instantaneous transition of a dream. The contrast between all the luxurious appliances of the house of Lady Darley, in one of the most aristocratic squares in London, and the cold formality, the stiff uprightness, that had pervaded even the furniture of Mr. Revely's, in the interminable and narrow High-street of Golding Magna, was hardly so palpable as the difference which existed between the inmates of the two mansions.

The very servants of Lady Darley were the antitheses of those who moved so gravely and grimly at the rectory. The whole aspect of the one establishment impressed on the mind the constant conviction that "few and evil are the days of the years of man's pilgrimage on earth;" while the other afforded a practical illustration of the experience of the preacher: "Then I commended mirth, because a man hath no better thing under the sun than to eat, and to drink, and to be merry; for that shall abide with him of his labour the days of his life."

Lady Darley's welcome of her niece was more than cordial; it was affectionate. She recognised with tears the striking resemblance which Catharine bore to her father; spoke of him with all the fondness with which an only sister may be supposed to regard the memory of a most be loved brother; assured Catharine of her sincere desire to contribute to her happiness and welfare in every possible way; told her she had given orders to be denied to all the world, that they might have a day to themselves to get acquainted with each other; and installed her in the possession of an elegant suite of apartments, in which, Lady Darley told her, she was to intrench herself whenever she was wearied with *her* or her guests, or desired to renovate her mind for society by the occasional cordial of solitude.

Catharine was enchanted with this display of affection. She had expected to find her aunt a woman of the world, resembling marble not only in its polish, but its coldness. The polish, indeed, was there, but a desire of pleasing and of being pleased seemed to shine in the playful eyes which beamed so kindly on her, incompatible with the haughtiness of rank in which she had imagined Lady Darley would intrench herself. Neither had her waking visions portrayed her aunt as possessing so lovely or so youthful a person. Independently of the accessories of the toilet, Lady Darley was, in fact, in excellent preservation. Her life had been checkered by as few cares as ever fall to the lot of humanity; consequently, time had touched her lightly. Physical circumstances had aided the effect of moral felicities; an excellent constitution had been unimpaired by the attacks of disease; a temper of imperturbable equanimity had preserved the smoothness of her brow; while the gratification of her ambition in all it had ever coveted, had guarded the dimples that surrounded her mouth from that fatal metamorphosis to which decayed beauties are subject, —wrinkles.

The first evening, as Lady Darley had promised, was spent *tête-à-tête* in her boudoir, in the fitting up of which consummate taste had aided the expenditure of lavish magnificence. In ministering to the gratification of the senses, the intellect had not been forgotten. Small but beautifully embellished editions of the standard writers adorned the costly book-cases; and a variety of delicate little musical instruments invited the touch and exercised the skill of those delighting in "the concord of sweet sounds." Catharine was entranced as Lady Darley touched the chords of a fairy harp, or awakened for a moment the pealing notes of an *accordion.* There was no appearance of display on the part of her ladyship. She did not profess to have much knowledge of music generally, but she had sufficient ear, she said, to gratify her niece's curiosity with regard to the powers of various instruments. If Catharine wished to amuse herself with any of them, she had only to direct that they should be carried to her own apartment. Every thing which she imagined could afford her gratification was at her disposal.

Catharine not only spoke, but looked her gratitude, and Lady Darley's countenance expressed the delight she felt with every new point of view in which circumstances led her niece to exhibit herself. And Lady Darley was a critic no less anxious than accomplished. No theatrical manager ever sat in judgment on the capabilities of a new actress with greater coolness and a more unprejudiced judgment, than Lady Darley examined every gesture, look, and tone of Miss Vernon on this memorable evening. Happy the actress with whom the results were equally favourable!

"So Mr. Revely has only one child,—a daughter?" said Lady Darley, as they conversed of Catharine's past life. 'What is her name?"

"Rachel."

"Rachel!—Just the name for people of their caste!—I might have guessed it. I see her exactly. Rather tall,—bony,—square;—thin lips,—sallow complexion,—long, thin, black hair, plainly braided;—is not that a likeness?"

"No, my dear aunt, you are wrong," said Catharine, with a smile; "a very petite figure, the gracefulness of which the plainest and most unbecoming attire in the world cannot conceal. Pale, but not sallow;—a fair cheek, blushing with the least excitement;—dark gray eyes, glancing timidly through long black lashes;—profuse dark hair, that *will* curl in her own despite;—a beautiful but rather full mouth;—the finest teeth imaginable;—and a voice scarcely louder than a whisper, but as sweet as the 'cuckoo's note.'"

"Poor thing!—What an assemblage of good gifts to be veiled under the gloomy bigotry of such a society as is to be found at Golding Magna! Has the little girl a lover?—or is the sentiment of love altogether too profane to be admitted within the precincts of the rectory?"

"Mr. Revely sees so few young men," said Catharine, evasively.

"But he has a curate, has he not?—Curates are personages in provincial towns."

"He has—Mr. Fulton," replied Catharine, and she blushed,—the slightest possible blush,—as she mentioned his name.

Slight as it was, it did not escape Lady Darley. "The first page of my niece's romance!" thought she.

"And is Mr. Fulton a lover of Miss Revely's? Perhaps he is an old man; I believe many curates *are* old, though that is a class of persons of whom, of course, I know little."

"No, he is quite young, and, moreover, handsome," said Catharine, composedly.

"And how is it that he and the little Rachel have escaped falling in love, as it is called?—Was the lady indifferent, or the gentleman unattainable?"

"I should not be surprised if they were to marry some time or other," replied Catharine.

"*You being absent*," said Lady Darley, significantly. "Am I to hear the history of the *prémices de votre cœur?*"

"I have none to tell," answered Catharine, with an air of veracity not to be mistaken. "The person to whom you allude understood me too well to attempt to soften my flinty heart. No people in the world could be better suited to each other than he and my cousin Rachel."

"Good:—with your personal advantages, and the blood of the Vernons to boot, a clergyman, at least, would be but an indifferent alliance for you,—and a curate!—

"'Who may be called the yeoman of the church,
That sweating does his work, and drudges on,
While lives the hopeful rector at his ease.'

No, my dear, I hope better things of you. Apropos,—how old are you?"

"Almost twenty."

"Is it possible?—I never saw a younger looking person; between *us*, you know, flattery would be ridiculous. However, there is no necessity for letting the fact transpire. *Eighteen*, even, is not juvenile enough for your looks. That is an advantage which we blondes possess. We retain the appearance of youth long after it has left us. Sir Greville Cleveland would not hazard a conjecture on your age;—*very young*,—that was all he vouchsafed on that point. It seems to me a much shorter time since your birth;—I was then little more than a child, staying with my brother; how delighted I was with the baby, only it would cry whenever I attempted to amuse it. What a melancholy thing retrospection is!—We must not sadden our first evening with it. Now tell me how you liked Sir Greville?"

"It was impossible that I could judge him fairly," said Catharine, laughing. "He rose before me with all the brilliancy of the first rays of the sun after a Lapland winter.

You could not understand the degree of—what must I call it?—admiration I felt for him, when I saw him in immediate contrast with the gloomiest portion of the population of Golding Magna."

"Sir Greville is certainly one of the most fortunate men in the world in making his first appearances. Adventitious circumstances are always in the way to aid the effect he produces. I am glad you like him. He is quite the man of the day *in our* world. Of ancient descent, immense fortune, fine talents—and *such* a person—*such* manners! Having seen Sir Greville, you have seen the bright peculiar star of our hemisphere, and must expect nothing beyond him,—of the masculine gender, that is. There is but one thing he is suspected of wanting—*a heart*. If he had one, it could hardly have escaped the efforts of the incessant artillery that has been plied against it. Sighs, smiles, the tender, and, as some hint, *the terrible*, have been employed in vain. He is as invulnerable as Achilles; happy the woman who discovers the *unbathed heel!*"

"Is he not married?"

Lady Darley looked at her niece keenly, to discover whether this question was asked in real simplicity. Satisfied with her observations, she replied:—

"I have always thought there is a certain something—a je ne sçais quoi,—a kind of delicate, scarcely perceptible freemasonry—which enables a woman of any tact to discover immediately, at first sight, whether a man is married or unmarried. Sir Greville would be horrified to learn that you, of all the world, had believed him in the bondage of matrimony; *you*, on whom he has lavished more admiration than he has vouchsafed to mortal woman these ten years!"

Catharine did not reply, for she was occupied in wondering whether Sir Greville, with all his graces and all his talents, were not one of those heartless egotists whom the votaries of fashion are wont to enshrine in the innermost sanctuary of their temple; chiefly, perhaps, because they have the courage to despise, or the art to conceal, their dependance on their worshippers.

"You will see Sir Greville to-morrow evening," resumed Lady Darley. "He petitioned humbly to be admitted to-day, but I am a despot, and must be obeyed. The best of all possible mottoes, and the only piece of Latin which a woman may be pardoned for knowing, is the pithy '*suaviter in modo, fortiter in re.*' To-morrow I shall introduce you to a few, a very few—the chosen of the *élite*—fashion twice distilled through the alembic of taste. Sir Greville will be among them, for he is *of* them. You will see more of the leaders of the great world in a *réunion* of this kind, than in ten crowded assemblies, where one meets everybody and speaks to nobody. Moreover—for he *is* over and above, being hardly within our peculiar pale—I have invited Mr. Stark, the clever epigrammatist. He is the son of Heaven knows whom, and has risen in the world Heaven knows how. One part by talent, *perhaps*—ten parts by impudence, *certainly*. He has, however, contrived to gain the *entrée* of some of the best circles—for, if not liked, he is feared, which answers his purpose as well, possibly better. You are new, and he will endeavour to occupy your particular ear, because all his clever points are novel to you, and he will be saved a world of invention. He piques himself on never repeating his bon-mots ; and, as he is wise enough to avoid inflicting them twice on the same person, one is bound to give him credit for an inexhaustible variety. Listen to him patiently, and you will find him quite the historian of the circle. He has acquired, nobody knows how, the most accurate information of every one's birth, parentage, education, and 'manner of life,' so that, to a novice, an hour's conversation with him is really an advantage. And now, my dear Catharine, a little music, which will at once gratify my taste and my curiosity. You sing, of course ; no human being ever had a voice like yours without singing. *Here* is the music-room, and *there* are innumerable folios of music—Italian, German, ancient, modern ;—choose."

And with music, and the almost enthusiastic approbation produced by the performance from Lady Darley, Catharine's first day in London closed.

CHAPTER XI.

It was a melancholy circumstance, and drew largely on Lady Darley's fortitude,—Miss Vernon was in mourning; all the visions of elegant costume in which her ladyship's imagination had indulged, necessarily dissolved *in nubibus*. She insisted, indeed, on her niece's laying aside her bombasins and crapes, and affording her dress the relief of a mixture of gray or white,—but even this amendment was capable of but little variety. To add to her distress, she was quite sure that Catharine's style of beauty would be exhibited to much greater advantage, if adorned with the more lively colours,—an error of taste, which proved that though Lady Darley's opinion in all matters of fashion might be invaluable, she had no eye for the picturesque,—she was no judge of pictorial effect. Catharine, who never contested trifles, would implicitly have yielded to her aunt's *dictum* concerning her apparel, while it outraged neither propriety nor prudence; nevertheless, she so far shared her sex's foible as to rejoice secretly in the very circumstance which Lady Darley was deploring. Her taste, cultivated by seeing the most glorious productions of the pencil and the chisel under the happiest auspices, was satisfied that the necessary simplicity of her dress would exhibit her rare beauty of complexion to far greater advantage than a profusion of the best assorted colours that Herbaut or Maridan ever combined. Catharine detested the frivolities of riband and gauze. A face that exhibited the purest rose-colour and white, the deepest blue, the brightest vermilion, the richest gold—required the relief of a sober drapery. And the effect of a profile so perfectly classical that Phidias himself could not have improved it, would have been as much disgraced by the fripperies of the toilet, as the Venus de Medicis by the eight breadths of silk or muslin which go now to compose that female garment ycleped a petticoat.

Perhaps, when Lady Darley saw her niece attired for the *soirée* in black satin decorated with a *very* few pearl ornaments, she suspected that her own judgment in matters of dress might not be so incontestably infallible as she had supposed, and her maid and milliner had declared it to be. She was generous enough to express her approbation of Catharine's appearance, even inclusive of the plain Grecian headdress, which must have exhibited any defect of feature had such existed.

"Mr. Stark, or Sir Greville Cleveland!" said Lady Darley, with a smile, as she heard steps in the anteroom.

Mr. Stark was announced,—a little dark man, of an insignificant appearance, with small, restless black eyes, shining, amid the gloom of his countenance, like glow-worms in a church-yard. He shook hands with Lady Darley,—bowed as he was introduced to Miss Vernon,—raised his glass to his eye, and examined her with a scrutiny which deepened her bloom into the flush of indignation,—smiled approvingly at Lady Darley,—and finally seated himself by her niece.

"Now tell me all the illnature you have committed this day," said Lady Darley. "You appear so exceedingly happy, that I imagine you have been rather more mischievous than usual."

"My vocation depends on the follies of mankind, and is likely to last while fools are to be found, which, thank the gods, will be as long as the sun and moon endure," replied Mr. Stark. "I flatter myself that, notwithstanding the innuendoes of your ladyship, I am one of the most benevolent persons extant. I labour for the good of my kind more arduously than any utilitarian of them all. They would reason man into wisdom, while I lash him into it; and which method is the more profitable, say, oh ye pedagogues, for ye know!"

"Does the world generally submit patiently to such discipline?" asked Catharine.

Mr. Stark employed a moment in glancing at Lady Darley with a look that seemed to say,—"There is a pretty question now for your young, timid beauty, fresh from the country!"—then replied:—

"The world, my dear Miss Vernon, cannot help itself. It may kick and plunge, like Balaam's ass, but is not likely to find an angel in the way, or a tongue to reprove 'the madness of the prophet.' The world, in its collective sense, is a dumb monster. As to its oracles, 'I will roar you by the hour with any lion of them all.'"

Other guests arrived, to whom Catharine was successively presented,—no very formidable ordeal, when there are good-breeding on one side, and self-respect on the other.

The great charm of Lady Darley's select soirées was the ease which pervaded their circle. There was an elegance of tone, purely the effect of habit, but no formality. Conversation never sank into insipidity, because it did not aim at brilliancy. It flowed in a uniform channel of good sense and good temper, which refreshed the mind without exciting it. Every thing was said well, but without effort. The grave and the gay afforded subject for discussion, as accident suggested the one or the other. Two or three members of the cabinet were of the party, and *therefore* good taste deemed the avoidance of politics imperative. But when general principles of government were touched on, everybody spoke without restraint, guiltless of meaning to offend, and consequently fearless of offending. The literature of the day,—the popular novel,—the successful drama,—were criticised with candour, and the natural collision of opinion on such topics elicited brilliancy, but *not fire*.

As the evening advanced, music added its charm to the hour; and Mr. Stark, who had been almost a silent member hitherto, betook himself to the task of entertaining Catharine.

"I hope you are not fond of music," he began.

"A strange hope!" said Catharine; "it is a real misfortune to be incapable of enjoying the most soothing of the fine arts."

"*Soothing*, do you call it?" said Mr. Stark, with a slight sneer; "that piece of elaborate noise from the perturbed brain of Moscheles, *par exemple*, with which Lady Adelaide Willoughby is at this moment afflicting the piano and our ears? Shakspeare was ignorant of the power of aural torture our modern composers would attain, when he wrote that much hackneyed passage

"'The man who hath not music in his soul,
And is not moved by concords of sweet sounds,'

&c., &c., &c.—I need inflict no more on you. Have you ever been to the opera?"

"Never in this country."

"Then beg Lady Darley to take you next Saturday. You will see Pasta* in the 'Semiramide,'—and you will also see the degree of love for music, in its divinest form, possessed by this most civilized British public,—ay,—by the 'Hebrews of the Hebrews,' the very most aristocratic portion of that public. You will observe the rapt attention with which, during the performance of some of the finest things ever produced by any thing short of inspiration, they listen,—*to themselves!*—Enjoy the hum of human voices,—the more than 'whisper of a multitude,'—and acknowledge how fine an accompaniment it constitutes to the most passionate acting of the most poetic actress in Europe!—Oh, yes!—we are a musical people. They who doubt it may be convinced by the price we pay to singers and musicians, to whom we do not condescend to listen!"

"You are adding a lash more to those you have already bestowed, are you not?" said Miss Vernon, with a smile.

"'Upon that hint I speak,'" replied Mr. Stark, quite pleased to have a *new* listener. "If we do not listen to the music, *en revanche*, we listen to the dancing. *Now* you *have* the look of a novice, and I am glad to see it, for hitherto I have been compelled to fancy you one of us, and any thing fresh is so *re-freshing!*—Yes,—we listen to the dancing!—As soon as the ballette commences, we not only lend our eyes, but our ears to our 'friends, Romans, countrymen!'—We cannot spare one of our senses from the entertainment;—all must be at their post to heighten this delectable enjoyment, which—no delicate woman ought to tolerate, and no wise man to allow his wife or daughter to behold!—Oh, we are a rational people,—we, the finest people in the world!"

Catharine did not answer;—her eyes were fixed on Lady Adelaide Willoughby, and her attention was at least divided by the brilliant execution of her ladyship.

"An interesting countenance, is it not?" said Mr. Stark, who observed the direction in which the glances of his companion were travelling. "And yet—*a pene si puo dir questa fu rosa.* A youth of uncommon brilliancy has passed rapidly away, and left her ladyship a melancholy memento of the past,—a noble ruin indeed, but a ruin still."

"I never saw a countenance so expressive of repose,—and yet I should think it the repose of resignation, not of content."

"A nice definition, and rather a subtle distinction," said Stark, with his usual sneer; "perhaps, however, you are

* An anachronism.

not so far wrong as ladies who dabble in metaphysics are wont to be. Poor Lady Adelaide has worn the willow these five years, and, instead of becoming a saint, has adopted the other alternative possible in such cases,—she is *a blue*, and looks upon human life from the heights of philosophy. She is the great refuge of genius in distress, and the great buyer of books which nobody reads. She is so charitable to literary unfortunates, that an author whose tragedy was damned,—the profits of which were to feed and clothe a sick wife and nine small children,—has a pension from her at this moment; and she bought up the whole edition of an unreadable poem, because she heard, by accident, that the writer had a blind mother, entirely dependant on him, whom he supported by following the profession of a diurnal and hebdomadal hack. Notwithstanding these eccentricities, however, Lady Adelaide contrives to make herself generally acceptable; and though the profane may sometimes call her mad, the *esoterics* of *the* mysteries generally consider her as one of the first among themselves."

"Her ladyship is not married?"

"Her ladyship is *not* married," replied Mr. Stark, most emphatically distinguishing the accent of acquiescence from that of interrogation. "Five years ago, Lady Adelaide had most convincing demonstration that

"'Man was inconstant ever;
One foot on sea and one on land,
To one thing constant never.'—

The circumstances were too sordid and too commonplace for romance. The youth who wooed and won her heart might not actually be guilty of malice prepense. Love comes upon a man like a fever;—perhaps the air brings it —perhaps the water,—but I am inclined to think it as involuntary as any other disease. He could not have meditated a folly of the kind; the thing would have been too absurd in a man who had been two or three years about town. Lady Adelaide had rank, accomplishments, beauty, —but, alas!—while all the other deities were propitious, Plutus frowned;—the two could not produce from their joint portions enough to furnish forth the goods and chattels fitting and respectable in such a case. What do you think, therefore, it was prudent and desirable that the gentleman should do?"

"Prudence should have been consulted before Lady Adelaide's affections were interested," replied Catharine. "The next best thing, doubtless, was to leave it to her to determine whether the ills of poverty were to be endured *together*, or the misery of disappointment *alone*."

"*He* took a wiser step;—he went to St. George's one morning with a new Birmingham heiress, who had precisely all that Lady Adelaide wanted, and wanted all that she possessed. What do you think of him now?"

"That, verily, he had his reward."

"Yes, he *had*, in your sense of the allusion. But the cup was more than full; it absolutely ran over. He had not been married three months when, lo! a cheesemonger, or a soap-boiler, or some such thing, died,—a relation, *maternally*, of Lady Adelaide's,—who furnished forth an adequate retribution by bequeathing to her his hoarded millions. My story is ended;—the moral—he that runs may read."

"Is my memory correct?—was the gentleman now placing the music-book for Lady Adelaide named to me as Lord Edmund Gresham?"

"Quite correct. In him you see an indifferent minister, and an execrable writer of tragedies. He has had the singular felicity of producing a tragedy damned so thoroughly, that not a single voice was raised in its favour. A palpable plagiarism from Sophocles, too;—but, in passing through his lordship's mind, it became tainted with the abominations it met in its progress. If you wish to understand, in all its sublimity, the beauty of bathos, read it. I shall be happy to lend it to you."

"No, thank you. I have no inclination to lose so much time."

"Or to destroy your temper, which a bad tragedy must do, and ought to do."

Lady Darley at this moment seated herself near Catharine.

"Well, my dear, has Mr. Stark amused you?—I hope so, for he has occasioned you the loss of Lady Adelaide Willoughby's playing, which, I assure you, is to be regretted."

"I ought not to complain. Mr. Stark has said as many severe things as could possibly be comprised in the same number of words," said Catharine, smiling; "and I am not ungrateful. I will confess that I have been amused."

"Of course you have had the history of all of us, and a critique on our various foibles?"

"Wrong not so your merits!" said Mr. Stark. "Lady Darley herself would afford matter for a folio!—But will your ladyship credit me?—Would he, 'the chief of men,'—the Agamemnon of our hosts, pardon me?—I have not once mentioned the name of Sir Greville Cleveland."

"The person in the world of whom I have been talking and thinking most this evening."

"Then you have obliged Sir Greville; for to be thought of and talked about is precisely the thing he most likes. It is the very 'end and aim,' or I wrong him, of his absence from your circle this evening."

"Every person of taste must value his society," replied Lady Darley. "No one has so good an excuse for his caprices as Sir Greville."

"Exactly,—the spoiled child of the world, it is but according to the natural course of things that he should spurn the parent who has cherished his foibles. If you, the élite, —would but administer a little of that wholesome chastisement, *neglect*, you would reap a rich reward in his increased observance. You will not see that you can do better without him than he without you, and he has the benefit of your voluntary blindness."

"I fear your satire has put Miss Vernon's mind out of tune;—I must endeavour to restore its harmony. Lady Adelaide has risen; will you try the harp, Catharine, and give us something of Mozart's?" and Lady Darley, putting her arm through her niece's, led her to the other end of the splendid apartment.

"Sir Greville holds Mr. Stark in utter contempt," she said, as they walked across the room; "compelled, by meeting him everywhere, to occasional notice of him, his address to him is marked always by stately politeness. You see how Mr. Stark revenges himself, and will understand the precise value which is to be given to his assertions."

Catharine had not time even to express her acquiescence, for they were close to Lord Edmund Gresham. Without farther solicitation she seated herself at the harp,—possessing too much simplicity of character to affect embarrassment at the display of a talent which had been sedulously cultivated, and too superior to vanity to be anxious about the impression produced on her audience.

The effect, therefore, was perfect. Lady Darley was satisfied that the success of her niece in society would be pre-eminent, and she reflected, with the complacency of a person enjoying a conscientious satisfaction, that, by her instrumentality, this "gem of purest ray serene" had been rescued from "the dark unfathomed caves" of provincial obscurity, to shed its lustre where the eyes of princes and peers might gaze at and appreciate its brightness.

"How is it that Sir Greville is absent this evening?" said Lady Adelaide Willoughby. "I imagined he always had a particular regard for Lady Darley's nights."

"Perhaps he was particularly expected, which accounts sufficiently for his being elsewhere," said Lord Edmund Gresham. "His *pre*sumption and *as*sumption are becoming really too absurd."

"It is our own fault," said Lady Adelaide. "We have submitted so patiently to his encroachments, that we have at length established him in a despotism from which we know not how to depose him, even while we sensibly feel his tyranny."

"Thank Heaven," said the Dutchess of Halifax, "I cannot charge myself either with submitting to the caprices of Sir

Greville Cleveland, or with courting his society. Having fortunately no daughters to dispose of, I had no inclination to purchase his favour at the expense of much of my own comfort. I have too many caprices of my own to endure those of other people."

"But Sir Greville possesses so much talent—so much taste—so many noble qualities," said Lady Darley, "that one may pardon him for showing occasionally that he feels himself superior to the rest of the world."

"An extensive supremacy!" said the dutchess.

"And a feeling which, I confess, I do not share with Sir Greville," added Mr. Stark. "His attainments are showy, —*conversational* I might almost call them—but they are not sufficient to place him in the rank of the first men of the day."

"He has the reputation of being among them, nevertheless," said Lady Darley.

"Where *we* have placed him," said Lord Edmund. "And, having enshrined the idol in the innermost niche of the temple, it is fitting that we should swear to his divinity, albeit we know him to be but of 'wood and stone.'"

"Allow that Sir Greville has paid the penalty of his absence this evening," said Lady Adelaide. "Not only has he lost the tribute of our wonted homage, but he is in danger of being deprived, by acclamation, of every claim to it."

"It would be a blessing to the world," said the dutchess, "if Sir Greville would either marry, or enter the society of La Trappe, one of which alternatives must, I think, be the termination of his extraordinary career."

"Or a retirement to Saint Helena," said Lady Darley.

"Which would be at the same time an exit à la Prometheus," said Mr Stark.

"Which would be any thing but a termination; the task of the vulture being without any prospect of completion," said Lord Edmund, who was indebted to Mr. Stark for a severe critique on his unfortunate tragedy, and who lost no opportunity of making a thrust at his enemy whenever he found him at advantage.

"I am corrected," said Mr. Stark, with a bow. "The accuracy of your lordship's classical knowledge is beyond dispute. How strange it is," he continued, turning to Mr. ——, the famous parliamentary orator, as if struck by a sudden thought, "that we, who are so early imbued with a reverence for the glorious productions of antiquity, should in our manhood, lose so much of our veneration as to pillage, without remorse, the finest of their sentiments, the noblest of their impersonations, and fit them into the Procrustes-bed of our own vile abortions and grovelling imaginations!—We take the head of gold from one, and the body of silver from another, and the limbs of brass from a third, and complete the misshapen monster by the feet of clay which we ourselves have manufactured, and then execrate the bad sense of the world, because our creation falls to the lowest abyss."

Mr. —— smiled, but he did not reply—first, because he disliked Mr. Stark; and secondly, because Lord Edmund, though but an official underling, was so far his colleague, and it is astonishing into what heights and what depths *esprit du corps* penetrates.

As to Lord Edmund, he turned away with just as much incivility as a gentleman can possibly allow himself to exhibit, and addressed himself to Catharine.

"We are entertaining you with a discussion," said he, "on the merits of a person with whom you are not acquainted. It will serve, however, as an introductory chapter to a new volume."

"It will, at least, serve Miss Vernon as a *carte du pays*," said the dutchess, "always an acceptable thing to a novice."

"If she have tact to profit by it, which in this case we cannot doubt," said Lord Edmund, with a bow.

His lordship, of course, expected either a blush or a smile—perhaps both;—his compliment, however, was as unsuccessful as his tragedy—a complete failure.

Lady Darley saw that Catharine was about to avow that she had seen Sir Greville Cleveland, a disclosure which Lady Darley had especial reasons for preventing. "Will not you, Lady Adelaide," said she, "you, who are 'fair charity's sweet self,' say one word in behalf of this unhappy man, whose character we are so mercilessly submitting to the torture?—While *we* are 'setting down so much in malice,' can you 'nothing extenuate?' "

"Much," said Lady Adelaide, with her usual placid smile; "but Sir Greville has a better advocate than I could be. He carries about him the magic of manners so irresistible when he is desirous of pleasing, that he will not have conversed an hour with Miss Vernon before all our slanders will be effaced. Sir Greville has achieved greater miracles than this."

"But who shall say whether he *will* be desirous of pleasing on the particular occasion alluded to?" asked the dutchess.

"In that case he deserves no mercy, and I leave him to the punishment he merits."

CHAPTER XII.

"You may estimate the importance of Sir Greville Cleveland by the quantity and severity of the censure lavished on him," said Lady Darley to her niece, as they breakfasted together the following morning. "People do not satirise the insignificant."

"And yet, I confess, the favourable impression Sir Greville made on me at Golding Magna is somewhat weakened. In his manner, then, there was not only grace, but so much simplicity, so much absence of pretension, that one had a sort of confidence in his good faith as well as his good sense."

"*At Rome, as the Romans*," said Lady Darley, with a smile. "A practised man of the world, like Sir Greville, understands perfectly the propriety of that rule, and is hardly likely to fail in its application."

"Is it the custom of the Romans, then," asked Catharine, "always to be absent when their presence is most desired and expected?—Do they find their satisfaction in being regretted,—in destroying the pleasure of a society of which they know themselves to be principal members?—Do they rejoice in imagining the forlornness of a circle of which they are the centre, and are they insensible to all the anger, and, perhaps, hostility, which 'small sins' excite more frequently than capital ones?

"'In heavenly minds can such perverseness dwell?'

Is Sir Greville Cleveland capable of enjoying so mean a triumph?"

"Alas, my dear, mortals are insects who are contented to derive a light from a very pale sunbeam!"

"Ordinary mortals, perhaps;—but I had—has not your praise of him justified me?—ranked Sir Greville above them. The statue has descended from its pedestal, and is but of common workmanship after all."

"This is all very well, *entre nous*. It is prudent, however, to restrain the expression of opinions so unusual in general society. The world may forgive a woman for being handsome,—even for being witty,—but not for entertaining opinions different from its own,—and thereby indicating that she sees and despises its errors. The world punishes nothing more severely than contempt. You may be a heretic in religion, but beware how you attempt to controvert, far less to reject, a simple point in the creed professed by the orthodoxy of fashion."

"But, to judge from the sentiments expressed last night, it is not an article of faith, even in the fashionable world, to believe in the perfection of Sir Greville. Mr. Stark detests him; the Dutchess of Halifax reviles him; and even Lady Adelaide Willoughby, to whom you appealed in his behalf, rested her defence solely on his manners."

"And what avails more?—Manners are to the character what fine eyes are to the person,—they cover a multitude of defects."

"Good as adjuncts,—bad as principals," said Catharine. "I always distrust a man who is commended wholly or chiefly for his manners. Such praise is like that assigned to good-nature;—we are, in either case, certain that nothing brighter or better lurks behind."

Lady Darley looked doubtingly at Catharine.

"I fear," she said, "your success will hardly be so great as I hoped. Analysis does not answer;—no one likes to expose his character to such a test;—what man would choose a wife who looks so curiously into the microcosm of the soul?—And, moreover, my dear Catharine, although it is the fashion to talk of the *march of intellect*,—and to indulge in most glowing visions of the future improvement of the human race,—believe me, men are not liberal enough to reduce their philosophical theories to practice where woman is concerned. They desire that she should remain where they, or destiny,—which is but opinion and circumstance,—have placed her. In the struggles of public life men find rivals or allies;—they are compelled to encounter opposing wills,—counteracting influences;—mind wars with mind,—and who is there that triumphs in every conflict?—*At home*, therefore,—at his own hearth,—every man likes to find *dependance*. It heals the wounds of his self-love;—it is a soothing balm to his mortified vanity;—it is a homage to his superiority, in which his spirit rejoices, and which, perhaps, may be necessary to recruit his mental energies. Now your very acquiescence implies that you are satisfied of the truth of what has been advanced;—not on the authority of the speaker, but because you have arrived at the same conclusion by some previous process of reasoning. One feels," added Lady Darley, with one of her blandest smiles, "how very unpersuadable a person you are. Men are not flattered by arriving at the heart only through the reason."

"And yet, what homage can be so worthy of both sexes?"

"Men—even men of the world—have in one respect something of Prior's Henry in their character. Satisfied with touching the feelings of woman, and engrossing her affections, they do not desire that she should sit in judgment on them,—that she should have the power to do so. They like to be *honoured*. If not heroes to their valets-de-chambre, to their wives they would be demigods. And it is on this principle, probably, that you see so many of the most intellectual men of the day choosing a simpleton as the mother of their children, without even the excuse of having their judgment blinded by exceeding personal attractions. In short, my dear, you must swim with the tide, or the chances are greatly against your reaching the shores of matrimony."

"I will not say, according to the wont of young ladies, that I do not mean to marry, but I *will* confess that I do not contemplate the passing of my life in single-blessedness with any thing like dismay. The term of 'an old maid' is hardly ever pronounced without intending to express something of odium or ridicule,—but I was very early made to see that happiness is not dependant on any relative position, and that a woman may be almost as useful, quite as respectable, and not unfrequently happier, unmarried, as if she had entered the 'holy pale.'"

"Useful!—respectable! - odious epithets: and how misplaced from lips so young and lovely! An old maid!—you—Catharine Vernon—the *last* Vernon—Lady Darley's niece—a débutante in life, under auspices of which it is not too much to say, that they are as brilliant as unexceptionable chaperonage can render them!—No, my dear Catharine, I cannot consent that all these advantages shall terminate in the insignificance of old-maidism. Nature never sent forth from her storehouse of beauty a face, a person, so perfect as yours, without meaning that it should be placed where it could be gazed at and admired,—that is, in the high places of the earth. Do not let us argue the point;—let us allow circumstances to shape themselves quietly; for, let us wrangle as we will, 'to that complexion we must come at last.' And now, my love, ring the bell, and tell me how you wish to dispose of yourself this morning?"

"I should like to call on my friend Mrs. Warren, if you can spare the carriage."

"By all means. I am a great advocate for the observance of propriety to people in every situation of life."

"I cannot take to myself the credit of consulting propriety; I am gratifying my feelings. I love Mrs. Warren for herself, and she was my mother's dearest friend."

"That is a sentiment I quite approve:—apropos,—who is Mrs. Warren, and where does she live?"

"She is the widow of a dignitary of the church, but not affluent. A vexatious lawsuit has diminished an income not very large originally. She lodges in Wimpole-street, Cavendish Square."

"Poor woman!" said Lady Darley, shrugging her shoulders, while her countenance expressed unaffected compassion. "Well, my dear child, it is certainly proper that you should go, and perhaps you had better invite Mrs. Warren to dine here;—you can offer the carriage;—it will save the *mal-apropos* of one of those horrible vehicles in which people allow themselves to be dislocated appearing at the door. Some day next week let it be;—let me consider,—yes,—on Tuesday;—a quiet evening, preparatory to your first appearance at Almack's, will be quite a beautifier. Say that I would have called on Mrs. Warren, but I consider a third person quite *de trop* when two friends meet after a long separation. I hope the neglect of this formality will not make her decline your invitation. I am sure *your* friends cannot be such as would inflict either mortification or discredit on you or myself. As to rank," said Lady Darley, with a proud smile, "I can afford to be condescending. It is only people whose position is equivocal that are compelled to build up their own consequence on that of their associates."

Catharine prepared for her visit with the greatest alacrity, rejoicing in the certainty that Lady Darley would offer no obstacles to her frequent intercourse with her friend. She was delighted to be able to invite Mrs. Warren to visit her; and this feeling prevented her from observing that the kindness of Lady Darley was but a modification of intense selfishness,—that the possibility of one of "those horrible vehicles" appearing at her door was to be averted only by a reluctant display of hospitality, for which she endeavoured to console herself by dwelling on the advantage of a quiet evening to her niece's appearance. The habit of investigating may be an advantage to the intellect, but it is questionable whether, in the present state of society, that advantage is not more than counterbalanced by the effect it has on our comfort. At the present moment, Catharine was indebted for one of the most delightful moods of mind,—when enjoyment and hope blend together,—to an illusion which could not have stood the test of the slightest scrutiny.

The anxious—the obscure—have not many temptations to quit the nook in which obscurity is not felt and anxiety concealed. Mrs. Warren was at home, and Catharine was clasped in the warm embrace of the beloved friend of her mother, for the first time since that mother's death. The tears of each fell plentifully, but Catharine felt soothed and softened with "the joy of grief."

"Your presence is indeed a cordial," said Mrs. Warren; "how I have longed for the freshness, the bloom of the country this spring, you may divine, when you look from my dusky windows into the duskier street. There have been moments when I have indulged the *young* thought of relinquishing my claims, and joining you at the dear cottage, content with the narrow stipend which would then remain to me."

"A thought which I should certainly have urged you to realize," said Catharine.

"It would be wrong, nevertheless, for it would be to offer a premium to fraud, while it would naturally confine my own means of doing good greatly within the limits which Providence had prescribed for them. However, now I see you, half the burden of 'the law's delay' seems lightened, and I shall begin to admit the hopes that have been held out to me, that, before your first season in London has closed, I shall be able to return with you to the dear cottage. And now,—how do you like Lady Darley?"

"As I am glad to feel for the sister of my father," replied Catharine; and she proceeded to deliver at once Lady Darley's apology and invitation.

Mrs. Warren graciously accepted the first, but she declined the second.

"No, my love;—I am not fit for the society of people of fashion. Their prejudices will shock me no less than mine will offend them. I have outlived the plastic season of youth, and find it difficult to yield to new impressions. Come and see me frequently, but let that be the limit of our intercourse, which, notwithstanding the courtly kindness of Lady Darley, I am sufficiently a woman of the world to believe will be quite as acceptable to her ladyship as if I punctually returned all your morning-calls, and appeared in answer to all her dinner-invitations."

Catharine offered an almost indignant dissent. "You greatly wrong my aunt," she said. "Polished as she is, she has evidently great warmth of feeling; and she was really quite delighted that I should come to you this morning. In all her elegance there seems not the slightest leaven of vulgar pride. How should there? Her claims are too well authenticated to offer any temptation to assumption. Pride is the chevaux-de-frise in which dubious pretensions encircle themselves;—there need be no preparations for defence where there is no danger of attack. I think you will like her;—there are necessarily points of difference between you, but it does not follow there should be repulsion."

"Very true;—for once, however, dearest child, let your abstract truths yield to the claims of my experience. Lady Darley will like me all the better if she hears of me only as your friend, and is not compelled to acknowledge me as her own acquaintance. People of fashion, good as their intentions may be, cannot help considering people of no fashion an encumbrance. And now, that point being settled, let me hear, not why Lady Darley sent for you at last, but why she had not sent for you before?"

"Circumstance, 'that most unspiritual god,' probably operated in both cases. It is an old maxim of yours, that we must not inquire too curiously into the motives of actions which benefit us, because such an inquiry would probably have the effect of greatly diminishing our gratitude. *Mine* to Lady Darley is very vivid; for, consider, that I was rescued from the solemn sameness—the monotonous commonplace—of the Rectory of Saint Andrew's, at Golding Magna. Can you wonder that, after my unwilling abode there, the house of Lady Darley should appear to me a Paradise?"

"And yet you,—young, lovely, prosperous as you are, may live to regret the safe dulness of Mr. Revely's household," said Mrs. Warren, with a sigh. "Disease often lurks in the most brilliant atmosphere; and the very clouds that dissatisfy us may be our safety. The paths of pleasure are seldom,—alas, are they ever?—the paths of happiness."

"This is rather discouraging to a novice. It is consoling that I am not very youthful, and have not lived a life of perfect retirement."

"Twenty is a very mature age,—there is no disputing it. Let me see,—yes, certainly that must be a wrinkle which I have been hitherto mistaking for the very nest of the loves, —a dimple. And truly, as you insinuate, you have seen the world,—France,—Switzerland,—have travelled by the Simplon,—looked at the Glaciers,—eaten macaroni at Naples, and learned *virtu* at Rome. Alas, my dear Catharine, there would be infinitely less danger in crossing the Arabian deserts than in passing through one winter of fashion in London. And do not forget that

"'. . . . . . Ships have gone down at sea,
When heaven was all tranquillity.'

I am not quite sure that your self-reliance is not as dangerous as your susceptibility."

"*Susceptibility!*" said Catharine, with a blush of slight indignation;—"my dear Mrs. Warren, I thought that was one of the last charges which could be brought against me. I, that have rather piqued myself on my coldness!—who have never had the least *penchant* for fancying myself in love!—who have arrived nearly at years of discretion without an entanglement!—who consider the passion almost as one of the bright creations of the poets,—a thing to be dreamed of, as one dreams of the sparkle of a star, or the flashing of the sunbeam on the wave. Susceptible! surely, my dear friend, that is not my besetting sin."

"That intense enthusiasm with which you admire what is most glorious in creation, most wonderful in nature, most beautiful in art, will, when excited by the real or fancied qualities of a living being, be the passionate love which sometimes,—too often,—'brings death into our world, and all our wo.' You are not the more strong because you believe yourself invulnerable. I fear there will come a moment when all the fences of reason and philosophy will

4

avail nothing, when you too will prove the destiny of woman."

"Be it so," said Catharine, with an attempt at gayety. "After all, love is a delightful sentiment. How many human beings are there of whom it constitutes the entire happiness! It is the parent of the most blessed charities of human life! In its purest state it is the least selfish of the passions, while it is the most engrossing. If love be indeed the destiny of woman, why should I strive against it?"

"But remember that, if happy love be the perfection of human felicity, disappointment is the most fearful of earthly ills. Old people, who are hardened by the trials of life, are apt to deride it;—but, if memory were not deadened, there are many statesmen, many warriors, many of the sternest and the bravest, who could testify that, sharp as may be the pangs which are to be endured in the most fortunate career, that earliest was the keenest. And to woman!—alas! —our answer is to be found in the churchyard and the mad-house!"

Catharine shuddered slightly.

"Lady Darley is prudence itself," she said, after a short silence. "I have seen quite enough to be convinced that she would consider a romantic attachment one of the most unpardonable follies a human being could perpetrate. In her circle there is not much fear of my falling into a danger of that kind. The opposite extreme might more reasonably be apprehended;—will you forgive me if I form *un mariage de convenance?*"

"Will you forgive yourself? would that be the fulfilling of your mother's hopes?" said Mrs. Warren, taking her hand, and looking on her with eyes that expressed even a mother's affection. "No, dearest Catharine, I would have you love,—but I would not have you taken at advantage. Temptation almost always assails us at the point where we thought no defence necessary."

"I will attend to your counsels as to the voice of my mother," said Catharine, tenderly embracing her friend. "I will not vainly imagine myself inaccessible to a sentiment which has marked the entire life of so many of the most gifted of the children of men. If I detect myself in being particularly gratified by the society or attention of any individual, I will endeavour to watch both him and myself. Youth is called the season of happiness;—how can that be so when the great event of our destiny is in suspense?"

"Because the young are accompanied by Hope.—Hope, blooming and beautiful as when she first sprung from Pandora's box,—not the Hope with faded colours, attenuated form, and sickly eye, that occasionally smiles on the care-worn, time-worn traveller in life's pilgrimage. One—yet one—word of warning;—you have seen in Mr. Revely's circle fanaticism in its most cheerless aspect;—beware lest, in Lady Darley's, you encounter skepticism in its most seducing form. True philosophy is inseparable from true religion. Eternity, awful even when illuminated by the brightness of revelation, is terrible indeed as the dark unknown of the skeptic. Do not be sneered out of your everlasting happiness. Many men have withstood an argument who fell before a sarcasm; and, to the young, what is so formidable as ridicule? Remote as I am from Lady Darley's circle, a whisper of its prevalent opinions has descended even to me. Mr. Revely considered a dissent from any of the articles of the Established Church infidelity, while others deem the belief of any superstition and credulity. Believe that the truth lies between the extremes; and do not, my dearest Catharine, allow the staff of the Christian faith to be withdrawn from you, on the assurance that the philosophy of modern schools will more than stand you in its stead."

"What shall I say to you? Only the words of the martyr of old,—'in this faith have I lived, in this faith will I die!' And now, my dear Mrs. Warren, how can I best contribute to your happiness?"

"First, by being careful of your own; and next, by coming frequently to see me."

Catharine promised both; and, after a visit of some hours' duration, she quitted Wimpole-street.

CHAPTER XIII.

The carriage stopped at Lady Darley's door,—the footman rolled the thunder of the knocker,—the prompt porter obeyed the summons,—and Sir Greville Cleveland appeared, to assist Catharine in alighting.

Miss Vernon blushed intensely. What a world of thoughts may crowd into the mind in the short interval that elapses between the first glance and the first word! She was not insensible to the homage of so unusual an act of condescension from a man distinguished for exacting tribute and paying none, nor did she reply to his warm and animated greeting with quite so much self-possession as usual. Sir Greville perceived her embarrassment, slight as it was, but he was not so flattered by it as a more intimate knowledge of Catharine might have made him; he attributed it to the natural diffidence of a novice, and he thought her rather less graceful than she appeared at Golding Magna.

"Catharine," said Lady Darley, as they entered, "Sir Greville has been here the whole morning to make the *amende honorable* for his last night's absence;—*compulsion*, he assures me."

"Miss Vernon appreciates herself too justly to doubt it," said Sir Greville, rather with the indifference of a man who has the habit of flattering, than with the empressement of one desiring to offer a marked compliment.

Catharine received it with even greater indifference than it was offered with.

"But now can you imagine," said Lady Darley, "how Sir Greville has been occupied since his arrival? In conjecturing where you were passing the morning, and meditating what he should conjecture. I hope you will think this a satisfactory method of disposing of two or three hours."

"Why did not you spare Sir Greville so much vain labour?" said Catharine, taking off her bonnet with the ease and the grace of a Frenchwoman, without displaying a single ringlet. "Or why, as curiosity is undoubtedly pain, did you not secure the cheap satisfaction of relieving it, by telling him that I was in Wimpole-street?"

"Oh, most unsatisfactory solution of the mystery in which I have delighted to envelop your morning's avocations!" said Lady Darley. "Sir Greville could not have imagined it. The most barbarous giant would not have been unfeeling enough to select such a prison for his fair captives."

"Why not?" said Sir Greville. "Do you not perceive, that the presence of those captives might have made even Wimpole-street the milky way of the stars of fashion? It is not the place, but the people, that sanctify the place *at first;* afterward, I agree that the place may distinguish the caste of the people. Before we venture to condemn Miss Vernon's taste, let us ascertain the *attraction.*"

"My mother's early—my mother's dearest friend," said Catharine, with a blush of emotion so beautiful that the most nonchalant exclusive might have pardoned it.

"And while Miss Vernon has enjoyed the luxury of pure and unvitiated sentiment, how have we been occupied?" said Sir Greville. "Do you think we have been so brilliant, so profound, so true, so amiable—I enumerate the last quality, insipid as it is, as the only valid excuse for the deficiency of the others—that her taste or feeling has suffered by her absence?"

"At least she would have had the advantage of making the experiment of 'strenuous idleness,'—a novelty to her, I conjecture. Moreover, she would have had the benefit of the lecture I have vouchsafed to you on your present fainéant mode of existence;—you—who have talent—more, who have *opportunity* to sway the destiny of a great empire

—to be the benefactor of your country—the friend of man kind."

"Miss Vernon is too unsophisticated to advocate the cause of ambition," said Sir Greville, gazing earnestly on Catharine, whose countenance was gradually losing its classical calmness for an expression of intense interest.

"Perhaps you mean that I am too naïve to understand it," said Catharine, with startling truth.

"If that be the case, be satisfied, my dear, that Sir Greville will think so no more," said Lady Darley, whose practised eye showed her that her niece and her visiter were about to change their relative positions—that the one was losing his conviction of superiority as the other quietly asserted her claims. "He will comprehend that there is a knowledge of the human mind independent of the knowledge of the world, *par excellence*, and sometimes quite as available."

"But, to return to the original point of dispute, grant that it is something to do no harm," said Sir Greville. "What is ambition? The fever whose raging pulse enables a madman to destroy or injure millions of his fellow-creatures. My love of ease—my indolence, if you will—is so far innocent, that none are injured by it but myself."

"Every one whom you might benefit by exertion," said Catharine, with sudden animation, as if surprised out of her reserve.

"Why should I sacrifice myself to those who will not thank me for my pains, and who would not suppress a smile, or stifle a groan, if I and all my race were to be extinct the day after I had effected their political regeneration?" asked Sir Greville, looking keenly at Catharine as he put the question. "Show me the public man whose sacrifice of private advantage has gained him the permanent gratitude of his kind? And for the temporary applause of the multitude! No! rather than strive for that, or before I enter the arena, I must become opera-dancer or fiddler."

"There is an applause superior to that of the multitude—one's own," said Catharine.

"That is so young!" exclaimed Lady Darley, who, with her conventional feelings and manners, dreaded that Catharine was exhibiting too much of *l'air romanesque*. "People do not labour *en philosophe* in the nineteenth century; and, if we were to fetch our Cincinnati from the plough, I much doubt whether, having been fanned by the breath of popular applause—that is, having tasted the sweets of office—they would return to it."

"Nevertheless, I agree with Miss Vernon—one's own approbation is a more comfortable thing than that of the world. It is to achieve *my own contentment with myself*, that I prefer the otium cum dignitate of my own house in town, and my own places in the country, to the intrigues, the mystifications, the vexations, or, in one comprehensive word, the diplomacy of Downing-street. Like other grown children, I have been delighted and dazzled with the colours of the air-blown bubble—fame—but I have lived long enough to deride a weakness that is vainer than vanity."

"Is every possible motive for ambition concentrated in Downing-street? Is there no fame but official fame?" said Catharine. "Must a man necessarily be of the cabinet to be the benefactor of his age? Can talent find no other goal worthy of its efforts than the premiership?"

"The greater the number of spectators, the more strenuous our exertions," replied Sir Greville, who began to think that the mind of Catharine might be as worthy the study of a connoisseur as her person. "We are very seldom wise or witty, and never eloquent, in solitude; I fear our very magnanimity derives a secret impulse from the hope that, if the present age is not just to us, posterity will appreciate and avenge us. We are early taught the homely precept, that 'a good action is its own reward,' but all our subsequent experience falsifies the assertion. We make a sacrifice to perform some great or benevolent action in behalf of an individual, and what is the harvest we reap? '*A thousand enemies, and one ingrate.*'"

"Still there *is* a reward,—the approving whisper of the mysterious spirit within us," persisted Catharine. "And in benefiting *communities* the remark of the French minister loses its poignancy."

"*Communities!*—the most ungrateful of ingrates!—standing, as, in England, the word does, for a mob who will deafen the patriot that devotes himself to its cause with acclamations at one moment, and,—lo, the wind shifts, and he is stoned! A mob—a community, if you will—derives its impulse from the breath of a demagogue;—when it thinks for itself, *then* I may attach importance to its opinions."

"*Teach it!*" said Catharine, with animation, unregardful of the admonishing looks of Lady Darley, who was absolutely aghast at this display of *blueism* in her niece. "The grand occupation for the higher minds of this era is to enlighten the lower. Knowledge has been deemed long enough an argand lamp to illuminate a drawing-room; it is time it should be known as a sun, the light, the splendour of whose beams, while it rests *first* on the tops of the mountains, penetrates at length into the depths of the profoundest valleys."

"*The schoolmaster is abroad!*—That is the watchword of the English illuminati, is it not?" said Lady Darley. "His first lesson is to teach the people that *knowledge is power*, and he will receive a practical proof of the truth of his maxim, by falling beneath the blow of the weapon he has put in their hands."

"He may teach them better things," said Catharine;—"that it is *enjoyment*;—because it suffices to itself;—because it opens the earth that seemed barren, and shows the rich veins of gold that run through it in all directions;—because it unlocks the mysteries of nature,—that exhaustless storehouse of grandeur, beauty, and wonder,—and reveals the sympathies that exist between the glories of the outer world and the inner world of man's heart. In the vast concert of creation, is there one thrilling tone but finds its echo within our spirits? Knowledge is a great, a glorious thing,—linking man with angels. Surely its best result is, when it demonstrates the real happiness of human beings,—that the calm shade of retirement is better than the turmoil of ambition, and that there is a holier, fuller bliss in communing with nature, penetrating her secrets, and benefiting our kind, than hero ever felt in the triumph of the battle-field, or minister in the ruin of a rival. *To know well* is the grand secret of content."

The enthusiasm of Catharine, so different from the ordinary *retenue* of her manner, absolutely illuminated her countenance. Sir Greville paused to enjoy it;—beautiful as he had pronounced her, it seemed as if half the perfection of her exceeding loveliness had never before even been imagined by him. As was said of Byron, by one perhaps as great as he, "her face was like an alabaster vase; it required to be lighted up before half its beauty was perceptible." Lady Darley, who saw with delight the admiration which Sir Greville was not only feeling, but absolutely enjoying, forgave Catharine the display of thoughtful knowledge,—the most unpardonable of all female offences in the fashionable code,—which had at first equally aroused her anger and her fear; and acknowledged that even *une tête un peu exaltée* was not without its occasional advantages.

"After all, then," said Sir Greville, "you do not insist on the absolute duty and necessity of my rising in St. Stephen's to bore the house every night for four hours, on a question on which the mind of each individual member has long been completely made up; nor do you think it essential that I should take possession of the premiership by storm, and insist on his majesty's permitting me to form a cabinet of confederates and slaves. You leave me in possession of my Tusculum, where I may solace myself with birds and flowers,—friends and books,—gazing, as Wordsworth says *and does*, 'into the deep blue sky,'—and occasionally penning an epistle to 'Tacitus,' or an ode to my 'jucundissime Martialis.' Forgive me;—I am unintentionally straying into *le pays latin*."

"I leave you certainly in possession of your Tusculum," said Catharine, playfully, and Sir Greville thought her as beautiful now, "when *this* change came over the spirit of her dream," as in the loftier splendour of her enthusiasm,—"but not that you should convert it into an Epicurean garden. Let benefits to mankind emanate thence; put a common into cultivation;—reclaim a marsh;—build schools, and search for fitting teachers; make a railroad, uniting thus the ends of the kingdom together; diffuse knowledge; in short, let every talent of every kind 'shine forth before men.'"

"The labours of Hercules!" said Lady Darley. "Try the effect of the perfumed atmosphere of *our* world, for a single season, on yourself, and then imagine the fitness of a man to whom for years it has been the breath of life, to breast the rough gale you assure him it is for his honour to encounter! You will find my prescription the pleasantest, Sir Greville; Catharine recommends you to be useful, I to be distinguished."

"There *is* a reward for which a man might undergo any toil," said Sir Greville, thoughtfully, while the intense expression of his powerful eye was fastened on Catharine; "there is a companionship which might give to the severest a character of delight. Unfortunately, girls of the present age are educated by the women of the last, who have the natural tendency of their kind to consider the days of their own youth as the brightest and the best, and who are not able to comprehend the characteristics which render *this* an era in man's history. Men, consequently, are so much in advance of their wives, that the latter must naturally depend on the *feeling* of their husbands, even when their appeals might more reasonably be addressed to the under standing."

"You are certainly exhibiting *en masque* this morning," said Lady Darley, in unaffected surprise. "*You*, who have insisted so much on *séduisant* softness as the *sine quâ non* of a woman's excellence! *Now*, the caprice of the moment would have her at the head of our armies and controlling the senate!"

"No," replied Sir Greville, seriously, "she should still be the Egeria of the grotto, whose agency, though always operating, is never perceptible. While man has passions and feelings, women will have influence. The page of history bears dreadful evidence of the fact. Since then she has, and ever will have, *power*, it is wisdom to teach her how to use it. Since a formidable weapon is in her hands and cannot be wrested from her, I would have her wield it for purposes of good, not of destruction. Yet do not mistake me; it is neither for her happiness nor ours that she should be dragged forward on the arena of public life. Her mind must not be soiled by contact with the baseness which more or less attaches to the struggles of political existence. *We* need a sanctuary in our home where shall still be found something to restore to us the freshness, the virtues, almost the romance, of our youth. Let woman still be among our household divinities, but let her be a tutelary one."

"Well," said Lady Darley, "after this, I really begin to think Don Quixote was a very rational person."

Sir Greville replied only by a smile. His eye had met Catharine's, and he had read there that which awakened thoughts, hopes, desires, such as he believed had departed for ever. Too skilful to weaken a favourable impression, he retired almost immediately, but not until he had ascer-.ained where Lady Darley would chaperone Miss Vernon during the ensuing week.

"My dear child," said Lady Darley, the moment they were alone, "if Sir Greville had been in his usual mood, you would have said too much. Young women should, above all things, avoid the slightest pretensions to *l'esprit fort* in its least objectionable sense."

"You will not have to complain of any public expression of my opinions," replied Catharine; "in society I shall be too much occupied in seeing and hearing to have the least inclination for talking. But this morning we were almost tête-à-tête."

"What!—with Cleveland as a third? My dear child, he *is* SOCIETY."

—And weeks passed away, and Catharine began to feel that to her also Cleveland *was* SOCIETY!

CHAPTER XIV.

It was in the midst of one of the most impassioned scenes in the Medea, when the whole being of Catharine was engrossed by the terrific truth of representation of the wondrous working of a powerful mind and outraged heart, where love that was idolatry leads to crime which is madness; when alternately excited and soothed by the miracles of

> "Dear music, that can touch
> Beyond all else the soul that loves it much,"

until life seemed the pageant, and the scene before her the reality,—that the illusion was destroyed by the most sudden transition from the highest poetry to the veriest commonplace, in the appearance of Mr. Stark, whose whole existence was an epitome of the cares, the blunders, the calculations, the sordidness, the bitterness, of this every-day working world.

Lady Darley was as little gratified by the unexpected, and

as she sensibly felt, unprecedented intrusion, as Miss Vernon. She had, however, too much worldly tact to allow her annoyance to manifest itself; and she consoled herself by reflecting that when Sir Greville Cleveland appeared, as he certainly would, before the commencement of the ballette, Mr. Stark,—who returned the contempt most demonstratively exhibited by Sir Greville, with all the interest of intense hatred,—would infallibly retire.

"Absorbed in the scene with as much *abandonnement* as the prima donna herself!" Mr. Stark began. "I envy you!—I envy the freshness of every tyro!

"'Ah, happy days, once more, who would not be a boy?'"

"That is a hackneyed commonplace," said Lady Darley, "and in point of sentiment untrue. There are very few men, especially young men, who have any tender regret for the days of school-bondage. A man might as reasonably lament his hard fate that he was not a young lamb,—that proverb of innocent enjoyment,—or any other animal, which has to fear only the whip or the goad, as *he* feared them. These have, perhaps, a more intense enjoyment of animal existence than he had,—and their intellectual pleasures must, I imagine, be pretty nearly equal."

"I am happy to err with Wordsworth," said Mr. Stark, with an expression as sarcastic as he ever ventured to exhibit to Lady Darley, of the éclat of whose patronage he was by no means insensible. "He has immortalized boyhood as retaining the last bright traces of the pre-existent state, of which

"'Our birth is but a sleep and a forgetting;
The soul which rises in us, our life's star,
Hath had elsewhere its setting,
And cometh from afar.'"

"Wordsworth never could have anticipated that his beautiful ode would be pressed into the service of such an argument," said Catharine, who read the writings of this most philosophic of the poets as she would have listened to the communings of a spirit, and who considered a quotation of this kind almost profanation.

"Wordsworth must be contented, like other dreamers, to have his visions turned to a useful purpose occasionally," returned Mr. Stark, who had not chivalry enough to repress a sneer which so many had deemed formidable, and from which he hoped so very young a woman as Miss Vernon would absolutely shrink.

"The utility of Wordsworth's poems is not dependant on a forced application of an insulated passage," said Catharine, with the simplicity and quietness of a person who thought only of supporting what she believed the truth. "None can read the wonderful pourings-out of a wonderful mind worthily, without becoming both wiser and better. That is a noble philosophy which demonstrates the blessedness that is around us and about us;—the beautiful, the true, the immortal."

"Some *will* regard the world *en beau*, while those who are nearest are compelled, for their misfortune, to see it *en vrai*," returned Mr. Stark, with a shrug. "The prism of fancy throws its own radiance on distant objects, just as you now, who are the segment of a circle distant from the Dutchess of Halifax, believe that her glittering turban is fresh from the looms of the gorgeous East; while I, who have just quitted her grace's box, vouch for its being manufactured of tarnished lama, which ought to have been inherited by her woman seven years since, and for which the said heiress of the wardrobe might have realized the sum of three farthings and a fraction."

"You are a most scandalous person," said Lady Darley, whose laugh, nevertheless, converted her reproof into applause.

"In this case, a most eulogistic one," said Stark. "In her Grace of Halifax, economy, always pardonable, is laudable. The wife of a poor nobleman, can we sufficiently commend the prudence that so palpably limits her own expenses?"

"Irony!" said Lady Darley. "It is a notorious fact, that the duke's income exceeds a hundred thousand pounds."

"And his expenditure a hundred and fifty thousand," returned Stark. "Whether that does not make out a case of very sufficient poverty, I appeal to Miss Vernon."

"At this moment she would assuredly give judgment against you," said Lady Darley. "She is prepared to visit you with the *peine forte et dure*, because you persist in engrossing one ear, while she would willingly give both ears and eyes to Pasta."

"Miss Vernon, when she has passed her novitiate, will learn that an opera-box is but a niche, in which the presiding divinities of fashion plant themselves to receive the homage of their worshippers. I shall consider my pardon conceded in the future tense."

Pasta was in all the wondrous agony of her best scene in the first act of the Medea; and Mr. Stark, who was desirous of propitiating a person so admired and *distinguée* as Miss Vernon, had the tact and *right* taste to allow her to enjoy it without interruption.

As soon, however, as the drop-curtain proclaimed that the efforts of genius after immortality had ceased, Mr. Stark resumed his very sublunary commonplace.

"I can scarcely credit my good fortune," said he. "During a whole act I have had the *éclat* of devoting myself to

Lady Darley and Miss Vernon, undisturbed by a single competitor! If it were not too egregious self-flattery, I should imagine people mistook me for Sir Greville Cleveland, and were cautious of standing between the light of Miss Vernon and her shadow. I hear there is to be a splendid réunion of the very élite at Cleveland House during the recess;—strange indeed, that the proceedings of St. Stephen's should affect those of Sir Greville!—that he should have permitted his thrice-sublimed exclusiveness to come into contact with the men of the people! It is a miracle worthy of the power that effected it."

"It is no miracle that at an important crisis,—an epoch in the national history,—a man of talent should sacrifice the elegant ease in which it has been his pleasure to pass existence, to the excitement of higher feelings,—the *utility* which you profess to advocate," said Lady Darley, who thought Mr. Stark had never been more disagreeable or more impertinent.

"But your ladyship will allow it to be a miracle that he, the most aristocratic of the exclusives, should appear suddenly as the apostle of the people,—the advocate for their initiation into all the mysteries of knowledge, and their consequent ascendency in the state," replied Mr. Stark.

"I do not see the absolute necessity of your consequence," said the Duke of Halifax, who had entered the box just in time to hear Mr. Stark's last sentence. "To excite in man the desire of knowledge as a means of *power*, politically so called, is to supply, in a certain point of view, a false motive. When knowledge comes to be universally diffused, it will cease to be political power. Power consists either in a real superiority, or the factitious superiority rooted in opinion and prejudice. There is not a vainer dream than the vision of the equality either of property or intellect. The immutable ordinances of Nature and of Providence are against it. Until all men have the same clearness and vigour of intellect,—the same industry,—the same constitutional strength,—although knowledge may be within reach of all, and all may benefit by it, there will be that infinite variety of *degrees* which will divide the highest from the lowest as immeasurably as at present. Power will ultimately be in the hands of the few. I am not asserting the necessity or the permanence of the aristocracy of mere rank, for the facts of history demonstrate it to contain the elements of decay; but an aristocracy of the mind will be lord of the ascendant, while one star continues to exceed another star in glory."

"There is an aristocracy which will always at least divide the empire both of rank and talent—I mean that of wealth," said Mr. Stark, gazing with unfeigned astonishment at that anomalous character—a radical peer;—"wealth will still give a certain ascendency to the possessor. It is the procurer of so much good, that the multitude always look with respect on the proprietor—their actuating principle being a desire to share the benefits of its diffusion."

"This is not precisely the most fitting scene in the world for a political discussion," said the duke. "I can scarcely explain how I came to be betrayed into it, except that I am here principally to congratulate Lady Darley—and"—with emphasis—"Miss Vernon—on the overwhelming eloquence with which Cleveland absolutely dazzled the house last night. We have so long considered him a man retired from the turmoil of public life, that to see him once more on the arena was hardly more agreeable than astonishing."

"To *one* party, I suppose," said Stark; "Sir Greville comes out, for the second time, on liberal principles."

"Sir!" said the duke, with an interrogative stare that would have done honour to the pride of the most unimpeachable tory.

"I say," persisted Mr. Stark, "that the present administration would be quite as well satisfied if Sir Greville had continued to be a silent member."

"Sir Greville probably consulted his own satisfaction rather than that of ministers," said his grace, with much hauteur.

"It is to be regretted that the constitution of the cabinet and the conscience are so often at issue," said Mr. Stark, who did not believe in the sincerity of the duke's political faith, and thought he hazarded nothing by a hint of the usually "impenetrable obscure" of his own principles.

"If ever I regret my birthright," said his grace, turning *from* Mr. Stark, "it is when I am obliged to content myself with reading the report of a speech in the lower house, such as Greville made on last night's important question. The countenance of a fine speaker is often an admirable accompaniment to a fine speech. I do not hold with Demosthenes, that the three great requisites of an orator are action—action—action; on the contrary, I admire that eloquence which disdains all other aid from the body than that of the voice and the eye. The effect of *these*, however, I confess, I am curious in observing."

The ballette was over—the prima donna was again on the stage—the hum of voices arose around—and Catharine was almost in despair. She was not exposed to the only interruption which, perhaps, she could have tolerated;—Sir Greville was still absent, and she would have found it difficult to decide at that moment whether his Grace of Halifax or Mr. Stark was the most disagreeable personage.

"As the protectress of Miss Vernon," said Lady Darley, who had no difficulty in penetrating the double cause of the dissatisfaction which saddened Catharine's countenance, "I am bound to defend her from the annoyance she is now suffering. I cannot permit your grace—I cannot permit *you*, Mr. Stark—to say a word while Pasta is within sight and hearing. Catharine is suffering martyrdom, which is a test of her musical faith to which I have no desire to subject her. Not a word;—this really *is* worth listening to."

The solemn, the magnificent strain, rose in full harmony on Catharine's delighted ear, filling her mind with those indefinite perceptions of grandeur and beauty which Madame de Staël has declared to be *religious*, and which *she* felt to belong to the poetry within the spirit, that cannot be written. But when did pleasure, even intellectual pleasure, add to its brightness, permanence? Who could expect the enjoyment of repose in the opera-box of Lady Darley? An irruption of three guardsmen—the only three patronised by Lady Darley—interrupted the comparative silence, and destroyed the enchantment for that night.

"Cleveland has absolutely astounded us all!" said one of them; "not the cleverness of his speech—no one doubted his powers—but such an application of them! He—the exclusive among the exclusives—converted into a radical! I should as soon have expected to find him with his gold toilet, and all his other decencies of life, as he calls them, in the back settlements of America. What *has* metamorphosed him?"

"*Oh, Dea certe!*" said Stark, with a glance at Catharine that was sufficiently intelligible.

"Do you tolerate a schism of this kind?" said another intruder, addressing Lady Darley. "We have yielded too much to Cleveland. I vote that he should be refused at Almack's—and, in short, sent to Coventry."

"That would not be convenient just now, as the world is engaged in struggling for invitations to Cleveland Park during the recess," said Lady Darley, coldly. "However, take my advice, and should you be among the invited, *decline*. You will have the satisfaction of being singular, which is achieving one step towards notoriety."

"I shall change my politics forthwith," said the third 'gentleman of the guards.' "We *may* live to see Cleveland at the head of affairs, and Brougham Chancellor of England. I shall begin to educate myself for the new era."

"It is well to begin in time, considering the barrenness of the soil you are intending to cultivate," said Mr. Stark, with his usual benevolence and good-breeding. "It is a long journey from the beginning of the primer to the end of the syntax of politics!"

"Suppose I place myself under your guidance; you shall initiate me into the mysteries of political economy, and I will repay you by teaching you somewhat of the *humanities*," retorted the guardsman, who cared nothing for Mr. Stark or his epigrams.

"Really, gentlemen, if you are here merely to exercise your wit, you have leave to retire; the lobby will answer your purpose quite as well. I never allow the atmosphere of my box to be vitiated by personalities," said Lady Darley, who was not particularly gratified by the presence of any of her visiters, and was compelled to conceal the disappointment she really felt at the nonappearance of Sir Greville.

"Then, my dear Lady Darley, expel Mr. Stark, for personalities are to him the vital breath of his wit;" said the senior of the guardsmen. "Promise me an invitation to Cleveland Park, and I will make my bow incontinently."

"No," said Lady Darley, "I never commit myself by a recommendation."

"Then my hundred guineas are as lost as Troy; your refusal deprives me of my last chance of going there. I flattered myself I was a favourite, and made sure of your interest, which, we all know, is omnipotent. I will never hazard a bet again which can be affected by the caprice of a lady."

"Petition Sir Greville himself;—*le voici*," said Lady Darley, turning round to welcome his appearance. "You are just in time for the crush-room, Sir Greville. We do not stay for the ballette; Catharine is Gothic enough to dislike it. Catharine, my dear, the opera and your sufferings are ended for this evening;—you are released from a purgatory to which that of Tantalus was paradise."

But Catharine had forgotten even those sufferings. A voice was whispering in her ear, which *to her* was as the music of an archangel. The weariness,—the disappointments of the evening,—were remembered no more. She was leaning on the arm of Cleveland;—she had heard that his hours had been spent at the post of duty,—a post to which *her* influence had recalled him,—and at that moment she felt that earth had nothing brighter or better to bestow than the emotions whose light stamped her brow with the impress of immortality.

CHAPTER XV

It was the middle of June, and Catharine had been in London nearly three months. How short a period, and yet how pregnant with those most important events in human life,—events which permanently affect the character! Able to appreciate the value of the elegance and splendour which surrounded her,—considering them as graceful appendages to existence, but entirely separating them from things essential to human happiness;—comprehending the *fatigue of pleasure*,—the toilsomeness of the incessant pursuit of fashion;—shrinking from the hollowness and heartlessness of ties meant to be the holiest and purest, but converted into mere modes of gratifying ambition or avarice,—a means of extending a connexion or perpetuating a name;—she turned from the gaudy world *without* to the serenity of that *within*, and lifted up her heart with a feeling of thankfulness, that, dazzled as she might have been by the meteors which were flashing before her, the light *there* still burnt steadily. She might not have *found*, but she *made* leisure, for the cultivation of an intellect already so carefully nurtured;—and there is perhaps but one higher delight than that of conscious talent,—the conviction that it is "as a gleam of immortality" to him who has reached the heart through the mind.

The secret of Sir Greville Cleveland's extraordinary distinction among the most distinguished, was, perhaps, that he did not affect an indifference to their opinion,—he really felt it. Careless of applause or censure, it was evident that his own will regulated his movements;—that he was gay, reserved, dissipated, or solitary, according to the prevalent mood of his mind, and for his own especial gratification. In society he was occasionally cold, but too well-bred to be brusque. Sometimes his conversation was animated,—even playful: sometimes—but rarely, and to particular persons—he was eloquent; and, on important topics, impassioned. Of his wonderful powers of mind, none doubted. During his short public career, when ambition seemed the idol of his worship, and its highest honours within his grasp, —when the eyes of all public men were on him, waiting anxiously for the result,—his entire abandonment of political pursuits, and his Epicurean indulgence of leisure, disappointed as much as they startled men of all parties. By the female world his secession was hailed with delight. Always now to be found in the gayest circles, mothers and daughters indulged in visions of splendour, in which Cleveland Park formed no insignificant object. His wealth, his ancient name, his influential connexions, were sufficient to attract speculators of this description. But when to these were united individual distinction, a magnificent person, splendid talents, and *at will* the most captivating manners, —the ardour of pursuit may be imagined, augmented too by his evident fondness for female society, and the curious fact of his avoiding even the appearance of a flirtation. Handsome as Lady Darley still was,—preserving a youthfulness of person which time seemed to attack in vain,—the tone of her intimacy with Sir Greville was so demonstrative of the soberest friendship, that even the bitterness of disappointed female aspirants never expended its venom on her. The *retenue* of her manner had placed her at the very summit of *respectability* as well as of fashion; and the whispers of slander never ascended high enough to reach her.

But when she produced a *protégée*,—a kinswoman,—so beautiful and graceful that the usual commonplaces of depreciation were felt to be pointless, even by those who ventured them,—Lady Darley's popularity with the whole class of matrimony-hunters, matrons, and damsels, sunk to a very low ebb. They had discovered now, they said, why Lady Darley had hitherto professed so disinterested a friendship for Cleveland. There was this niece *in petto* to be produced on a favourable opportunity, and thrown constantly in his way by the inimitably ingenious manœuvre of fixing him, previous to her appearance, on such terms of intimacy as would render his withdrawing impossible. And everybody knew what "blind contact" would effect. No man—no disengaged man—could resist the influence of daily association. Doubtless Miss Vernon was well tutored by her clever aunt, and was perfect in her *rôle*. And as the attachment of Sir Greville became more evident, people began to express doubts whether, after all, his attentions would ever lead to that consummation which, beyond doubt, Lady Darley and her niece devoutly wished. Would a man, whose private associations were conducted on a principle as aristocratic as the bias of his political prejudices had an opposite tendency, marry so completely out of his caste? Miss Vernon was just of honourable descent,—no more,—the daughter of an officer,—a soldier of fortune, probably:—her mother, the sister of a country parson, or some such thing. What a *mésalliance* for Cleveland! It was quite impossible he could seriously contemplate encountering such a phalanx of evils as a connexion of this kind would oppose to his comfort. How would he feel himself in the midst of the Bloomsbury gentility of a spruce parsonage,—at a table redolent of ducks and peas, port and sherry? How would he endure that the elegance of Cleveland Park should be polluted by the presence of a man in "a suit of rusty black," whose parish formed the boundaries of his travels and understanding;—who, having no idea of *les convenances de société*, would be in everybody's way, and find everybody in his? Then the wife,—always, in such cases, the *ursa major*,—a slattern or a notable!—proclaiming her affinity to the lady of the mansion, by constant quotations of "*my niece's*" opinions! Then the half-dozen little stars who doubtless would complete the brightness of the domestic constellation! No!—the thing was altogether impossible. Cautious as Sir Greville was,—shrinking almost instinctively from the approach of any plebeian contamination,—it was not to be supposed that he would allow his admiration of a person that might be pretty, to entail such intolerable horrors on his futurity. Miss Vernon would find that the intellect on which she evidently valued herself was not of an order to effect a miracle of this kind. A man in Sir Greville's position could not overlook the claims his own family had to his consideration. What would the haughty Countess of P—— say to such an accession to the honours on which she piqued herself,—she whose vaunt it was, that, since the days of the Plantagenets, *her* blood had flowed in the purest channel, undefiled, in a single instance, by mingling its stream with that of *the people!* How would Ponsonby of Ponsonby receive *such* a Lady Cleveland,—he who, in the pride of heptarchial descent, had said, that "although as a subject he honoured his king,—as a man of family he could not condescend to measure himself with a Guelph!"—who deemed the Bourbons *parvenus*,—and derided a nobility derived from a *maire du palais*,—a Capet! There was not a man in England who might not perpetrate such an alliance with greater impunity than Sir Greville! for not even the Howards were fenced round by such a bevy of uncompromising aristocrats. By these and similar considerations, mothers and daughters brought themselves to a comfortable conviction that Sir Greville never would commit an error of so grave a kind,—and they had still a farther consolation in the reflection that if he *were*, notwithstanding their convictions, infatuated enough to be guilty of so unpardonable a sin, he would find his punishment in being one of the most miserable of human beings.

Reckless of all these prospective evils, Sir Greville Cleveland still remained at the side of Catharine, drinking in, at ear and eye, a love of which he had believed himself incapable. The human heart may be so exhausted by passion, that no flower of feeling will bloom on its parched and arid surface; and Cleveland rejoiced to feel that all within *him* was *not* barren,—that he could yet breathe the sigh of love, —that he was yet sensible to the ecstasy of its hopes,—to the not unpleasing torment of its fears. And how grateful to Catharine the secret consciousness that *she* had roused such a mind from inactivity to exertions which might be of incalculable benefit to a whole community,—that *her* smile was prized as an adequate reward for the labour to which it animated him. Yet the world was so far right, that Sir Greville was not the plighted lover of Catharine. Each aware of the feelings which existed in the other, words had not breathed them. It seemed that Cleveland, with his usual Epicurean sensitiveness to whatever heightens either the sentiments or the sensations, desired to prolong that poetical epoch in the life of love which precedes its avowal, —when all is told by looks, by actions, even by voice,—and by words every thing concealed;—when love converts every commonplace of existence into a romance, by abandoning itself to the imagination; and almost hesitates to utter or to hear declarations which are to disperse its dream, and set around it all the thorns and fences of reality.

Lady Darley had penetration enough to see exactly how matters were progressing, and tact enough to abstain from any, even the least direct interference. Fashion was the goddess of her idolatry,—that after which she was constantly crying, "*per fas, per nefas, rem;—rem, rem, quocunque modo, rem;*"—and to see her niece the wife of him who controlled its oracles, would be the complete gratification of the highest ambition of which she was capable.

With unequalled adroitness she contrived to place them constantly in positions calculated to exhibit in each those peculiar traits of character most suited to the taste or feelings of the other:—and all this management was effected with so exquisite a regard to delicacy, that neither was startled for an instant with a suspicion of the possibility of being manœuvred into an engagement.

The assembling of a large party at Cleveland Park during the recess was a thing of annual occurrence when its proprietor was in England. Lady Darley anticipated with delight a period always fraught with enjoyment, but now pregnant with higher interest. Drives, walks,—even the scenery of such a place in the summer season, when all creation bloomed and sang in the spirit of love,—must necessarily lead to the declaration which, it was evident, was only just not made. There was not the shadow of a doubt on her mind that it would ultimately be made and accepted, but she felt that it was necessary to the perfection of her triumph that this should be effected before the completion of Catharine's *first* season in town. But she was careful not to alarm Miss Vernon's delicacy by avowing the full extent either of her observations or her hopes. She spoke often of Sir Greville, but *wisely;* not as one of those *maladroit* persons who, wishing to impress their hearers with one sole idea, are, in a perverted sense of the words, "instant in season and out of season," but rather following the train of Catharine's thoughts, and avoiding all those allusions in which underbred people indulge as an outlet for all the wit and piquancy they have treasured up for similar emergencies. She left his eloquence to the tender mercies of newspaper editors, secure that, whatever might be their comments, his speeches would reach Catharine's understanding and heart by the aid of their own high deservings. His importance was sufficiently authenticated by the evidence of the world at large, and the admiration with which her own sex regarded him was neither silent nor restrained. When the carriages were at the door to convey them to Cleveland Park, Lady Darley regarded them with the agreeable certainty that, when they again entered the square, they would convey thither Sir Greville's bride elect. She had the satisfactory consciousness of having done all in her power to produce so desirable a consummation, and she reflected with considerable complaisance on the munificence with which she had embellished Catharine's jewel-box and wardrobe, feeling convinced that, "if the spirits of the departed were cognizant of what passed on earth, her poor brother would be gratified with the sincere affection she testified for his orphan, and her constant regard to the dear girl's best interests."

In the happiest frame of mind, therefore, Lady Darley drove up the noble avenue that led to Cleveland Park,—the hereditary residence of Sir Greville.

CHAPTER XVI.

The party assembled at Cleveland Park was even more splendid than usual. Those who composed it were not only persons possessing a certain degree of rank and fashion, but also a considerable elevation in the scale of intellect. Sir Greville did not consider that the production of a clever work necessarily rendered a man an agreeable, or even a suitable, member of his domestic circle, but he regarded it as a recommendation,—an excuse for minor objectionable qualities, and a claim to forbearance, if not approbation. No man of genius, whose manners and morals did not disgrace his mind, had reason to complain of the exclusiveness of the owner of Cleveland Park. On the contrary, Sir Greville was fond of showing how highly he appreciated intellect, by bringing its possessors into a society capable of understanding, and, in a certain degree, of rewarding their efforts. These persons were naturally less conventional than those whose whole existence has been spent in one peculiar sphere, from the tone of which they have never departed, and which they almost believe the universal attribute of mankind. The variety was novel, piquant, and consequently agreeable to people to whom change itself is almost always a relief, and who do not undervalue attainments for which they are not ambitious of being distinguished. Intrenched in the superiority of rank, they allow that of genius to a race whom they consider its professors; and if any of their own class aim at plucking the laurel, they draw that line of demarcation between him and other literateurs which separates the amateur from the artist.

No part of the existence of Catharine had been more delightful than the present. It excited and gratified both mem ory and hope. It recalled the brightest days of her past life, and it opened a vista of future happiness such as realized her wildest dreams. Even in his character of host, when compelled to give much of his attention and observance to his guests generally, he never lost the power or the wish of distinguishing Catharine by a word,—a look,—a movement,—an inflection of voice,—something which spoke to her heart, and, delicate as it was, was sufficient to secure her the deference of all around, who felt that she was to be the mistress of Cleveland,—the future distributer of its hospitalities. The most reluctant matron was compelled to admit the belief that this *might* possibly occur, and to shape her proceedings accordingly. Even young unmarried women were sinking rapidly from the rank of rivals to that of flatterers and expectants of future favours. Every look of Lady Darley's bespoke her entire satisfaction with all around her;—not a cloud seemed to dim the brightness of Catharine's horizon, and, that its splendour might be the more per ceptible, a letter from Rachel, arriving when " hope was at the highest," placed vividly before her the contrast of the obscurity, the wearisomeness, the insipidity, of the existence to which she had been condemned at Golding Magna. Even the contents of that letter threw *one* drop into her " cup of joy;" for a creature so pure in heart as she was could not but rejoice, in the midst of her own happiness, to learn that one she esteemed and loved was escaping from the severity of a sorrow which Catharine now was well able to comprehend.

Rachel wrote thus :—

" If my former letters, dearest Catharine, have been occupied chiefly with *your* interests, and inquiries after all that amuses or surprises you, in a mode of existence of which my imagination,—always a sober painter,—cannot even conceive a picture;—if, as you complain, I have said little of Golding Magna or its inhabitants,—it has been because I was reluctant to touch on topics which I knew most excited your curiosity,—shall I not rather say your sympathy? —while so much uncertainty involved them. Now that feelings,—and feelings, in the High Street of Golding Magna, must, you are aware, constitute my events,—which have hitherto been fluctuating, seem to become more steady;—now that I can write what will contribute to your satisfaction, I fear I am in danger of wearying you with egotism. I have much to tell, and the temptation of opening to you thoughts which none around me would pardon, or perhaps understand, is too strong to be resisted. I know that you love me, and I do believe that you will rejoice to learn, that a prospect of happiness opens to me sufficient to satisfy the humble hopes of one who knows that, at least, this world is a succession of trials. To be the first, sole occupant of *his* heart, might have filled me with overweening self-confidence. I might have learned to value too highly those poor endowments which had attracted him, and I am satisfied to believe that it was necessary to the security of my soul, that I should reap only the fruit of patience, and have to be satisfied with an affection that results perhaps from gratitude, perhaps also from compassion.

"Believe not, dearest Catharine, that this conviction is as humiliating to me as to you. Taught to judge with lowly humility of mankind in general, and of my own sex in particular,—to estimate myself as a poor shred of mortality, with no inherent value, except as I served to exhibit my Creator's power and goodness,—I cannot but receive the affection, even the good-will of my fellow-creatures, rather as an emanation of their own benevolence, than a tribute to my deservings. What is there in me worthy to engross the entire heart of one so gifted as George Fulton? Endowed with the best power,—that of being eminently useful in the great field of man's salvation,—how wide an interval separates him from me, whose highest honour it must be to contribute to the comfort of his hours of retirement,—to share the meanest of his cares,—and to participate in such duties as admit the association of a woman? How little real partner ship can woman have in the higher exercises of man's duties, or his ambition! In her it is hardly becoming even to understand the extent of her husband's attainments, fully to comprehend the efforts of his eloquence, far less to assist them. Even I, with the cumbrous waste of learning it was my poor father's pride and pleasure to bestow on me, have learned the wisdom of concealing it, and blush more for my knowledge than my ignorance. *You* have combated such opinions more than once, but happy is it for me that they are mine. My humility makes my felicity; and do not, dear Catharine, tell me that I am under a delusion, for to wake from the dream would be—*not to live.*

"Your departure, deeply as I felt it, and sincerely as I regretted it, has led to my happiness. How little do we feel that Providence

"'Behind the darkest cloud
Conceals a smiling face!'

How much wisdom is there in the declaration, even in a worldly sense, that 'patience worketh experience, and experience hope.' Gradually, as Fulton's mind admitted the certainty that you were really gone and for ever, that you were as the inhabitant of another world to which he could not follow you, his regrets partook more of the character of resignation. The first symptom of this improved state of feeling was his speaking of you—a topic which, at first, he had sedulously avoided; and the fear of hearing your name mentioned made him, I think, reluctant to visit the rectory, where he was quite sure that it would be introduced. At length, however, he came as usual, inquired whether I had heard from you, and what impression the new scenes to which you were introduced had made on your mind. By reading passages in your first letter I was able to satisfy him on this point, and I saw that he evidently was affected by the picture you gave of the elegances surrounding you. Your portraits of your new acquaintance mortified him, I perceived, by forcing him to remember how far he fell short of them in all the qualities which you notice most approvingly. He felt also the impassable gulf that *position* had put between you and himself, and he *almost* despised the *littleness* of such distinction as had hitherto been the object of his warmest ambition. 'How little do the high and mighty ones of this earth think of such as we are!' he said, with bitterness. 'How we toil after an honourable fame, in the miserable delusion that the best of our fellows will hear at least of our doings, while they look not down, from their heights of grandeur, on the crawling of the worms on which they hardly condescend to tread! Men waste health, strength, existence in the struggle, but how vain their most strenuous efforts to rise above the obscurity of their condition!'—'Surely,' said I, 'that is not always true; and, even if it were, a minister of God ought to find no subject of regret in such a circumstance. He seeks the glory of his Master, not his own; he aims at increasing the real happiness of his fellow-creatures, not at obtaining their applause. His object surely is to be useful, not distinguished. The laborious servant of the sanctuary may better do the work of his Creator, than the High Priest on whose brow flame the gems of the tribes of Israel!'—'My spirit is too worldly,' he replied, with a sigh; but afterward he spoke of you with less interest, as one may recall a bright day that has departed. As he began to talk less of you, I found he said more of myself. He inquired after my pursuits;—recommended books;—read to me when I worked;—walked with me;—explained his own views of things; his plans of future life;—and, two days since, asked me to share that life with him. He described to me honestly the difference of the love with which you had inspired him, and that tender friendship which he could offer me. 'Every man has his dream,' said he; 'I have had mine, and I have now been awake long enough to be sensible that it is not the part of wisdom to dim the sober brightness of the reality by contrasting it with the unreal splendour of the vision. I loved Catharine neither *with* nor *against* my reason, but independently of it. In her presence feeling only was awake,—such delight as thrills us when we hear wild and intense music,—or as if we were suddenly ushered into a scene where all the glories and wonders of the world were gathered together, absorbing us in such a madness of delight, that, while we are sensible of feeling, we know not what we feel. It is not thus now. I seek you, Rachel, as the partner of the pilgrimage of human existence,—who will alleviate, by your sympathy, the toils that must necessarily beset it,—whose love will sooth the evils and the troubles to which "man is born as the sparks fly upward."' What answer could I make to such an avowal?—I could but weep, and answer him in the words of Ruth the Moabitess, —"'The Lord do so to me, and more also, if aught but death divide thee and me!'

—"How tranquil is happiness! My father's step is lighter, and his voice more glad, as he sees how his dearest hopes are advancing towards accomplishment;—my mother looks happier than usual, as preparations for our marriage make larger demands on her activity. For myself, the quiet of my heart resembles the sleep of a child who has been rambling abroad until fatigue has driven it to repose;—too great excitement has forced rest upon me. Satisfied with feeling that I am happy, my exhausted spirit desires not to draw aside the veil of futurity. When *he* is near me I am too well satisfied, even to recollect that there *is* a to-morrow.

"How shall I conclude this volume? Not by apologizing for the length of details which I know will interest you, but by praying sincerely that God may bless you, as he has blessed me, and, if it be possible, more abundantly."

—"So much for the eternity of human affections!" said Catharine, as she folded the letter. "Wisely and mercifully are we constituted, who in a world of change are ourselves so changeable. Is not mutability a condition of our being?—mutability of body—of heart—of mind? What is *brokenness of heart?* Is it not when *we* remain unchanged, while all else obeys the impulse of its nature, and we expiate the discord created in the universal harmony by everlasting silence?"

How melancholy a reflection for the young!—for a woman, too, just entering on the experience of the heart! Just embarked on the dangerous sea in which so many have been wrecked! *Mutability!*—how much of fear—how much of sorrow—how much of despair—is comprehended in that one word!—that our very best and brightest feelings must, even against our will, *change!*—that our love itself must lose its "bloom and perfume" even under the happiest auspices!—that the romance which renders our youth noble and generous must pass away!—that we must outlive the poetry of existence!—that we must live to gaze at the bright stars, and feel no more that they are "the poetry of heaven,' —on the fair earth with a deadened sensibility to its beauties! Alas! that time, which lays its decaying hand on our bodies, stealing away a grace—a charm—a beauty—with each touch, should deal even more remorselessly with our affections! Blessed sunshine of youth! Who has not lived to regret the dreams which were begotten by its brightness! Who has not wept on being rudely awakened from the illusions which rendered earth a paradise! Who has not smiled over the vexations and the follies which threw a transient cloud over those days of spring, as he contrasts them with the errors and the trials of advancing life! Well has "*immortal youth*" been described as among the joys of heaven. In that alone is a perpetual fountain of happiness. With that we associate all the glow, the freshness, the buoyancy of spirit—

> "Which, out of every lovely thing we see,
> Still extracts something beautiful and new!"

This is indeed to be regenerate;—to throw away, with our worn-out bodies, the sordid cares, the debasing passions, the ignoble purposes which have marred our early promise! To regain not only youth, but *immortal* youth!—to escape not only sorrow, but *change!*

CHAPTER XVII.

Lord Bacon says, "A man that hath no virtue in himself ever envieth virtue in others, for men's minds will either feed upon their own good or upon other's evil; and who wanteth the one will prey upon the other; and whoso is out of hope to attain another's virtue, will seek to come at even hand by depressing another's fortune."

Independently of that producing cause of envy, "the having no virtue in herself," the Dutchess of Halifax had an active, restless mind, which, being always idle, was always mischievous. She had successively produced three awkward daughters, intending that one of them should engross all the wealth, and honour, and dignity of sharing the fate and fortunes of Sir Greville Cleveland,—in which praiseworthy design, having endured three several defeats, it is by no means unnatural that she should regard with considerable ill-will the individual likely to appropriate the good which she had found unattainable.

"Sir Greville," said the dutchess,—it was Sunday evening, and there was a tolerably general *réunion* of the inhabitants of Cleveland House in its splendid music-room,—"do you always go to church on Sunday in the country?"

"Generally,--the example is good."

"Yes,—but it might produce as much effect, and be offered with greater comfort to one's self, if you would alter the arrangements of your pew. I suppose you are here to *fête* the tenantry during Christmas, and how you manage to endure its unsheltered situation at that dreadful season I cannot conceive. It is bad enough even at Midsummer."

"I flattered myself it was a perfect *bijou* of a pew," said Sir Greville, to whom it was new to listen to a breathing of censure on any one of his appointments.

"Oh, *tout au contraire;*—those crimson cushions and curtains are the most unbecoming things in nature. Then the fireplace is most awkwardly situated. One must sit with either that or the preacher behind one, having either at disadvantage. Miss Vernon's complexion, I observed, looked quite faded, and, after that, judge of the rest. Pray, Miss Vernon, had you a comfortable pew at Golding Magna?"

"Yes, for we heard well and saw nobody."

"Humph! You lived with the parson, did not you?"

"Yes, with the vicar, my mother's brother," returned Catharine, coolly.

"Should you like to be a parson's wife, Miss Vernon?" *vulgarly* persisted the dutchess.

"It would depend on the man," returned Catharine, rather amused than provoked.

"You don't object to the profession, then?"

"No."

"'Did this in Cesar seem ambitious?'" said the dutchess, turning to Lady Darley. "Miss Vernon is a beautiful pattern of humility."

"Your grace's discoveries are as notable as they are pleasant," said Lady Darley, pointedly.

"Don't be angry, my dear. It really only amuses me to imagine Miss Vernon in a straw bonnet and a black silk gown, leather shoes, and white cotton stockings—the uniform of all parsons' wives in the country, I have heard."

"Possibly," said Lady Darley, "for I know nothing of the class in general."

"But Miss Vernon must know a great deal. I suppose, my dear, after church, you spent Sunday at Golding Magna in singing psalms."

"On the contrary, much as we do at Cleveland Park—that is, in abusing our neighbours."

The dutchess was in the smallest possible degree disconcerted; but she rallied again, and resumed the attack with the greater vigour, because she perceived that Sir Greville was listening with an air of interest.

"Well, that must be more amusing. But what kind of people were your neighbours?"

"Good, bad, mediocre; pretty, ugly, plain; poor, rich, and *between*," said Catharine, calmly.

"Just the kind of people of whom one knows nothing," said her grace, petulantly.

"Let us hope something of the good, and in all humility let us confess, something of the bad," said Sir Greville, coming to the rescue. "The shades between these two great extremes exist all over the world."

"If it be not impertinent, what was the name of your Golding Magna friend?" said the dutchess, turning from Sir Greville to Catharine.

"Not impertinent!—I can only be obliged by the great interest your grace is pleased to take in me," said Catharine, so demurely as to excite a general smile. "Revely is my relation's name."

"If the dutchess ever troubled herself about controversial divinity, or divinity of any kind, she would recognise that as a name not unknown to fame," said Sir Greville.

"*If* I did—but as I never do, I plead guilty to knowing nothing in the world about Mr. Revely. I dare say he has a son, has he not?"

"None."

"Fortunate enough—was it not, Lady Darley?" said the dutchess, flippantly. "Pray, Miss Vernon, is it true that curates always make love out of the book of Ruth?"

"My dear," said the duke, "your wit is too brilliant to be wasted on people who don't understand it, and are in danger therefore, of undervaluing it. Miss Vernon, shall we have some music?"

Wearied with the flippancy of the dutchess, Catharine willingly assented. Sir Greville arranged the lights and the music-books, and placed himself in such a situation as, while he heard the divinest of Handel's songs to advantage, enabled him to enjoy a complete view of the countenance of the beautiful musician.

"Well, I confess I am not moved by the 'concord of sweet sounds,'" said the dutchess. "I detest all singing but Pasta's, and all music except at the opera."

"Perhaps you have not before heard Miss Vernon," said Lady Adelaide Willoughby, who was always amiable, and particularly observant of the *bienséances*, which it was the dutchess's pleasure to violate, as a Frenchman eats bread *à discrétion*.

"Indeed I have—at Lady Darley's—on the first night of her exhibition:" she added, in rather a lower voice—"Now, my dear creature, can you conceive any thing equal to the folly of Lady Darley? Knowing Cleveland as she does—the most fickle—the most insensible—the most exacting—the most tenacious of human beings—it is really beyond *be-*

yond that *she* can contribute to the infatuation which is making her *protégée* perfectly ridiculous."

"Her *penchant* for Sir Greville?" said Lady Adelaide with a smile. "Look at him at this precise moment, and judge whether he be not doing his best to strengthen the delusion."

"You do not actually believe that an obscure nobody is to share the honours and dignities of Cleveland Park and its appertenances?"

"Most devoutly and most contentedly."

"Oh, if Miss Vernon be under your special protection—not that her being thrust into our particular set has ever been satisfactorily explained to me. The transition from a country parsonage to Lady Darley's dressing-room was sufficiently great—but to Lady Darley's boudoir, and the Cleveland drawing-rooms—is rather too immense. If the absurdity of Cleveland's committing such a *mésalliance* were possible, only conceive the rage of all the Ponsonbys! That is precisely the only thing which would make me forgive it."

"And your cross-examination of Miss Vernon, on the merits of her uncle's parsonage, was undertaken in the benevolent design of demonstrating to Sir Greville all the horrors into which he is about to fall?"

"Precisely;—if one had but a few allies!—But was there ever such a set of frights at Cleveland as this year? One would think Lady Darley had had the selection of them all, and had invited them with a view to affording her niece the advantages of contrast. Lady Paul Lorimer—'deeply, darkly,' but *not* 'beautifully blue'—with her chymistry, her botany, her poetry, her metaphysics, and her omnium gatherum albums—'her eyes in a fine phrensy rolling,' as she fixes them on Miss Vernon's face; pretending to be absorbed in admiration of her beauty, when all the time she is really making eyes at W., the poet, whom she is toadying beyond all experience, to get him to dedicate his next volume to her—which he will not do, because he abhors all blues in general, and Lady Paul in particular. The verses she was showing about yesterday, pretending they were her own, were actually a folly of W.'s, sent ages ago to a country newspaper. Only read them, and fancy Lady Paul, large as Hercules and strong as a porter, '*the trembling leaf.*' There they are—and the identical newspaper."

Lady Adelaide read:—

"'Were I a trembling leaf
On yonder stately tree,
After a season gay and brief,
Condemn'd to fade and flee;

"'I should be loath to fall
Beside the common way,
Welt'ring in mire, and spurn'd by all,
Till trodden down to clay.

"'I would not choose to die
All on a bed of grass,
Where thousands of my kindred lie,
And idly rot in mass.

"'Nor would I like to spread
My thin and wither'd face,
In *hortus siccus*, pale and dead,
A mummy of my race.

"'No,—on the wings of aii
Might I be left to fly,
I know not, and I heed not where,
A waif of earth and sky!

"'Or cast upon the stream,
Curl'd like a fairy boat,
As through the changes of a dream,
To the world's end I'd float.

"'Who that hath ever been,
Could bear to be no more?
Yet who would tread again the scene
He trod through life before?

"'On,—with intense desire
Man's spirit will move on;
It seems to die, yet, like heaven's fire,
It is not quench'd, but gone.'

"Lady Paul might have plagiarised worse verses," said Lady Adelaide, returning them.

"Yes,—but the jest of their being W.'s own! Just conceive it!—and the gravity with which he paid the proper compliments to Lady Paul's vanity! Now can you fancy the equal to *that?* Lady Jane Pierce absolutely singing a second to Miss Vernon!—with her peacock voice, just as if she intended showing how very absurd some women can be! See;—Cleveland cannot stand it; he is absolutely walking away."

"What a delicious voice Miss Vernon has!" said Lady Adelaide, as he approached.

"Very, but—"

"Not powerful enough to drown Lady Jane Pierce's, is not that true?" said the dutchess.

"I am glad to have been spared the pain of saying it."

"After all,—who would marry a woman for an accomplishment, all the enjoyment of which he may have by paying for?" said the dutchess.

"Men have done it from time to time," replied Sir Greville, carelessly.

"And *so* 'gone mad,'" added the dutchess, supplying the *misquotation*. "But do for once tell me, my dear Sir Greville, on what principle you selected your present party?"

"Harmony, my dear dutchess, harmony!—While Mr. W. and Lady Paul talk poetry together, Lord Paul amuses himself by quarrelling with Villiers about politics. Lady Jane

Pierce is here to praise my musical instruments, while her sister, the Lady Alice, botanizes in my conservatory, and pronounces my collection of plants unequalled. Lord Henry Mackenzie makes love to Miss Austin, much to the satisfaction of her excellent mother, while Sir Harry and Lady Beaumanor, in all the rapture of the honey-moon, make love to each other much to their own contentment. Then Miss Bertram, assisted in her geological researches by Stanhope, has enlightened me as to the various strata on which this, the mansion of my ancestors, is reared. The duke praises my schools, projects rail-roads, and favours me with occasional lectures on political economy. Lady Archer pours into the sympathizing ear of Lady Darley her lamentations on the never-ending topic of her lord's extravagance and her children's *gaucheries*. Yourself and Lady Adelaide find employment in criticising me and my guests, doubtless with a view to our amendment. Well,—*que voulez-vous?* I really pique myself on the general satisfactoriness of my arrangements."

"But Miss Vernon!—for Heaven's sake don't let us omit Miss Vernon!" said the dutchess, affectedly.

"Miss Vernon!—Ah, true," said Sir Greville. "Well, she and I amuse ourselves with looking on."

"Being at leisure,—having decided your own game," said the dutchess, rising and walking away.

"No, my dear dutchess,—unfortunately for *me*, not decided!" and Sir Greville walked again to the side of Miss Vernon, affording her grace leisure to pursue her benevolent remarks.

"After all, every rational woman would refuse Sir Greville," said she, lowering her voice to a whisper. "It is astonishing what dreadful tales were rumoured when Lady Sophia Barron first went to Italy. If he *be* to marry, it is wise in him to choose a woman who knows nothing of his past."

"But all the world *has* known of his past for these last ten years, and yet any one of us would have made our best courtesy for the honour of his alliance," said Lady Adelaide.

"Then his conduct is abominable in bestowing on such a person that which *we* should have vouchsafed to accept," said the dutchess, with an affectation of sportiveness.

"But what a gifted creature she is! We may contrive to render birth and rank exclusive, but beauty and talents are dreadful democrats. If ambition be Miss Vernon's foible, she will find hundreds willing to gratify it quite as able as Sir Greville."

"My dear Lady Adelaide, that is so like you!—Always *un peu romanesque*. After all, your own romance was not pleasant enough to be remembered."

"The dutchess's reminiscences always furnished her with

the means of punishing a disagreement of opinion by darting at the offender a very pointed shaft from her quiver.

"Suffering has taught me good-will to others," said Lady Adelaide, gently; her short history—how few words suffice to tell the wreck of woman's dearest hopes!—being too much public property to permit her to affect unconsciousness. "Miss Vernon loves Cleveland, not the *Cleveland estates*, and I am benevolent enough to wish no woman to endure a disappointment of her first young affections."

"How very odd!" said the dutchess, languidly. "I thought, my dear, you had really lived long enough to have got beyond all that."

"Does woman ever get beyond it?" asked Lady Adelaide, quietly.

"Experimentally I know nothing. I married the duke because I was desired to do so; and, if not particularly happy, we have been at least too well-bred to render each other miserable."

"You are fortunate," said Lady Adelaide; "but the mode of life which you find endurable would be positive wretchedness to many,—to Miss Vernon, possibly."

"To all *têtes exaltées*," said the dutchess, looking considerably bored, and varying her amusement by an assiduous observation of Sir Greville and Catharine.

"You are not aware of the great interest you have excited in the dutchess," said Cleveland;—her examination of you has been—nay, continues to be—intense. Lady Darley, you perceive, is sufficiently wearied to find a ramble in the conservatory refreshing. Shall we join her?"

Catharine took his offered arm, and they walked away. It was but the length of two apartments from the music-room to the conservatory, yet Sir Greville found time to congratulate Catharine on her taste for walking, and to inquire how she would like the next morning to be employed,—whether they should ride, drive, sail, explore the country or the town, or, if no party were formed—if all were left to amuse themselves, would *she*, at her own hour, allow him to be the companion of her ramble?—He particularly desired to show her his late improvements,—to have the benefit of her taste on those he projected. Catharine blushed—hesitated—assented,—and found herself at the side of Lady Darley.

* * * * * *

It was one of those bright and sunny mornings in June, which seem to realize all that the poets have sung of the loveliness of spring. The party at Cleveland had divided into sundry sets,—driving, riding, sailing, fishing, walking, as caprice or inclination prompted; but all were abroad, wooing the glad influence of a blue and beaming sky. Catharine, also, was inhaling the balmy air, her heart bounding with the joy of its own hopes, throwing its own gladness over "the universal face of things," and gratefully exulting in the deep, internal consciousness, that in this fair world there is, if somewhat to be suffered, more—much more—to be enjoyed.

"If life were ever thus!" said Sir Greville, who had walked for some minutes in silence at her side; "the vicious and the trifling far away;—all creation radiant as if the angels were abroad, and it rejoiced in their smiles,—no clouds,—the very shadows rendering the sunshine more beautiful,—what could one crave more than its eternity?"

"*Change*," said Catharine, smiling at the unwonted mood into which he had fallen.

"Such a thought is rather premature in early youth,—a youth so bright as yours," returned Sir Greville, thoughtfully. "The lesson it inculcates should be learned only from experience."

"An experience, however, which commences in childhood," said Catharine, playfully. "The flowers I loved bloomed with equal beauty in my presence for many hours, but *one* sufficed to send me to my birds,—and their warbling, in turn, was enjoyed, until satiety compelled me to employment, and employment again to amusement. Even *I* have lived long enough to feel that the mind requires variety, and is not only refreshed, but strengthened by it."

"You rest your argument on sensations; *but sentiments*—you ought hardly to have awakened from the beautiful illusion of their immutability."

A cloud shaded the brow of Catharine. "*She remembered her dead*," and the anguish which had passed away, leaving a tender regret unmingled with repining,—too soothing to be painful. Cleveland saw the shadow, but he misinterpreted its source.

"You cannot have lived long enough to feel that all the happiness of life consists in illusions? You cannot have experienced the withering fact, that to be happy is but the result of skilfully deceiving ourselves?"

"Far from it," said Catharine. "The true is to me likewise the beautiful. I cannot allow that there is no reality about us,—that all the noble feelings of our nature are mere vanities. There is truth in religion,—truth in philosophy: let us hope there may be truth *within* man as around him."

"Philosophy should be true," said Sir Greville, with a smile, "for it has divested life of much of its poetry. We smile at the thunder which our ancestors regarded as an omen, and calmly calculate the period of a comet, which they deemed a messenger sent to warn the nations of impending fate. After all, are we the happier for our knowledge?"

"Are we happier for civilization? Do we value the reason which elevates us above the brute?" said Catharine, the glow of animation spreading over her countenance. "You, who are the owner of palaces enriched with the most elaborate workmanship of art—the most splendid efforts of genius,—would you contentedly return to the barbarous magnificence of the Saxon, whose floor was strewn with rushes, and his naked walls stained with smoke? Surely we should rejoice in the greater light of the present, and in measuring our ascent from the past, anticipate, with rapture, the progress of the future. A thousand years since, what *were* our countrymen?—A thousand years hence, what *will* they be?"

"That is a splendid vista," said Sir Greville, gazing on her with delight.

"What a happiness to you, who have such means of advancing the improvement which is to give it its splendour! Your rank,—your influence,—your talents,—your time,"—Catharine paused, for the expression of his eye caused hers to droop.

"Catharine," said he (it was the first time he had ever so addressed her), "shall I tell you what *yet* I need?—An impulse! By what you *have* done judge what you *may* do! Invest my existence with new charms,—share with me the pursuits—the duties you inculcate. Be yourself the blessing of my home, the angel of my destiny—be *mine!*"—

* * * * * * * * * *

Catharine had returned from her ramble. She sat in the window of her dressing-room, her fair hand supporting her yet fairer cheek, and her eyes fixed on the smiling landscape spread out beneath, yet evidently seeing none of its beauties. Her spirit was too intensely occupied with its own workings to be conscious of aught external, and Lady Darley stood unperceived a few minutes by her side, watching, with the most pleasurable feelings, her absorption.

She spoke at length, and her voice restored her niece to consciousness, or, as Lady Darley called it, to a capacity for commonplace. But her start, as her day-dream was so suddenly dissolved, was succeeded by a blush of "celestial rosy red," which an observer far less acute and less interested than her ladyship would have known to be of "love's proper hue."

"My dear child, only one word; I will not trespass on your solitude, which your face tells me is peopled just now with bright and beautiful thoughts," said Lady Darley. "All that has passed this morning I do not inquire;—give me your confidence when you like it;—you have not quitted Cleveland in coldness or displeasure? Assure me of it."

"I have *not*," said Catharine, blushing still more brightly. "I meant to seek you this evening before you retired to rest;—I am not insensible to your claims on my confidence;—how can I ever forget that all my happiness is owing to you?"

"Then I am satisfied," said Lady Darley, with a countenance expressive of the exultation she actually felt. "You *must* endure my presence a little," she continued, seating herself by her niece; "I see—I feel—that all my hopes for you are on the eve of accomplishment. Cleveland has proposed?—is accepted?"

"He has,—he is;—incapable of trifling with the feelings he had excited,—which he had been at pains to excite,—he has said,—imagine every thing that woman would most wish to hear."

"From the man she loves," added Lady Darley. "I understand it all, my beloved Catharine. You are the future mistress of Cleveland Park: you will fulfil a destiny worthy of your graces and your talents. I could not select, from the most distinguished in England, another man to whom it would give me equal pride and pleasure to see you united. A name so ancient,—a position so well ascertained,—such a place here,—such a villa at Richmond,—a residence in the north, quite baronial,—a palace in town,—such a person,—such manners,—such genius,—the most *distingué* personage in Europe! I foresaw it all. You were precisely intended for each other. You are the most fortunate of women; and, I assure you, I think him the most enviable of men. And the family diamonds, Catharine,—of course they will be re-set. There is not a peeress in England who will eclipse you:—not the Dutchess of ——;—not the *parvenue* Mrs. ——, who blazed at the Pavilion in the rental of a palatinate. What arrangement have you made? When is it to be declared? Is the Bishop of —— to marry you?—He was Sir Greville's tutor."

Catharine smiled at the rapidity with which Lady Darley had recollected so many details, of which neither she nor Sir Greville had even spoken. Satisfied with hearing she was beloved; that she was sought, as the companion of his existence, by the being whom she loved with all the warm and passionate enthusiasm of a heart hitherto untouched,—with the holiness, the devotedness of unsullied first-love,—her imagination had rested in the sanctuary of such blessed feelings, and had not shaped one vision of the future. And Lady Darley looked almost disappointed, when she learned that the fact of the engagement of her niece and Sir Greville was all on which her mind could feast itself for the present.

"How gratifying to me, Catharine, that you should form so brilliant a union while under my protection! How rejoiced your poor dear father would be with this alliance! I am persuaded Sir Greville is precisely the kind of man he would approve as a son-in-law, independently of those extrinsic advantages which render him, in every respect, the most desirable *parti* in the kingdom. We must not, however, for a moment depreciate these. After all, rank, wealth, distinction, have their advantages. They are the setting round the precious stone, which exhibits its brilliancy and lustre to a thousand spectators, who would never have vouchsafed a glance at it as it lay in the obscurity of a cabinet. We must always prefer Cleveland Park to your other places, Catharine,—it has been the scene of the most fortunate event of your existence. As for myself, I am not sure that I was so much gratified when poor Lord Darley proposed,—although I really was in love with him. Of course we shall not quit Cleveland sooner than we originally intended."

"It was Sir Greville's particular request that we would remain; which renders it necessary that what has taken place should be known only to ourselves. Otherwise, I could not endure the embarrassment of such a position. If we go, he says he shall break up the party and follow us."

"That would be very selfish in us. No, I cannot possibly consent to that. Yet it is hard to be compelled to conceal an event which almost overwhelms me with delight. You and Cleveland have so much *retenue*, you will be able to appear as usual; and his attentions to you have already been sufficiently marked; and, in any ordinary case, I flatter myself I am a perfect Spartan in self-command. But this is not an ordinary affair. Is it not permitted me to hint—just to hint the *possibility* of such an event—to the Dutchess of Halifax? Consider her impertinence last evening! She has always been convinced that Cleveland's attentions to you meant no more than a flirtation. She says he has so long been accustomed to the most flattering pursuits from young and beautiful women, that he would never relinquish their homage for the *homeliness* of matrimony. I *must* undeceive her: it is really uncharitable to allow her to remain in error."

"She will forgive us," said Catharine, with a smile. "The dignity of the dutchess does not prevent her being very communicative; and I am sure that even Sir Greville will see the necessity of our immediate departure, should the fact of our engagement transpire."

"Well, my dear, I submit. This is your day of power. Brides elect are despots by privilege: and it would be as well not to leave Cleveland until Sir Greville himself can attend us. I have the greatest reliance on his honour. But, after all, inconstancy is the prerogative of man; and the more he is accustomed to your society, the better. It is astonishing how many engagements have been preserved only from habit. Your acquaintance with Cleveland has not been a long one; he has not been accustomed to spend a part of every day with you for months. The loss of you would not cause a chasm in his existence."

Catharine sighed as she listened, and felt that—

"Man's love is of man's life a thing apart."

"And now, my dearest child," resumed Lady Darley, "do allow me to offer one word of advice. You have managed admirably hitherto."

"*Managed!*" said Catharine, with a glow on her cheeks, and a kindling eye.

"Be not indignant, love; it is of no advantage to show *me* the improving effect of a blush. *Managed*, child:—you must take the words as they occur to me. In this world of ours nothing is to be done *without* management. Tact—intuition—woman's instinct—have effected wonders for *you;* and, after all, what are these but address?"

"If that be the correct interpretation, I am well content," said Catharine. "Truth and nature are the only allies I could consent to employ."

"Well—I ask no more. Will not nature and truth teach you to evince your attachment to the man to whom you are shortly to be united for ever? Believe me, Cleveland has been too long used to the homage of women to brook cold ness from the single one whom he has selected to bear the honours of his name. Sometimes, perhaps, his opinions may rather startle you. Men who have lived so long in the world as he has, *will* have theories and fancies of their own, which it would be prudent in you to smile at—or approve."

"*Smile at*, if you will," interrupted Catharine, "but *not approve* by the sacrifice of truth. Sir Greville understands me now well enough to detect when my approbation is real—when feigned; and do you believe he would esteem his—his affianced wife the more, because she preferred being false to inflicting a slight wound on his caprices? No, my dear aunt; if prudence were all, and self-respect nothing, you must not counsel such a degradation."

"But Cleveland, my dear love, would forgive the possible error in the flattering motive. He has been so long accustomed to act dictator—"

"That it would be well to teach him his new *rôle* in time," said Catharine, playfully. "My dear aunt, let us leave things, as we have hitherto done, 'to shape themselves.' Cleveland has lived long enough in the world to prefer honesty, were it but for its novelty."

"But do not believe that life has always been, even to Sir Greville Cleveland, the bright and brilliant series of enjoyments which the world has deemed it. He has had to endure the common lot of man—disappointment. Be therefore tender of a heart which the lightning may already have scathed."

"*Scathed!*" repeated Catharine, gazing with pained surprise on the unusual gravity of Lady Darley's countenance; for the word grated unpleasantly on her ear.

"Not *literally*, my dear child. My regard—my interest—for you and him, exaggerates my anxieties for you and the expression of them;—not *scathed*, but *irritated*—rendered doubtful—suspicious, perhaps To distrust the sincerity of the attachments wo inspire, is one of the penalties we pay for continuing to live. In short, my dear Catharine, I fear your coldness."

"*Coldness*,—and to him!"

"*That* promises well," said Lady Darley, with a smile of approbation. "Let Sir Greville be made to feel and understand that you love him,—that that love is the grand actuating principle of all your thoughts and actions."

"Love him!" said Catharine. "Can there exist a *possible* doubt? Have I not accepted him?—bound myself to him through life, for weal or wo?—avowed that my happiness is dependant on him, and believed that I have sufficient guarantee for its security in his faith—his honour? Needs there more?"

"My love, remember the *accompaniments* of an offer such as Sir Greville's. He has no opportunity of making *you* play a part in the tragedy of 'all for love, or the world well lost.' He cannot prove your disinterestedness. Not a woman in England would have refused him. Why should he believe that, for the sake of a silly and unintelligible romance, you would have done otherwise than they? Nay, dear Catharine, let me not chase the bright rose from its proper seat. Believe that my anxiety may have heightened things which do exist, and fancied those which do not."

"I will believe it," said Catharine. "The possibilities which you suggest are too humiliating to be real. Could Sir Greville believe me mercenary enough—"

"You would refuse him, of course," interrupted Lady Darley. "But hark!—the first dinner-bell! Well, my dear, I must leave you. I will send Willis, and take your Lucy to-day. Willis arranges your hair so beautifully!—And wear your black satin, my love. Cleveland says, nothing exhibits the perfection of your beauty so much as that dress. You have had great success in society, Catharine; —yet, when I look at you, it is not wonderful that you bewitch everybody. It is not your regular features;—a mere outline, however perfect, cannot produce enchantment:—your complexion,—beautiful;—but yet Lawrence has painted as well; and men do not pull each other to pieces for his prodigies. Is it your hair,—that bright coronal of gold?—why, mine glitters as bravely, if more darkly. You smile,—is it that smile? Nay,—the spirit that dwells there—

"'The loveliness ever in motion, that plays
Like the lightning in autumn's soft shadowy days.

I am glad you do not blush, dear: you are not humble enough to be pleased or pained by such a subject. You are worthy to be Cleveland's wife." And affectionately kissing the forehead of her niece, Lady Darley left her to the silence of her own deep contentment.

Willis must have officiated with more than usual skill this day; for, when Lady Darley returned to Catharine, before descending to the drawing-room, she said and felt that she had never seen her look so lovely. Willis received her approbation as a tribute to her own success. "Really, my lady," she said, with a simper, "I must say it is a pleasure to dress Miss Vernon. She is always pleased: she sees I do my best, and she is satisfied. Do what one will for some ladies, they are never contented: then they get an ugly frown, and look ill, and think the fault rests with me: and, as you know, my lady, no face ever did or ever can look handsome in a passion. Allow me, Miss Vernon,—that fold does not fall gracefully."

"Really, Catharine, I think, if ever you marry, I must transfer Willis to you," said Lady Darley.

"Indeed, my lady, it would give me great uneasiness to leave your ladyship," returned Willis; "but, if you positively ordered me to go, of course it is my duty, my lady. And there is no lady in the world I would sooner serve than Miss Vernon. Indeed, I must make so bold as to say, all Sir Greville's people are of the same opinion. Servants, you know, ma'am, cannot help having eyes and ears. All *us*, my lady,—the second-table people,—make a point of drinking every day to Sir Greville and Lady Cleveland that is to be. Dear me, ma'am,—I hope I have not offended. Sir Greville is the best of masters;—and, as I say, you will be the best of ladies. To be sure, as we say, you might go through the world and not find such another beautiful couple; and, as Sir Greville's own gentleman was observing, if ever a marriage was made in heaven, this will be. You know, ma'am, Raith has lived with Sir Greville these many years, and he says Lady Sophia Barron was no more to be compared to Miss Vernon, than paste to a diamond. Those were Raith's own words, my lady."

"Lady Sophia Barron!—And who was she?" said Catharine, with a curiosity not wholly unmingled with anxiety.

"La, ma'am!" said Willis, in the eager desire of giving intelligence, common to all her class; "Lady Sophia Barron was in Italy long before you came out, because of Mr. Barron's health. She married Mr. Barron after it was all off between her and Sir Greville; but, as Raith says, ma'am, 'my master,' says he, 'was born under a lucky star; for if him and Lady Sophia hadn't quarrelled, they would have been man and wife, and we should never have seen Miss Vernon mistress of Cleveland Park'"

"Hold your tongue, Willis," said Lady Darley, angrily; for she saw that Catharine had not heard this allusion to Sir Greville's former attachment and engagement without emotion. "Look at that ringlet behind Miss Vernon's ear: it should fall lower on the shoulder: it is not becoming."

"There, my lady," said Willis, whose soul was immediately absorbed in the suggested alteration. "Well, it is an improvement. It has the sweetest curl! As I said to Raith, said I, 'Look at Miss Vernon's hair, and place Lady Sophia Barron's by the side of it, and then tell me who's who.' La, ma'am! why it a'n't to be compared to it! And her ladyship is not so young as she was."

The second dinner-bell rang:—Lady Darley drew her niece's arm through her own, and they descended to the drawing-room.

Sir Greville's glance of admiration repaid Lady Darley even for the sacrifice of her invaluable Willis. Catharine had never looked more lovely. Her eye was more softly, more darkly blue; a warm rose hue glowed on her cheek, and there was a pervading *consciousness* in her expression, which more than compensated for the absence of her ordinary self-possession. Perhaps, too, the slight shade of pensiveness, resulting from the Lady Darley's suggestions, and from Willis's hints of a certain Lady Sophia, added a greater charm to the general interest of her appearance, for it was *new*. The ordinary expression of Catharine was serene, not sad; and even while Sir Greville admired the unusual grace, he sought by a thousand assiduities to replace it by a smile.

With the tact of a woman of the world, the Dutchess of Halifax arrived at the conclusion that an éclaircissement had taken place, and that Catharine Vernon would shortly become Lady Cleveland. She had just that dislike of Catharine which inferior minds always have of superior; and she had a particular malice to gratify against her dear friend Lady Darley, to whom it had occurred to be always the successful rival of the Dutchess of Halifax. Now the story of Lady Sophia Barron was much better known to the dutchess and her *clique* than to the ladies and gentlemen of the housekeeper's room; and it was a notorious fact, that the attachment and engagement had been of very different materials from the ordinary attachments and engagements of people of their caste. Nevertheless, it had passed away, and *therefore*—the dutchess cherished the consolatory thought—so might this.

Not that the three Ladies Halifax were yet to be disposed of. Under the able generalship of their noble mother,—backed by their father's influence, interest, boroughs, and every desirable *et cetera* but money,—all had married. A splendid governorship in the East had provided for Lady

Mary and her husband, where she was magnificently dying of bile and indolence. The heir to the countless millions and billions of an avaricious banker, had, by the irresistible charms of a *cadeau* of unequalled diamonds, won the Lady Emily,—the beauty of the family; while the third had bestowed herself on a detrimental, who, when the distasteful marriage had absolutely been perpetrated, was of necessity provided for by being returned for one of the duke's boroughs, and enriched by one of those government appointments which fill the purse without particularly distressing, by labour, either the mind or the body. The dutchess therefore might charitably have allowed the course of true love, or love of any kind, to run smooth, but she could not. She had never forgiven the disappointment inflicted by Sir Greville. And it was intolerable that a little *parvenue*, whose existence was unknown but yesterday, should "achieve honours" which ought not to fall on one who was not "born to honour."

The dutchess was too much a woman of the world, and estimated Sir Greville too nearly at his proper worth, to believe that *she* had the power of breaking off his marriage, if really decided on. But she possessed, nevertheless, the consolatory conviction, that the means of annoyance were in her power, and that, if unable to injure, she could at least torment. She believed Sir Greville quite vulnerable on the score of the plebeian connexion he was about to entail on himself; and she gave Catharine credit for having "brought away from a country parsonage" sufficient of its romance to feel considerable uneasiness when allusions were made to the past loves of Sir Greville. Having no heart herself, the dutchess nevertheless had arrived at the knowledge that such a member was to be found in the organization of others; and she had not lived so many years amid the throng of mankind, without having learned somewhat of the means by which wounds may be inflicted on it,—those deep wounds which "never heal without a scar."

CHAPTER XVIII.

As if to authenticate the proverbial uncertainty of English skies, the morning succeeding the important yesterday threatened a second deluge. The whole party were confined to the house, half of them engaged in regretting the state of the weather, and insisting on the impossibility of getting through a long day tolerably within doors;—others in writing letters, that necessary evil, wisely performed when *ennui* renders it almost a duty to bestow our tediousness on correspondents whom we cannot offend, but for whom we do not care a straw;—others again in reading newspapers, the refuge of the intellectually destitute;—some yawned over a new novel; a very few quietly pursued their habitual occupations, and of these two or three were in the adjoining music-room. Sir Greville and Catharine were among them,—conversing in so low a tone as, under the shelter of the bravuras with which, as usual, the Ladies K. were delighting themselves and torturing their hearers, to be in the actual enjoyment of a tête-à-tête.

Every thing spoken in the drawing-room *might* have been audible to them, if they had been less engrossed with each other. As it was, they heard only the sweetness of "lovers' whispered words," until the voice of the Dutchess of Halifax touched "the electric chain wherewith we are darkly bound,"—and both Catharine and Sir Greville paused.

"Really, Stark is an amusing creature," her grace began, "although I almost wonder how he ventured on the impertinence of writing to *me*. He knows I never allow my name to appear in a dedication, and he has the assurance to make a request of the kind. At least that is the ostensible object of the letter;—perhaps, after all, it is a *ruse;* he wants to boast of my correspondence. He was almost broken-hearted on being excluded from the Cleveland réunions. I rather think the intelligence he sends is *en revanche.* Has any one heard lately of Lady Sophia Barron?"

It was at the utterance of this name that Sir Greville and Catharine paused. It produced a startling effect on both; but, as the colour of Catharine deepened, the cheek of her lover became more strikingly pale.

"It is nearly a year since I heard from Lady Sophia," said Lady Adelaide Willoughby; "she was then at Florence, and great hopes were entertained that Mr. Barron's constitution would be completely renovated by the climate."

"Fallacious as hopes dependant on climate usually are," said the dutchess; "Stark writes that poor Barron died some months since, and his widow, Lady Sophia, has returned to England."

"Poor Lady Sophia!" said Lady Adelaide Willoughby, with a sigh. "Her destiny was a singular one. Mr. Barron appears to have been a very eccentric person."

"But one most honourable and upright," said the dutchess. "Women are not to be pitied whose happiness depends on the principles of their husbands, not on their taste, or, in other words, their caprice."

"But still first love," persisted Lady Adelaide—

"Is generally first nonsense," interrupted the dutchess. "A girl goes into the world with *le besoin d'aimer* strong upon her, which is naturally gratified by the first tolerable man who amuses himself with talking romance to her. I always consider that first love in a girl is coeval with a taste for Mrs. Radcliffe's things, which expires as soon as she has escaped from the namby-pambyism of the teens."

"Love in Lady Sophia was more than a mere fancy," persisted Lady Adelaide. "She was a very superior young woman,—so carefully educated,—so amiable,—so pious."

"A Methodist," sneered the dutchess, "who, if report says truth, in the odour of her superior sanctity, could not forgive a youthful folly in the man she affected to love. If there be one character more detestable than another, it is a Puritan or a Pharisee of this kind."

Once or twice during this dialogue Catharine had attempted to converse with Sir Greville, but her effort had failed; with pale cheek and perturbed brow, his faculties were evidently engrossed by it; and, after a moment's struggle, he quitted her side and entered the drawing-room.

"Oh, Sir Greville," said the dutchess, as soon as her eye rested on him, "here are news for you! Lady Sophia Barron is actually in England."

"So I hear," said Sir Greville, with a calmness of tone which, to a man of his habits of self-command, was hardly an effort.

"Do you know, Sir Greville, I am very curious to witness a meeting between you and your sometime ladye love," said the dutchess, with her usual nonchalant impertinence.

"Your grace may rely on the gratification," returned Sir Greville; "the chances of society must inevitably bring Lady Sophia and myself together."

"Mr. Stark informs me that poor Mr. Barron has left every thing to Lady Sophia, and his income was immense," said the dutchess. "The world are already speculating on the second choice of the wealthy widow. If I were she I should accept nothing beneath a royal duke,—but then some of the royal highnesses are terribly bad *ton*."

"How long is it since Lady Sophia married Mr. Barron?" inquired Lady Darley, who was conscious that Catharine overheard the whole conversation.

"Sir Greville, I dare say, can inform us," said the malicious dutchess. "I have heard that disappointment is an accurate chronologist."

"I am bound to rely on the experimental knowledge of your grace," said Lady Darley, who could, on occasion, equal in impertinence even the Dutchess of Halifax. "Pray, Sir Greville, how long is it?"

"More than ten years, I think," he replied, "so that the green willows with which the dutchess liberally crowns 'the man she delighteth to honour,' are fallen into 'the sere and yellow leaf.'"

"They will bloom again when you meet Lady Sophia,"

persisted the dutchess. "*On revient toujours à ses premiers amours.*"

"Weak minds may;—minds all feeling and no knowledge," said Sir Greville, thoughtfully. "Where conviction of the unworthiness of the object, moral or intellectual,—nay, where even the conviction of an unapproachable dissimilarity in taste, and habits, and objects, possesses a mind able to think, *on n'y revient jamais.* Moreover, time,—experience,—the first properly spent, the other rationally used, may have enlarged the intellect of one party while the other may have been stationary. And this may be the result of 'the omnipotence of circumstances,' which have bound down one in a narrow spot to which that faculty, so merciful a condition of our being, of adapting ourselves to almost any mode of life, may have at length accommodated even the mental powers;—while the other may have visited almost every possible haunt of civilized man,—have been an actor in scenes of the highest excitement;—tell me, then, the fitness of those for each other? There is, doubtless, identity between the lovers of twenty and the acquaintances of thirty, but there is no longer sameness. The chances are ten thousand to one against both parties having made equal advances. Each is changed, and the object of the *premier amour* is but a phantom of the past. It does very well to talk about in a romance, and to sing about in choice Italian, or Moore's as sweet English, but reason and experience *prove* it an absurdity."

"I hate metaphysics," said the dutchess: "however, in the present case, you will find your system consolatory. Stark declares that Lady Sophia's second choice is already made."

"Mr. Stark being in her ladyship's confidence," said Lady Darley, with a smile of disdain.

"He must have a divining-rod," said her grace; "for he is always in possession of the first intelligence of every thing that is likely to happen, and that never *will* happen. He is a very disagreeable person, doubtless, and I give him up to dissection with the greatest satisfaction. However, I will read you what he writes.

"'It is a pity that the season is at an end, just as a star of the first magnitude is about culminating at our meridian. Lady Sophia Barron has arrived at Mivart's, accompanied by her most unintelligible brother, Stracey Hamilton, and attended by a suite almost as numerous as that of a monarch of Irân. My comparison hopes for favour in your grace's sight, as it is suggested by my knowledge of your taste for orientals. As it is six months since Barron died, her ladyship is justified in discarding that *ne plus ultra* of dowdyism, the bonnet of a new-made dowager,—beneath whose terrific shadow the fairest face becomes as petrifying as that of a Gorgon. It is said that Mivart's is quite filled with cavaliers expectant of her ladyship's favour. Unhappy train,—predoomed to disappointment!—Poor Barron's successor was elected some time previous to his decease, in the person of an Italian principe, a besom friend of Stracey Hamilton's, who very properly has himself fallen in love with the *illustrissima Signora Sorella.* Stracey Hamilton, with only a younger brother's fortune, will find his advantage in his sister's affection, and poor defunct Barron will have the happiness of providing for *two* families. My informant says, that the bridegroom elect has been Lady Sophia's cavalier servente these last two years, enjoying the full privileges of that character. He and Barron were the best friends in the world, and the whole affair was conducted after the most approved Italian model. Lady Sophia has taken the usual course of your superexcellent people. They who stand on the very pinnacle of virtue have no power of moving but by descent; and as there is an inherent principle of nobility in the human mass of matter, we arrive, by the usual process of deduction, at a moral of which none of us can doubt the benefit.

"'Meanwhile, what will the lord of Cleveland Park say to this arrangement? If, as the German proverb says, "old love never rusts," we may conjecture that he, with all his dignity, will not hesitate to run a tilt for the hand of the Lady Sophia. An attachment strong enough to drive him into exile must have left, if not wounds, at least scars,—and who shall conjecture what the very first interview with one so beloved may not effect?—Farewell, then, to the hopes of——.'

"There, that is the whole," said the dutchess, closing the letter. "Stark's letters are merely a vehicle for public report; we may be tolerably certain that what he writes all the world have been talking about and believe."

"The world must have a 'most rapacious maw,' if its credulity can swallow all that Mr. Stark amuses himself with propagating," said Sir Greville, with a smile, in which there was more derision than scorn. "He is one of those unfortunate persons who, putting their memory to the torture to furnish their wit, are compelled to draw on their invention for facts. Lady Sophia has a purer and a loftier mind than Mr. Stark is capable of appreciating, and the calumny he has propagated is worthy of one of that wretched tribe who exist by slander."

"That is very generous of you," said the dutchess, with an affected drawl; "I thought forsaken swains avenged themselves by saying all manner of evil of the fair inconstant. And a very natural result too!—They must find a scapegoat to carry their own sins into the wilderness, and the follies or frailties of the lost one offer themselves so readily!"

"Your grace and I do not understand each other," said Sir Greville, with as much hauteur as the host could possibly exhibit to the guest. "Honesty, I suspect, is too homely a virtue to be cherished by the courtly, but *honour* is the vaunted virtue of the aristocracy, and I am bound to defend your grace's ORDER even against yourself. No man of honour—no *gentleman—can* commit the crime of traducing the woman he has once loved. There is something so wretched in a baseness of this kind, that the veriest reptile among us would shudder at the possibility of being suspected of it. To assert the excellence of Lady Sophia Barron is not, however, a necessity of honour, but of integrity; and Mr. Stark exhibits less than his usual prudence in aiming his venomous arrows at a mark too lofty indeed for him to reach, but not too lofty to prevent the recoil on himself."

"Poor Mr. Stark!" said the dutchess, with her usual *nonchalance;* "It is a pity he should be ignorant of the scene he has produced, he who is so fond of making an effect! If he should ultimately arrive at the honour of being shot at by the chevalier *sans peur et sans reproche*, Stracey Hamilton, he will acknowledge that he has not lived in vain. Lady Darley, why have you patronised Mr. Stark with so much empressement?"

"For the same reason which makes *you* find his letters endurable, my dear dutchess; he amuses me, and in this monotonous world it is something to be amused."

"In truth it is; and so, Sir Greville, you perceive how impossible it is that I should give up poor Stark, especially in the country," said the dutchess. "And as to Lady Sophia, she would certainly forgive the scandal for the sake of the defence which it has elicited."

"Lady Sophia would feel, that to refute falsehoods so contemptible would be to confer too much honour on them," said Sir Greville, returning to the music-room.

"Poor Cleveland!" said the dutchess, in an affected *sotto voce;* "faithless or fickle as Lady Sophia was, it is evident he has not forgotten her. It would not surprise me if they were to renew their engagement; after all, real life is full of romances Be it as it may, I should not envy the woman on whom Cleveland, in a fit of capricious preference, might bestow the *débris* of his heart. What can be so annoying to a second love, or a second wife, as a constant recurrence to the charms and graces of the first? Don't you agree with me, Lady Darley?"

"Perfectly," replied Lady Darley, with an acquiescence, the freezing contempt of which was felt and understood even by the frivolous Dutchess of Halifax, who avenged her insulted dignity by leaning back on the *fauteuil*, and reading Mr. Stark's letter with an *enjouement* too demonstrative to be natural; ever and anon smiling as she came to particular passages, intending her companions to observe how interesting and amusing its contents must be, and to feel an intense curiosity to penetrate a mystery so studiously concealed from them.

Poor human nature !—How constantly it

> "Resembles ocean into tempest wrought,
> To waft a feather, or to drown a fly."

CHAPTER XIX.

"Catharine," said Lady Darley, one evening, when her niece had retired for the night, just two days preceding that fixed for their departure from Cleveland Park, "I do not recollect ever mentioning to you the name of Lady Sophia Barron."

"You never did," replied Catharine, turning pale as at a sound of ominous import.

"She was a Hamilton, the most distinguished beauty of the circles ten years since. At seventeen she was beloved by Sir Greville, if not with the reality of first love, at least with all its devotedness. It would be too ridiculous to suppose that he, with his infinite advantages, had lived to be five-and-twenty without previous, and, perhaps, extensive experience of *la belle passion.* Nevertheless, Lady Sophia had the advantage of being his first *fiancée*, which is much the same."

"It is," acquiesced Catharine, with a sigh.

"But I do not expect in you, Catharine, the childish romance of believing, that because he loved Lady Sophia before even the fact of your existence was known, he therefore loved her more. All the sing-song nonsense of first-love, of which one used to read in trashy romances, has gone by with moonshine soliloquies and sonnets. The world has outlived its babyhood, and we look for common sense even from tolerably well-educated girls, whether in their teens or their twenties."

"You are angry," said Catharine, raising her eye with that expression of serene integrity so peculiar to her noble countenance, "because I appear less happy than usual—less satisfied or less at ease with Cleveland. But you mistake the cause. He was aware that I could not avoid overhearing Mr. Stark's letter read by the dutchess, or her comments on it, and I think he should have considered my feelings sufficiently to have spoken openly to me afterward. It is not of a former attachment that I complain; I am not young enough to indulge for a moment the dream of being the first and only object to excite his love. He has injured me by his want of confidence in me—of consideration for me; by putting it in the power of such a person as the dutchess to enlighten me in the most unpleasant manner. It was hardly possible that I could escape hearing, from some envious or malicious person, that Cleveland had but the *débris* of his heart, as her grace expressed it, to bestow on me. It would have been better if he had confided in me."

"Are you mad, my dear child, or do you suppose that men of the world, like Sir Greville, keep a *catalogue raisonné* of their *liaisons* for the purpose of entertaining each successive woman who is to be placed on the list? You must be terribly in love, Catharine, to allow your fine understanding to be enveloped in such a misty maze of absurdity."

"I did *not* expect to hear of Cleveland's *liaisons*," said Catharine, with a blush; "but the particular instance of Lady Sophia,—an engagement so notorious,—all the world were aware of it,—surely it would have been prudent,—it would have been kind,—if he had prevented the malice of others by his own candour."

"Quite nonsense, my dear! Past loves are good for nothing but to be forgotten. Cleveland knows human nature, especially *woman's* human nature, too well to put jealousy in the way of his future wife. If she stoops aside to pick it up, it is not his fault."

"I did not stoop aside," returned Catharine, discomposed; "and at all times confidence and truth are better preventives of jealousy than concealment. If Cleveland's engagement with Lady Sophia were broken off from caprice,—faithlessness,—the natural tendency of human beings to change,—why did he hesitate to speak of it? If I had venerated him less after such an avowal, I should have relied on him more. But is there not an evident change in him since he heard of Lady Sophia's return? Is he not occasionally melancholy and *distrait?* Is it tormenting myself with vain fears to suppose it possible he may regret the precipitancy with which he bound himself to me, and sigh for her, once so beloved, and now free to reward his constancy? Is it not true that the desires of man become but the more vehement for the obstacles which oppose them; and that Lady Sophia, whose image must in his mind be surrounded by so many memories of the past, appears to Cleveland tenfold more worthy of his regard, because—yes, even *because*—the bonds he has so lately imposed on himself place his honour and his heart at variance?"

"A young lady resolved on being miserable is too ingenious a casuist for my poor common sense to cope with," said Lady Darley, evidently angry. "However, unless you are resolved to lose Cleveland for the sake of a phantom conjured up by yourself, I should advise you to discard that cold and ungracious air with which you receive all his efforts to testify the sincerity of his love. That he will, in the intercourse of society, encounter Lady Sophia, is a certainty not to be doubted. At seven-and-twenty, with all the graces of foreign courts upon her, her beauty will have gained in elegance what it will have lost in bloom. Under the irritation of your coldness, is it not natural that he should remember the silken chains of former days, and seek again the flowery wreath whose sweetness he has tasted? Besides, as the dutchess told him, '*on revient toujours à ses premiers amours;*' and, notwithstanding his eloquent *tirade*, meant probably to be heard by you, such things do happen, and in *this* case the supposed difference between the two, on which he founded his argument, does not exist. Lady Sophia's mind was of the finest order, and she has not passed the interval in obscurity."

Catharine *felt* she was too agitated to reply. Every woman naturally shrinks from the prospect of her lover's again associating with the object of former—perhaps first—affection; and Catharine, conscious that the atmosphere which surrounded herself and Cleveland was less sunny than usual, experienced all the anguish of a vague jealousy, a dim sense of impending evil, that chilled her heart with an iciness almost as that of death.

"Lady Sophia Barron," resumed Lady Darley, "was a Hamilton. The violence of Cleveland's passion for her was notorious. He was at Lord Edinburgh's seat in Scotland a whole grouse season. All the Hamiltons were, what is called, seriously brought up, that is, they thought themselves wiser and better than their neighbours; they were saints and Christians, and the rest of the world heathens and idolaters, publicans and sinners. I dislike them all; and, when Cleveland was so fascinated, or rather infatuated, with Lady Sophia, it proved the attraction of opposites. To be sure, there was no denying her beauty—that glorious oriental beauty,—intense black eyes,—cheeks of carnation,—lips of ruby,—the most profuse hair, gathered round her head like a turban of black velvet; yes, she *was* beautiful in *her* style, as you, Catharine, in yours. Hers was the beauty for the voluptuary, yours for the man of intellect,—the attractions of both of you suited to the different periods of life in which Cleveland bowed to the power of each. Well—a second season in town dawned, and just as people expected the usual *dénouement* to an engagement so publicly avowed, the affair was off. Lady Sophia returned to Scotland, and Cleveland went to Italy."

"And Lady Sophia married!" said Catharine, with something of contempt for her ladyship's power of change.

"Married!—Certainly. Why not?" asked Lady Darley,

in unaffected astonishment. "Cleveland is not the only man in the world worth a woman's acceptance; and, if he were, very few are in a state, either of mind or circumstances, to say, '*aut Cesar aut nullus.*' Lord Edinburgh was not rich, so that in one point of view an alliance with Cleveland was highly desirable. Mr. Barron, however, answered quite as well; and though he was somewhat old and a *parvenu*, Lady Sophia, according to report, passed with him through a very amicable matrimonial existence, and has found her reward. He had the good manners to die before she had attained to that mature age when a successor becomes an object of indifference, and she enters a second time on the arena of English fashion, probably with quite as much beauty as she possessed in her days of girlhood, a manner perfected by travel, prejudices corrected by experience, and a dower to make her worthy the consideration of every younger son throughout the British dominions."

"Still, why Sir Greville and Lady Sophia did not marry, remains unexplained," said Catharine, thoughtfully, and looking quite as unhappy as the occasion warranted.

"That is the keystone of the mystery," returned Lady Darley. "After all, it is the very height of folly to dim the brightness of the present, because we cannot explain the past. How very few of the motives which influence human actions are visible to us!—and how many engagements have been dissolved—how many foolish hearts broken, for a word or a look!

"'A something light as air, a look,
A word unkind, or wrongly taken,—
Oh, love that tempests never shook,
A breath, a touch like this, hath shaken!'

There is poetry for you, Catharine; when I am drawn into discussing romance or sentiment, I am glad to borrow the language, shall I not say also the ideas, of others, to supply the deficiency of my own. In one word, which is entirely my own, do not pluck up the tree beneath whose shelter you repose, because the shadow which it casts is rather darker than you like. Be satisfied that the honour of Sir Greville will ratify the engagement into which he has been tempted by love. Of the sincerity of that love you have the best guarantee in its disinterestedness. In a worldly point of view, there is nothing either in your position or circumstances which could have tempted either the ambition or the avarice of any man, least of all of Cleveland Rely on it, his taste is all he has sought to gratify in his love, and is not taste identified with love itself? I forget the beautiful allegory of Cupid and Psyche, but I think I am inculcating its moral. *Addio carissima;* sleep well, and smile on Sir Greville to-morrow; consider how much 'food for meditation' an adieu bequeaths to a lover, and let yours be so sweet as to occupy him only with halcyon thoughts."

Catharine returned the "*good night*" of Lady Darley, that commonplace farewell which leaves the sufferer a prey to the long lingering hours of sleeplessness and sorrow; but, instead of slumbering, she looked upon the moon, and "communed with her own heart." How often the memory dwells on a word spoken perhaps thoughtlessly, and draws from it "food for meditation even to madness!" Catharine felt that if, as Lady Darley had said, in her attempt at consolation, the love of Sir Greville were the mere gratification of his taste, it had nothing in common with the passionate attachment which engrossed *her* whole being. If it were this, it was a preference which found a counterpart in the choice of a gem for his cabinet, an ornament for his princely hall! If this were *all*, could *it* contend with the fond memories of his early love, when the enthusiasm of youth had lavished all its own treasures on his idol? And how deeply is the present always touched by the past! Even the contrast of his tame and subdued feelings or affections *now*, might throw him upon the recollection of what *had been*, when his heart was as bright as his youth, and the world within reflected the gladness of the untried world without. And he had not wearied of the love of his early years; it had been *withdrawn* from him; it appeared that hearts "*had* been torn away by a sudden wrench." There was no evidence of satiety—of inconstancy in *him*. When "hope was at the highest," Lady Sophia had given the signal of eternal separation; *eternal! would* it be eternal? Did *she* hold Sir Greville only by the bond of that honour in which Lady Darley had placed her security? Was there hereafter to be within his spirit a perpetual conflict between his honour and his love? No!—Catharine felt, that if a pang *must* be endured, that would be the lightest which separated her from him for ever. To owe his constancy only to his honour, appeared to her so intolerable a misery,—a degradation,—that—and she shrank as she contemplated the alternative—to see him no more would be the less terrible.

CHAPTER XX.

Catharine had quitted Cleveland. She was again in Grosvenor Square with Lady Darley, feeling in the heat of the air,—the clouds of dust,—the emptiness of every place of fashionable resort, the desolation and dirt which *brooded over* all the aristocratic mansions from whose walls the pre siding divinities had departed, and which had lately echoed with the footsteps of pleasure and the voices of mirth—how very miserable a place London *can* be, and how pleasant it is that there *are* such things as gardens and green fields in existence! that England is not *yet* one vast metropolis! Yet she carried within her a hive of delightful thoughts and hopes. The last day of her sojourn at Cleveland had been most satisfactory, if so tame a word can convey any idea of the feelings it excited. Nearly every guest had departed, and the rest were making arrangements to follow them. She had spent all the morning in rambling about the grounds with Sir Greville, in enjoying the beauty of one of the finest parks in England, with its romantic dells, its miniature forests, its haunted echoes, the very refinement of solitude. His manner—his words—had satisfied even *her* doubting heart, her craving love,—and she ceased to remember in his presence the existence of Lady Sophia, far less did she regret that he never spoke of her or his former engagement. Catharine could deride the weakness of her former solicitude, and stigmatize her jealousy of feelings, probably forgotten, as a most unworthy weakness. She could believe that Lady Darley's experience and her worldly knowledge rendered her a competent judge even in matters of the heart,—that empire so completely beyond the jurisdiction of experience and even of reason! Sir Greville was to join her at Darley, as soon as Lady Darley despatched to him intelligence of the arrival of herself and her niece at that her elegant jointure-house, and Catharine had nothing to do but to wander from one room to another, watching the preparations for their migration, and bewildering the methodical delay which seemed to retard their progress.

With something akin to remorse, she recollected her friend Mrs. Warren, and reproached the selfishness of that love which was absorbing all other sentiments. Since her return to Grosvenor Square, so much had she been divided by memory of the past and hope of the future, that all the duties belonging to the present were in danger of being neglected. And so it is with every passion, whether love, or ambition, or fame; it is the Aaron's rod which swallows up all thought, all feeling, unconnected with itself.

But with Catharine repentance was followed immediately by reparation. In as short a time as possible she was in Wimpole-street, embracing her friend, and pouring forth apologies and regrets, the sincerity of which was attested by their earnestness.

"I *have* felt your absence, dear Catharine," said Mrs. Warren; "but how natural that the pleasures which surround you should occasionally engross you! I heard of your return from Cleveland Park by the Morning Post, the only medium by which I attain to any knowledge of fashionable movements. But independently of my chancery-suit, that never-failing source of excitement and irritation, I have had something to interest me during your absence. I have seen again, I had almost said an old friend, at least the acquaintance of former years, one for whom I might be supposed to feel affection, for the relation of governess and pupil, before my marriage, existed between us."

Catharine *looked* the inquiry prompted by a not very unpardonable curiosity.

"One of the many children of a poor clergyman, that class which supplies nearly the whole tribe of female professors of all kinds, I was actually educated for a vocation, which, to your apprehension, must be one of misery and dependance," said Mrs. Warren, replying to Catharine's *thought*. "To me, however, it was fraught with no such burden, either in expectation or experience. The eldest daughter of a large family, in very moderate circumstances, is early inured to self-denial, trouble, and annoyance of every kind; and after all it was rather an improvement in my destiny to find myself in the school-room of the Ladies Hamilton, instead of the untidy, thickly-populated nursery, half nursery half sleeping-room as it was, of my father's parsonage."

Catharine's attention was indeed excited, but this time she had not voice to speak.

Mrs. Warren proceeded:—"Lady Sophia Barron is so distinguished by the advantages of wealth and widowhood, that you have probably heard of her at Cleveland Park; it is of her I am speaking, as my frequent companion since her return to England."

"I heard of her arrival," said Catharine, as calmly as she could, affecting to be occupied with something passing the window, that she might not expose to the searching eye of her friend a cheek which she was conscious was pale as death.

"Of all the Hamiltons," said Mrs. Warren, too much engrossed with her subject to notice the emotion of her companion, "Lady Sophia was the one who pleased me least as a girl. There was too much *adroitness* about her, if I may call by that name her tact in escaping both the punishment and the odium of every fault of which, in common with her brothers and sisters, she might be guilty. To use a word of Miss Edgeworth's, she appeared to me an embryo '*policizer*,' and I suspect now I did her injustice."

"Is she beautiful?" asked Catharine,—that question which every woman who loves first asks concerning her rival.

"Exceedingly beautiful," replied Mrs. Warren, with an earnestness more expressive even than her words. "The first gloss of youth seems hardly fled, while all the polished graces of maturity contribute a thousand charms to its brightness. I never saw a person for whom society and travel have done so much. And the charm of her voice!—You, Catharine, who consider the voice so much an index of character, would be really enchanted by it."

"A fine voice *is* an attraction," said Catharine, compelled to express the necessary acquiescence.

"Time appears to have improved Lady Sophia's temper and character as much as her person and manner. Formerly there used to be so great a degree of *fierté* about her. that in the midst of great natural attractions it acted as a principle of repulsion. Now, there is a union of dignity and softness, more becoming than I can attempt to describe. Sorrow has touched her, and there is a kind of beauty which suffering serves, as a fourth grace, to embellish; of this kind is Lady Sophia's. I never saw a woman in whom the absence of extreme youth was less to be regretted. While she is with me I always feel that I did her injustice in preferring her sisters to her; and yet, perhaps, the change is less in me than in herself."

"There was a report at Cleveland of her engagement to an Italian nobleman," said Catharine, with all the composure she could assume.

"Which she repeated to me; and, though indignant at the indelicate disregard to all proper feeling with which it charged her, it was rather a matter of amusement, because, she assured me, that there does not happen to be a single Italian of her acquaintance in England. Independently of her own assertion, a disregard to appearances is the last error of which I could imagine Lady Sophia guilty. She has already sacrificed sufficiently to propriety. You have heard of the engagement that formerly existed between herself and Sir Greville Cleveland?"

"I have," said Catharine, and her voice, notwithstanding her habitual self-command, faltered.

"It was the result of an attachment of no ordinary strength,—severed by circumstances which proved Lady Sophia's no ordinary character," resumed Mrs. Warren, too much occupied with her former pupil to observe the embarrassment of Catharine. "The fault committed by Sir Greville was what the world terms venial in all men who have the excuse of youth, rank, and fashion;—to me it appears a moral delinquency of a flagrant kind; but I rather imagine that Lady Sophia's resentment was caused by the *infidelity*, not by the *sin*."

Catharine felt that her silence was almost falsehood,—that she was intruding into a confidence which, were her real situation with regard to Sir Greville understood, would be studiously withholden. Yet how difficult to declare to

Mrs. Warren that *she* was the bride elect of the once plighted husband of Lady Sophia! How impossible an act of self-denial to shut her eyes to the opening of the early life of her lover, in the only portion of it to which mystery attached,—all that had embarrassed and distressed her! Catharine continued silent.

"Lady Sophia," resumed Mrs. Warren, "married Mr. Barron too soon after the separation between herself and Sir Greville to render it possible for any unprejudiced person to believe that her union was the result of affection. I do not think it was a happy marriage; but *she* speaks of Mr. Barron in terms of gratitude befitting rather the magnificent bequest by which he has marked his attachment, than their manner of living together. Yet I am sure my conjecture is correct. There are no allusions to past happiness,—no domestic recollections,—no tears that will *not* be restrained. If Lady Sophia weeps, it is gracefully, and as a proper tribute to decorum."

"How artificial!" said Catharine, not insensible to so unamiable a trait.

"Women of the world—the best of them—*are* artificial," said Mrs. Warren. "Lady Sophia is the world's pupil, and she does credit to her instructer. The redeeming touch of nature in her character is the constancy of her heart to Sir Greville,—concealed, perhaps even unknown to herself, during the existence of former ties, but now betrayed by every look, every inflection of voice, when she speaks of him. Perhaps the finale of her romance, after all, may add another to the triumphs of first love."

"My dear Mrs. Warren," began Catharine, now resolute to speak, "I meant to tell you,—in confidence,—as my mother's friend,—that Sir Greville is not *free;*—that, in short, if Lady Sophia were not in existence, your friend's child would now be the happiest of women! My dear Mrs Warren, *I* am the affianced wife of Sir Greville."

It was now Mrs. Warren's turn to be silent from irrepressible amazement; and, even when that subsided, violent emotion rendered it impossible for her to speak. She embraced Catharine with a mother's fondness, and wept over her with a mother's kindness, but she found no words of congratulation, for there was no hope of future happiness in her heart.

"Lady Sophia never loved him as I love him," said Catharine, with fervour; "did she not sacrifice his happiness to her pride?—entail years of misery for what, after all, was a fault,—a fault *now*, not only pardoned, but forgotten by herself? What possible error could alienate *me* from him?"

"If it were *crime?*" said Mrs. Warren, still in tears.

"Crime!—no; that is not within the compass of possibility!—*That* might indeed effect our separation, and leave for me the single refuge of the grave; but crime cannot taint the name of Cleveland!"

"The world pardons its prosperous children, and has courtly names for their lapses from rectitude, which are branded with strong stigmas when low men fall," said Mrs. Warren, sorrowfully. "Error may entail dreadful—awful consequences."

"But are not human actions to be judged by the principle, —not the effect?" said Catharine, with strong emotion. "Were we accountable for all the evil that resulted from our actions, even the best of them might be recorded against us as sins, and the fallibility of man would be a reproach to the justice of Providence."

"Effects which may in some degree be foreseen, become parts of actions," returned Mrs. Warren. "However, my dear child, to descend from generals to particulars, let me assure you that the error or fault, whichever we may term it, that dissolved the engagement of Sir Greville and Lady Sophia, was no inexpiable offence, according to human judgment. Years have elapsed since it occurred, and repentance may have effaced the stain, if stain there were."

"If Lady Sophia's pride *only* led to such a display of resentment; if, after the lapse of so long a period—after new connexions of so sacred a nature, she still recurs,—notwithstanding her improved power of deciding between right and wrong, to the hope of again winning the love she rejected, —I do not think that I am to be condemned for clinging to the belief that Sir Greville's mysterious error was a mere inadvertence of youth. Have I ever indulged in the vain dream of finding in the partner of my life *perfection?* Can I suppose that an existence passed, like Sir Greville's, in the midst of splendid temptation, has been sinless? No; for he is a human being. I have loved him,—I *do* love him, as a man, not an angel; and who and what am I, that I should venture to search into the records of the past for matter of reproach to him to whom I am bound by ties only less sacred than those pronounced at the altar."

Mrs. Warren sat for some minutes in silent reflection.

"Dearest Catharine," she said at length, "I hardly know how to pardon myself for agitating you thus, when I reflect how vague, after all, are my suspicions relative to this unhappy affair. I knew nothing but by report of the engagement existing between Lady Sophia and Sir Greville, for at the time of its occurrence I had been married nearly three years. It was not a subject to which, under existing circumstances, I should have thought of alluding when I saw Lady Sophia on her return to England, if she had not, with all the frankness of intimacy, introduced it, and spoken of her hopes and fears regarding the future. It was from her hints that I have been led to suspect a result of a peculiarly painful nature from the original error of Sir Greville; but they were *only* hints. I do not consider my plain *straightforwardness* by any means a match for the tactics of a skilful female politician, and Lady Sophia *may* have been in possession of a fact of which I am only just aware,—that the child of my most beloved friend has succeeded her in a heart which she still covets. If I do not now judge her ladyship uncharitably, she has reason to rejoice in the completeness of her triumph, for no human being could in that case have forwarded her views with more entire unconsciousness than I have done. The voice of kindness is so welcome to the unhappy, that they are reluctant to doubt its sincerity; but what if the improvement in Lady Sophia should be confined to manner, and the *policizer* of childhood be a policizer still? How she contrived to introduce the subject of Lady Darley's lately acknowledged niece,—to elicit from me all I had to tell of your person,—your mind, —your history! Age is said to bring suspicion in its train; *I* seem to have been credulous as a child."

"There is comfort in this supposition," said Catharine; "and now, friend of my mother, breathe a prayer for the happiness of her child!"

Mrs. Warren folded Catharine in a long embrace, and she invoked for her all the blessings which can attend the lot of mortals; but still she wept, for to experience the future is always darkened by a shadow.

Catharine quitted Mrs. Warren with a heart how much less tranquil than when that morning sun dawned on her! No woman can be conscious that mystery attaches to the man she loves, without desiring to penetrate it,—without dreading a thousand ills which she will hardly acknowledge to herself. Catharine believed it possible that the youth of Cleveland might be stained with folly—perhaps, morally speaking, with guilt,—but she rejected with indignation the mere supposition of its being a proper ground for distrusting him now in his years of maturity, when thoughtlessness had expired beneath reflection, and the truest philosophy had succeeded to the extravagances of imagination. Yet she was not happy. To a heart filled with unbounded love, not only willing, but desirous of laying open to him who engrossed it every memory of the past, every feeling of the present, every hope of the future,—the consciousness that in *him* there was reserve, perhaps distrust, was in itself painful. Moreover Catharine, without a distinct apprehension of the fact, was tormented with a thousand jealous fears; she dreaded the possibility of future intercourse between Sir Greville and Lady Sophia; the natural recurrence to former scenes enjoyed together; her power of bringing back, in all the vividness of reality, the blessed feelings of the springtide of life, flinging again into his lap the prim rose and violets of existence,—appealing to him through the past, yet standing before him in the splendid colouring of the present. Above all, Catharine had to keep her misery within her own heart, conscious that Lady Darley would combat her fears only by sarcasm and raillery, weapons which may be useful in attacking fanciful miseries, but which add to the keenness of real misfortunes.

"At least the season is over," said Catharine, when she retired that night. "Oh that we were once in the country! When I see him at Darley I shall be happy. Lady Sophia will feel that he belongs to another, and perhaps—oh, that she would!—she will return to Italy, and leave England to him and me!"

CHAPTER XXI.

As Catharine stepped into the carriage which was to convey her to Darley House, she turned to take one lingering look of the mansion in Grosvenor Square, perhaps with that feeling of reluctance so general in human nature, to quit a residence to which we are accustomed, even for one which we approach under the happiest auspices, and to which our desires have long pointed. The carriage rolled along, and she could not help wondering what had been the mighty preparations which had caused their detention until this day The windows were still adorned with their accustomed draperies;—Persian and Turkish carpets lay upon the floors;—the usual paintings adorned the walls;—or-molu and buhl exhibited themselves as before;—*bijouterie* was scattered in all directions;—and the plate and diamonds had been deposited at the bankers' only this morning. All that was to be done was left to the performance of the housekeeper, who remained in town another week for the purpose of making the necessary disposition of furniture, &c. Why, therefore, had Lady Darley, with all the importance of necessary occupation, remained until now,—protesting daily against a delay which, after all, had effected nothing?

Alas, Lady Darley would have been embarrassed to find a substantive reason for almost any action of her life! Fine ladies do not reason; they feel, or affect to feel, which answers their purpose quite as well, because it creates very nearly as much *sensation.*

Darley House, though far inferior to the magnificence of Cleveland Park, was as elegant and well appointed a mansion as could be desired by the most aristocratic dowager To Catharine, its gardens and shrubberies were delightful Since she had parted from Sir Greville nothing had been so soothing, so consolatory, as the long solitary ramble in the evening through an avenue arched over by foliage so dense that the rich autumnal sunset could not penetrate it. Above that bowery walk was the glowing crimson sky, but within it the sober twilight, whose *grayness* harmonizes so well with *reflection* and memory.

It has been ably said by a female writer, that "passion, when we contemplate it through the medium of the imagination, is like a ray of light transmitted through a prism; we can calmly, and with undazzled eye, study its complicate nature, and analyze its variety of teints; but passion, brought home to us in its reality, through our own feelings and experience, is like the same ray transmitted through a lens,—blending, burning, consuming, where it falls." And so it was with Catharine. She who had hitherto considered reason and principle as the lawful directers of human conduct,—who, in theory, had acknowledged the necessity of the subordination to their supremacy, of every feeling, every thought,—who had contemplated *passion*, properly so called, as an enemy whose approaches should be dreaded, guarded against, and prevented,—*she* had now admitted that very enemy into the citadel, and found evidence of his presence in the agitation,—the unnatural light and darkness which attended him.

There had been a time when she would unhesitatingly have pronounced it the duty of every woman similarly situated, to state to her future husband that a mysterious charge of error was hinted against him, to ask an explanation, and to observe for herself whether it had been repented or remedied. She would have deemed it culpable to shrink, as she was actually doing, from the possibility of knowing *that*, which duty, delicacy, perhaps religion, might enforce on her conviction as a necessary ground of eternal separation. She would have considered the jealous dread with which she regarded Lady Sophia Barron as a weakness unworthy of a generous mind. In theory she had contemplated love as a high, ennobling, and exalted sentiment, preferring in its perfection the happiness of its object to its own, in the train of which perfect confidence followed as naturally and fitly as the shadow the substance. And here it was with the base alloy of jealousy,—that most humiliating of all human passions,—that destroyer of all mental dignity, placing its unhappy subject at the mercy of the meanest informer,—filling her with a thousand painful suspicions of her own inferiority,—degrading her far, far below the scale which Providence had assigned her among his intelligent creatures,—the sport of every accident,—the slave to every caprice. Jealousy is the torture-bed of the *passion* of love;—happy they who have felt it only as a pure sentiment!

"A letter from Sir Greville, Catharine," said Lady Darley, as she examined the contents of the Darley post-bag. "Do read a line or two, that I may know when he will be here; I am tired of the vague kind of expectation implied by the indefinite '*week or two.*'"

Catharine obeyed.

"It contains hardly more than the number of lines necessary to tell me that he will be at Darley House on Wednesday evening," replied Catharine.

"I hate Wednesdays;—I have, you know, my white-letter days, and that is not one. Old women talk of the bad omen of beginning work of any kind on Fridays;—Wednesday now is my very black day. The most unpleasant circumstances of my life have always happened on a Wednesday."

"Superstition is the last weakness I should have expected to find in you."

"Ah, my dear, it is the common disease of human nature. Some of us have strength of mind sufficient to conceal it, but none to escape it entirely. Who among us does not cherish certain sounds as indicative of good or bad? Who has not his *pressentimens*, the shadow of the coming evil? Who has not on more than one occasion found himself suddenly in a new spot,—perhaps in a strange country,—and yet all around strikes his eye as familiar and accustomed,—and he feels that his *dreams have been prophetic?* The least imaginative have certain commonplace auguries of their own;—*esprits forts* have not been insensible to omens;—and I, you see, soiled, and sullied, and hardened, by perpetual contact with the world, I have my own peculiar pets of fancy. We are strange beings, we human creatures;—neither knowledge nor experience, nor scoffing nor reasoning, can divest us of our yearning after the supernatural."

As Lady Darley spoke, she employed herself in carefully opening a letter of voluminous folds, in the contents of which she was presently absorbed.

"Well," she said, as she refolded it, "this might also destroy a theory of *pressentimens!* That such a thing should happen, and my little familiar vouchsafe no whisper! Do you remember, Catharine, a very beautiful and embellished cottage-ornée, which I pointed out to you as we drove to Reading yesterday morning, about two miles from the Park gate? It extorted from you some little sentimentality on the joys of the golden mean, while I magnanimously defended the *more* golden extreme of Cleveland Park."

"Yes, I remember perfectly; there was a beautiful arbutus, and —"

"Yes; it reminded you of *your* cottage, where you once had some plan of rusticating with poor dear Mrs. Warren. This place,—the Grove, as it is called,—has been just a month untenanted; its owner, a stockbroker, who furnished it in the most costly style; after all, what is the extravagance of the most aristocratic of the *haute noblesse*, to that of your *parvenu*—your man of millions? The owner is ruined, in prison, a candidate for the benefit of the Insolvent Act. And now, observe the coincidence, or fatality, or malignant aspect of the stars, or whatever you may choose to call it,—who do you imagine is its new occupant?"

"Mr. Stark, perhaps; he talked of a new poem, the in spiration of the country, and the comfort of a cottage."

"Mr. Stark! That would be a common pebble set in curious mosaic! *His* cottage is the antithesis of the Grove; a thatched, mud-walled, whitewashed building; a small window at the side, which enlightens his private sitting-room; another, a pent-house kind of thing in the roof, which does the same good office by his chamber. In the front is a porch where his landlord drinks ale in the evening with an accompaniment, 'lending its sweetness to the desert air,' but not to be named 'to ears polite,'—the clumsy substitute for the oriental hookah. Beyond, you behold ten square feet of garden, crowded to suffocation with the most pungent of the esculent vegetables, from which a small green paling and a dwarfish gate keep off the inroads of carts, horses, and other passengers along the turnpike road. *Behind*—stables, cow-houses, piggeries, surround a farmyard littered with straw, and musical with the various voices with which nature has gifted geese, ducks, and hens, and similar of the feathered generation. A small pond, covered with duckweed, is in one corner, and *that*, my dear, is the 'Pierian spring' from which Mr. Stark's genius drinks deep. No, no; the Grove was not built for Mr. Stark. Try once again."

Catharine owned herself at fault.

"In charity, then, I terminate your suspense,—Lady Sophia Barron! There, my dear, acknowledge that I have made what playwrights call a very fine point. Your start, Miss O'Neil never surpassed it! Your look of dismay, quite Siddonian! Behold us then within *indispensable* visiting distance of the whilom ladye-love of your knight."

Catharine was silent.

"Now, my dear," resumed Lady Darley, "do me the favour to be sincere, and tell me truly, Do you not wish Lady Sophia with Glendower's spirits, in the 'vasty deep?'"

"Not quite," replied Catharine, with a languid smile, "but certainly in Italy."

"A most foolish wish. You have too much faith in the potency of Lady Sophia's spells, even supposing, which by no means appears on the face of the record, that her ladyship has even the will to make the experiment. And if she *had*, remember Sir Greville's bonds, and *then* ask yourself, 'What's Hecuba to him, or he to Hecuba?' Above all, dear Catharine, be counselled by me; when we meet—as meet we must—this formidable Lady Sophia, do not permit the slightest change of colour, the smallest inflection of voice, to indicate that her presence discomposes you. Be as cold as you please; *that* may pass as a fault of temperament: but be always, and undeviatingly, calm. The slightest symptom of agitation, and her ladyship is master of the field!"

"Her presence will not discompose me," said Catharine, thoughtfully. "I am not subject to nervous agitation, you know. It is *on reflection* that I connect disagreeable consequences with her return to England, and a renewal of intercourse, should that take place, between her and Sir Greville. But, if I *am* to endure the pain of his inconstancy of *heart*, the sooner it occurs the better for me. I am yet sane enough to say, that I will never owe to his honour a fidelity denied by his affection."

"I detest romance, Catharine; what other tie than hon our have ninety-nine women in every hundred on the men whom ultimately they marry? I strongly suspect, and I have the observation of years as the basis of my suspicions, that very few men approach close to matrimony without sundry misgivings, and that, at *that* point, honour, not love, is the spur which compels them to advance. With all your talent, Catharine, you are yet very young, and quite new to the world; and as for your education, you yourself must be sensible that it has given a bias to your mind which prevents you from viewing things as people in *general* view them."

"True; for I have been taught to separate the right from the expedient, and to consider that prudence which prefers a less degree of present pain to a greater degree of future pain. Could the pang of separation from Cleveland, *my lover*, equal that inflicted by the coldness, the disgust, or even the distaste of Cleveland, *my husband?* No, my dear Lady Darley, you would not wish your niece to be scorned by the man whose name she bore, as the *enforced* partner of his existence,—one who derived all her social claims from his unwilling bounty,—who, by the very fact of appealing to his honour instead of his affection, proved that her selfishness was stronger than her love,—that she preferred the indulgence of her own feelings to his happiness. No, no, my dear aunt, my education was not wrong because it was unusual. Would not our sex be happier if their hearts were strengthened by early lessons instead of softened? Does moral courage necessarily render a woman unfeminine, and is she less worthy of love for thinking rightly, than when enveloped in those charming errors which men cherish and flatter, *because* they are a delightful homage to their own superiority? Or do you think the present condition of woman the best possible for herself, or for those beings whose early nurture—whose first impressions—*must* be received from her? Do you think an improvement in *her* would not effect a material improvement in the whole range of society? Or do you think virtue the stronger because the means of defence are few and weak, and those of attack many and strong? Pardon my warmth," she continued; "I *must* defend my education, for an imputation on it is an injury to my mother, who directed it."

"I have not a word to say against it," returned Lady Darley, with one of her blandest smiles; "you have acquired so charming a bloom by your defence of it, that whatever may have been its errors, I look in your face and I forget them all! Only, my dear child, many theories are very excellent, which do not answer in practice because they are *premature*. It may be a mark of talent to outrun the spirit of the age, but it is rarely prudent to manifest it, and almost always dangerous. Galileo was in the dungeons of the Inquisition for a discovery in natural philosophy; and you may find a novelty in moral philosophy as severely punished *now*. To return, however, to Sir Greville. Why *should* the mere fact of Lady Sophia Barron's return to England disturb either you or myself? How little leisure has a man of the world for the cherishing of those youthful fancies which make solitary men poets, and sometimes maniacs! You will see the two meet as polite acquaintances should meet,—or perhaps as strangers, if such be the lady's will; the more discreet, perhaps, in all cases of this kind, when the love on both sides was ascertained beyond all possibility of doubt. We *must* call on Lady Sophia as soon as we hear of her being settled at the Grove. Can you rely on yourself sufficiently to promise me that you will be just the same self-possessed, graceful personage as usual?—that I shall have the pride and pleasure I always feel in introducing my niece,—the last of the Vernons?"

"I can," said Catharine, calmly.

"Catharine, you *force* praise from me," said Lady Darley, looking on her with unfeigned admiration. "With all your—*grandeur*, I must call it for want of a better name,—there is nothing theatrical about you,—nothing for effect,—not a look,—not a gesture,—not a tone of your voice. Perhaps, after all, your very simplicity *is* grandeur. Yet there is nothing cold, nothing austere, in your *reasonable* method of viewing things. You are a creature breathing poetry and feeling still,—full of bright and happy thoughts of sunshine and starlight, and great and glorious things, about which even I—woman of the world as I am—may have had my reveries; and without which, in youth, there is an unloveliness in the most gifted mind. Time acts by our minds as our faces,—it deprives them equally of their bloom. And *here* you will have an incalculable superiority over Lady Sophia,—a superiority to which a man like Cleveland, wearied with the hardness of the world, will be acutely sensible. There is a *freshness* about you,—'the delicate dew of the rosebud,' which never survives youth,—least of all a ten years' married life. To *him* even Lady Sophia's acquired graces must appear hackneyed, for he has withstood the artillery of the most polished women in Europe unscathed. Yes, my dear Catharine, let us discard all fear of *ourselves*,—all doubt of *him!* Cleveland Park will be yours, and the heart of its master with it; so let us put aside these letters — you are tenderly cherishing Cleveland's half dozen lines, I perceive,—and regain our cheerfulness by breathing the sweet air of this bright day. We will call on half a dozen people, and hear, or report, the acquisition our neighbourhood is to enjoy in the society of the accomplished Lady Sophia Barron. For once, Catharine, I am absolutely tired of talking, for I have made a speech long enough for one of Mr. Canning's electioneering addresses."

CHAPTER XXII.

If the happiness of Catharine had been regulated by the tenderness of her lover, she must at this time have been one of the most blessed of human beings.

She had before enjoyed the society of Sir Greville with all the adjuncts of that romance and poetry peculiar to a highly picturesque country, but at Cleveland Park the commonplaces of existence had continually broken the charm. A large party of the fashionable and the frivolous were there, demanding a share of the time and attention of both; their occasional *tête-à-têtes* were short and unsatisfactory, disturbed even during their enjoyment by a conviction of the observation they were exciting; and even the most legitimate love likes not that stranger eyes should be watching its progress. But at Darley there were whole days of leisure, and almost of *tête-à-tête*. Lady Darley was often present, certainly, but she knew so well how to dispose of herself,—had so ready an art of becoming, or appearing to be, absorbed in the occupation or the idleness of the hour, to the exclusion of all other persons or thoughts unconnected with it, that the most *exigeant* lovers could not consider her *de trop*. And Catharine and Cleveland rambled together through the lonely woods and glades that embellished the neighbourhood round Darley, acquiring a deeper insight into each other's tastes, minds, and feelings,—rejoicing, *she* especially, as this intimate communion displayed to her a world of intellectual and moral beauty, from the stores of which she might daily gather new and purer mental aliment. It was impossible to doubt the sincerity of any sentiment professed by such a man. Sir Greville appeared to have left the dross of his artificial manners in that society which was their congenial element. In the country he was manly, true, rational, sometimes imaginative. Conscious of the indisputable extent and depth of his own attainments, he did not deem it necessary to mark his own elevation in the scale of rational beings by depressing, below her proper position, the woman he had chosen. He disdained the petty despotism by which mean men secure themselves from the rivalry or the scorn of the other sex; he was glad to feel that the being he loved was able to appreciate him. It is only those on the confines of the empire of intellect who dread the inroads of their neighbours, or believe that the settlement of others around them will render their own a debatable territory.

It was now July, and it was decided that the marriage should take place in September, as soon as the year of Catharine's mourning for her mother had expired. What an invisible chain connects the most joyous events of human life with the saddest, as if it were an ordination of Providence that they should exercise a mutual influence over each other, lest in our prosperity we should become presumptuous, and in our adversity we should despair! To a daughter, in whose heart the memory of her mother was placed in its most hallowed shrine, the prospect of a marriage, which was to be the consummation of her dearest hopes, was shadowed by the reflection that the voice whose blessing would have rendered it doubly holy was silent for ever;—that the prayer which would have pleaded so tenderly for its happiness was to be uttered no more on earth! Again and again Catharine asked her heart, would her mother's approbation have sanctified this union? And she endeavoured to take comfort as she listened to the *hope*, the *faith*, of that heart, that it would.

"Are you aware," said Lady Darley to Catharine one morning, "that Lady Sophia Barron has received the visits of every person within visiting distance, and that, on every account, it is advisable we should call on her without farther delay? Sir Greville is bound to Abingdon this morning;—a more favourable opportunity for our driving over to the Grove is not likely to offer."

Catharine assented reluctantly, as people perform an unpleasant but inevitable duty.

Lady Sophia was at home, and in a few seconds Catharine found herself gazing, with intense interest, on as fine a head as ever started into life beneath the pencil of Leonardo da Vinci. Glowing, animated, brilliant,—with an expression ever varying, but always attractive,—Lady Sophia, if she had lost the characteristics of girlhood, still preserved all the graces, and much of the bloom, of youth. Nothing could exceed the easy dignity of her reception of Lady Darley and her niece; there was one moment's—only a moment's—earnest scrutiny of the latter, so transient indeed that it must have escaped the observation of any individual not prepared to detect the least palpable indication of extraordinary interest. Otherwise, her calmness, her suavity, her self-possession, were the only characteristics of manner that offered themselves to the animadversion of the most critical.

"Italy is the country of my *taste*,—shall I say my *mind?* —England of my heart," Lady Sophia replied to some commonplace inquiry from Lady Darley of her national preferences. "Existence there is picturesque, and one looks on every thing through a dazzling medium, which, perhaps, is injurious to our perceptions of truth. Here, on the contrary, we regard life more nearly, and see it in its reality; not so beautiful, not so graceful, it is true, but with a consciousness that we are not walking in a dream from which we may presently be aroused by some tremendous shock, in the shape of an assassin or a carbonaro. There is an epoch in human life in which we feel the full value of the true, and are contented to forgive the absence of the beautiful."

"But the true and the beautiful are so closely blended in the perceptions of all well-regulated minds!" said Lady Darley, affecting philosophy, an affectation the most unsuited imaginable to her usual *manière d'être.* "Moreover, our tastes are more flexible than we are willing to allow; and if your convenience or your inclination fix you again as a resident in England, I do not despair of hearing you, at some future period, advocating the gloom and the irregularity of its climate."

"It is possible," said Lady Sophia, with graceful acquiescence; "and, in the design of making England my permanent abode, I have brought with me as many reminiscences of Italy as could be deposited in any dwelling of moderate dimensions. Perhaps you will look into my magazine of curiosities; it is in a terrible state of confusion, but its contents are, I flatter myself, sufficiently valuable to dispense with the accessory of accurate arrangement. There are some gems of art which have not been despised by the first connoisseurs in Europe."

Lady Darley and Catharine accompanied Lady Sophia, with the usual exp essions of courteous and grateful assent, into a large drawing-room, converted into a cabinet of *virtu*, in which very few marks of the derangement of which her ladyship complained were perceptible.

No person who has understanding enough to appreciate, and taste enough to love, the *chefs d'œuvre* of the masters of painting and sculpture, can gaze upon them without losing much of that selfish dwelling upon personal considerations which forms and occupies so much of human existence. Catharine was speedily engrossed in the contemplation of the splendid gems of art around her; and, in conversing with Lady Sophia on the history of the production of many of them, often so curious an illustration of the wondrous working of the human understanding and affections, she escaped from the recollection of the singular position in which they stood to each other; she lost the reserve in which she had hitherto involuntarily infolded herself, and she exhibited to Lady Sophia the extent of knowledge, the elevation of thought and feeling, which distinguished her so remarkably from the frivolous mass of her sex. Lady Sophia herself was too hackneyed a worldling to be enthusiastic even in the arts she affected to admire;—too intensely occupied with her own interests ever to overstep the threshold that leads into the enchanted hall of poetry and imagination. She was therefore sufficiently unoccupied to be able to observe every indication of Catharine's mind and feeling which was thus manifested. If, however, she had not the reality of enthusiasm, she had learned its language, and she replied to the remarks of her guest in a tone correspondent to her own.

"It is a real misfortune not to be bound by some ties of preference or sentiment to a peculiar place," said Lady Sophia. "I should feel it a cause of thankfulness if duty, or prudence even, recommended to me one spot as a permanent residence rather than another. When one has unbounded freedom of choice, one hesitates so long, in the fear of making at last an unfortunate selection. A house I must have, and the Grove, with all its recommendations of situation and neighbourhood, is so mere a cottage, that, if large enough for my ambition, it would not contain the half of my accompaniments. One picks up so many things in travelling,—not valuable perhaps, but appealing to one as reminiscences,—emblems of past thoughts,—souvenirs of agreeable hours recalled,—mortifying consideration!—so much the more forcibly by palpable objects. I could not consent to part with the most insignificant of my pebbles. Can you, Lady Darley, name any place to me likely to afford space enough for a tolerable arrangement of them and me?"

"Not unoccupied, I fear," replied Lady Darley; and it occurred to her to add, "nothing less magnificent than

Cleveland Park would suit you," when a fortunate recollection of the embarrassment the malicious remark might cause to Catharine prevented her.

"Berkshire is a pretty county, but hardly romantic enough for my taste," said Lady Sophia. "I am young enough to like to ramble over 'hill and valley, fountain and fresh shade,' and have actually indulged in the fancy of settling myself on the banks of Winander Mere. The only objection is its remoteness."

"And its climate," said Lady Darley; "to you its mists and clouds must be doubly terrible, considering the sunny land in which you have so long dwelt."

"Human nature,—*my* human nature, at least," replied Lady Sophia, with a smile, "delights in contrasts. One tires even of perpetual sunshine, and I am not quite sure that I should object to a short experience of the bleakness and mists of Westmoreland. Besides, you know, I am a 'child of the mist' by birth, and Scotch men and women are proverbially national. If it were not that so many painful recollections are attached to my native land, *there* would I sojourn, for I love the mountain heather still."

Lady Darley was silent,—her perfect good-breeding rather shocked at Lady Sophia's allusion to her private history,—explaining taste and actions by hints at causes with which her hearers were bound to appear totally unacquainted. Catharine wished that more had been said, or not so much, but she felt how impossible it was to insist on such a topic.

"I am very solitary just now," Lady Sophia resumed, "but I mean shortly to fill my house with as many of my friends as will consent to be cabined within its narrow limits. When Mrs. Warren is my guest, I shall hope, Miss Vernon, to see you very frequently. I do not venture to flatter myself that I *divide* Mrs. Warren's love with you, but I have at least some claims on her affection; and, wayward pupil as I was, she still feels an interest in me and my welfare. Apropos, of old friendships;—I am told that Sir Greville Cleveland is at Darley House;—I hope he will resume his acquaintance with my favourite brother Stracey, who is here with me; and who, though given to solitary meditation, is not quite hermit enough to admire a *tête-à-tête* with me daily."

"Sir Greville will of course call on your ladyship as soon as he is aware of your being the occupant of the Grove," said Lady Darley, with some *retenue*.

"I assure you I expect no less of him," returned Lady Sophia, with a gayety which became her exceedingly. "Our ancient enmity is gone to the tomb of the Capulets, I hope. We have lived long enough in the world to know that charity and forgiveness become poor human nature better than the bowl and the dagger."

Lady Sophia sighed, and looked pensive, as if to demonstrate how equally playfulness and gravity became her exquisite beauty.

"I shall have great pleasure in renewing my own acquaintance with Mr. Hamilton," said Lady Darley. "I remember him—must I confess it was ten years since?—a very young man, and quite a *héros de roman*;—he was wounded in the early part of the Spanish campaign, under circumstances peculiarly desperate;—I think he succeeded in rescuing the colours of his regiment from an overpowering superiority of numbers. I am ashamed to have so vague a recollection of an action, the gallantry of which was, I remember, universally acknowledged."

"Stracey, I am sure, will be delighted to claim your acquaintance. Darley House has an attraction, of which even I, wanderer as I have been, have heard, but of the potency of which I have only been sensible this morning. I shall be too happy, Miss Vernon, if you allow me to improve this introduction into intimacy, and you will not be very much offended, I trust, if I return your call immediately."

Catharine was obliged to reciprocate a wish so gracefully expressed; but her colour deepened as the insincere compliment escaped her lips, and her coldness might have chilled any one less resolved to carry her point than Lady Sophia.

A few more courtesies—a few more commonplaces—and Lady Darley and her niece, nothing loath, re-entered their carriage.

"How agreeable—how fascinating—if she were not Lady Sophia Barron!" said Lady Darley. "Confess that Cleveland had at least a very fair excuse for feeling the force of her ladyship's attractions."

"She is beautiful," replied Catharine, thoughtfully; "so beautiful that one wonders, not at the attachment, but that it could ever be forgotten."

"To forget is the condition of human life," returned Lady Darley, with some impatience. "No man in his senses would sigh for perfection itself when convinced it was unattainable. Lady Sophia is a very beautiful woman, but I am not quite sure that her great charm is not in her manners. They are very captivating—so soft—so feminine. It is pleasant to be the dupe of so exquisite a deception."

"Are we sure that there is deception?" said Catharine. "I fear that the relation in which Lady Sophia has stood to Sir Greville makes us harsh judges of her."

"Will you be good enough, my dear Catharine, to tell me what particular object you imagine powerful enough to decide Lady Sophia on taking a house avowedly too small for her—in a neighbourhood with which she is unacquainted—which is not recommended by any of those associations that occasionally induce romantic people to establish thems in the least desirable spot in the world? Do you suppose she is particularly anxious to watch, with a disinterested eye, the progress of your wooing, or is desirous of being a spectator of the ceremony which is so shortly to proclaim you *won?* No, my dear, Lady Sophia is not a woman likely to be so *inconséquent* as to expose herself to inconvenience without a motive. Moreover, I always distrust the compliments one woman pays to another, and Lady Sophia's expressed and implied admiration of you affords to my mind unequivocal evidence of her insincerity."

"Do you really believe that Lady Sophia indulges the hope—the desire—" Catharine began.

"Of dividing you and Cleveland?—Yes—unhesitatingly, yes. But, Catharine, although such is my conviction, there are no reasons why you should be melancholy or fearful. Lady Sophia hopes against hope. The thing is utterly impossible. Even if you were less fair—less attractive—less the object of Cleveland's devoted attachment—still would *she*, in seeking him, pursue a phantom. Remembering, as he must, all the pain—all the agony of the disappointment she inflicted on him—do you believe that *he*, the spoiled child of the world, would be so far pacified by her tardy repentance as to seek again to rivet the chains so rudely snapped asunder? Admire, however, the address of Lady Sophia, in making us the bearers of her overtures. Why should she suppose that *I*, at least, was so little experienced in the wiles of women of this goodly world, as to be the dupe of the ancient friendship of Sir Greville Cleveland and Stracey Hamilton—men, the moral antitheses of each other—between whom there never could have existed one congenial sentiment?—If she persuades Stracey Hamilton into seconding her efforts so far as to vouchsafe us a visit, you will see immediately the desperate manœuvre on which his sister has ventured. If he is with her, it is from a conviction of the propriety of his guardianship; Hamilton was always engrossed in the pursuit of some Utopian good to mankind in general, to which he sacrificed all the time other men of rank spend in a search after pleasure, or perhaps fame. I would engage that at this moment he is hunting out some morass to be drained—some common to be enclosed—for the diminution of poor-rates and such like parish concerns. On second thoughts, I really wish he *would* call; his eccentricities will amuse you."

"Were he and Cleveland really friends during the time of Lady Sophia's engagement?"

"Why yes, child, certainly; how could it be otherwise? Even to the seventh generation, all the kinsmen and acquaintance of the woman beloved shine with a reflected light in the eyes of the lover. When the affair ended the friendship terminated, as usual since the days of Pylades and Orestes."

"Do you think Cleveland is aware that Lady Sophia is in our neighbourhood?"

"I do not think on the matter. It is not of the least consequence; he *must* know, and yesterday or the day before would have answered as well for the communication as to-morrow. On the whole, I am glad that Stracey Hamilton is in Lady Sophia's suite; he will answer very well as an object to whom Cleveland may dedicate his courtesies, while he leaves the task of entertaining Lady Sophia to you or me."

Catharine was silent, and, sooth to say, disturbed. What her reflections were Lady Darley found it easy to conjecture, from the exclamation that escaped her almost involuntarily after a long pause—"How exquisitely beautiful she is!"

"Granted," said Lady Darley, with a smile; "but even *then*, Catharine, you surpass her, for your beauty is of a rarer character. As a general rule, however, let me advise you never to praise the beauty of another woman; it is only just in rather better taste than to depreciate it. You are suspected of a desire to show your superiority to envy, and your consciousness that you have higher claims to consideration than mere personal attractions. It seems to insinuate that you pique yourself on the superiority of your mind, and even beauty itself is much more easily pardoned than wit—perhaps because it is more completely an accident. No young woman should criticise the personal attractions of another;—if she admires—it is affectation;—if she condemns—it is envy. Let her wait until she becomes a matron, and then she may fall into the usual duties of a chaperone—to *prôner* her own protégées, and find fault with those of every other person. Oh, my poor purchased roses, hide your diminished heads! Catharine, what a blush is there!—Sir Greville, you are the most gallant of cavaliers—always at hand just when your liege lady requires your services. I am tired to death; I have been talking these two hours—a monologue that might tire Mathews. Will you forgive me if I run away for a little, and condemn you to a *tête-à-tête?*"

CHAPTER XXIII.

"This is certainly the happiest period of my life," said Cleveland, as he stood with Catharine on the bow of a fairy bridge which spanned a miniature river, the chief ornament of the grounds round Darley House. "Youth had its seasons of rapturous excitement and ecstatic dreams, but *here* there is 'a sober certainty of waking bliss' which promises duration. I look beyond the present not only without fear, but with hope; there is something so holy, Catharine,—if I may so characterize any sentiment of mine,—in the love you inspire, that I feel not only a happier, but a better man by indulging it. It is something, too, to know that I have such a wealth of affection hoarded within my heart; I, who have so long imagined that every spring of feeling was exhausted; I, who, having drunk so largely, had a right to believe that I had drained the cup! If it were not presumptuous, one might almost believe that there is what certain religionists denominate a special Providence, watching over us, miserable, weak, and erring as we are."

Catharine looked at him doubtingly, and the colour mounted even to her temples. "It is not presumption, but faith, to believe that which is revealed," she said.

"There shall be no religious controversy between us," replied Cleveland, with a smile. "Such a doctrine is beautiful creed for tender, dependant, injured woman; it is right and wise that she should believe there is a retributive power on her side, an eye that watches over her wrongs, and punishes. Your sex are placed in so unjust a position here, that it is policy to ensure their submission by presenting to them a religion which promises them an equality with their oppressors hereafter."

The colour which had just bloomed so brightly on the cheek of Catharine was succeeded by the paleness of marble. She was silent; and Cleveland, looking, as was his wont, in her face, to read there the sentiments her tongue sometimes hesitated to pronounce, was alarmed at her death-like appearance. "Are you ill, dearest Catharine?" he asked. "Let us sit on yonder bank; we have walked too long; you are quite fatigued."

"No; it was a sudden pang—it is over; a few moments' rest will restore me," replied Catharine, but so faintly, that Cleveland, without speaking, supported her to the bank and placed her on it.

"Catharine," he said at length, as he watched the colour returning to her cheek, "I have observed you so closely, and I comprehend you, I think, so well, that I am convinced you were, and are, suffering from mental, not bodily, distress. You are shocked at believing that I regard religion rather as a theory than a fact?"

"You are right," replied Catharine, regaining her wonted calmness, and inexpressibly relieved that he voluntarily afforded her the power of ascertaining what were his real opinions,—"you are right in part, but not wholly. I *was* shocked that you should lightly speak of a subject, to me too sacred to be approached without reverence;—I was more,—I was self-condemned. Was it possible that I then, for the first time, remembered that your sentiments on such a point were all-important?—that I have allowed my whole heart to be engrossed"—she paused, conscious of the extent of the avowal into which she had been betrayed.

"Self-condemned!—for that which is the proudest triumph of my existence!" said Cleveland. "Do you think, Catharine, that a love which pauses and hesitates at every step,—looks round cautiously to discover whether any obstacles are likely to impede its progress,—shrinks if the path appear not all verdant and flowery,—think you such a love would satisfy me?—No, Catharine; I am yours thus devotedly,—thus eternally,—because your heart *has* rushed forward to meet mine, regardless of aught but the joy of meeting 'its other self!'—Far from us be the selfish calculation which measures our love by the standard of a rigorous judgment, which gives just so much as we believe will produce our own happiness, and shrinks at the point where pain begins. No, Catharine;—for weal or for wo you must love me, now and ever!—Where I am in error, my guardian angel;—where I am right, my disciple."

"Alas," said Catharine, "what woman can venture to say, that even the errors of the man she loves shall not become hers?"

"She who is guarded by him against himself," replied Cleveland, with far greater earnestness than his ordinary manner exhibited. "Neither you nor I, Catharine, are bigoted in our opinions;—we know enough to be conscious 'how little *can* be known.' I reverence,—I love, your religion;—I am not an infidel, at worst, and, I may add, only *occasionally* a doubter; there are times when convictions are much stronger than at others,—when, perhaps, the internal voice speaks loudest. I am a speculator, not a theorist: a seeker after truth, ready to adopt it, were it to be found in the caves of Mithra, or in the temples of the Buddhists. The *precepts* of Christianity no sane mind can impugn;—happy for mankind if the world were regulated by them. Some of its peculiar doctrines *may* be open to cavil, and some minds, perhaps, are so constituted, as to be absolutely incapable of receiving them. For my own part, I avow to you, that I never saw a sincere Christian walking humbly with his God that I did not envy him; and if sometimes I am assailed by doubts whether all be true, still more frequently do I question, is it possible that this can be false? Remember, Catharine, that no man would voluntarily doubt, for doubt is a state of torment; not a breathing of unbelief, in my darkest moments, shall be whispered by me to you; far be it from me to attempt to snatch you from the rock of certainty, to plunge you into the whirlpool of speculations! In that, as in all else, your happiness shall be my only object; and what may not your example effect?"

Catharine smiled, but it was through tears, for the war between her heart and her principles was not pacified by all the specious eloquence of her lover. Cleveland saw that it was not peace within her, and he hastened to divert the current of her thoughts.

"How many hours we have been separated this morning, which we might have enjoyed together! No man can live in the world without making daily sacrifices of his inclination. It requires the solitude and the privileges of a hermit to employ time according to inclination. My morning was not a morning of enjoyment, for it was occupied in observing the misdirection of intellect, and the unfortunate effects of a false system. I visited the son of a tenant of my father, who, discovering early talents which were deemed worthy a higher destination than that of a tiller of the soil, was educated at a public school and at college, by my father's bounty, for the church. He did not disgrace his patronage, but he disappointed it. Sufficiently imbued with classical literature to take a very high university degree, and to be pronounced eminently qualified for the living which he now holds, he was, and he remains, in all real knowledge, all that can benefit his species,—perhaps all that can enlarge his own mind,—in a state of ignorance with which even an American Indian might be reproached. His mind is so darkened with the dust of antiquity, that the light of the present cannot penetrate it. Impressed with the conviction of the high importance of the Greek and Latin classics, the slightest hint that their knowledge was in a great measure erroneous,—that their theories were absurd,—and their hypotheses mere reveries,—startles him as a heresy. He shares, with many of his class, the error of believing that an acquaintance with the classical languages, as they are called, is *knowledge*,—knowledge in its enlarged application. I almost think that his veneration for the *vehicle* of the thoughts of the ancients exceeds that with which he regards the thoughts themselves. He has employed years in the composition of a laborious treatise on the Æolic digamma, and meditates a volume of essays on etymologies, that idlest of all elaborate trifling. The most lamentable fact connected with him is, that, not satisfied with so grievous a perversion of intellect in his own proper person, he is educating his only son to tread in the same miserably narrow path, in the delusion that eminence will be found at the end of it. It is in vain to endeavour to open the eyes of the blind; and what blindness equals his who treads for ever the same circle,—meditates always on the same subject,—until he believes that the progress of the human mind, instead of carrying mankind for ever onward, makes perpetual revolutions in *his* orbit, and that *he* is on a level with it."

"You are describing a species of insanity," said Catharine.

"Insanity of a kind so common as to pass for learning, as the vulgar understand the word, and perhaps not incorrectly, for it rather expresses the signs of ideas than ideas themselves. He is but the victim of a false system of education, and he believes that he is doing his duty by making another in the person of his son. The boy already presents that most miserable of all spectacles, a melancholy, spiritless child,—his bodily energies enfeebled, and his intellect inert,—an embryo drone in the great human hive."

"My morning was spent with a person belonging, one would think, to a species that had neither thought nor feeling in common with your protégé," said Catharine. "I have called with Lady Darley on an acquaintance of yours,—Lady Sophia Barron."

"Lady Sophia Barron!" said Cleveland, with a slight change of voice, but not of countenance; *that* was too much under the command of the practised man of the world. "She is, or rather *was*, an acquaintance of mine; but I had not the remotest idea of her being in Berkshire."

"She is the tenant of the Grove, a beautiful cottage *orné*, in our immediate neighbourhood."

"It is nearly ten years since I saw Lady Sophia Barron;—she was then unmarried," said Cleveland, thoughtfully. "Time must have altered her greatly."

"I cannot decide on that point," replied Catharine, affecting a gayety she did not feel; "if Lady Sophia were more beautiful, more charming, ten years since than now, she must have been more than woman. A lovelier creature I never saw."

Cleveland looked earnestly at Catharine.

"It is not generally policy in one woman to praise another; one always suspects her sincerity," he said, apparently satisfied with the survey. "I remember Lady Sophia not *more* than woman, but in person perfect as the most finished model of her sex. In short, Catharine, her lovers followed her like the tail of a comet or a Highland chief, and," he added, in a more earnest but rather subdued tone,—

"'Among the rest, young Henry bowed
In perfect adoration.'"

"I knew it, Cleveland, "said Catharine, with an animation that testified all the satisfaction she really felt at the avowal; "and I thank you for ceasing to make a mystery of the matter with me. Mr. Stark's letter to the Dutchess of Halifax, at Cleveland—"

"I remember it all, Catharine; I have thought of it again and again, and as often I have resolved to state the fact to you with my own lips. And I was deterred,—will you forgive me that I judged you by—your sex?"

"I will forgive every thing but future distrust," said Catharine, gently. "Let our confidence henceforth be mutual and implicit."

"Be it so," said Cleveland, but his voice was less clear than usual. "Shall I venture to tell you with what love—what madness rather—my soul doted on that woman? The more I doubted her capacity of returning any part of that furious passion, the more it grew; her coldness never chilled me, but it inflamed,—it *forced* my unnaturally kindled feelings into another channel. There was no infidelity of the heart, Catharine, in the crime by which I lost her. I did not for an instant prefer, even equalise, that other far, far more unfortunate being with her; I was like a traveller in the desert, who sees afar off the pure and bright stream at which he may safely quench his intolerable thirst, but who, parched and panting, turns aside to taste of the unwholesome spring that is recommended only by its proximity. Sophia did not reason thus; my ravings—they were ravings—were unheeded by that proud, cold woman; and I fled, smitten by the lightning of her words, from her presence, into the vortex of a world too ready to welcome me. There is my history, Catharine; so did I last part from Lady Sophia; judge now with what feelings I contemplate the possibility of meeting her again."

"No, I cannot judge," replied Catharine; "I cannot even comprehend how such love as yours could cease,—could be succeeded by the faintest semblance of attachment to another."

"I will not reply to your implied question by any commonplace assurances, Catharine; let our present situation—let my future life testify,—that I *have* found it possible to love again,—even with a deeper, a holier, a worthier love than that of my young days. Months of that despair which exhibits itself in utter recklessness succeeded my separation from Lady Sophia, but the mind of man is not made to be crushed by one storm, how fiercely soever it may assail him. Other interests attracted me,—by turns, ambition—pleasure,—the pleasures of intellect as well as the pleasures of the senses. The hour of reflection—of cautious examination of the past, also arrived,—and I came to understand that Lady Sophia had sacrificed me to her pride, not her principles,—that she avenged my momentary infatuation for her unhappy rival, not my forgetfulness of the ties of honour and probity. Resentment succeeded to grief; and, though there was still a strife of feelings which imbittered my existence, love sank in the conflict. Lady Sophia married; it *was* a pang, but it passed, and left me a wiser, a freer, if not a better man. Inhabiting the same sphere, it was not within the compass of my expectations that I could live on without occasionally meeting Lady Sophia in society, and I learned to contemplate such a contingency as a thing neither to be avoided nor dreaded. And *now*, with *you* by my side, Catharine, *you* on my arm as the chosen partner of my life, *can* you wrong me so greatly as to believe that I shall regard Lady Sophia as other than the passing acquaintance of the hour,—that I shall see her with less indifference than the thousands of lovely women with whom I exchange courtesies daily?"

"I will *not* so wrong you," replied Catharine, earnestly. "I will tell you that Lady Sophia has sent by Lady Darley *almost* an invitation to you to call on her. Her brother is with her at the Grove,—an old friend of yours, she says,—who will find your acquaintance an alleviation of the dulness of his sojourn with his sister."

"Is it Stracey Hamilton?" inquired Sir Greville, slightly discomposed.

"I would gladly be spared that meeting," said Cleveland. "He is so connected with the painful episode of my story, as to view my error through the exaggerated medium of its unfortunate consequences; and his inclinations, as well as my own, will, I am sure, place us on the footing of strangers. Stracey Hamilton is not a man to be despised, and I should prefer encountering him only in general society; there *are* feelings, dear Catharine, which resist the alleviation of time, and remorse is one of them."

"Remorse!" repeated Catharine, with a slight shudder.

"Even so," replied Cleveland, with a sadness of manner most unusual to him. "The woman whom my crime destroyed had interested Hamilton more deeply than myself; he did not seek the gratification of an idle vanity—an unoccupied love; he *would* have saved her,—but, with the unhappy credulity of her sex, she listened to the temptation, not the warning,—she fell,—and, to complete the tragedy, she died."

"Fearful!" said Catharine, in irrepressible emotion.

"Do not hate me, Catharine,—for the bitterness of my repentance might wash out a stain even deadlier,—if deadlier there be,—than that!" said Cleveland, with stern composure. "I have laid bare my heart to you, Catharine; but I will do more. I will tell you that, notwithstanding all, I deserve your love still. If penitence *can* expiate crime, mine has been expiated; if an intenseness of love unequalled can merit return, mine for you merits it. If the past were for ever to fling its shadow over the present, who might abide it? Accept my confession,—my long repentance,—as security for the future; and believe that he who has for years carried within his breast the fire that has preyed on mine, is tenfold better fenced against crime than he who sees it only as a glittering temptation. For the present, at least, we will speak no more of this; but in your solitude, beloved, think of me mercifully,—and love me not the less because I have pleaded for your compassion."

CHAPTER XXIV.

Catharine *did*, in the solitude of her own apartment,—in the depths of her too devoted heart,—think mercifully of Cleveland. But her thoughts were not the thoughts of the happy,—her love not the blissful confidingness of the undoubting. She had learned that between her own principles—those, too, affecting the very highest interests of morality—and his, there existed a gulf which she, at least, *willed* not to overpass, and which he, in his present state of proud intellectual self-dependance, *could* not. She felt that the test of her moral strength had been applied, and that she had been found wanting. A voice louder than the clarion of the voice of the multitude,—the *speechless* voice within,—warned her that her hour of proof had passed, and she had failed. The chosen of her heart had avowed principles which, if not those of the absolute infidel, were at least those of the skeptic, and she had not rebuked, far less had she shrunk from him. She was conscious that he deemed her religion—her cherished immortal hopes,—a beautiful dream to solace a woman's imagination,—a staff on which her credulity leaned for support, and which sufficed for *her* weakness. She saw that, from the heights of his philosophy, "of the earth earthy,"—he looked down on *her* faith as the pardonable credulity of a child,—a fable not unbecoming its lisping accents, its feeble voice. Even now, in the very extreme of her passionate love, her mental vision was sufficiently clear to enable her to discern that he considered Christianity as a beautiful system on a level with that of Plato and Socrates, to be admired by every right-judging mind, but to be adopted or rejected at pleasure,—a matter of taste, not of vital importance, and little influencing the eternal destiny of man. How fearful an apprehension to her who clung to those hopes as the shipwrecked mariner to the last mast of his shattered and sinking vessel! And yet, fearful as such a conviction was,—painful as was the vista it opened of her future *mortal* existence,—the influence it must inevitably exert on the minds of her children, for whose earliest impressions at least she was accountable,—she shrank from the endurance of the present agony,—the pain of voluntarily severing her interests from his who had neither part nor lot in the matter which all *her* convictions, her reason, her principles, her mind and heart, felt to be the casting of the lot for eternity.

Catharine Vernon was a gifted, an endowed woman,—one to be classed with the best, the most elevated of her sex,—but *woman* still. Moreover she was, in those humble but emphatic words, *a lonely woman*,—with a heart full of love, yearning to bestow it on something of her own kind, but with only one solitary outlet for the stream that flowed within, longing to gush forth. *How* she loved him let those feel who have experienced the desolateness of a situation like hers,—who stand alone in the world,—or, more barren still, among those with whom they have no thought or feeling in communion, whose every word jars on their holiest and best sympathies, or outrages their most cherished principles. Catharine's weakness was an error, but let such answer whether it were unpardonable.

Yet how much less happy was Catharine than yesterday! How she indulged the vain, the undignified wish, that the knowledge which had so diminished her felicity had been still withholden,—that she could, as heretofore, shape forth a vision of her lover's faith and feelings accordant with her own. The history of his attachment to Lady Sophia was painful, but what was it to the bitterness of the thoughts which now oppressed her? And yet,—when she felt it possible that she might, by struggling, by meditation, perhaps by prayer, gain strength to do that which she felt it to be her duty to do,—the prospect of the possible triumph of Cleveland's first-love unnerved her resolution, and confirmed her in her decision to love him, as he had said, through good and ill, through weal and wo.

It was the very day after the conversation with Cleveland which had left so painful an impression on her feelings; they were at the breakfast-table, the letters were distributed,—put aside,—all but one,—and that Cleveland, having examined carefully the handwriting of the address, opened immediately.

"Such is the constant course of man's life," he said, with an air of undisguised vexation, as soon as he had mastered the contents of the letter; "if he plucks a flower, it is snatched from his hand ere its sweets are half enjoyed; if he strays by accident into a pleasant path, he is compelled by some necessity—the irresistible necessity of circumstance—to turn aside into a rocky and rugged road, beset with briers and thorns; in plain prose, his enjoyments are constantly interrupted by his duties. Yes, Catharine, I must for one week leave Darley. Read the letter; I have a troublesome executorship to fulfil, to the family of a man to whom I was once greatly obliged, and my presence in town at this juncture is indispensable."

Catharine read the letter.

"You must go, doubtless," said she, smiling, in aid of her effort to subdue a sigh. "This is a case which puts mere inclination quite out of the question."

"It is," said Cleveland; "strong as that inclination is *here*, it is impossible to consult it. But a whole week?—I trust you will not be too happy during that week, Catharine."

"We shall get on very tolerably;—we shall put up prayers for your speedy return, and hang up votive offerings to every god in the Pantheon," said Lady Darley. "Moreover, we have the promised visit of Lady Sophia Barron in prospect, and Catharine will have an opportunity of doing justice to the merits of that whilom hero, Stracey Hamilton, a thing which could not possibly have occurred in your presence."

Sir Greville looked uneasy.

"I must not have you deem too largely of his merits, Catharine," he said; "all your admiration of him will be so much censure of myself; this world hardly contains two beings more opposite."

"Do not fear," replied Catharine; "I almost doubt that the faculty of admiration is not sufficiently developed in my mind; I cannot often, and I assure you I try sufficiently, persuade myself into admiring what all the world besides is raving about. Perhaps my perceptions of the beautiful and good are not so keen as they ought to be."

"Perhaps your *conceptions* of the beautiful and the true are too elevated to be easily satisfied; that is the more probable metaphysical solution of the difficulty, I suspect. However, Lady Darley, in intrusting my treasure to you, I shall depend on your not permitting too great a degree of intimacy with this hero; and on your abusing him in exact proportion to the pleasure you find Catharine deriving from his society."

"Rely on my vigilant guardianship; and a week, you know, is not exactly long enough to permit the establishment of any violent intimacy between us and the party at the Grove,—a morning call and a dinner must necessarily be the limits of our intercourse."

Cleveland departed that evening, and it did not displease Catharine to find, by his whispered caution at parting, that he was really uneasy at the possibility of her thinking Stracey Hamilton too agreeable. No woman resents a doubt of this kind, because, while it impugns her constancy, it evinces the anxiety of her lover,—that anxiety by which she is accustomed to test the strength and sincerity of his attachment.

"Good night, my dear," said Lady Darley, as they retired to rest; "I must do you the justice to say, that you have been quite as dull and *ennuyeuse* this evening as the departure of Cleveland required you to be. I shall have to report very favourably of you. Be just as dismal to-morrow morning, which will assuredly bring Lady Sophia and the noxious Stracey Hamilton, and my eulogies will be unbounded. After all, Cleveland's short flight is rather apropos; it will disappoint her manœuvring ladyship, who considers *him* the chief—the sole attraction—at Darley. That was a very convenient letter of his, for I suspect he would rather not meet Lady Sophia at present. Do not blush so violently, my dear;—you saw it, and there could be no juggling, even were Cleveland—which he is not—capable of the baseness. *Why* did you blush, child?"

Catharine hesitated for a moment.

"I will not distress you, my dear. Give me only so much of your confidence as you choose."

"All—all—my dear aunt," said Catharine, earnestly; "in truth, I believe I blushed because you suggested the possibility of Cleveland's desiring to avoid Lady Sophia. Why should she now be of sufficient importance to him to excite a feeling of the kind?"

"Alas! my dear, the human heart is a mysterious world, with the workings of which we have a very shallow acquaintance," said Lady Darley, with a shrug. "One has so many inexplicable sympathies with people for whom one has once had a *tendresse;* and things went very far between *them*, you know,—marriage decided,—*trousseau* prepared,—every thing but the ceremony. Once more, my love, good night; don't torment yourself with vain curiosity about feelings you can never know, and which, I hope, you will not experience. We will enjoy our security;—Cleveland is this night in London, and Lady Sophia in Berkshire."

CHAPTER XXV.

The morrow came, but brought not its expected visiter—a real disappointment to Lady Darley, who, knowing that there was no danger to Catharine's heart—no dread of a foolish attachment and imprudent marriage—really wished her to become acquainted with Stracey Hamilton, as a man very much talked about, and despite of—it might almost be said *through*—the want of the advantages of primogeniture and fortune, distinguished. The want in this case, as in so many others, might have wrought out the distinction.

Catharine was not sorry that Lady Sophia and her brother still deferred their visit. She was too deeply, too entirely engrossed by Cleveland, to feel curiosity about any other individual of his sex, far less interest. And, indeed, it must have been a feeling of no ordinary intensity that could compensate to her the positive pain occasioned by the mere sight of Lady Sophia. Accustomed to search into and analyze her own emotions, she was not ignorant of the unwarrantable—she did not scruple to call it, the unworthy—jealousy which was the root of this pain: and she struggled to set her right principles—her reason—in array against it, but she was taught that in this, as in every disease moral and physical, prevention is easier than *cure;* the passion had been permitted to gather strength, and now the more she strove against it, the more deeply she involved herself in its inextricable folds.

The second morning brought,—not Lady Sophia,—but her brother.

His person, not strikingly handsome, but commanding, notwithstanding the deficiency of height, had that indescribable air of distinction which warns the multitude that they see a superior—and the few that a spirit of the very highest order is within. His eyes, of that colour which is said to be most expressive,—a dark gray,—were so searching, so penetrating, as to be almost severe, aided, too, as their effect was, by the firm compression of his handsome mouth. His broad forehead was of a dazzling whiteness, which indicated that the bronze of his complexion was not natural, but the result of the fierce suns of inhospitable climes. His address was somewhat cold and reserved, but perfectly well-bred, and even Catharine thought that the voice of Cleveland himself was not *very* much sweeter.

"I am charged," he said, "with Lady Sophia's written apologies. She is wise enough to know that she will be able to offer a more satisfactory explanation of her non-appearance than my diplomacy would achieve. You will find that indispensable business has summoned her very suddenly from the Grove."

Lady Darley could only bow and express a few words of polite regret; it was not for her to appear surprised at Lady Sophia's movements, or to question concerning her arrangements. Then she read the billet.

"Will you pardon me, my dear Lady Darley, if I assume so much importance as to believe that you have remembered my promise of returning very speedily the visit with which you and Miss Vernon honoured me? It was indeed a pleasure which I promised myself, and which circumstances compel me most reluctantly to defer, I will not say *relinquish.* Trifles indicate character; and I fear you will think mine very vacillating by this sudden change in my plans. The fact is, the lawyers imperatively require my presence in London for a few days, to complete some arrangements in the transfer of an estate, and the mandate of a lawyer is, as you know, absolute. Stracey remains at the Grove, and promises himself the happiness of walking to Darley with my *billet*, and he will assure you of the sincerity of my regret, that I have not been able to improve my acquaintance with Miss Vernon, to whom I beg you to offer my compliments.

"Yours very truly,

"SOPHIA BARRON."

"My sister has said more than I shall venture to say for her, I am sure," began Hamilton, when Lady Darley refolded the note,—he had employed the interval of her reading it in a very scrutinizing examination of the person of Catharine; "in my private opinion, the little word caprice,—or, to be more lenient, inclination,—would explain the origin of all Sophia's actions."

"Brothers are privileged satirists," said Lady Darley; "Lady Sophia is paying the penalty of great wealth and independence, by being compelled to come into personal contact with that vulgar thing called business."

Colonel Hamilton's brow slightly contracted, and he made a remark on the beauty of the view from the window near which he sat, evidently with the design of changing the subject.

"It *is* beautiful," said Lady Darley, replying to his observation. "Your admiration of it reminds me that it is a favourite point with Sir Greville Cleveland, and reminds me also to tell you that he is in London on unavoidable necessity, or I am sure he would be delighted to renew his acquaintance with you."

"It would be pleasure to neither of us," said Colonel Hamilton, abruptly, with more truth perhaps than politeness. "I beg your pardon, Miss Vernon," he added, seeing the colour deepen on the cheeks of Catharine; "I am a rough soldier, and consider plain truth the badge of my profession. Cleveland is too much of a courtier to fall into a similar error, and it is the unapproachable dissimilarity between us that renders it impossible that a renewal of our acquaintance could be desirable either for itself or its results."

Catharine bowed; it was impossible to reply to so unusual a remark as this.

A few commonplaces passed, and Catharine listened with interest. There was much originality in Colonel Hamilton's opinions on the most ordinary topics, and novelty itself compels attention; we are anxious to discover whether this new mode of viewing things be correct, and whether it be possible that we, all our lives, have been in error. There was a slight vein of severity perceptible in his remarks, indicating a mind that dwelt rather on the weaknesses and faults of his species than on its capacity for good, and its frequent production of good. In short, he evidently saw the world as it exists in its bad reality, not in the *possible* excellence with which the philanthropist delights to invest it, either present or prospective. Cathârine suspected that he had proved the falsehood either of love or friendship,—those two passions or sentiments which the young believe to exert so mighty a power over the whole human race! As if the waters of avarice, or ambition, or even poverty, were not bitter enough of themselves to taint a human mind!—As if no disappointments could shadow existence but those of the heart!

Colonel Hamilton spoke of Italy,—of Scotland,—climates, countries, he said, the antitheses of each other,—producing different races of men,—proving beyond controversy the influence of physical circumstances on the intellect—of climate on moral character. He considered it the blessing for which he owed the highest gratitude to Providence, that he had not been born an Italian. Their bravery, he thought, was that of banditti,—such as the handful of men were that fathered the Roman name,—the Romans themselves being but the result of a curious combination of circumstances,—occupying a certain cycle in time,—the necessary product of the succession of centuries in which they existed.

Catharine was amused at an eccentricity which evidently smiled at itself, and threw forth its odd *déraisonnemens* as a child blows air-bubbles—for the pleasure of seeing how far they will float. Colonel Hamilton, as he spoke, gave her one of his searching glances, and seemed pleased to find himself understood.

"Have you been in the Highlands, Miss Vernon?" he asked; and receiving a negative reply, continued, "It is not the place which I should propose as the most likely spot in the world to attract the attention, the admiration of a very fine lady;—you are *not* an ultra fine lady, Miss Vernon?"

"No."—Catharine smiled as she added, that many years of her girlhood had been spent in travelling; France, Germany, Poland, Italy, the Alps of one country, the forests of another, had made her familiar with *some* hardships, and had robbed her of all claims to be enrolled among the class of delicate hothouse plants to which he alluded.

"It is a trite remark, and, *being trite*, *true*," said Colonel Hamilton, "that the English see more of the country of their neighbours, and less of their own, than any other nation under the sun. There is a peculiar anomaly in our national character. While we consider ourselves the first people under the sun in our national capacity, we yield to almost every other people in our individual pretensions. I do not think I am very intelligible;—I mean, that while we claim a superiority for our *nation*, we prefer foreign artists, artisans, fashions, modistes,—all the appendages of that luxury which marks the height of civilization; a tacit tribute paid unconsciously, and falsely, to the higher refinement, taste, cultivation,—of our neighbours."

"But we avenge ourselves by asserting our superiority in the higher grades of human pursuit, both intellectual and useful," said Catharine. "We claim the meed of the world's admiration for our legislators, our generals, our philosophers;—we are the first in the progress of scientific research;—we place our authors, our dramatists, our poets,—in the foremost rank in the universe. We demand the tribute of the homage of all people, nations, and languages, for our Shakspeare; and we feel a contemptuous pity for those who are unable to comprehend the might, the majesty, of that wonderful '*barbarian!*' We place Milton by the side of Homer, and we demand that all nations should concede to him a place on the same pedestal. I almost think we gratify a secret pride by preferring foreigners as the ministers to our lower tastes,—we affect to think our countrymen above so ignoble a rôle. Even music we consider a recreation and an amusement,—and we are contented to be indebted to other nations for its beauties and its pleasures; we think the chronicles of our fame complete without enrolling the name of one of the masters of the mighty art among our archives. And even in painting,—I do not believe our enthusiasm would ever have carried us so far as to deck with the laurel wreath the dead brows of Raffaelle himself."

"I will not find fault with your special pleading," replied Colonel Hamilton, "for I, too, am proud of my English half-brethren—prejudiced as we Highlanders are said to be, and limited in our patriotism."

Colonel Hamilton looked at his watch, apologized for his unwarrantably long intrusion—received, with evident satisfaction, Lady Darley's assurances that his visit had conferred both honour and pleasure,—and, finally, accepted an invitation to meet a small dinner-party at Darley on the morrow.

"A clever and amusing man," observed Lady Darley, as she watched him riding down the avenue, "but not a Cleveland, Catharine."

"*Not* a Cleveland," acquiesced Catharine, as she thought of Alexander and his *two suns*. "Nevertheless, I am glad to have seen him; he is a man worth knowing."

"Why, yes;—he happens to be one of those whom not to know argues one's self unknown. I assure you Hamilton, when he chose it, divided the empire of fashion with Cleveland himself, notwithstanding his inferiority both in person and that greater source of power, fortune. The pursuit, however, wearied him;—he has made no efforts after fashionable notoriety, but *great actions*, which, having a higher end in view, sometimes, as in his case, draw the lesser in their trains."

"That is saying much for him," said Catharine; and she felt a painful—an almost indistinct consciousness, that Sir Greville was *not* altogether the superior.

"When you answer Cleveland's letter"—Catharine had heard from him that morning—a few lines expressive of his hope of returning even the day before that originally fixed, but certainly on that day;—"when you answer Cleveland's letter, do not omit to mention Colonel Hamilton's visit; a possible rival is always a stimulus to fidelity."

"I shall assuredly do so, but not from that motive. How lowly must I deem Cleveland's love if it required so unworthy a stimulus!—I shall tell him I have made Colonel Hamilton's acquaintance, because I think there ought to be perfect confidence between us, and he may attach importance to the circumstance from his former acquaintance with Colonel Hamilton; he appeared unwilling that there should be any intimacy with him."

"A very natural unwillingness;—every unprejudiced man must deem Hamilton a dangerous rival with a woman capable of appreciating his intellect through the whimsical, or perhaps cynical, veil in which he chooses to invest it. Stracey Hamilton is not a man to be despised."

"To be *respected*," said Catharine, calmly; "there is an evident truth—an integrity about him, in which one is inclined to confide without question. I never saw two people so nearly related, whose manner, countenance, conversation, were so different—who made impressions so opposite,—as he and Lady Sophia Barron."

"Yes,—and for the reason *you* have detected: he is all truth,—she all artifice. It was more than kind—it was wise in him—to leave England, and give her the benefit of his protection, as soon as he heard of Mr. Barron's death. I suspect he has no particular esteem for this *bella sorella* of his. If Cleveland's journey to London had not been so recent and so unexpected, I should have some suspicion that *his* lawyers had drawn her ladyship to London at this particular juncture."

Catharine *had* some such suspicion; and, though reason and probability were against it, she could not escape from the haunting thought.

CHAPTER XXVI.

The second visit of Colonel Hamilton to Darley House did not by any means diminish the favourable impression he had made. There is a class of females who deem it imperative on them to prove that they are *fiancées*, by assuming an air of languid reserve in general society, and exhibiting a haughty, and almost always an *affected* indifference to all mankind save *the one*. Catharine did not belong to this class. Her high-breeding was quite as conspicuous now as formerly; and, *in Cleveland's absence*, she had as much courteous attention to bestow on her temporary associates as had ever distinguished her. At dinner, Colonel Hamilton was on her right, and an old and very deaf divine on her left, too engrossed in discussing the delicacies of the table to wish to partake of "the feast of reason," even if conversation had not been so laborious as his infirmity rendered it. Colonel Hamilton therefore engrossed Catharine's nearly undivided attention; and as she listened, she was compelled to feel that the characteristic grace of a manly mind is not its elegance,—hardly its literature,—but its strength. There was a vein of lofty principle—of unshrinking integrity—running through all his remarks, which demonstrated that they were the habits of his life,—the leaven pervading his whole moral being. It seemed evident that the erectness of his bearing was that of rectitude, not arrogance,—and that the terseness of his speech was not the result of insolence or presumption, but the natural effect of concentrated thought. It might be that the striking contrast he presented to Cleveland afforded a wilder field for the indulgence of Catharine's curious observation; her attention to him was indubitably intense, and Lady Darley observed it with an amused wonder, which might, if she had been less assured of the constancy of her niece, have become alarm and anger.

The day of Cleveland's expected return arrived and wore away, and he came not. Catharine was less disturbed by the disappointment than Lady Darley, who expressed considerable indignation at so unlover-like a want of punctuality, and harangued on the topic with a volubility that had a far more depressing effect on Catharine than the cause which had produced it.

The next morning brought—not Sir Greville, but a letter explanatory of his absence. He reprobated the tediousness of lawyers,—described the emptiness and dulness of London,—deplored his separation from Catharine, and then wrote :—

. . . . "Are you aware that Lady Sophia Barron is now in town? According to Lady Darley's report, she seemed so fixed at the Grove, that I was amazed to meet her at the chancellor's *house*,—not *court*,—a day or two since. Legal business, she said, had compelled her to her very unpleasant journey, and to delay her improvement of your acquaintance. Colonel Stracey Hamilton, she added, is still at the Grove, commissioned to make himself acceptable at Darley House, and to prepare *you* especially for a favourable reception of his sister on her return to your neighbourhood."

There was nothing here to excite the indignation and alarm apparent on the countenance of Lady Darley, as Catharine read the extract to her,—but she *was* indignant and alarmed.

"Is that the whole, my dear?" she asked, with a rapidity very seldom apparent in her graceful and polished address. "Does he say nothing of the impression Lady Sophia made on him?—of her altered person?—Surely there must be something; you cannot have read all."

"All relating to Lady Sophia," replied Catharine, gravely. "Possibly Cleveland did not imagine the subject very acceptable to my feelings."

"He who says little thinks much," observed Lady Darley. "So short a notice of one once so interesting to him! —Just as if he were compelled to give you intelligence you were likely to hear from another source, and withheld all that he alone could tell, and therefore the most interesting! —Has he called on Lady Sophia?—*That*, at least, you ought to know. I am very angry with Cleveland,—*very*;—I am responsible for the preservation of my niece's dignity, and I shall write to tell him so."

"No, my dear aunt," said Catharine, firmly; "*I* must be the guardian of it, and I am bound to believe in the faith, the honour of my affianced husband. Why should I doubt the truth of his plea of protracted business? Why condemn his accidental meeting with Lady Sophia Barron? Why disturb the happiness of implicit trust, by permitting every event to fling a dark shadow on my path? I will reply to Cleveland's letter, and tell him that I await his return patiently. If—" continued Catharine, and her voice faltered, —"If I *am* to lose him, it shall not be by evincing an unworthy doubt of his fidelity,—a mean jealousy of his renewed acquaintance with a woman who, he himself has assured me, has been long since forgotten."

"As you please," said Lady Darley, who, undecided whether to approve or reprobate Catharine's declaration of confidence in Cleveland, was happy to leave the matter altogether in the hands of her niece.

Catharine wrote, and another week wore heavily away. Sir Greville was still absent, and Colonel Hamilton reported that *law* still kept his sister in the torrid zone of London. Lady Darley's indignation, as usual, exhausted itself in words,—inflicting on Catharine the additional pain of defending the conduct from which she was actually suffering, and the more severely because no expression of grief or anger escaped her.

And Catharine *did* suffer: she felt that there was, in the letters of Cleveland, a tone of constraint too intelligible to the heart that loved him so entirely: a change had evidently passed over him. His expressions of affection were more polished and less warm;—his explanations of the causes of his prolonged absence more and more involved, and less satisfactory. In one letter was the following extraordinary paragraph:—"Rely on me entirely, my dear Catharine, and trust to nothing you may hear of me but from myself With such as we are, slander is always busy; and the hundred tongues of scandal are ready to spread abroad our least significant actions in so misshapen a guise, that we ourselves cannot recognise them. Believe that every decision of my reason more and more approves the choice I have made of the partner of my future existence."

"*Every decision of his reason!*" How Catharine pondered over these chilling words! How she wept over the conviction that he was endeavouring to control the wanderings of his heart by the dictates of his judgment! But her letters studiously concealed the doubts—the suspicions—that harassed her. She was anxious to display the same chastened tenderness that had formerly characterized every sentence; and when she felt how great was the effort to suppress the distracting thoughts—the jealousy—which struggled within her bosom, she sighed in bitterness under the sorrowful certainty that it was not now with them as in times past.

Cleveland's absence had extended a month beyond its anticipated duration. Catharine's heart sank as she read the reiterated complaints of the law's delay, which now nearly occupied his less frequent letters. Lady Darley was full of a thousand projects, of which the chief fault was that they were utterly impracticable. She even threatened to quit Darley, and return to Grosvenor Square, apparent as the object of so extraordinary a movement, at that season of the year, must be to the whole world, and consequently certain to incur that world's "dread laugh." Catharine's stronger resolution conquered hers. She positively refused to accompany her, and declared her intention of reclaiming the protection of Mr. Revely if Lady Darley carried this imprudent design into effect, with an earnestness and calmness that assured Lady Darley it was not a mere threat, and compelled her to relinquish a scheme so incompatible with the dignity she professed herself anxious to uphold.

Then she entreated Catharine to allow her to write one very short letter to Cleveland, merely to say that she and her niece were quite happy, that the visits of Colonel Stracey Hamilton were frequent, and his society delightful;—that it was really something to be on terms of intimacy with a man so distinguished, with whose name all the world was familiar,—who had done more for his generation, in his short life, than the whole host of fashionable dictators, whose existence was unknown beyond the limits of May Fair, had achieved in the aggregate of their added existences. But Catharine implored her to lay aside her too fluent pen, and her prayers were heeded, for they were evidently sincere.

An unopened letter from Mrs. Warren was in Catharine's hand, when Lady Darley entered her dressing-room in unusual haste and evident trepidation.

"Read,—read!" she said, almost breathless with agitation, extending the Morning Post. "That abominable woman!—the most artful person! Could you have believed any thing so shameless?—after her notoriously bad treatment of him too! My dear Catharine, why do you not read?"

In her eagerness, her ladyship had not perceived that she had extended, without relinquishing, the paper. She apologized petulantly for her *bêtise*, as she called it, and Catharine read:—

"At this season of the year our columns are necessarily dull and uneventful in all that regards the occurrences of the beau monde. It is therefore with no ordinary pleasure that we are able, from personal observation, to report on the improved beauty of the lovely Lady Sophia Barron, who, as Lady Sophia Hamilton, shone in our hemisphere, a few short years since, as a star of the first magnitude. Her ladyship is now in town, and rides almost daily in the Park with Sir G—— C——, a well-known leader in the fashionable world. The existence of a former engagement between this distinguished pair is matter of notoriety, and nothing would less surprise us than its renewal.

"We have heard rumours of the attachment of Sir G. C. to a rustic fair one, to which, however, we yield no credence. The gentleman may have amused himself with a little gentle philandering; but we are assured that nothing of a serious nature exists anywhere but in the imagination of the rural Phyllis. We will only add our ardent wishes, that a union so every way desirable as that of the probability of which we flatter ourselves we give the earliest announcement, may restore to her proper place, in her own country, a lady whose beauty, elegance, wit, and accomplishments have for years rendered her the highest ornament of the most distinguished continental courts."

Lady Darley attentively observed the countenance of her niece as she read the noxious paragraphs, but its calmness was hardly disturbed.

"*Well!*"—a petulant and emphatic exclamation from Lady Darley.

"Evidently intended as a means of annoyance to me, and therefore failing of its effect," said Catharine. "That Cleveland has seen Lady Sophia I know from himself,—that he has ridden with her is possible, but I shall not allow myself to regard a probably accidental circumstance as indicative of such results as the writer of this paragraph desires me to suppose. Mr. Stark conferred on me one benefit; he initiated me into some of the smaller mysteries of the press,—of which this is one."

Lady Darley walked rapidly up and down the room, hardly able to suppress her own doubts and suspicions, and yet unwilling to disturb the mind of her niece with the feelings which discomposed her own.

"Cleveland is a man of honour," she said at length, interrupting her own meditations. "*There* you are safe."

"Yes,—while his inclinations are under the convoy of his honour,—no longer,—no farther," replied Catharine, seriously.

"You do not mean to say," exclaimed Lady Darley, turning her eye hastily full upon her niece,—"you do not mean me to understand, that, for the sake of a mere affectation of refinement,—a spurious sentiment,—you would break off an engagement which ensures you the very first match in the kingdom, and afford a triumph to a woman who would give half her existence to snatch the prize from you?"

"It is unwise to boast of the extent of one's courage," replied Catharine, with a faint smile; "I am secure at least in the certainty that your voice will always animate me to act as becomes my father's daughter."

Lady Darley hastily quitted the room.

Catharine glanced once again at the newspaper, and then betook herself to the perusal of Mrs. Warren's yet unopened letter.

"To secure your permanent happiness even at the expense of some present suffering is, my reason tells me, the part of a true friend, my dearest Catharine. And yet, so unwilling am I to inflict pain on the beloved child of my dearest friend, that I have been cowardly enough to postpone writing to you from day to day during the last week, until I blush at the selfishness which sought indulgence of my own feelings at the expense of your interest.

"I will not ask you if you remember a conversation we had together just before you last quitted London, in which you avowed your engagement to Sir Greville Cleveland, and I—did I more than hazard a conjecture that Lady Sophia Barron indulged the hope of once again engrossing the heart that had formerly acknowledged her empire? I need not tell *you* that Sir Greville is in town even now; but I fear that I shall have the pain of communicating a startling novelty when I add, that Lady Sophia is here also, and that Sir Greville's attendance on her is too public and too constant to be compatible with his honourable regard for any other engagement.

"I have seen Lady Sophia,—I see her frequently, for I have no pretext for forbidding her visits, and I am the unwilling witness of a triumph she is not anxious to conceal. She does not plainly tell me that Sir Greville is desirous of renewing his former bonds, but she insinuates more, and—difficult as it is to judge so severely of a human being, to think so ill of human nature—one's own nature,—I cannot help believing that I am the confidante of these insinuations because, knowing that child was never dearer to mother than Catharine Vernon to me, she judges that, *through me*, she shall be able to alarm and wound the heart of a dreaded rival.

"And indeed, dear child, her ladyship judges wisely that nothing affecting your interests could be withholden from you by your faithful friend, when the knowledge was likely to be profitable to you; and I think that these circumstances do affect your interests—your dearest interests, Catharine, *if* you love Sir Greville, of which how can I doubt? Is he not your betrothed husband,—the accepted lover of your heart? Could any worldly advantages place a man in such a situation with regard to you, unless your best affections were entirely his? *Now*, then, my dearest child, is the moment in which the happiness of your whole existence is at stake. If Sir Greville be unworthy of you, he must be relinquished with whatever pain—whatever agony. *Your* knowledge must decide whether his remaining here is necessary,—what is the tone of his letters to you,—whether the assertions and insinuations of Lady Sophia are merely malice, or have a too sure foundation. But weigh well, my Catharine, the immense importance to your future happiness of the decision you now take. Inquire of your own heart how you would hereafter regard the *husband* who voluntarily incurred temptation, or, if it overtook him, had not resolution to flee from it,—who perilled his own honour and *your* happiness in a game, the successful results of which could bring him no higher gratification than the mere triumph of vanity."

Catharine read no farther. Every sense seemed paralyzed. Wo appeared to accumulate upon her from every source, and to gather strength in proportion as she resisted its approaches. There was on her mind a vague but dreadful consciousness of Cleveland's unworthiness, and she was roused from the anguish of that painful conviction by the rapid driving of a carriage up the avenue—by the sight of Cleveland himself alighting in evident haste, and with an air of impatience which it required no great flight of fancy in her to believe the result of a love as devoted as her own.

So mutable, so varying, are the effects of this tyrannising passion over the purest and most highly-gifted women!

CHAPTER XXVII.

CATHARINE was too much occupied with attempts at preserving her own calmness to be able to examine Cleveland's manner, especially as the surface was smooth as before. But Lady Darley, not engrossed by any deep internal emotions, had leisure to perceive that, though the polish and the courtesy remained, there *was* a change—a slight embarrassment seeking to conceal itself beneath a multitude of inquiries and explanations, poured out with a rapidity and an animation very different from the usual quiet composure which distinguished him. She did not attempt to veil her own displeasure, but was as cold and distant as if she were avenging a pointed neglect to herself—the most unpardonable offence to a woman who, during her whole existence, had been accustomed to the homage of countless votaries Cleveland could not but be sensible of such a demonstration of anger: frowns on a brow habitually placid, coldness on a lip always smiling, serious formality in an address distinguished for its playfulness. But he continued his anecdotes of his law business, rendered amusing by his description of the habits of law life, as he called it. He had dined, he said, once or twice in the chambers of his man of business: and even Lady Darley began to thaw beneath the interest of his graphic details.

It was evident, however, that in the whole party there was that effort at ease which is the most painful evidence of want of confidence in each other. When Cleveland was compelled to quit the precincts of the Temple, and relinquish his caricature of the miseries of legal life, he must necessarily listen to Lady Darley's volunteered history of their proceedings during his absence—a history which, he knew, must be connected with topics he was most reluctant to discuss. But Lady Darley was resolved to make a sortie from her garrison, and take the strongholds of the enemy by surprise.

"Very few people are in the neighbourhood at present," she began. "Lady Sophia Barron, who promised to be an amusing acquaintance, left the Grove, as you are aware, the morning after you bade farewell to Darley."

"Yes—I saw Lady Sophia in town," returned Cleveland, with a coldness evidently assumed for the purpose of concealing his embarrassment. "We met accidentally at the chambers of my lawyer."

"Quite a woman of business, Lady Sophia, to be visible in such a place," said Lady Darley, sarcastically. "The possession of a strong mind is of great advantage even to one's purse; it is a satisfaction to be able to investigate the mysteries of law for one's self, and it may be profitable; the pleasure I shall take leave to doubt. Lady Sophia's taste differed from mine, fortunately for you; her society must have rendered London less wearisome in this its dullest season."

"The newspapers have given me credit for being largely indebted to it," said Cleveland, whose eye had caught the Morning Post, and who now put his hand on it. "Editors must fill up their columns, and their accuracy is too well understood to render their reports dangerous."

"Annoying, perhaps, nevertheless," said Lady Darley. "Women are tormented occasionally by seeing their empire transferred to another, even in print. *I* should be perfectly *enragée*, for I do not affect to be above the little jealousies of my sex."

"Some are so without affectation," said Cleveland, looking at Catharine, who was glad to divert the undignified sarcasms of Lady Darley, by remarking on the beauty of the portfolio of fine engravings which was just brought in from Cleveland's carriage. But Lady Darley had yet another point of attack from which she was not to be driven.

"Very fine—very fine," she said, looking over Catharine's shoulder at an engraving she was admiring: "after all, the Italians understand these things better than we do: Colonel Hamilton—Stracey Hamilton, Sir Greville—has some very fine specimens in this line; he was good enough to send them to Darley for our gratification, or rather, I should say, for Catharine's; I fear I have no taste for *virtù*.'

"I hope you like Colonel Hamilton," said Sir Greville, a sudden gleam lighting up his eyes, and an expression in his countenance altogether unintelligible.

"Do you *hope* so?" said Lady Darley, hastily. "That

hope is not exactly accordant with your injunction to me regarding this very Stracey Hamilton when you quitted Darley."

"Perhaps both were but idle expressions," said Catharine.

"Capricious, perhaps," returned Sir Greville with a smile, "an illustration of the inconsistency and versatility of all things human. Laying aside, however, my own particular predjudices, I am bound to declare that there is, in Colonel Hamilton, much that is worthy of the esteem even of Miss Vernon."

"I quite agree with you," retorted Lady Darley, "and in my opinion Miss Vernon will act but fairly in reciprocating the very exuberant admiration he is pleased to lavish on her."

And her ladyship disappeared.

"My long absence has offended Lady Darley," said Cleveland with some petulance. "You, I trust, do me the justice to believe that it was not voluntarily prolonged."

"I at least do you the justice of admitting that your own judgment ought to regulate your own actions," replied Catharine, seriously. "I cannot venture to attribute to you any other motives than you avow; I dare not so impugn your honour, your principles."

Cleveland's brow contracted slightly, but almost instantly regained its usual smoothness.

"Noble in all!" said he; "above suspicion, as above deceit yourself!"

"I have a letter to read and ponder on," said Catharine, rising; "meanwhile look over the paper under your hand, and you will see that, if Lady Darley's anger be unfounded, it has a cause of apparently reasonable excitement."

Catharine *did* ponder over the letter—Mrs. Warren's letter; and she felt that the hour of suffering had come on her, and despite the whispered doubts of her own heart, the questionings of her reason had found her unprepared.

She was now to bring to the most rigorous test those principles which had hitherto been the rule of her life; the unerring guide of her actions—never surrendered in the hour of difficulty, never failing in the day of distress. But how few shadows had fallen on her young and sunny life compared to the years of darkness, "which are many!" The single great sorrow of her experience had been the death of her parents; her father's, the gloom of her childish days, her mother's *still* the grief of her solitary hours. But death, the immediate dispensation of Providence—the bereavement in which an Almighty hand is visibly apparent—generally leaves the human mind, if humbled, submissive, and there is no suffering that sooner yields to the always irresistible influence of time. But the trial which awaited her was the severest that can befall devoted woman. To feel that he, in whose love she had garnered up her dearest earthly hopes, was betraying her;

that falsehood lurked within a breast which she had believed to be the abode of pure, unstained truth; that he to whom she looked for protection, for happiness, was ready to sacrifice her on the altar of his own selfishness; or, at best, if still yielding to the bonds imposed by honour, bringing a reluctant heart, a resisting will, to the sacrifice. "Not that; not that!" said Catharine, in the anguish of her spirit; "better to resign him for ever; to restore his freedom of choice; to pass my solitary life in cheerless apathy, than to be the hardly tolerated wife of an unloving husband! No, no, mother, no! Your child shall better honour the precepts your hallowed lips taught her."

Catharine's cheek, that day, was very pale, but in the expression of her eye there was a holy calmness, in her whole manner a self-possessed dignity consistent with the utmost gentleness; and even Cleveland, with his divided heart, for it *was* a divided heart, confessed that loveliness might exist in perfection apart from the seductive brilliancy, the animated playfulness, which had of late so enthralled him. His own manner was attentive, even tender, all that became a betrothed lover, Lady Darley acknowledged, and her coldness vanished as she made this observation. But what can deceive the instinct of a woman who loves? Catharine saw that his eye was occasionally fixed, as if on an absent object; that his remarks were confused; and he so *distrait* as not to reply to questions positively addressed to him. The feelings of a polished man of the world must indeed be agitated beyond all control, when they thus influence his manner; manner which all the habits of his life combine to render independent of any emotion, and to place as much under his command as the motions of his muscles. If Catharine had indulged a secret, almost an unconscious hope, that the hard trial which awaited her might yet be averted, it faded at last, and she at length almost ceased to converse, for every sentnece cost her an effort. But Lady Darley, as her anger wore away, became more than usually animated, and talked so vivaciously as to allow her companions to act audience with great propriety. Cleveland remained longer in the dining-room after the ladies had quitted it than usual, but even this circumstance did not abate the cheerfulness of Lady Darley, to whom indeed good-humour was so natural that it cost her an effort to wear the semblance of displeasure. When he joined them he looked, Catharine thought, very miserable, and his inquietude was the more apparent because he affected to meet Lady Darley's raillery with correspondent vivacity, while, even when he smiled, his countenance was cold and perturbed. He asked Catharine for music, and she seated herself at the harp, glad to find refuge there from the necessity of speaking. He did not, as usual, approach the instrument to hang over it, and to whisper those half-breathed words which are dearer evidences of love than volumes of well set speeches. Catharine felt the change, and her heart trembled. She was sensible that her trial had already begun; that between her and Cleveland the faith of love was broken.

Cleveland did not ask Catharine to sing, and she was grateful for a negligence which spared her a trial she felt must be insupportable. It was easy to press the strings of her harp, and to draw forth melody which habit had rendered mechanical. Her execution was as brilliant as usual, and if the feeling, the expression, which was the chief grace of her music, was not there, none remarked its absence. Cleveland's eyes were fixed on her, and she met their gaze once—that altered gaze, in which there was pity, melancholy, but *not* love—not that glance of secret intelligence which revealed that heart was understood by heart—that there was a language more eloquent than words. Catharine played piece after piece, unwilling to surrender the defence music afforded her, until even Lady Darley, proud as she was of her niece's excellence in this, the most brilliant of accomplishments, wearied of the "concourse of sweet sounds," and noticed the lateness of the hour. Catharine rose instantly and approached the open window. Late as it was in the season, the air was mild and balmy, and the stars shone out in their unspeakable lustre—the most wondrous display of omnipotent power. Cleveland stood by her side, and he, the hackneyed man of the world, was not insensible to the influence of the hour. His manner assumed somewhat of the softness which had marked it before his unfortunate visit to town, and his voice "sounded sweet in every whispered word."

"You look coldly on me, dearest Catharine," he said, "and I do not deserve it. All is not at peace within me, and I require sympathy from my affianced wife—not doubt—not mistrust—not pride."

"*Pride!*"

"Yes—your calmness, whether real or affected, is pride—in the relation in which we stand to each other, *unbecoming* pride."

"You have at least the merit of being candid."

"I hope so; between us there should be no mystery: perhaps there has already been too much."

Catharine felt as if the moment that was to decide her destiny approached, and she leaned against the window for support. She did not, could not speak.

"It was a fault, an error, wholly mine, but it is not too late to repair it," resumed Cleveland. "It is wisdom to show ourselves to each other as we really are; the revelation may give pain, but it may prevent despair."

He paused; both were silent.

"*You*—your innocent youth—has nothing to reveal. The

secret of your heart is the mystery of its love for one unworthy of it. And yet, Catharine, not so utterly worthless but that he can prize the treasure of such love—such pure devotion can feel—at some blessed seasons—that the whole empire of world-tainted passion can offer nothing half so precious. Will you, Catharine, save me from my destiny?"

"Will you save yourself?" said Catharine, recovering her energy.

"Ah—there—eternally reasoning! Are you quite sure, Catharine, that you do not deceive yourself when you fancy you love me? Are you quite sure that your sentiments are not the result of some process of thought, which has led you to the conclusion that there is no apparent cause why we should not be happy together, and this conviction you call love?"

"You are unintelligible," said Catharine, with a glow of insulted feeling.

"It is no time now for the discussion. Shall you walk, as usual, early to-morrow morning?"

Catharine replied in the affirmative, but her voice faltered, for she *knew* that it was the last ramble they would take together, and she felt how different it must be from those which had lately been the most delicious hours of her existence.

"I will meet you at the trysting place," added Cleveland, sorrowfully, but with that touch of sarcasm in which spirits of a certain order indulge in the hour of grief.

And Catharine, pale, but not shrinking from the trial, retired to her sleepless pillow.

CHAPTER XXVIII.

"I HAVE waited for you," said Cleveland, advancing to meet Catharine, and drawing her arm through his. "And yet this is a somewhat early hour for a sybarite of the aristocracy to be abroad, is it not?"

Catharine said something, not very intelligible, about the fineness of the morning and the fragrance of the air.

"Add a commendation of the warbling of the birds, and then you will have made as pretty a young lady's speech, and one as unlike Catharine Vernon, as heart could desire," said Cleveland, with the bitterness of a man who is playing with his own misery. "Never tell me you are not changed, Catharine; tell me truly, frankly, honestly, *what* has changed you?"

"And do you need to ask?" said Catharine, striving to be

firm. "Have you no secret consciousness that I ought to be changed?"

"My want of punctuality impugns my sincerity, perhaps, and you would punish my error by your coldness. I am no schoolboy lover, Catharine. Spoiled by the adulation of the world, goaded by thoughts which your calm soul could not understand and would probably despise, I am not in a temper to endure petulance even from the woman I so ardently —admire."

How Catharine felt that word!

"I will strive *not* to be petulant," she said, mildly, "and if I err, forgive me; *you* may, for you know best why I should be petulant."

"For the report of a stupid, lying newspaper, perhaps!" said Cleveland, with some violence and more haughtiness. "No!—I must not be weighed in that worthless balance, Catharine! I will not defend myself against accusations drawn from such a vehicle! Slander in all its shapes is abhorrent, but most when its source is nameless."

"Let there be no anger between us," said Catharine, calmly: "there needs none. I am here, by your own appointment, to hear the explanation of some mystery which, last night, you avowed ought to be made, and of which there had already been too much between us."

"And it *shall* be made. First of all, tell me, Catharine, what is *love*—ay, *love*—in your thoughts, feelings, heart—understanding, if you will?"

She could not speak a word, and she would have wept, but how could she forgive herself for tears at such a moment —at a question so cruel?

"Forgive and pity my waywardness, Catharine," he said, changing his tone. "It is but the thunder of the fearful storm within. Have you not read of the violent convulsions of the elements which, at intervals, agitate the most sunny climes of the earth, unknown to more temperate latitudes? Even thus it is now with me. My calmness yields to the voice of the hurricane; human nature is too mighty to be bound in the trammels of convention when the hour of conflict comes. And it *has* come."

"I do pity you," said Catharine, gently; "yet, Cleveland, since a word—a wish—might terminate this conflict, why not speak it?"

"A word!—a wish! The struggles of man's passions are not to be so quieted!" said Cleveland, gloomily. "It is my misfortune to be under the dominion of opposing feelings: my judgment, my reason, my honour, all point alike to one path; but memory—the wondrous power of the unforgotten past—agitates me with a thousand hopes, fears, wishes: why, I am 'puling' like a schoolboy," suddenly changing his tone for one of self-contempt; "you do not recognise me, Catharine, in this guise."

"'Some have died for love, and some gone mad,'" she replied, with womanly scorn.

"I am neither dying nor maddening," said Cleveland, coldly; "and you may believe my entire sanity when I tell you, that I am persuaded my happiness will be secured by our union, and that I implore you—if indeed you love me, Catharine—to hasten the bridal, that certainty may bring rest."

"I *have* loved you, Cleveland," said Catharine, earnestly "as woman may, in all honour, love. But if, with you, to love be to forget principle, judgment, propriety—the prudence of providing for the happiness of the future rather than for the gratification of the present—such love I have not. I am still capable of so much consideration for myself as to assure you, that no inducement you could offer—no temptation the whole earth could afford—could humble me into accepting the hand of a man whose heart led him to another. Sir Greville Cleveland, *you are free*. I will not tell you to be happy. I cannot so soon relinquish my belief in your nobility of soul as to deem you capable of being speedily reconciled to yourself. Consolation, however, you will quickly find—may its balm be not only healing but safe!"

"You do not, cannot mean that we should separate!" and his countenance expressed sincere distress. "My happiness is in your hands, Catharine; my convictions—my heart itself, assure me that it is so. Be the guardian angel of my destiny. If you believe that I am worth salvation, preserve me, Catharine, from the abyss into which, with open eyes, I feel that I shall rush, if you withdraw yourself. With you is my safety; with you are honour, happiness, dignity, all that can render human life worthy of immortal man! Pardon my error—the wandering of a moment's thought. I cannot, must not lose you."

"I dare not intrust my happiness to your keeping," said Catharine, firmly.

"Do you doubt my honour?" he asked, with the sternness he had occasionally manifested throughout their interview. "I cannot bear such a doubt from you. If you could conceive the extent of the sacrifice I am ready to make—"

"I require none, I will accept none," interrupted Catharine, resolute to terminate a conversation which must evidently be their last, without any display of that anguish which even now was hardly to be restrained. "We have not hitherto understood each other. You have estimated me more humbly than I have estimated myself; and in a point where a woman true to herself deems it least pardonable. Here we part, and *both free*. I have a right to request that you will not pain me by remaining at Darley, and that you will believe our separation final."

"You shall be obeyed to the letter," said Cleveland, bowing with haughty composure, and turning away.

Fortunately they were near the house, and a hurried walk brought Catharine, in a few minutes, to the shelter of her own apartment.

She did not weep, agony such as hers finds not the relief of tears. She sat on her couch fixed as a statue; her thoughts, her feelings benumbed—oppressed by a weight which seemed to stifle the breathing of her soul. Then succeeded that whirlwind of emotions in which all the past, the present, the future, present images of grief to terrify the heart of the bereaved. But amid all her thoughts, fears, terrors, the one feeling rose—the spectre that could not be laid—she had voluntarily relinquished Cleveland for ever. Oh, that sickness of the soul, which succeeds so terrible a crisis in the destiny of woman!—woman, whom the necessity of honour, of principle, of duty, so often compels to become her own martyr! Catharine felt as the mariner who has run his vessel by his own hand upon a rock, when all the winds of heaven seemed to blow favouringly, and knows that nothing but the most desperate efforts can enable him to breast the waves and reach the shore, while his exhausted strength warns him that his hope is in impossibilities!

A voice at her door roused her. It is not the least of the sufferings of the wretched, that they are compelled to attend to the thousand trifles whose minuteness composes human existence. It was Willis, from Lady Darley, desiring to know whether Miss Vernon would choose breakfast in her room—her ladyship waited.

"Dear me, ma'am," said Willis, as Catharine admitted her, "you look quite ill. Shall you like to see my lady?"

Catharine assigned a headache as the cause of her wretched appearance, desired Willis not to trouble Lady Darley, and requested some tea might be sent to her. The obsequious waiting woman retired, quite confident, however, that Miss Vernon's altered looks were the result of something much more serious than a mere headache, a conclusion that did honour to her penetration, and of which she gave Lady Darley the full benefit.

The information of Willis brought Lady Darley very soon to the side of her niece. "What on earth is the matter?" she asked, as she gazed in dismay on the pallid and almost rigid cheek of Catharine. "I detest early rising and early walks—the worst things in the world for delicate people Cleveland is not risen yet; Raith has taken breakfast to his room; do not think of leaving yours. If you would lie down and endeavour to sleep, your headache would be cured Sleep is the best remedy in the world for all complaints of the kind."

"I *will* try to rest," said Catharine, with as much calmness as she could assume. "I requested Willis not to disturb you with any report of my bad looks; I. shall be better soon."

"I hope so, for, to tell you the truth, Catharine, you look dreadfully wobegone. If you had seen Cleveland this morning, I should suspect a lover's quarrel. He certainly deserves your displeasure, and I thought you really too gentle last night. It is well that men should occasionally feel the pressure of their chains."

"I *have* seen Cleveland this morning," said Catharine, in a low voice, unwilling to speak, but adhering to her usual habit of inviolable truth.

"Ah—then there has been a fracas. Well, my dear, do not quite weep yourself into a Niobe, and if you have courage to remain a prisoner here until dinner time, you will inflict a very proper penance on your knight, and bring him to your feet. So, *au revoir!*"

And playfully kissing the fair neck of her niece, Lady Darley glided gracefully from her presence, with all the buoyancy of a heart at ease.

Catharine once again alone, endeavoured to bring her thoughts under control—to contemplate the future through a medium—how different from that in which, a few short hours since, she had viewed it! It was a fearful thing to *hope* that Cleveland would quit Darley before that day's bright sun waned, and yet Catharine did hope it. She felt that, even if he attempted it—a thing, considering his character, quite beyond all rational expectation—no explanation could remove the impression made by the involuntary admissions which had escaped him. She knew that the heart she had believed wholly hers yearned after another; that she had never engrossed it; that while reason had selected her, feeling coveted that other. It was an inexplicable mystery that, with the secret consciousness of lingering love for her who had been the betrothed of his youth, he should simulate an attachment which promised nothing to gratify his ambition, and which must fail to satisfy his heart. Catharine was bewildered as she attempted to fathom causes so impenetrable to her unworldly vision. But she knew—felt—in every burning throb of her indignant heart, that she had been unworthily—falsely—despoiled of her young affections, and that there *is* a dishonour, foul as the darkest stain to which infamy attaches, for which the world has no punishment, the sufferer no redress, and which in the code of courtly morals is branded with no stigma.

Noon had passed before Catharine was conscious of the flight of time. It was three hours since she had quitted Cleveland: was he preparing to depart?—was he really gone? A throb of pain warned her of what was yet to be endured; that—such is the weakness of the strongest heart—

while here she believed him not wholly lost. She trembled lest the sound of his chariot wheels should smite her senses; shrinking from the anticipated agony, she pressed her hands on her eyes as if the very light of the sun were hateful, and doubted whether her conduct was actually right—whether she did not delude herself by believing she was making a sacrifice to principle, when she had but laid an offering on the altar of pride.

A gentle tap at the door—her own maid entered; a letter from Sir Greville. She took it in silence and was again alone.

Too agitated to read it immediately, she paused to recover composure; and it was, at length, with a trembling hand that she broke the seal and read:—

"Although you have pronounced the fiat of our separation, I cannot leave Darley without once again placing my destiny at your disposal. And in doing so, Catharine, I shall endeavour to paint for you as clearly as I can, a full-length portrait of the man who aspires to be your husband, that you may not be betrayed into union with an unknown, or, on the other hand, that you may rejoice as *they* rejoice who *escape*.

"I will not repeat to you the tale of my early love for Lady Sophia Hamilton; you have heard it from a thousand tongues, for the world long made it a theme. But 'all my madness none could know,' nor shall I detain you with an attempt at portraying a passion, the violence of which would terrify your calm mind—its idolatry shock your piety. Such as it was, however, it made my happiness *then*, and my torment *for ever*.

"*Crime* parted us—myself and Sophia I mean. Yea, crime; and it was a crime also which was allied with infidelity to the master passion that threatened to ingulf my being. How such things *can* be, it befits not your pure mind to learn; that they *are*, the story of many wretched as myself may prove.

"The woman—alas! she was but a girl; a pure fair girl, the single hope of a widowed mother—who betrayed my senses into a momentary infidelity to Sophia, was too young in the experience of this world to comprehend the depth of shame and misery into which she was hastening; and when, at length, she *did* comprehend it, and saw that though her mother's heart 'did brokenly live on,' still it *was* broken, was it madness that overcame, in her, religion—love—the feelings of woman—the 'love strong as death' of the mother? I know not. Perhaps it was your sex's inherited dread of *shame;* like the Hebrew tale of her the first woman who sinned and cast the guilt upon her husband; and she had no husband on whom to cast it, and the child—*her* child—*my* child, died—by violence!

"Well, there was discovery, and the trial—*her* trial—came on, in virtuous, harsh, severe Scotland. The evidence was perfect, and she was condemned—*condemned and executed!* Handled by the accursed hands of the common hangman!—the fair creature whose holiness I had profaned —I *only*—the gaze, the scorn, the mockery of a multitude! You have dreamed of hell! What was my heart, Catharine, when, with all my power—all my influence—I strove to save and *could* not!

"She died, and I became———! Do you not think my breast was the meet abode of a devil? The law could not reach *me*—the law, that unequal-handed monster, which grasps the lesser criminal with a gripe that crushes to the death, and lays not even a gentle finger on him whose damnation is begun even in this world!

"*You* will say, that if any other evidence were needed of a future state of retribution, *this*, this burning fact would seal its truth, and assure everlasting perdition to the spoiler of as fair a flower as ever bloomed out of paradise!

"I have paused; memory has done her work of torture, and I breathe to ask you, Will you still chain yourself to him who is tormented with a memory of—*is* perdition more?

"My secret—my whole secret—*was* known but to one—to Stracey Hamilton, the sternly upright stoic, Stracey Hamilton.

"Between him and me there was ever a gulf fixed. We could not pass over to each other. His aspirations and mine were—how widely different! Love for Sophia was the single bond of union between us, and he, who discovered, from his close companionship with me, my temptation to infidelity, became more jealous for his sister than she for herself. And the poor unfortunate victim, too—he strove to warn her; but when is it that the whispers of warning are not drowned by the eloquence of—*dare* I call it love?

"Sophia discovered and rejected. In vain—in vain—my supplications—my agony—my temporary madness. During its access my victim paid the horrid penalty of her transgression, and I awoke to consciousness, and she was not! What mortal man could do to alleviate the agony of such a death, Stracey Hamilton had done. He had sustained the widowed mother during her few surviving hours, and had finally laid her in hallowed ground. He had attended my couch of suffering, but, when I revived, he conveyed to me the mandate of his sister, that the bond between her and me was eternally severed—and, Catharine, thenceforward I was desolate!

"She married—another. With me time did its usual work. It mitigated both anguish and remorse. *Fashion* is not the atmosphere most congenial to either, and I lived the life which men like me—rich, highly descended—do live, of adulation and homage, when one learns to despise the wretched, blind, grovelling world, that can abase itself to bow the knee to things so miserable, so greatly guilty, as my most miserable, most guilty—self.

"But again time progressed, and the adulation which at first shocked me by its contrast to my own terrible thoughts, became the habitual aliment of my being. It did not longer excite, but it was necessary. *It was the bread of my mind.* The world smiled on me: woman wooed me; wealth accumulated round me the treasures of the East and the West; song and music shed their light on my path; and I dreamed that happiness was with them.

"But the voice of the heart is not to be so stifled; I yearned for *love*.

"The friendship between myself and Lady Darley afforded the most pleasurable recreations of my life. She asked no greater attention than it pleased me to offer. If I visited her, she received me with smiles: if for weeks I neglected her house, she pardoned me and welcomed my return. I desired to marry; men of ancient name wish to perpetuate it, and as the summer of my life declined, I thought more of the forefathers of my race among whom I ought to be enrolled. The nieces of Lord Darley were paraded before me, but my fastidious taste rejected the want of cultivation, of refinement, for which the robust health and untutored vivacity of country romps afforded no promise of compensation. And *then*, Lady Darley bethought her of the orphan of her brother.

"I listened long, and thought deeply of the graces, the beauty, of your mother, Catharine; the integrity, the firm, manly, noble mind of your father; and I wished ardently to see if in their only child were united the characteristics of both. Dream not that my visit to Golding Magna was accidental. It was the result of a design penetrating far into the future: it was the first step in my progress towards the attainment of you. The succeeding steps you know.

"And yet accuse me not of falsehood, Catharine. If I deceived you, it was because I myself was deceived. What living man, with a keen perception of grace and beauty, could be insensible to the surpassing loveliness of your person? What understanding, capable of appreciating intellect, could be unconscious of the superiority of yours? Taste is not always perverted with the morals, and mine was yet unwarped enough to esteem the perfect rectitude of your heart. To call this union of esteem, admiration, approbation—*love*, was no impossible mistake. It was a sweet dream in which my reason itself was awake, and of which, infatuated as I am, I am still sane enough to say, would that it had never been broken!

"*Infatuated!* Yes, Catharine; and with perfect consciousness of my infatuation. Why I have lingered with *her* days, weeks, you can understand. And yet was it in the power of mortal man to resist the persuasions of that voice, whose tones always awoke the echoes of his deepest feelings? To withstand the seductive softness of those eyes into whose depths he had looked until reason—feeling itself—melted away in the fires of intense passion? Smiles shone on me which, in my bright youth, had been the sunlight of my soul—and years had not taught me the power of resisting them. In one word, Catharine, the spell that bound me was the conviction of being beloved by her who had so long been the goddess of my heart's idolatry, and in the delirium of my passion, all else in this wide world was forgotten.

"*Hers* was the admonishing voice that warned me of my bonds, and compelled me to reflect on the requirements of honour, principle, and feeling. Even now, Catharine, even now, I value, I prize inestimably, the love of your pure and noble heart. Even now I ask you, with all earnestness, to forgive the momentary thraldom to which I have bowed, and to receive vows offered in all honour and sincerity. I have parted eternally from the siren, whose voice had nearly maddened me; and she knows that I am here bent on fulfilling vows not less dear than binding. Be mine, Catharine; trust me, we shall yet be happy: I in the consciousness of my honour and your love, you, in the tenderness, the affection, which shall labour to crown with blessings every hour of your life.

"I have written incoherently, I fear; but I have neither time nor will to measure my phrases. This day must bind us more firmly than ever or our separation must be final. Mystery *has* ceased; my heart has been bared before you; its wounds have been probed—its darkness displayed: such as it is, if you spurn it not, its dearest hopes centre in you; but if you *shrink*—a word, and I go—for ever.

"No need now for reflection. For once obey the dictates of feeling, and let reason act in a calmer crisis of destiny. I await your reply in impatience not to be described—in anxiety, of which it boots not to speak. I love—I honour you. Give me a wife whom I may revere. Give me the benefit of your society—your example—and make me what you please.

"CLEVELAND."

No! there needed no reflection! In the storm of conflicting feelings which raged in the breast of Catharine, there was no space for it. Horror, jealousy, pity, indignation, shame strove for mastery, and by turns attained it. But, above all, the whisper of reason—the still, small, *accustomed* voice was heard—saying, "With him thou canst have no communion!"—and before the hour ended she was able to write her decision:—

"I thank you for your confidence: with me it shall be sacred. Nevertheless we have parted for ever. Existence could afford me no happiness, unless I felt that the light of my husband's virtues was reflected on me. I cannot wed to be the soother of remorse. May God pardon your sin, for it has been great. May you live to feel the necessity—the wish—for his pardon.

"I do not affect to deny a love which was sufficiently avowed by our engagement. My present pain is the proper penalty of my fault; for I loved you not only without the sanction of my conscience, but in opposition to its warning voice. It is well for me that you should be the avenger.

"Do me the justice of believing, that in Lady Darley's plans, whatever they may have been, I have had no participation. Our first meeting has never appeared to me other than an accident; and the consequences which have flowed from it have not, on my part, been premeditated. It is, indeed, painful to believe that my father's sister could so wrong his orphan. *This*, however—the severing of the tie between us—will, in some sort, repair that wrong.

"I do not presume to point out what your future conduct should be. Wherever you go—in all seasons and situations—my prayers will follow you. Would that they may bring a blessing upon you—that best of blessings, peace!

"Farewell. Believe me cold, calculating, unfeeling—what you will. *Now*, at least, my reason, my conscience, are strongly on my side, and methinks that in their strength I shall be strong.

"Once more, farewell; but—it is my last request—spare me another meeting."

One weary hour—another passed—and Catharine heard the sound of a carriage. An inexplicable and irresistible impulse bore her to the window. It was Cleveland's. Woman's instinctive pride kept her concealed from observation, but she saw all. The packing was completed in a few minutes. Cleveland himself entered: and she could see, even there, that his face was very pale. His servant sprang on the box—a word was spoken—and they disappeared.

Catharine was alone—to feel the deadly calm of the desert shore, on which the shipwrecked has found a temporary security

CHAPTER XXIX.

"In Heaven's name, Catharine, tell me what all this means?" said Lady Darley, rushing into her niece's apartment—her cheeks pale, her eyes kindling with unwonted fires, and an open billet in her hand.

Catharine took the note in silence, but she held it some minutes before the mist that obscured her sight permitted her to read it. It was from Cleveland, containing his adieu—the ordinary thanks for hospitality—regret at the unexpected circumstance which had enforced on him the necessity of so speedily absenting himself—and referring for further explanation to Miss Vernon.

"What *is* all this?" repeated Lady Darley, when Catharine had two or three times reperused the note, and still spoke not—was unable to speak; "this is carrying matters rather too far; a fracas I thought there had been, but are you aware of the danger of permitting him to leave Darley angry—offended, when every allurement awaits him elsewhere?"

"There is no danger now," said Catharine, with as much calmness as she could assume; "we have parted, not for a day, but for ever. Our engagement is at an end."

Lady Darley seated herself in speechless astonishment.

'And may I, in all humility, be permitted to ask," she said, at length, "what mighty event has produced an effect like this, so suddenly that there was no time to consult *me*—a person who might be supposed to feel some trifling interest in the matter?"

"No, my dear aunt, there was neither time for consultation, nor need of advice," said Catharine in a low voice. "You will agree with me, that as soon as I saw clearly that Cleveland still loved Lady Sophia Barron, delicacy, principle, all womanly pride, all womanly feeling, required that I should release him from an engagement which could no longer constitute his happiness."

"Then you really and positively mean to say," replied Lady Darley, with a calmness that was much more indicative of anger than the most violent indignation, "you really mean to say, that you have restored to Cleveland his freedom, and have absolutely left a clear field to Lady Sophia?"

"It is wiser to relinquish a heart than to contest it under such circumstances."

"My nature is not so happily constituted as to find shelter from annoyance in an apophthegm," said Lady Darley, with as near an approach to a sneer as her countenance could exhibit. "I am quite alive to the misery of seeing you—you, Catharine Vernon, my niece—pointed at by the world as deserted! Who will suppose it possible, that, in the nineteenth century, a woman, from a mere superfine refinement of sentiment, relinquished one of the first *partis* in the kingdom, for the benefit of a rival whom she had every reason in the world to dislike! It will be a fine recompense for the kindness which led me to snatch you from obscurity, to hear on all sides that, after a season spent under my guardianship, my own niece, spite of her personal attractions, was left *plantee!* No, no, Catharine, this is a mortification I cannot endure, and I insist on being allowed to write Cleveland's mandate of recall forthwith."

"If that were possible, it would not be obeyed," said Catharine. "But it is *not* possible; my sentiments are the result of convictions founded on circumstances over which I have no control—over which none has control, for they are in the irrevocable past. Pardon, my dear aunt, the disappointment I grieve to cause you, but pity me, for *I* am not on a bed of roses!"

But Lady Darley could neither pardon nor pity. She could not forgive the overthrow of all the magnificent *chateaux d'Espagne* with which she had been delighting her imagination, since the formation of Catharine's engagement. As the aunt of the mistress of Cleveland Park, one of the finest baronial seats in the kingdom, she had anticipated a vast accession to her own popularity—an increase of that homage which was the very aliment of her happiness. And now not only were those brilliant castles overthrown, but she was doomed to endure the dread of seeing a woman whom she had always disliked, and now positively detested, in possession of the reality of her own brilliant visions; the substance, of which the shadow had so captivated her fancy. But in vain she argued—entreated—threatened—ridiculed—raved; Catharine was firm, and for the first time since she had called her aunt's house her home, Catharine retired to rest the object of Lady Darley's unmeasured anger.

The next sun arose but to witness the renewal of her attacks and Catharine's resistance, mild but unbending. Repeatedly Lady Darley reprobated her own weakness in allowing her happiness to be disturbed by the folly of any other person, however nearly she might happen to be connected with her. Then, like all people pampered by prosperity, on a first disappointment, she raved at the ingratitude of the world, declared she would never more interest herself for human being, then wept over her wrongs, and then recurred to entreaty and persuasion; and, in fine, added such a weight to the unhappiness of her niece, as rendered the burden nearly intolerable.

Anger—violent emotion of any kind—was always a real

evil to Lady Darley. It disturbed all the enjoyment of her existence—it necessarily prevented *the indulgence of herself.* To have the usual equanimity of her temper agitated by anger was a serious misfortune to her; and having tried all other efforts in vain, she settled herself into a cold, serious, frozen formality of demeanour, which, though painful in itself, at least allowed Catharine to collect her scattered thoughts, and to make an effort for the recovery of her tranquillity.

This assumed calm was not, however, of long continuance. The fashionable newspapers, those which constituted Lady Darley's diurnal recreation, put forth daily paragraphs referring to the renewal of Cleveland's engagement to Lady Sophia. With the usual scurrilous wit of some of them, allusions, often of the most mortifying nature, were made to the obscure beauty whom a few ignorant persons had described as Sir Greville's fian ée; barbed arrows which were dipped in venom for Lady Darley. Nor was Catharine herself free from discomposure, to find her name thus publicly set forth to the world as a vain and ignorant person, who had misinterpreted attentions meant to be nothing; or, equally mortifying, as an unfortunate doomed to reap the fate of those who aspire too high. She longed for retirement; to withdraw from that world, with whose splendour she had been dazzled, but which she had found hollow and unsatisfactory. She longed to hear words of counsel and consolation from the lips of friendship, and she felt, with a sigh, how empty a thing was the affection lavished on her by Lady Darley, when her prosperity was at the highest; when triumph marked her path, and when the future was arrayed in the most glowing colours of hope. The period of that affection had passed with the prosperity that had excited it; it was quite beyond the extent of her ladyship's philanthropy to be faithful in adversity, or ever to forgive the hand which had, even remotely, wounded her selfishness.

Indeed it appeared from her reproaches and remarks, that *she* had been the person most exposed by the whole affair; that the inroad had been made on her happiness, not on that of her niece; and that Catharine, not Cleveland, had throughout been the aggressor.

Moreover, as the more decided displays of her anger ceased, she began to feel that the society of Catharine was by no means essential to her comfort; that on many important points they differed entirely; and that it would be an exceedingly inconvenient thing to her, to have her as a permanent appendage to her family. She felt persuaded—at least she persuaded *herself*—that no one could exact from her more on behalf of her brother's orphan than she had already done. She had introduced her into the very first monde, had put her in the way of making an excellent establishment; had even secured an admirable match for her, and *she* had voluntarily destroyed her own prospects by a proceeding that none but a *tête exaltée* could ever have meditated. Then Lady Darley, though really indignant at the conduct of Sir Greville Cleveland, would have found it excessively inconvenient to relinquish his intimacy; a result which must be the inevitable consequence of Catharine's remaining with her, for it was out of the question to suppose that he would submit to the awkwardness of constantly meeting the person who had so recently rejected him. Even if he did eventually marry Lady Sophia Barron, Lady Darley felt that she could not relinquish his acquaintance: but, on the contrary, meditated the prospective sacrifice of her dignity, the propitiating of *his wife*, who would doubtless become the presiding divinity of fashion.

Conscious of much that was passing in the mind of her aunt, Catharine could not but welcome, with tears of joyful thankfulness, a letter from Mrs. Warren, in which that excellent friend announced the termination of her lawsuit by a compromise, and placed herself at the disposal of her "child."

"That I sincerely pity your present sufferings," she wrote, "I need scarcely say, for you are too well assured of my affection to doubt that I grieve for your grief. And yet, dearest Catharine, I see cause for thankfulness in your escape from a union with a man the half of whose private hours must be given to remorse, and for whom your tenderest feeling must have been pity, instead of that veneration with which your noble heart *should* regard the moral character of him, whom it had chosen as 'guide and head.' It is not at present a season for reasoning. For some time we will weep together, but still do allow me occasionally to feel that you have *only* dissolved a connection which your sainted mother never would have approved."

Lady Darley offered no word of persuasion to induce Catharine to remain with her. She expressed a courteous hope that her niece would recover serenity and bloom in the retirement she loved; that they should meet again, at some future time, under happier auspices; promised to write, and begged to be written to; lent her carriage to London; waved her hand from the window, with a graceful resignation, as Catharine stepped into it; and then turned to make arrangements with her maid for joining immediately a large party of fashionables at Brighton.

CHAPTER XXX.

Once more Catharine was the inhabitant of the beloved home of her youth, but with a heart how wounded, how changed!

As she gazed around her—visited each accustomed spot, the garden, the scene of her infant gambols, still redolent of the fragrance of the very flowers which had then bloomed in beauty beneath her glad eye, the furniture selected by her mother's taste, the sofa on which the declining form of that mother had reposed, the couch which had been her bed of death—no marvel if the tears gushed from her eyes, and if sighs burst from her aching bosom. She felt that the prayers breathed by the tenderest of parents for her happiness had not been answered, and she shuddered as a faint *first* whisper from the sleepless monitor within, warned her that her own hand had mingled "the bitter drop with the waters of her existence."

A few days sufficed to establish her and her friend at the cottage. Their life subsided into the ordinary routine of *home;* their domestic arrangements had become mechanical; everything was regular, and, on a moderate scale, well appointed; Mrs. Warren, approaching the decline of life, felt the luxury of the repose around her, as the bird, chased by the tempest, rejoices in the at length attained shelter of its own nest. She had outlived the period when excitement is necessary to happiness. The monotony which chafes more ardent spirits, soothed and refreshed hers. "A pleasant abode, a lovely country around, the poor to befriend, the suffering to cheer, books to instruct, religion to elevate and exalt, and *you,* Catharine, to love—must I *not* be happy?" she was wont to say to her young companion; and she *was* happy.

But, alas! it is not in the power of mere place—of mere external circumstances, to hush the storm of passion. *That* requires a power which must be supplied from within; and Catharine, with all her natural and acquired strength of character, was not *yet* capable of exerting it. The calmness which surrounded her, contrasted painfully with the vividness of the scenes she had quitted. The first agony had indeed passed away;

> "The storm was hushed, but still the waves ran high."

Apathy—indifference to the milder stimulants o´ existence,

succeeded. Pursuits which had formerly interested her became tasteless and insipid. That taste for reading which, if once thoroughly acquired, is, perhaps, the most valuable which the human mind is capable of attaining, was not, indeed, lost; that was impossible. But too often *itself* was a source of suffering, by recalling more vividly all the past which it so concerned her happiness to forget. *Here* was a sentiment which *he* had formerly expressed in language far more glowing; *this* was a description too applicable to her own disappointment; *that* graphic sketch was a portrait of her rival; everywhere the shadow of the past fell on her. From intercourse with the commonplace families who constituted the usual society of a country neighbourhood, she shrank with nervous susceptibility. She dreaded being compelled to appreciate the high value of what she had lost, by the contrast of the worthlessness of what remained. In her poor pensioners—the village school—she compelled herself to manifest some interest, but her heart struggled against it, and after every such exertion shrank into yet profounder listlessness. Her mental enjoyments sensibly diminished. She had proved the emptiness of the world, and disdained it as a theatre for the display of intellect, forgetting the noble theory she had hitherto professed—that knowledge sufficeth unto itself, that it is its own recompense and reward. In a word, with all her fine endowments, her careful cultivation, her rectitude, her strength of mind, she was in danger of being utterly wrecked by a passion stronger than either intellect, principle, or reason.

Mrs. Warren saw the dangerous crisis in the history of her beloved ward, and she essayed to apply what she deemed the only available remedy.

They had been reading a record of the disappointments of the heart—a *true* record, for it belonged to the page of history. It was that of the amiable and unfortunate Jane of France.

"It is a trite remark," said Mrs. Warren, "that scarcely any woman marries her first love."

Catharine changed colour rapidly—red and pale by turns—thinking that her friend had thoughtlessly touched on a very painful topic.

"Trite as it is, I am inclined to think the remark true," continued Mrs. Warren, unmindful of Catharine's varying complexion. "And what a moral we may gather from it, if we be inclined to 'gather sweetness from every flower!' Believing, as *we* do, that a supreme and merciful Being superintends all the events that agitate this state of existence, we must necessarily suppose him careful for the happiness of so large a proportion of his creatures. We cannot, therefore, for a moment believe that perpetual misery is the inevitable consequence of a disappointment of woman's earliest affections."

"Storms devastate the earth—inundations sweep away whole provinces—still they are permitted," said Catharine.

"Your illustration hardly applies to a moral truth of almost universal application," said Mrs. Warren. "Man cannot resist the convulsions of nature; he must still see his property ingulfed by the earthquake; his vessel wrecked by the tempest; but industry may retrieve both. But human beings *can* resist the whirlwind of passion; for God has given them, in their reason, a counteracting power: and that being imperfect, he has added religion, and enforced its precepts with the most awful sanctions."

Catharine shuddered slightly, and remained silent.

"A human being who, forgetting the responsibility of his position, neglects the duties of the present in regrets after the past, is entitled neither to respect nor commiseration," pursued Mrs. Warren, "except such commiseration as every Christian is bound to feel for the blindness of his brother. After all, this is a sentiment one would not be ambitious of exciting in one's fellow-creatures, although it has been my fortune to meet occasionally with young ladies who always showed themselves to the public eye with the willow bound round their brows."

Catharine's complexion heightened into an indignant blush. "Whatever my sufferings may be, I am careful to confine them to my own heart," she said with some asperity. "Not caring for the sympathy of the world, I am not desirous of drawing on its commiseration. I have seen enough of it to despise it."

"We will qualify your assertion, my dear Catharine, by limiting your contempt to the world of *fashion*. None can —you least of all—despise the intellectual, the good—those from whom we draw instruction and example. None can defy the opinion of such, without becoming worthless, and consequently useless—the most dreadful evil that can befall a mortal. There is a sphere of utility for the humblest of us; and wo to us, if we permit it to be narrowed by our selfish tenderness for ourselves—the egotistical spirit which finds the review of its own sorrows more interesting than the power of adding, according to the capacity given to each, to the general benefit of its species."

"You judge hardly of me," said Catharine, the tears rolling down her pale cheeks.

"Better are the wounds of a friend than the caresses of an enemy," said Mrs. Warren, taking the passive hand of her companion in her own. "Can I see you, my beloved child, sinking into a blameable indifference to every social duty, without seeking to arouse you to a conviction of your sin? Must I only in silence bewail that lamentable love of sorrow which encloses your thoughts in the past, and resolutely shuts out the future from you—that future which, I believe, never yet was unconnected with hope to any sane human being? No, dearest Catharine, your mother's friend has to perform a task, painful indeed, but from which that tender mother herself would not have shrunk—of condemning the being dearer to her than any other on earth, and endeavouring to rouse in her the conviction, that repining for the irrevocable past is impious—and that to regret the dispensations of Providence is no part of the resignation of a Christian."

"Religion does not forbid man to weep," said Catharine, gently.

"But it commands him to run the race set before him. Can she do that who is constantly looking back, and regretting the things that are behind?—things, too, defiled and impure, and with which it was sinful in her to come in contact? Wiser than I, Catharine, have said, that no human being ever yet suffered, who might not trace the origin of his suffering to his own folly or his own crime."

Catharine was weeping bitterly.

"Let me tell you the story of a woman who suffered as severely—was it not more severely?—as you have done—one not gifted with half your endowments, not intrusted with half your talents—and yet capable of feeling, in all its extent, the torment of betrayed affection—the story of *myself*, Catharine—and then answer me whether it be not easier to *relinquish* than to endure desertion.

"I was a poor man's daughter, Catharine, and he whom I loved was not born to greater worldly advantages than myself. We were lovers in youth—yea, in childhood. I cannot draw on memory for a thought—an association—*before* he was dear to me. We did not exactly, like Jeanie Deans and her Reuben Butler, tend our flocks together on the mountainside, and imbibe the elements of a pure, and, on one side at least, a strong affection, with the perfume of the mountain heather. He was a pupil of my father's, and I, who was educated, you know, to instruct others, shared with him his tasks, and, for I was the senior pupil, though not the senior in years, aided him, smoothed down the difficulties of *tyroship*, and, possibly, divested the vestibule of learning of some of its terrors.

"He went to college, but part of every vacation was spent at the parsonage, and I was there, for I was still too young to commence my foreign labours; I remained yet amid the drudgery of domestic hardships. But it was something to look to the epochs of happiness which his regular visits constituted in my almanac. *Something!*—it was as the sun to animal existence, imparting a radiance and a splendour to objects which did not, never could, possess them in themselves.

"At length time came, the time so dreaded by him, when I was to step beyond the limited horizon of my home, and to view the world on a comparatively large scale. It is a bitter draught, that draught of dependance, *pecuniary* dependance, Catharine, on mortal man. To *me* its irksomeness was softened by the thoughts of *him*, the hope of the future, the dream of the past. His letters were constant; twice a year I saw him at my father's house, when I sought there to recruit strength of mind and body to encounter the toils by which I repaid my yearly salary! Imagine all that he was to me! the single star of hope—of memory.

> 'I loved . . . . . .
> Tenderly, passionately, madly loved him.
> Sinful it was to love a child of earth
> With such entire devotion as I loved,
> The imaginative passion seemed so pure:
> Quiet and calm like duty, hope nor fear
> Disturbed the deep contentment of that love:
> He was the sunshine of my soul, and like
> A flower, I lived and flourished in his sight.'

"When I wished to be happy, Catharine, and to catch a gleam of sunshine in the sober twilight of my dull existence, my thoughts naturally flew to him from whom alone it could shine on me. Amid a deluge of those daily cares, trials, and sorrows which, in the aggregate, make up a lifetime of misery, his love was the ark which bore me above the waters. I endured the present in uncomplaining, even cheerful patience, for the future—the future full of hope was before me. My love for him was unconnected with a single doubt, a single fear. He stood before my mental vision as the image of truth itself. I loved—I revered him, with too perfect an esteem to dream, for a single instant that the idol of my worship owed his awful beauty to the drapery which my fond imagination had thrown over him.

"As soon as he had obtained orders, he came to a curacy within an easy distance of the house that was my present home. How I rejoiced, when I found that he would be within my daily sight, that an hour's walk would give us the power of sharing those thousand thoughts and feelings which make so much of the happiness of love. Poor short-sighted mortals! how little inclined are youth and inexperience to believe that there may be a curse in granted prayers!

"Well, Catharine, to shorten as much as possible a long story, we saw each other frequently, in openness and sincerity, for our, *my*, attachment did not blush to meet the eye of day. My patrons esteemed me, and they spoke jestingly of future patronage for the man of my choice, but *so* that I shed tears of thankfulness, in my solitude, over those promises, for I knew that they were spoken in all sincerity. He was an occasional guest at their table, and his own manners seemed to add to their prepossession in his behalf, and surely no creature was ever more blessed in quaffing the bitter draught of dependance than I at this period!

"My eyes opened at length. I became sensible that his manner was embarrassed—his professions equivocal, and he began to speak of our union as an event that could take place only at a very remote period; he, who had dwelt so much on the energy, the industry, the exertions, which should enable him to effect it with love's own rapidity! He saw a thousand obstacles which had before escaped him. He sighed over the privations to which, he said, a narrow income would subject *me*, so little able to cope with them; *me*, who would have endured any suffering, any *want*, for his sake!

"I was not naturally jealous, but I could not always be blind. The eldest sister of my pupils was eighteen—pretty, gay, volatile, inclined to flirt, and to make a property of every decent-looking individual of the other sex who fell in her way. He was not insensible to her attractions, her youth, superior connections, fortune. A correspondence was discovered by her parents, which served but to confirm a jealousy that had already been poignant enough to chase the colour from my cheek, and happiness from my heart. Their indignation was surely justified by the double treachery. He was forbidden the house, and my grief—for grief it was—was sufficiently considered to be recognised as a plea for my immediate return to my home.

"Alas, Catharine, there were none there to pity or understand me. I stood as one apart from the rest, who had no feelings in common with them but the instincts of near affinity. A maiden aunt, who had hitherto had but little intercourse with us, felt, in her declining years, the need of companionship, and the universal voice of our household said, that I was the proper person to accept her invitation. In fact they felt, and I felt, that I was not one of them, and they were not averse to getting rid of a companion whose sad looks and quiet demeanour were perpetual reproaches to their boisterous cheerfulness, and the bustling vivacity, which was to them the happiness of existence.

"To my aunt's I went—a reserved, placid, ladylike personage, whose first address rather chilled my hopes of feeling or inspiring affection. In her sober household everything proceeded with clocklike regularity; every fraction of time seemed to have its proper and allotted occupation. Yet there was no severity in her manner; its gentle composure indicated a heart at peace with itself, its neighbour, its God. But I had not yet arrived at the power of appreciating the value of such a state of mind. My feelings had so lately been stretched on the rack of perpetual excitement—alternating between the most passionate love and the most distracting jealousy—that the calmness of my relative appeared apathy, her air of contentment selfishness. How I wronged her, dear Catharine! How incapable I was of comprehending the blessings of the peace 'which passeth all understanding,' the peace of a Christian!

"But by degrees my aunt's excellences stole upon me, not dazzlingly and bewilderingly, like the flash of a meteor, but cheeringly, consolingly, like the light of a balmy morning after a dark night. As soon as I understood her, I poured into no unwilling or unsympathizing ear the story of my disappointment, my grief. If she checked my repinings, it was with compassionate gentleness; if she opposed my assertions that this world could never henceforward afford me one enjoyment, it was by elevating my thoughts to the higher destiny which is assigned to human beings, by opening to me the sublime hopes and consolations of religion. I did not yield willingly or immediately to her arguments, drawn from things which were indeed 'too high for me,' but her beautiful example bore them gradually upon my mind—my convictions—with irresistible force. Racked by a disease which, at intervals, stretched her on a bed of agonizing torture, no murmuring mingled with the groans which bodily suffering wrung from her pale lips; as I wiped the cold dews from her contracted brow, I heard the whispered prayer, the confession of one of the humblest of mortal hearts, that, in the midst of her chastisement, mercy had been remembered even to her, for there was within the peace that no corporeal anguish could disturb. Was not *this* a lesson for me, Catharine? Was it strange that I humbled myself before my Maker, and bewailed the impious selfishness which had made me, on the first severe trial, exclaim, 'Never sorrow was like my sorrow!' The hours that I passed by the side of that saintly martyr were pregnant with the most awful, the most spirit-stirring lessons. From her I learned the value to our own happiness of marking every hour with some object of utility to ourselves and our kind. I was instructed in the sinfulness—the meanness—of that miserable sorrow which rejects all the alleviating circumstances Providence scatters around, and finds or fancies an enjoyment even in its own indulgence. I was taught to discriminate between the grief natural to suffering, and the nurture of it by a sickly sentiment which loathes the possibility of its days of mourning being shortened. In one sense man is *not* made to mourn, but to bestir himself in a scene making daily, hourly demands on his exertions. My eyes were opened to the fact, that employment is a duty; and blessed are we that it is so, for in occupation we find security from sin, forgetfulness of sorrow. By being occupied—

laudably, I trust—memory was necessarily silenced. I desired to do my duty in the first instance, as a slave, perhaps, strives to propitiate a severe taskmaster. But in time a better frame of mind succeeded; I rejoiced in 'labours of love:' I had been tranquil, I became happy; and I had gathered strength to bear the stroke which fell on me, when I learned that he had become the husband of the woman whom his ambition, if not his heart, preferred to me, the opposition of her parents having yielded in his, as in so many other instances, to the perseverance, the obstinacy of *persuasion.*

"Yet it *was* a blow, Catharine. I could not derive any satisfaction from the consciousness of having rejected an unworthy suitor. I had been deserted, even when I was most devoted to him. My pride afforded me no aid. I was bereft of all external support. I was sustained only by the conviction that *this* was my appointed trial, and to sustain it with fortitude, a proper discipline.

"A few weeks—*prayer*—the society of my incomparable kinswoman—sufficed to restore my tranquillity; and then succeeded *another* trial, but one which, while it wounded, exalted and purified.

"My aunt, my best benefactress, died. Until within a few hours of her decease, her sufferings were dreadful, but endured with a submission, how perfect, how beautiful, how awfully instructive! I witnessed the strife between the body and the soul; and I saw how the latter achieved its triumphs through the might of Him 'who *is* mighty.' I saw and trembled; but while I trembled, my desire to appropriate to myself those blessings which cheered *her* bed in sickness became more intense, my efforts after its attainment more earnest, less self-relying, more humble. Her grave became to me as the altar of my dedication to the service of *her* Master; and I left its hallowed precincts subdued, mourning, fearing, trembling, but submissive.

"The little she had to bequeath—it was a mere trifling legacy—some books, a few jewels—for her income had been held by a life tenure—was mine: but I was compelled to quit, in a few short weeks after her interment, a home which had been my own during the most interesting, the most important epoch in my existence—when I learned to measure the world and its enjoyments accurately—to form a just estimation of the relative value of time and eternity. To quit it was a trial—like a second parting from the dead. But my repining sighs were checked—for I remembered *Whose* providence had ordained that I should again seek shelter, as a dependant, beneath the roof of the proud.

"In the family of the Earl of Edinburgh I passed the three succeeding years; and then, Catharine—a practical infidel to the creed of the eternity of first love—I married Mr.

Warren; and gave him, heretic that I was, more tenderness, more esteem, more veneration, than it had been possible for me to bestow on the lover of my youth. No woman was ever more blessed in married life than I was; and it is my conviction of the absolute necessity that a highminded woman should rely on—confide in *implicitly*—the moral dignity of her husband—which assures me, that in a union with Sir Greville Cleveland, you would have found only splendid misery; for, believe me, the brilliant attainments which captivated you, are little adapted for the narrow sphere of domestic life, and would demand the whole range of fashionable society as their arena; neither are they satisfactory substitutes for that integrity which, *you know*, Sir Greville had lost with peace of conscience, or that 'religion, holy and undefiled,' which, if he had too much good taste to deride it, he disbelieved."

Mrs. Warren paused, and she was well satisfied that Catharine should be silent, absorbed apparently in deep communion with her own heart. And the result of her self-communion was manifest in the regularity with which she sedulously applied to those pursuits best calculated to strengthen her mind—to open to her the great truths of religion. Poetry, romance, she rejected, as dangerous food to feelings too much excited. She sought all that could exalt her faith, establish her principles, ennoble her reason: and in such cases, the mere pursuit is success. Effort is the first grand step to victory; and when Catharine retired to her pillow after the day's labours—for she had voluntarily, *and wisely*, made her studies laborious—she felt happier, more satisfied with the present, more resigned to the past, than she had ventured, a few hours before the trial, to believe possible.

Then plans were invented and tried for doing good, according to her moderate means, to all within her reach. Projects which the death of her mother and her own subsequent removal from the cottage had suspended, were renewed. Pensioners, the regular payment of whose small stipend had not compensated to them for the loss of the occasional visits of her whose hand bestowed it, were again revived by her presence—cheered by her conversation, by that feeling which never forsakes the human heart, of pleasure in being cared for by its kind. And Catharine felt the benefit she bestowed return into her own bosom; it is impossible to see the countenances of our fellow-beings lighted up with joy at our approach and be insensible to some responding feeling of gladness. And it is thus that "mercy is twice blessed; it blesses him who gives and him who takes."

Winter had worn away not all in gloom, and spring had touched that point where it is softening into summer, before Catharine, notwithstanding the regularity of her letters, received any reply from Lady Darley. And then she wrote in evident anger, announcing the marriage of Cleveland—the splendour of the bride—and reprobating the perverse folly which had led Catharine to prefer the dreadful obscurity of her present situation to one so brilliant and distinguished. She complained, in a tone of unabated resentment, of the ingratitude which had so repaid all her exertions—all her kindness. Then she charged fickleness and caprice on Cleveland, who had of late, probably prompted by Lady Sophia, shamefully neglected her who had so long been his ally. She seemed to find consolation only in predicting all manner of unhappiness from the marriage which now formed THE *event* of the beau monde, and wished both the *nouveau maries* and Catharine might not live to repent the rule they had severally chosen to perform in this disagreeable business.

Although Catharine had believed that she had tutored herself to regard the union of Cleveland and Lady Sophia as a probability little short of absolute certainty, still when she found it had actually occurred—that he to whom she had once looked so fondly for the whole happiness of her existence was indissolubly bond to another—it seemed as if she had only now lost him. Her head fell upon the open letter, and sobs of unutterable anguish burst from a heart that felt, for an instant, as if its burden was too heavy to be borne. But Catharine had acquired the habit of *resisting* self, and her *abandonnement*, intense, wretched as it was, did not long continue. It is true, that it seemed to her, for a short time, as if all her efforts to forget had been but miserable folly—an abortive attempt to escape from the overwhelming wretchedness which was her lot. But *this* also passed away. She was able, at length, to pray—to reflect—to comprehend the reasonable truth that, as the wife of Cleveland, neither happiness nor honour could have been her portion, for in ceasing to respect her husband, must she not cease to respect herself? And knowing the history of *his* fearful past as she did know it, how could she have honoured him whom, nevertheless, it was her duty, as it would have been her happiness, to honour?

"From first to last, I always doubted the result of your engagement with Sir Greville Cleveland," said Mrs. Warren, when, in a few days, Catharine took courage to mention to her the contents of Lady Darley's letter. "Never before did I comprehend the extent of the selfishness of men of fashion! I trace him from the first moment of his acquaintance with you—his *designed* introduction, so well contrived as to wear the appearance of accident, or at least of being merely *incidental*—contrived, nevertheless, by him and Lady Darley, that he might judge whether he thought you worthy of being honoured with the *débris* of a hea t seared by a thousand passions, polluted by the contamination of the world, disgusted with the very height of its own prosperity, incapable of one true, one generous emotion! Charmed with your beauty, your talent, your graces, and above all, the admiration you excited in others, he sedulously strove to inspire you—*you*, pure, unworldly, noble in Heaven's best blessing, innocence, with such love as might add to the happiness even of a *good* man, and which to *him* was the excitement his exhausted mind required, the novel aliment that was to give zest to enjoyments satiety had loathed! In the whole engagement there appears but one predominating thought, how to secure his own happiness! And when a meeting with a woman he had formerly loved reawakens feelings which *ought* to have been extinguished, does one tie of honour—even of compassion, fetter his actions, or arrest his career? No! no! Self, self, is the monstrous idol of his worship, and to that he has sacrificed principle, honour, feeling—all that restricts the actions of better men. And, in short, he has qualified himself to be the husband of Lady Sophia Barron, and he will have his reward!"

Catharine wept, but hers were tears of gentle sorrow, and were succeeded by a long period of such sweet tranquillity as the heart unwillingly relinquishes, even for the admission of the most joyful emotions.

PART THE SECOND.

CHAPTER I.

THOUGH early in April, the sun shone with a brightness sufficient to penetrate, albeit with the faintness of its beams, the Cimmerian darkness of the most densely populated narrow streets of London, while it illuminated Portland Place with a splendour which gave warmth enough to permit the large windows of a drawingroom in one of its best houses to be open, thus admitting the fragrance of the various plants that occupied the balcony.

In the full enjoyment of the luxury of the scene, the balmy air, the warm sun, the elegant apartment, a lady sat with her eyes fixed, in abstraction, on a newspaper she still held in her hand, the columns of which had offered deeply interesting matter to her perusal. Her mind had been intensely occupied, and was now enjoying that dreamy repose which commonly succeeds great intellectual exertion. It was with a momentary impatience, therefore, that she heard the door open and a visiter announced—Mr. Stark.

"I could not deny myself the pleasure of congratulating Mrs. Stracey Hamilton personally on the brilliant success of Colonel Hamilton," he said, advancing with a smile intended to express every amiable and cordial feeling; "to congratulate myself, also, on the reappearing above our horizon of a star whose brightness shone on us three years since, with the transience of a meteor. Who, more than I, regretted the sudden retirement of Miss Vernon, at the termination of her first short season?"

Catharine bowed coldly, a manner observed by Mr. Stark, and attributed by him to her year's rustication in the ultima Thule of the Highlands.

"I heard from the queen of these our realms, Lady Sophia Cleveland," resumed Mr. Stark, pronouncing very distinctly each syllable of her ladyship's name, and keeping his eye steadfastly on Catharine's serene countenance as he did so, "that Colonel Hamilton and his lady were expected last week in Portland Place, and on the privilege of old acquaintance I have ventured thus early to remind you of my existence. But how in the world, my dear Mrs. Hamilton, for I conclude you have the leading voice in such matters, came you to choose a residence in this resort of ambassadors and nabobs? It is quite a journey to travel from *our* part of the world to these tramontane regions."

"Alas," said Catharine, "my tastes will, I fear, never stand the test of the standard of fashion."

"You will improve," said Stark, with a patronising smile; "under the auspices of your inimitable sister-in law, the deity of our worship, you cannot fail to become at least the high priestess of our temple. Do you not think Lady Sophia exceedingly improved? Time seems to reverse his usual proceedings in her favour, and to impart new lustre to her charms instead of diminishing their bloom. Of course you have seen her since her arrival."

"I have," said Catharine, quietly, "and can imagine nothing more beautiful."

"I dare not venture the proof of the possibility," said Mr. Stark, with an application too palpable to be mistaken. Mrs. Hamilton neither bowed nor smiled. There is but one worse reception of a compliment than a calm silence, and that is, to request its repetition. Mr. Stark felt obliged to resume. "Have you seen my kind friend, Lady Darley? May we hope to welcome her in town this season? Her distressing accident has deprived our society of one of its most delightful leaders."

"It *was* distressing," said Catharine. "On our return from Scotland we remained some weeks at Darley House, and rejoiced to find that, dreadful to a human being, in the prime of life, as the loss of a limb must be, my aunt had learned to bear it with resignation. The retirement to which she has condemned herself, has invested her accident with a gloom which, to one of her habits, must be almost insupportable, but I trust the arguments of Colonel Hamilton have so far influenced her, that she will be our guest in Portland Place before the expiration of the season. Her house in Grosvenor Square, as of course you know, is let."

"That most delightful of mansions!" said Mr. Stark, with a sigh of unaffected regret to the memory of the departed fêtes in which he had there sustained a part. "Really it embarrasses our philosophy to explain why such direful visitations should overtake poor mortals."

"Our religion helps us out of the difficulty," said Catharine, mildly. "Trials are one of the necessary conditions of a state of probation."

Mr. Stark shrugged his shoulders, and flew from a subject which he thought beneath his wit, and ridicule of which, he had tact enough to suspect, would be most unacceptable to the wife of Stracey Hamilton, who, in Mr. Stark's phraseology, was suspected of the sin of saintship.

"Three years have made sad alterations among us," he said. "While you were improving—*preserving*, I ought more properly to say—your beauty in the healthy retirement of the country, we have been getting old, and what is worse, looking so. Their graces of Halifax are recruiting at Rome, —financially recruiting, I mean. I had a letter from the duchess yesterday, complaining of the wearisome existence she was obliged to pass in the 'city of the soul,' a most unmeet abode, you must confess, for a person in whose idiosyncrasy that material article—by-the-way, I fear I have touched on a pun—is wanting."

Catharine hated personalities, and knew too little of the duchess to be interested in her adventures or feelings. Mr. Stark felt that he was in danger of sustaining a monologue, without the advantage of an attentive audience. He had, however, the strongest division of his forces in reserve.

"Could you believe that Cleveland—Cleveland, who shunned the precincts of a court as a place pregnant only with dulness and flattery, is now one of the most frequent, as the most favoured guests at Carlton Palace? His burst of liberalism has been pardoned in a certain quarter, in consideration of its being an access to which Sir Greville had never before been subject, and with which he has never been attacked since. Lady Sophia and his majesty—*rex meus et ego*—have changed all that, and the Cleveland House coterie is ten times more brilliant than ever."

"Lady Sophia with her wit and beauty must add to the brilliancy of every circle in which she appears," said Catharine, with a quietness which Stark, who had not that principle of internal truth which, as an instinct, enables its possessor to understand what is true in others, mentally pronounced the climax of hypocrisy and a proof of the most consummate self-possession.

"His majesty thinks so, for he deems none complete ungraced by her presence, and all Europe bows to the perfect taste of George the Fourth. And apropos, of courts, when, my dear Mrs. Hamilton, are you to be presented? Under Lady Sophia's fostering wing, you cannot fail to be received with favour."

"I am vain enough of my wife to think that she need not shine by the reflected lustre of another," said Colonel Hamilton, who had entered unperceived, and knew quite enough of Mr. Stark to understand an impertinence which Catharine, for her comfort, did not even suspect.

Mr. Stark rose to pay his compliments to a man whom he feared, and consequently disliked; and the cordiality, the obsequiousness of his manner were a tolerably accurate measure of his secret antipathy. Where he knew he had much to conceal, he thought it necessary to profess much. His praise of his enemies, like a drum, was loud in proportion to its hollowness

"Radicalism is not the fashion of this era," said Colonel Hamilton when Mr. Stark was once again seated, "nor is it likely to become so during the reign of the most exclusive monarch in Europe. When the Pavilion is permitted to be visible to the public eye, and the mysterious beauties of Virginia Water exposed to that *profanum vulgus* which his majesty *odit et arcet*, then may the wife of Stracey Hamilton hope to be received with favour in a court at which, by-the-way, it is not an honour to be received at all—and not until then."

"I have no desire to be presented," said Catharine. "I love the quiet life I have lately lived, and court its continuance so far as the keeping up of your connections, Colonel Hamilton, will permit."

"Tell it not in Gath!" said Mr. Stark, lifting up his hands in affected horror.

"Your presentation is necessary, Catharine," said Colonel Hamilton; "but it is *not* necessary that you should grace his majesty's private society, even if, under the auspices of Lady Sophia Cleveland, you were courted to become a member of it."

In Mr. Stark's apprehension, human life offered nothing more desirable to the ambition of man and woman, than the power of entering "into the secret chambers" of a prince's palace. He began to feel something very like contempt for the understanding which was unable to appreciate the glories, the possibility of approaching which dazzled his own mental vision.

"Mrs. Hamilton has been studying that *chef d'œuvre* of eloquence with which you startled the house last night," he said, looking at the newspaper which now lay on the table by Catharine; "a study which, I conjecture, she has shared with the whole reading public of England."

"I have no eloquence, properly so called," said Colonel Hamilton with a *downrightness* that passed Mr. Stark's understanding. "I have told the truth in a plain, unvarnished manner, as becomes a soldier whose sword is hardly yet turned into a ploughshare."

"Its transformation into a *pruning hook* may be deemed perfect," said Stark with the smile he always wore when he meant to say a witty thing; "his majesty's minister, at least, would think so, were your bold plans of retrenchment to be carried into effect."

"The day is not so far off as you and your party delude yourselves into believing, Mr. Stark," said Colonel Hamilton. "We hear the distant growl of the thunder, and we are led to expect the approach of a storm—perhaps of an earthquake. There are moral symptoms no less infallible: why should we resolutely close our minds against the receiving of warnings, which at least might afford to those whom they threaten, the power of preparing to meet the coming danger, or of betaking themselves to the security of shelter?"

"Interpretations of prophecies differ," said Stark. "We do not deem the discontented grumblings of a few factious demagogues the portentous thunder which you appear to consider it."

"We must refer the accuracy of the interpretation to the period of the fulfilment," said Colonel Hamilton.

"Meantime is it not philosophy to enjoy the present?" said Mr. Stark. "In putting Mrs. Hamilton *au courant du jour*, so far as regards Lady Sophia's great popularity in the very highest quarter, I have taken the privilege of old acquaintance, and I hoped to be of service to one"—bowing to Catharine—"whom it was impossible to know and not regard with the most unbounded admiration."

"Compliments to my wife are my property," said Colonel Hamilton, laughing. "I thank you, therefore, Mr. Stark, on her behalf. Your politeness, you perceive, is quite overwhelming to the timidity of her inexperience."

Mr. Stark could not but feel the rebuke, for his eyes were at that moment fixed on a countenance expressing intellectual and moral dignity, with a majesty not to be mistaken. Probably he found the atmosphere of the room uncongenial to the health of *his* mind, for after a few desultory commonplaces he retired.

"Lady Sophia's *hired* parasite and flatterer," said Colonel Hamilton, as soon as he had retired. "A lampoon on her ladyship began their acquaintance—continued on condition of its being answered and refuted. Henceforward Mr. Stark was my sister's *chargè d'affaires* in all those petty intrigues which constitute the diplomacy of fashionable life. Doubtless his visit here was to reconnoitre—and my Catharine fears not that, even though the spy be sent from Cleveland House."

"You do me justice, Hamilton," she replied, gently. "There has been perfect confidence between us, and we have that friendship for each other which ensures mutual reliance."

Colonel Hamilton gazed on her for a moment with one of those looks of inquiry which she felt were not always intelligible, and he seemed immediately to occupy himself with the newspaper.

CHAPTER II.

When Stracey Hamilton won from Catharine her consent to become his wife, he was confident of possessing her affectionate regard—her undivided esteem; and he felt that in them there was a better foundation for matrimonial happiness than in that more passionate—that blinding and bewildering love with which she had regarded Sir Greville Cleveland. And when he examined his own heart, he believed that with that affectionate regard—that undivided esteem, he should be satisfied. But he deceived himself.

Loving Catharine with that intense love which her personal loveliness, her endowments of mind, her charm of character, could hardly fail of inspiring in one so enthusiastic as Colonel Hamilton, he had believed that satisfied with calling her his—with the security that her principles would prevent her from ever regarding another with warmer sentiments than himself—he should be content to live with her in the perfect confidence of trusting friendship, not craving that participation in the boundless love which filled *his* whole being, and *for* which he was now athirst.

And even as his utmost desires could have craved, Catharine did love Hamilton. From day to day, during the first happy year of her wedded life, esteem, friendship, admiration had gradually ripened into that deeper, that tenderer sentiment, which it is the highest happiness of woman to feel for him to whom she is for ever united. But deep as this love was, its stream flowed on tranquilly. Satisfied with the constant society of Hamilton—with being the bosom confidant of all his cares, all his hopes, all his thoughts—she did not dream that he cherished one single doubt of the entireness of her affections; far less that he had ever permitted that whisper so fatal to his tranquillity to suggest to him, whether he had done wisely in seeking the hand of a woman who had conquered, with so much difficulty, a first absorbing passion—and who had confessed, even in accepting him, that she deemed it a point of duty to guard against the admission of a second sentiment as engrossing as the first, and proffered in exchange for his heart of hearts, only cold esteem and the reliance of a confiding friendship.

Perhaps the calmness and *rétènue* which constituted so principal a grace in Catharine's manner, were, in the peculiar circumstances of herself and her husband, unfortunate. Never did the devoted heart of Hamilton for one moment condemn the wife he adored, but he did occasionally—when her playful smile had been the only reply to the outpourings of his passionate love, or her calm kindness had checked his enthusiasm—reproach himself for the selfishness with which he had so ardently sought to make this bright creature his own, without more clearly ascertaining that *her* heart was in the matter.

Catharine, meanwhile, satisfied of the love of her husband—confiding in his honour as in the brightness of the sum or the lustre of the stars—enjoyed a happiness pure as earth *can* give. She walked in a delusion—little dreaming that her smile of perfect content—her smooth calm brow, the seat of tranquillity—the gentle welcome with which, after his temporary absences, she received Hamilton, were to him so many sources of a bitterness to control the expression of which cost him an effort almost beyond his strength.

But he unfortunately *did* control it. Regarding Catharine's intellect as something altogether brighter and more exalted than any other of her sex possessed, he shrank from the possibility of lowering himself in her eyes by the confession of the thousand indefinable jealousies and torments which racked him, driving peace from his heart, and sleep too often from his pillow. He suffered in silence, and when Catharine perceived the cloud on his brow, or the paleness of his cheek, her soothings did but increase his pangs, for they were only chidings that he allowed his ardour in the success of his various plans of public utility to make such inroads on his health and tranquillity. He felt—he believed—that if there were aught of love for him within her heart, she could not fail to trace to its source the agitation, the moodiness, which would not always be suppressed.

Moreover, when Stracey first proposed to stand for his country, and forsaking their beautiful retirement in the Highlands to plunge at once into the cares and turmoil of public life, Catharine offered no word of opposition. *He* did not know that she was thus evincing the strength of her affection by sacrificing the undivided enjoyment of his society in the retirement she loved, to the belief that, to his active mind, public life offered the most desirable objects of pursuit, and that he would find more happiness in the conflicts of the legislative arena, than in the prosecution of those more limited projects of good among his own people, which had hitherto been his occupation. Little did she suspect that Hamilton sought in the excitement of politics a counteracting influence to that restless and unsatisfied love for herself which ought, united as they were, to have constituted his felicity, but which, in their mutual misunderstanding, threatened to become fatal to the happiness of both.

To Catharine herself the prospect of again entering the London world was exquisitely painful. If the love that has passed away, do not become indifference, it becomes aversion, and it was with this latter sentiment that Catharine justly regarded the selfish man of fashion who had so wantonly trifled with her happiness. If it had been practicable to decline his society altogether, she would have done so but the near relationship between his wife and Colonel Hamilton rendered that altogether impossible. Lady Sophia's letter of congratulation to her brother on his marriage, if not cordial or affectionate, was at least polite, and the correspondence subsequently existing between them had preserved precisely the same tone. When he announced his projected visit to London, there was indeed no offer on her ladyship's part of accommodations in the princely mansion of Cleveland House. Colonel Hamilton was quite aware that his sister had long been wearied of the censorship of his presence, and suspected that she would never invite a renewal of it, and he was right. But Lady Sophia was influenced by a double motive. Whatever might have been her sentiments for Sir Greville Cleveland, it is quite certain that, from the moment when marriage had sealed her triumph over her innocent rival, and established her firmly as the wife of the autocrat of fashion,they had gradually been declining to indifference; and, probably, even in that selfish region which constituted their world, there did not exist a more coldly courteous pair than Sir Greville and Lady Sophia Cleveland. But there is a jealousy whose origin is vanity, as well as one which is the offspring of love. Lady Sophia could not endure that the graces—the superiority of her sister-in-law—should be exhibited daily to the eyes of her husband in immediate contrast with herself. She was conscious that she should sink immeasurably in such a comparison, if made in the privacy of domestic life; but she gave herself credit for too much of the *esprit de societié* to dread losing her supremacy in the haunts of fashionable splendour.

Nevertheless it was no part of Lady Sophia's plan to be on distant terms with Mrs. Stracey Hamilton. She secretly did Catharine the justice of feeling that her character must demand the respect of society, and would be of weight sufficient to guaranty, in some measure, the respectability of all those who were admitted to her intimacy. Lady Sophia had her own private reasons for coveting the sanction of Catharine's acquaintance, or, if possible, her friendship, and the visit of Mr. Stark was, as Colonel Hamilton had said, one of reconnoitring; to prepare the way for the favourable reception of her ladyship, by hinting at the facility with which her introduction would ensure Catharine's admission into that very highest, that most *récherché* society, which drew a magic circle round itself over which no profane foot was permitted to pass, even in that most extensive of all capitals, the metropolis of free, civilized, *commercial*—Britain!

Mr. Stark, on leaving Portland Place, flew instantly to Cleveland House to report progress.

CHAPTER III.

Lady Sophia was in her boudoir, and Mr. Stark was admitted instantly within that generally inaccessible sanctuary, for the *entrée* of which many fashionable aspirants would have given—*almost* their reputation.

"At home?" inquired her ladyship.

"At home," replied Mr. Stark.

"Indulging in the Vandal practice of receiving morning visiters, I presume?"

"I was admitted. I wish I could flatter myself it was an exception in my favour."

"You have achieved higher honours, for you are *here*," said Lady Sophia, coolly. "And did you see Stracey also?"

"I did."

"Laconic!" said her ladyship, with a sneer. "I do not tolerate the epigrammatic style from any one, judge if from you."

Stark smiled and bowed as if he had received a compliment.

Lady Sophia averted her eyes—proud eyes as they were—and smelt to her eau de cologne.

"Playing turtle doves still, were they?" she asked in a tone somewhat subdued. "Very well for the Highlands, but I suspect Stracey tired of *toujours perdrix*, or why bore himself with parliament, and speeches, and all that kind of thing?"

"I must do them the justice to say there was nothing *maussade* about either of them. They appeared satisfied with each other, as well-bred friends might be; nothing more—at least not exhibited to the eyes of the curious. And yet a man might be excused a little extravagance in favour of that splendid woman. With all due deference, your ladyship's self hardly surpasses her."

"Hardly *equals*, you would say if you dared. But have a care, my power brooks no partner even over my abjects," said Lady Sophia, with unequivocal contempt. "So Mrs. Stracey Hamilton's beauty is in high preservation, is it?"

"Upon my honour you might swear she was not above seventeen, judging from her bloom. It is the—the reserve—the loftiness, I should call it—of her expression which compels you to believe there must have been more years of thought to form the mind it indicates. If her manner had a little of the airy grace of your ladyship's, she would be irresistible."

"But wanting her cestus—the girdle of taste—Venus herself was powerless," said her ladyship with a complaisant smile. "Well, about myself?"

"I obeyed your commands with a dexterity which I flatter myself you would have admired—insinuated the success of a *debût* in the presence of majesty under your auspices and boldy asserted that, with the said majesty of England, your ladyship's influence was all-sufficient—which had the merit of being as nearly true as bold assertions in general are expected to be."

"Well, well—the text; no comment, so please you, Mr. Stark," said Lady Sophia, her little foot impatiently beating the silken cushion on which it reposed.

"Colonel Hamilton, with the austerity of a Cato Major, depreciated the value of royal approbation, and denied that gold was at all the more precious for being stamped with the royal image; declared, against the lady's avowed wish, mark you, that Mrs. Stracey Hamilton would be presented, but declined the honour of a more particular acquaintance with the illustrious gentleman in whose gift are stars and garters."

"Stracey always was the most unmanageable barbarian in the universe," said Lady Sophia, indignantly. "Mr. Barron wronged me cruelly by inflicting him on me as one of his executors. The annoyances he has caused, and continues to cause me, are beyond endurance. He seems to have made it his pleasure to search for all Mr. Barron's kinsfolk, for the purpose of impressing it on me as a duty I owe to his memory, to bestow on them some portion of the wealth I derive from him. As if I had any superfluities! As if all I possess, and ten times as much would repay me for the succession of sacrifices made during the dreadful ten years I spent with Mr. Barron! As if Mr. Barron himself were not the proper judge of the extent of his relations' claims on him, and as if his utter neglect of them had not sufficiently proved his conviction of their worthlessness! In my view of the case, to shower benefits on those whom he virtually declared unworthy, would be rather an extraordinary method of evincing my respect for his opinions."

"And an inconvenient one," said Mr. Stark, with a smile. "Colonel Hamilton's theories are as absurd as his practice."

"Yes; only conceive his persisting so long in his extraordinary passion for Miss Vernon, hoping against hope; with the knowledge, too, of her attachment to another man—an attachment she had found it so difficult to subdue! Imagine the *bonhommie* of his assuring me, when I ventured a little gentle raillery, that the fact of Miss Vernon's accepting him was so convincing a guarantee for her having entirely subdued any former feeling for an object every way unworthy of her, that he would feel no anxiety were it possible that that object—released from his present ties—were to attempt to revive her former feelings! But mark the inconsistency! The ceremony is no sooner completed, than Stracey flies off with his lady to the retirement of the Highlands, lives during a whole year in the profoundest obscurity, and emerges just at the precise moment when his passion, being on the decline, no longer fears to expose its object to the temptation to inconstancy."

"Inconstancy of the heart *only*," said Mr. Stark. "That is the only species of inconstancy of which we can venture to hope Mrs. Hamilton capable. For my own part, far from believing in her attachment to Sir Greville, I deem her incapable of any warmer sentiment than a cold, calculating preference with which reason, and possibly *prudence*, had at least as much to do as the heart."

"Do not rob me of my laurels," said Lady Sophia, with unwonted earnestness. "I would not relinquish the satisfactory certainty of having had the power of wounding that woman, for any other triumph this world could afford me."

"How unintelligible is your sex!" said Mr. Stark, with his bitter air of irony.

"To those to whom we do not condescend to manifest ourselves," returned Lady Sophia. "Has it never occurred to you to penetrate so far into the arcana of *man's* motives as to understand, that his own success fades beneath the pleasure of crushing a rival? Human passions are of neither sex. It was something to gain Sir Greville Cleveland, but oh! how infinitely more, to hurt—trample on—triumph over—the niece of Lady Darley!"

Mr. Stark smiled—his detestable smile.

"Yes," said Lady Sophia, gazing proudly and unshrinkingly on him, "I understand you; it exalts you to feel that you are receiving a confidence from Lady Sophia Cleveland. But you and I, Mr. Stark, have at length touched that point, where our intercourse resolves itself into the mere fact of being useful to each other, and the one who can confer most is superior to the one who *only* dreads least. You will never betray me while silence is your interest, and it will be your interest until this world and its conventions, its splendours its honours, its temptations, shall have passed away. During your life therefore. And not fearing you, I use you as is most pleasant to myself. Now, being woman, it is a humiliating consciousness that after all I am *but* woman, I *must* occasionally speak of myself, my wishes, my hopes, my loves, and my hate. Partly necessity, partly convenience, have rendered you my confidant, and I seek, in speaking unrestrainedly in your presence, that relief which every day human nature requires. Do you think this is a state of things with which a man may feel abundantly flattered?"

"*I* do," replied Mr. Stark; "it is sufficient to my ambition to be necessary to Lady Cleveland."

All the scorn of her proud spirit was expressed by a look, but it was not Mr. Stark's policy to be affected by a contempt which did not manifest itself in words.

"You," resumed Lady Sophia, unobservant of his sickly compliment; "you, who have not the heart to feel one strong emotion, can comprehend nothing of my hatred for Lady Darley. When I heard in Italy that she was about to achieve for her niece the first alliance in England, for so the surface-judging world deemed Sir Greville Cleveland, I put an oath on record in heaven, that if man were to be won by woman's effort, Cleveland should be mine. Believe not, Mr. Stark, that love for him formed one single actuating impulse of my conduct. He had already injured me beyond forgiveness. No! in avenging myself on others, it was something to feel that I avenged myself on him also; and have I *not* been avenged?"

Her dark eyes flashed with terrible expression, as she observed the acquiescing bow of her servile auditor.

"The very act of separating him from a woman who might have loved him, who possibly did love him, was revenge. But when I added to this the final triumph of binding him for ever to a woman who had, for ten years, been the all-complying, the subservient, the *tender* wife of a man she loathed! Great Heaven, how a woman's soul must be debased, her heart seared, her feelings perverted, her instincts trampled on, before she could become this very wretched thing, a ten years' hypocrite! Well, well, Cleveland's misdoings were at length amply, most amply revenged! A little allurement, a few tears, a few protestations, and he, the *intellectual giant*, wavered, and wavering, was won! The very same want of principle which divided us before, united us at length and for ever."

"But Lady Darley," urged Mr. Stark, who was resolute in allowing no opportunity to escape of penetrating mysteries, which he might hereafter render subservient to his interests.

"Yes, Lady Darley. In my very early days she and I exhibited the effects of instinctive antipathy. The discipline of a rigid education had not qualified me to become one of her *coterie*, *then* the most distinguished coterie of the world. Delighted with her softness, her suavity, her polish, my inexperience led me to a very pertinacious courtship of Lady Darley's intimacy; but she, by no means captivated by the stiffness and formality resulting from the narrowness into which my mind had been educated, contrived to keep me at a distance, which, while she skilfully avoided the odium of repulsing a youthful aspirant, continually made me understand, 'Hitherto shalt thou come and no farther!' *My* day, however, arrived at last. My *naïvete* attracted Cleveland—do not understand me to depreciate the power of my beauty, *that* too had its spell, perhaps the very contrast between me and himself contributed to inspire the deep sentiment which, I verily believe, he *did* once feel. Ah!" said Lady Sophia, with a sigh, "after all, those young feelings had their charms, and *I* too may say with one *as* world stained,

> There's not a joy this world can give
> Like that it takes away,
> When the glow of earthly thought declines
> With feeling's dull decay.'

Even then, however, Lady Darley was my enemy. She ridiculed my rustic notions, as she called them, my Puritanical strictness, and predicted a reaction which might hereafter leave my husband to regret the *first* error. I had numerous good-natured friends happy to enjoy the pleasure of inflicting mortification by repeating all these criticisms, and when the day of reaction did come, as come it will to all who are trammelled by forms instead of principles, don't you think it was something, even after ten years' *not* patient waiting, to deal out retribution to Lady Darley?"

"The unkindness of the prediction should have been forgiven for the sake of its truth," said Stark, who never lost the opportunity of making a point.

"*Truth!* It was a truth a child might have discovered. A human being, unless cursed or blessed with a very timid mind, who begins by believing too much, ends by believing too little. On this point, however, Cleveland—the skeptical Cleveland—has no ground for complaint. He himself infused into *my* mind the first fatal doubt, and 'the fruit he reaps is of the tree he planted.'"

"The wisdom of doubting is precisely the wisdom man generally would deny to woman," said Mr. Stark, with the air of a person enunciating an aphorism.

"Because, in all ways, her faith is his security," said Lady Sophia, "as in her ignorance consists his superiority. Subsequently, when domesticated at Rome, what constant matter of curious speculation was offered to a mind that dared to be speculative! So many trappings, so much mummery, such hardly concealed jugglery, environed the thing the priesthood and the priestridden called religion, that in learning to apply to it its own degraded, prostrating name *superstition*, one was in danger of forgetting, one did forget, that the word *faith* was applicable to anything true or elevated."

"And having once attained to that conclusion, from what an 'infinite deal' of restraint one is emancipated!"

"But after all," said Lady Sophia—"for while we are

philosophizing we may as well consider the question in all its bearings—is woman the happier for the removal of those restraints? Does your definition of happiness, Mr. Stark, place me among its possessors?"

"*Happiness!* As Pilate asked of truth, so do I ask of happiness, *what is it?*"

"The same answer would have satisfied your question and his," said Lady Sophia, with an expression of such peculiar pain as to startle her companion into something like compassion. "Happiness lies in truth; they, at least, deem thus, who can declare the unutterable bitterness which taints the prosperity of the most prosperous, who have ventured to seek her in falsehood."

"These are but names, however," said Stark, with a shrug. "Those who have made the political laws, by virtue of which the few rule, and the many obey; those who have made the conventional laws, by which the links of society are bound together, have established a certain arbitrary code, in which they have assigned to certain actions the terms best suited to their own convenience. In fact, good and bad are but artificial results, existing only in relation to our position, abstractedly, nonentities. A man who lives in utter solitude can neither steal nor murder; is he, therefore, good? A patriot kills a tyrant and frees a people; is he, therefore, good? A patriot, *against* public opinion, attempts the life of a tyrant, and is torn to pieces by wild horses; is he good or bad? History, the mighty fiction, pronounces on actions by events. If the American war had had a different termination, Washington would have been a warning instead of a model. We who dare judge and examine, are not to be duped by words."

"Experience, experience, Mr. Stark," said Lady Sophia, bitterly. "Our own hearts give the lie to our sophistry. We know, we feel, there is something to be grasped which we cannot grasp; something to be found which we cannot find; to be done, and we do it not; to be avoided, and we hug it to our bosoms. Has it ever occurred to you to endeavour to comprehend what *remorse* may be?"

"Never," said Mr. Stark, composedly. "Considering the brief duration of life, I do endeavour, on principle, to occupy every moment with pleasurable sensations 'doing or suffering.' Remorse! what is it? If it be regret for having thrown away a portion of the past in pursuit of the folly of which the present assures me, I understand it. I am too philosophic, however, to suffer even that regret to be mingled with bitterness. I mitigate it by the resolution to shape the future by the new rules my wisdom has acquired. Placed on this globe by accident, controlling neither the day of our birth nor the day of our death, unable to direct or arrest the progress of circumstances, whose irresistible impulse hurries us whither we know not, and often where we would not, the victim of events which compel on us a line of conduct contrary to all we had previously marked out for ourselves, what avails it to us to shape for ourselves rules of action we can never apply, or to judge ourselves by principles adapted only to free agents, which we are not? Remorse is a mode of mind in the highest degree unnatural, considered with relation to us, the bondsmen of an invincible necessity."

"And yet, neither effort, nor argument, nor reflection, can chase the phantom, and we are driven to a crowd where there is no room for it; or to an opiate which enables us to shut our eyes upon it," said Lady Sophia. "I remember once being struck by the force of an argument advanced by an author against the eternity of punishment; that, according to the present constitution of the human mind, pain could not be eternal, because, such is the force of habit, that it becomes at length indifference; the ordinary state of its being, therefore, not felt, since we feel only by the succession of sensations. Now that man never knew remorse—never had a remembrance, the poignancy of which was not mitigated by time—never imagined what it was to escape from the one dreadful idea, for a brief moment, to feel it recur with additional horror, like what one experiences on the first awakening from sleep, after some great sorrow. In fact, if death were not a state of nothingness, remorse must surely be the worm that never dies. Do you think that I have never regretted the most rigid restraints imposed on my youth, when I have felt the more galling bondage of the present? Happy they who are content to be bound by the safe errors of the world's narrowest prejudices!"

"It is strange that your ladyship should be the person to convince me that novelty is *not* charming in every shape. This is a mood to be painfully regretted by one so devoted to your interests."

"Why, in truth, it would hardly furnish matter for an epigram," said Lady Sophia, with an entire change of manner. "Let us amuse ourselves by contemplating my fair sister-in-law, the beautiful, the intellectual, the conjugal Mrs. Stracey Hamilton, a convert to our theory of emancipation. Do you think it would have a tendency to increase her present stock of—happiness, let us call it, for so she herself would, I suppose, term the illusion that surrounds her?"

"Even to dream of the possibility requires a stretch of imagination beyond me. She exists in the comfortable belief that her creed is truth, and its deductions certainties, real, tangible certainties, which will neither deceive nor escape from her. Not daring to overstep the limits prescribed by her religion, she rejoices in the consolatory assurance that she is among the wise, regarding the great stars which shine over the gulf of daring speculation as lights that lead astray. Even in matters of very inferior moment, I have heard poor Lady Darley regret the unpersuadableness of her niece."

"*Poor* Lady Darley!" exclaimed Lady Sophia. "What a pleasure to be able to say 'Poor Lady Darley!' and oh, the yet greater pleasure of saying it to herself! Would that she were among us in this her day of humiliation!"

"It is to escape that sort of commiseration, I suspect, that Lady Darley buries herself in such rigorous seclusion. Mrs. Hamilton *sentimentalizes* much on the occasion, and eulogizes with considerable emphasis the resignation with which the calamity is borne; a resignation kept so carefully from the eye of the world you perceive! I suppose, now, it would be consistent with her creed to find a moral good in this bodily evil. It will be charity to wish Lady Darley the benefit of a conversion."

"To a woman to whom the world was all, what a dreadful trial! the weariness of a solitude without occupation! To-day the twin brother of yesterday, and to-morrow of to-day! nothing can prolong her life but to become blue or devout, and I question whether her vocation be to either alternative!"

"It will be easier to turn Darley House into a Methodist chapel than into a museum," said Mr. Stark. "Lady Darley is a wealthy dowager; on the consideration of an adequate legacy, I would offer my services in either line."

"The appointment is already filled up, I fancy. There are certain sects who have women preachers, are there not? Now Mrs. Warren would answer the purpose admirably well: you have heard of Mrs. Warren? A prosing old woman, ages ago my *gouvernante*, and until her marriage, Miss Vernon's *chaperone*. After all, Stracey made a scandalous alliance; neither birth nor fortune."

"Lady Darley's in reversion, possibly. Report spoke largely of her liberality to the bride."

"Report was in good humour; it is always tenderly disposed to those who are never likely again to awaken its echo, just as we push into the abyss of ignominy a man unfortunate or imprudent enough to be detected in flagrant wrong, and then look down on him with an eye of commiseration, because we are sure we shall not be entreated to lend a helping hand. We are in an excellent world!"

"The world has its flowers yet, and while within my reach I will not quarrel with them."

"*Revenons á nos moutons*," said Lady Sophia, after a short pause. "These Hamiltons—*gènant* as intimacy with them will be, it suits me to cultivate it; albeit Stracey, I suspect, will endeavour to preserve a certain distance between his too amiable sister, and his most correct wife. He will fear that I shall labour to impress on her the foolish idea that women really are not mere machines, but may occasionally be permitted to decide on the agreeable and disagreeable, without looking through the spectacles with which a husband may be pleased to invest their eyesight. However, if war is to be between us, let Colonel Hamilton look to it; *nous verrons!*" And her ladyship's cheek flushed, and her eye sparkled.

"But the lady appears at present to sustain the rôle of Griselda. It is quite edifying to witness the deferential air with which she listens to the opinions of her husband."

There was a pause, and Lady Sophia was thoughtful. Her remark, when she broke the silence, revealed what had been the theme of her meditations.

"After all, if not capable of love, why did she marry Stracey? What had he to tempt her ambition? neither title nor wealth. They commenced with the prospect of retirement, and the late addition to his fortune was a legacy as unexpected by himself as by all his family."

"You must allow her to have suffered much from the loss of Sir Greville Cleveland, and this, too, without giving her credit for any extraordinary susceptibility," said Stark. "There never yet lived a woman of any talent who was not ambitious. In neither sex can there be talent without ambition. She had fixed her eyes on an eminence, the path to which lay smooth before her; she was approaching the summit when an obstacle intervened, which increased until she was compelled to retrace her steps, and sink into her original obscurity. Was this nothing? On the contrary, an incalculable disappointment. Do you think she was likely to undervalue the means of escaping the mortification of the world's dread laugh?"

"A very satisfactory solution of the difficulty, could you but prove that she was within hearing of that dread laugh," said Lady Sophia; "but she had the wisdom to remove herself into a solitude it could not penetrate."

"Did not the tidings of Sir Greville's marriage and your ladyship's triumph penetrate that solitude? When whole columns of the daily press were filled with the history of your bridal splendours and bridal triumphs, do you think no pang was felt?"

"Allow me, in turn, to question. Do you think they were read? Do you imagine our fashionable journals are particularly inquired after, in the plain country seats or humble cottages, which contribute so large a proportion of the population of Great Britain? Or, to descend from generals to particulars, do you believe that, at *such* a crisis, the eye of the chaperone would not *first* glance over the said journals, and carefully put aside any which contained the means of wounding the feelings of her *protegée—a protegée*, too, beloved with all the romantic warmth that seems to have taken refuge with her class, as its last abiding-place on earth? No, no! There is no explaining her marriage with Stracey, but by supposing her capable of something like the folly of a second attachment—as if the first had not been painful enough!"

"Some one of her friends—Lady Darley, possibly—was kind enough to propagate in her behalf the monstrous fiction that she—she—Miss Vernon—dissatisfied with Sir Greville's conduct or principles, had refused him, and that he had betaken himself to Lady Sophia Cleveland for consolation!"

"True in part, but not wholly," said Lady Sophia, more calmly than Mr. Stark expected. "It suited the stilts of magnanimity on which Miss Vernon chose to exhibit herself to the wondering eyes of human nature, to relinquish her claims on Cleveland's honour as soon as she suspected the wanderings of Cleveland's heart."

"*Heart?*"

"Yes, *heart*—the world may have petrified it, but once Cleveland had a heart;" and Lady Sophia breathed one sincere sigh of feeling to the memory of the past.

"You persist, then, in believing that Mrs. Hamilton is really attached—as the phrase goes—to her husband?"

"*Husband!*—well—yes—not to cavil about a homely word—attached, certainly; but not so entirely, perhaps, as to escape the melancholy softness with which one recollects that dream of one's youth which 'lingering haunts the greenest spot of memory's waste.' It will be a matter of some interest to me to behold her first meeting with Cleveland. If Stracey exhibit but 'the twentieth part of one poor scruple' of jealousy, their lot is marred for ever. His pride would never forgive her who inflicted the self-humiliation, nor hers the distrust which ventured to doubt her."

"You have looked deeply into their hearts?"

"With the keenness of hate," said Lady Sophia, earnestly. "Talk not of the intense watchfulness of love for the interests of its object; commend *me* to the vigilance of hate. There is no sharpening of the perception like that produced by an intense, insatiable, unappeasable desire to wound. Not the slightest gesture, even to the falling or the raising of an eyelid, will escape my observation, or be too minute to convey a token. Yes—nothing shall prevent my seeing the first meeting between them," she added, with a sudden glow; "I will, for once, exhibit myself in a *tête-à-tête* drive with Cleveland. That will give us a domestic air, and Stracey will congratulate himself on the effect of the admonitions for which I used to be indebted to him."

"It has been whispered that Lady Sophia Cleveland is omnipotent with all but with him whose name is honoured by being also hers," said Stark, with his peculiar sneer.

"The whisperers might have added, that that is the precise quarter in which Lady Sophia Cleveland never troubles herself with any exertion of her influence," said her ladyship, haughtily, brooking, with difficulty, even after her unlimited confidences, that Mr. Stark should venture to hint at a truth of which, she was too conscious, and which, if it did not wound her heart, mortified her vanity; and this, to a woman of her character, was probably the less tolerable grievance of the two.

The door of the boudoir opened; the cheek of Lady Sophia crimsoned at the presumption of the unannounced intruder It was Sir Greville Cleveland himself.

"I thought your ladyship had been alone," he said, slightly bowing to Mr. Stark, now as ever his aversion. "I have just heard of the arrival of your brother and—" a slight pause—a scarcely perceptible change of voice—"and Mrs. Hamilton. Were you aware of their intended removal from Scotland, or have they declined our hospitality?"

"It was not offered," said Lady Sophia, hastily. "Stracey and I are never cordial, and it would not be agreeable to me to have him an inmate in my house."

"It would have been a pleasure to me to see him in *mine*," said Sir Greville, with haughty emphasis; and Mr. Stark, who had no desire to behold the bursting of the impending storm, nad the tact to rise and make an effort to withdraw.

"Do not go, Mr. Stark," said Lady Sophia, "I have a thousand commissions to give you, and Sir Greville will not remain a moment."

"Good-morning, Mr. Stark," said Sir Greville, with a manner not to be mistaken, and—Mr. Stark was gone.

"Before resuming the subject I came here to discuss with you, I cannot help expressing my surprise at finding Mr. Stark *tête-à-tête* with you *here*, where you profess to admit only a privileged few."

"Of whom Mr. Stark is one," said Lady Sophia, flippantly.

"I interfere so little with your ladyship's arrangements, that you seem to be in danger of forgetting I possess the right of doing so," said Sir Greville, with a very *translateable* expression of displeasure in his eye. "You know that I have a particular objection to your intimacy with Mr. Stark; it is neither dignified nor creditable. He is a mere pander to the meanest passions of those who pay him for his services."

"He is amusing, which explains everything," said Lady Sophia.

"A most unworthy explanation," said Sir Greville, half grieved, half disgusted. "One of the base herd who go from house to house gathering and scattering scandal in their progress, caricaturing their last hostess for the amusement of their present, and so on in an everlasting circle! While you permit yourself to be gratified by his sarcastic remarks on your intimates, do you suppose that you alone are spared?

While you applaud the epigram which so keenly satirizes the foibles or the vices of your neighbour, do you imagine that you are not made to afford equal matter of amusement to her?"

"*Ainsi va le monde*," interrupted Lady Sophia, with an impatience not affected. "For Heaven's sake, spare me a lecture, or reserve it until I make a demand on your purse, which will be immediately."

"*More* money!" said Sir Greville, with undisguised surprise. "Even *your* unbounded expenditure cannot already have exhausted last week's supply."

"It has," said Lady Sophia, angrily; "once for all, understand that I claim a right to the unquestioned disposal of my own income."

"For your own sake, I will not acknowledge such a claim. If it be possible, I would preserve you from sinking into that most shameful, most execrable of all characters, a female gambler."

"Gambler!" repeated Lady Sophia, turning visibly pale even beneath her rouge.

"Yes, gambler, Sophia," said Sir Greville, gravely, but more gently than before. "Well may you shrink—well may you tremble, to know that all your early promise has sunk to this!"

"Remember *who* first blighted my early promise," said Lady Sophia, with bitterness. "*You—you—Cleveland*—preaching morality to *me*—to *me*—to whom *you* presented the first dark realization of crime my youthful mind had ever contemplated! Silence to *me*, Cleveland, and carry your morality to those who do not know you. It is my misfortune that *I* do."

"A misfortune voluntarily incurred—*courted* by your ladyship," said Cleveland, with a flushed brow. "I recovered my happiness, and was on the eve of securing the best, the fairest guarantee for deserving it, when you, like my evil genius, came between me and my hopes, dragging me back to the wretched world of vice and folly I would—how very fain!—have quitted!"

"Heroics always pass my understanding," said Lady Sophia, regaining her composure in proportion as the perturbation of her husband became apparent. "If you drove away Mr. Stark, who is at least amusing, for the purpose of an exhibition of this kind, I owe you small thanks for the favour."

"Happiness I have long since ceased to hope for at your hands, but I *will* exact from you a regard for my honour—for the preservation of my dignity in the eyes of the world. You *may* make me miserable, you shall not make me ridiculous! beware how you provoke me to exert the power of controlling you."

"Threaten not me, Cleveland," said Lady Sophia, with calm defiance. "I fear not, care not, for living man—least for *you*. I am not your dupe, neither are you mine; we know each other; our wisdom will be to keep that knowledge from the world. Leave me to my own devices, I do not interfere with yours."

Cleveland walked up and down the highly decorated apartment in perturbed silence: altercations of this kind were not new to his experience, and he was not ignorant that the results had generally led to more firmly establishing the independence of Lady Sophia, and consequently to the endangering of that fair reputation in the eyes of the world which was absolutely necessary to his existence. Affecting as he did to scorn the homage of the satellites of fashion, he had never outraged their usages by his caprice, or violated their prejudices by any daring aberration, until he had first put forth his feelers, to ascertain that his footing was secure, that he might venture to do so with impunity; that by arousing the curiosity of his worshippers, he obtained a more elevated position in their temple. He affected to disregard the world—*his* world—as a means of securing its homage, and his success had attested the shrewdness of the observations on which the experiment had been founded. But when he married, he deprived himself of many of the adjuncts by which he had achieved his triumph. Fashionable mothers, blooming beauties, no longer courted the smiles of a man who had not a hand to bestow; the struggle had ceased, for the prize was won. Cleveland House, it is true, was as magnificent as ever. Brilliant crowds filled its stately saloons; genius flew to the shelter of the patronage that issued thence, but the presiding genius of the scene was changed. Lady Sophia had usurped the throne of her husband; and so gracefully did she wield the sceptre, that the glories of the former reign were forgotten in the elegances—the novelties, of the present.

Yes—*novelties*, for the multitude—even the aristocratic mob—love change. All the usages of Cleveland House were familiar to those who thronged its halls: its scrupulous etiquettes, strictly enforced by its master, who ventured, elsewhere, to violate all. Lady Sophia was the most daring of innovators. She threw down—she set up—she arranged—she deranged. Sir Greville, who was wont to consider the house of his fathers as part of himself, ventured a gentle remonstrance—a whispered hint—the shadow of a frown; but Lady Sophia exhibited her designs—her plans—to a party of the choicest spirits of the day assembled round his board, and the universal voice was in her favour. Then her ladyship had more dilettanti jargon than he had. She possessed, moreover, in perfection the feminine accomplishment of pouring forth a deluge of eloquence in defence of her own views of things, which, if it did not convince, at least overwhelmed. She had the art also of insinuating the ridiculous; that is, though she was too well bred to quiz her husband herself, she gently opened the eyes of others to the ridicule of the position he was maintaining. Sir Greville, for the first time in his life, felt what it was to writhe beneath "the world's dread *smile*." In the first few months of their wedded life, Lady Sophia had completely established her ascendency, but she had gained her points by steps so imperceptible, that Sir Greville had hardly felt his degradation until the sceptre was actually wrested from his grasp.

Time, that mighty worker of miracles, revealed at length to Cleveland what he had gained—more painful still, the value of the pearl he had cast away.

"To resume the business which brought me here, Lady Sophia," said Cleveland at length, "it is my desire that your brother Stracey and his wife should, at least, be offered the accommodations of this house, and I request you to make this sacrifice to propriety immediately."

"I make no sacrifices to propriety at the expense of my inclination. I do not choose that my brother's wife—your whilome ladye love—should bring the splendour of her charms into close contact with mine. Do not be alarmed; I shall make her acquaintance because it suits me, but I shall not put you to the pain of making comparisons which may probably lead you to very unsatisfactory suspicions of the existence of your own taste or wisdom. Stark says Mrs. Stracey Hamilton is lovelier than ever—and I—can you pay *me* the same compliment, Cleveland?" said Lady Sophia, looking maliciously in his face.

Cleveland turned away in disgust.

"I meant to propose to you," resumed her ladyship, "that we should go together, in the dignity of our connubial state, to pay our dutiful respects to our well-beloved brother and sister. To-morrow morning—will that suit you?"

"Yes," said Sir Greville; "the presence of your brother will be my security for your propriety: shame to both of us that it should be needed."

"You are welcome to your share of it, but I beg you will exempt me. And now—pray act on the hint—whither shall you betake yourself?"

"To the nursery; may I ask when your ladyship last entered its precincts?"

"I cannot accurately remember, but then consider Fanchon is no inducement to me. I give you credit for your good taste, for she is really pretty enough to excuse your condescension."

"Whatever may be my vices or my follies, want of parental affection is not among them," said Cleveland, with unusual emotion. "Would to Heaven that the absence of all natural feeling on the part of one of their parents, did not render it necessary that my children should experience a double proportion of tenderness from the other!"

"So overflowing a proportion, that part of it extends even to their attendant!" said Lady Sophia, with a sneer. "You are welcome, however, to the flirtation, for I assure you nothing could tempt me to the vulgarity of being jealous."

How untrue! and she was conscious of the untruth; yet she spoke without embarrassment, for she knew the falsehood of the humiliating accusation she made, and felt that there was but one woman on earth whose influence over Cleveland she really dreaded, and that was the woman from whom she had separated him.

Sir Greville *did* go to the nursery, where, intrusted to the care of their attendants, his two children were literally exiled from the presence of their mother. The eldest, a girl, was a lovely and healthy child; but the youngest, the boy —the heir of the House of Cleveland—whose birth Sir Greville had hailed as ensuring, in his own immediate line, the continuance of the honours of his race—delicate and sickly, depended for existence on incessant care. All that wealth could procure for him, Sir Greville did procure; but the child needed that which wealth cannot purchase—for which no stranger can furnish a substitute—the unwearied, watchful tenderness of a mother's love. With an aching heart the unhappy father listened to the feeble, painful cry of his boy; and with remorse "sharper than the serpent's tooth," he felt, that in outraging the woman whose principles—whose feminine feelings—would have ensured his children the fostering nurture of maternal love, he had incurred the righteous punishment of seeing the pride of his heart withering before his eyes—unpitied, untended, unthought of by the unnatural being his infatuation had selected as the mother of his heir.

With all Sir Greville Cleveland's worldliness, his heart had not yet entirely shut out the conviction that affection is the best blessing of human life. He had quaffed deeply of the draught of pleasure, of ambition, of passion; but the unappeasable yearning for love—that evidence of a nature not wholly lost—had never yet been gratified. No exertion of pride or self-love could effectually blind him to the fact, that he had been his own destroyer; that he had wantonly put from him the means of happiness; had turned away from the light of the star which shone so benignly on his path, to follow the misguiding meteor which but led astray. To escape the haunting consciousness of unredeemable folly, he had rushed with renewed avidity into the pursuits—the trifling or the serious pursuits—of the multitude; seeking everywhere a substitute for the lost blessing, unwilling to believe that the whole universe has none to offer. The worthiest, the most dignified occupations of the intellect, do not suffice to the happiness of men. A universal love to mankind, an active desire to advance the interests of his race, an extensive benevolence diffusing his bounties on all sides, cannot satisfy the incipient craving for sympathy. There is within us a voice which, if it awaken no responsive echo, is silenced for ever; and man, "not born to live alone," finds his noblest purposes perish, his best intents but vanity, his existence a toilsome progress through a barren desert. The birth of his children had awakened in the breast of Sir Greville new hopes, new affections; and as he bent over the couch of his young, he had occasionally hoped to find with them a haven where, in the evening of life, his painful career might find a soothing close. But it is the punishment of a depraved moral appetite, of a vitiated enjoyment of the world, to find in innocent affections no substitute for the stimulating food to which it has been accustomed. Sir Greville continued to love his children as the sources of future comfort to himself; he continued his daily visits to their nursery, to encourage their attendants to proper vigilance; but he lived with and for the world still, a dissipated, a disappointed, and a wretched man, with the sleepless consciousness at his heart, that he was daily meriting the punishment of him who, having many talents, abused all.

Lady Sophia did not recover her tranquillity with the departure of Sir Greville. Fearlessly as she had defied him, remorselessly as she had trampled on his feelings, deeply as she had humbled his pride of heart, it was now her turn, in solitude, to quail. Indifferent to the husband she had so assiduously courted, so hardly gained; negligent of the children to whom, in giving them birth, she had become responsible for as much happiness as infancy can enjoy, she had not courage to despise the world in the throng of which alone she silenced the tormenting voice within. Even when she so haughtily disregarded his accusations, her heart trembled as it admitted their truth, and prompted the sudden question whether, if so far enlightened, he knew no more? No, surely, he did not, could not! Did not she *still* preside over the splendours of Cleveland House—share his name. Would these things continue to be, but that Sir Greville's knowledge stopped at a certain point? Accident must have led to the discovery of so much, for virtually separated, each having a distinct set, distinct associates, meeting only casually within the vortex of the world, it was hardly possible that he was aware who constituted the coterie with which she had become inextricably involved. Perhaps, after all, her demand for money had excited in his mind the suspicion of her gaming; little guessing to what extent! how deeply she had drunk of that, the only excitement which afforded her perfect escape from herself.

The enormous income of Sir Greville had not sufficed to his lavish expenditure, nor did the addition made to it by his marriage free him from his embarrassments. Moreover, Lady Sophia's large fortune had been so tied up by the prudence of Colonel Hamilton, as to be secured to their younger children, uninjured by the possible extravagance or folly of their parents. Lady Sophia had already so largely anticipated her own income, as to feel all the pain of pecuniary involvements. A desperate effort, the courage of the moment, had produced her application to Sir Greville, but his accusation terrified her from its repetition, and it was with feelings better imagined than described, that she read the following note from Mr. Stark.

"My dear Lady Sophia,

"All my representations can wring from R. no more than three thousand for the diamonds. He says there is a flaw in the central stone, which considerably diminishes its value. The paste substitute will cost fifty guineas, which, under the unfortunate circumstances, is a large deduction. Lady Paul Lorimer would, I am persuaded, give twice the sum, but then the *exposé!* Do not think so lightly of my discretion as to think that I have given the slightest hint in that quarter. I do but throw out the suggestion for your especial consideration; unless you should approve another plan which an accident enables me to propose.

"It happened, unfortunately as I thought, that Lord Vere found his way into R.'s private room, just as I was placing the bracelet so as to give it the full advantage of a proper fall of light. Whether he recognised it I cannot say, but its peculiar form renders it more than probable. He had too much tact, however, to evince any interest beyond the proper admiration, inquired of R. whether it was to be sold, and offered to make the purchase on the terms of the owner. Shall he have it? Lord Vere is too much your slave to permit any uneasiness on the ground of such a trifle's being permitted to fall into his hands. I have promised R. that a decision shall be sent to him by five this evening."

That decision cost Lady Sophia a severe struggle. She felt that it was the first step of the "facilis discensus Averni." Would it not be wiser to take R.'s three thousand than the larger sum from such a quarter? What would be the result? Should she once again apply seriously to Sir Greville? No, no; *that* at least was a humiliation not to be thought of! Lady Paul Lorimer; no, she detested Lady Paul. Besides, Cleveland was too intimate there not to recognise the toy, his own present on the birth of their firstborn. After all, if it were a *galanterie* of Lord Vere's, no particular mischief was involved in it. If it were his generous foible so to dispose of his wealth—what then? Besides, she was not necessarily compelled to know that he had been the purchaser. Stark must manage all that. And instructions were despatched to Mr. Stark accordingly.

The money was in Lady Sophia's possession—had passed into the hands of her noble *female* creditor; her present embarrassments were at an end, yet her night was one of wretched splendour. She was tormented with an incessant curiosity to examine the jewels of every woman around her, in the dread that she should among them recognise her own. But surely, if the real sentiments of Lord Vere were what she had so much reason to believe, he would not betray her! Yet what human being was to be relied on? False to herself, what reason had she to believe that others would be true to her? Lord Vere had in his power such a means of gratifying his vanity, if that were not under the dominion of some stronger passion!

The next day terminated her doubts and her fears. A carefully sealed envelope lay on her magnificent toilette, placed there by her woman, who had received it, she said, from Mr. Stark. The heart of Lady Sophia throbbed with an unwonted pulsation. She put the packet aside until able to open it alone. The moment came at length, after a weary and unaccustomed longing for solitude. The bracelet sparkled before her with its wonted brilliance. A three-cornered note of the brightest rose colour, and breathing of the most delicious perfumes, lay upon it.

CHAPTER IV.

"*To Mrs. Warren.*

"As if there needed a monitor to remind me of writing to my dearest friend! Ever since I despatched my last bulletin to the cottage, Stracey has been urging me to report of our daily doings to our common mother; and if I have not acted in obedience to his wishes, it has been because I had nothing to communicate more important than our settling ourselves in Portland Place, and receiving quite as many cards as convince us we shall not find this vast metropolis a desert, even though we inhabit so unorthodox a locale of it. But now, that interview has taken place, which so strongly excited your interest. Sir Greville and Lady Sophia Cleveland drove from this door an hour since; Stracey has flown to one of those places instituted to render home an unnecessary comfort to man, his club; and I have passed a short time in looking into my own heart that I may endeavour to describe what my feelings are and were, in a situation which was sufficiently singular.

"Ever since Stracey first resolved on coming to town, I have been accustomed to consider the renewal of my acquaintance with Sir Greville Cleveland as a matter of necessity. *You* know how strongly the prospect of being even remotely connected with him operated, in the first instance, against Stracey's suit; how I shrank from marrying the brother of Sir Greville's wife; and how your arguments, his pleadings, were insufficient, until the voice within my heart told me loudly that I was destroying my own happiness with *his*. That the love which unites me to my husband is a sentiment of no ordinary strength, has been sufficiently evinced by the fact of its overcoming an obstacle which did certainly once appear insurmountable. After our marriage, during the happy, happy year in the Highlands, so wide an interval, both of this material world and the immaterial one within, separated us from the hemisphere of fashion and its population, that I rejoiced in the security of having escaped all possible collision with the Clevelands. To relinquish that dear abode, cost me more pain than I would care to confess to any one but you; but I offered no opposition, because Stracey seemed to desire it so earnestly, and acquiescence in all his wishes is not more my duty than my pleasure. And, indeed, there were moments when I thought that retirement, that entire living for each other, which was so abundant a felicity to me, did not suffice for his. I fancied that the desire for a wider field of action, the impulse of his sex, became too urgent to be subdued; and that the occasional gloom I remarked in him, originated in the unsatisfactoriness of our uneventful life. All this, you know, is natural; and if I was foolish enough to feel a very slight pang on first suspecting the real state of things, I was wise enough to repress every expression of my secret sorrow, and to enter, with apparent alacrity, into his plans for emerging into public life, that scene of bitterness and disappointment, where *one* successful man grasps all his ambition covets, to find he has chased a skeleton; and ten thousand others never reach the goal. This, however, is but a woman's view of the matter: man is educated for action—we for endurance; and the same verb is conjugated very differently, you know, in the active and passive voice. Well, when Stracey was really returned for ——shire, I began to accustom myself to the certainty of meeting Sir Greville and Lady Sophia, and of maintaining such an intercourse with them as befitted the relation in which we stood to each other, or rather, as the world would expect us to maintain. None are better aware than you, that Stracey's intimacy with his sister has long been a mere sacrifice to appearances; for when there are no common principles, feelings, modes of conduct, how can the mere accident of consanguinity suffice to ensure friendship? Happy are the families where characters harmonize as features resemble; but in how few instances does this occur! I was quite sure that Stracey, far from desiring, would not even approve anything like a confidential friendship between me and Lady Sophia; and I thought that, by intrenching myself within the *cheveaux-de-frize* of perfect politeness, I could give such a tone to our intercourse as would save me from any of those embarrassing allusions which I had no reason to suppose Lady Sophia would, otherwise, have the delicacy to avoid.

"I will not affect to say that I thought on seeing Sir Greville with indifference. It was impossible to forget how we had last met—how we last parted; and it is one thing to cease to love, but another to forgive the selfishness which has caused you to suffer. I could see, with thankfulness, the benevolence of that Providence which has preserved me from the misery of a union with a man whose idol was himself, which had given me in exchange the warm affection of a heart glowing with love for its Maker, and benevolence toward his species. But I could not justify the *instrument;* I could not cease to condemn the wrong, although up to that might be traced my happiness. He contemplated no such results; and he did that greatest injury to woman—he despoiled my heart of its first fresh feelings—its *first love:* he turned into gall that which ought to be the honeydrop of life: he robbed me of months of happiness, rendering me a creature useless to others, and burdensome to myself. The world laughs at such sorrows; but I have not yet reached that period of life where feeling changes into satire. I still look back on all I can remember of my past existence: I have known sorrow under many shapes; but I still point to the wretchedness *he* inflicted, as the darkest cloud that has ever hung over my horizon. I felt that his presence would necessarily bring all the misery of the past more forcibly to my recollection, and that it would at least interrupt that calm frame of mind so essential to human happiness and human improvement; it would disturb the spirit of universal charity I had so sedulously cultivated, and excite feelings of dislike—perhaps of animosity, as painful to their subject as to their object. I *did*, therefore, shrink from the coming trial; and it required no small portion of reflection, no slight exertion of self-command, to enable me to meet it with firmness. To add to my discomfort, I fancied that the eye of Stracey was fixed on me with an expression strange to it, and, for a moment, the fearful question suggested itself, did he really believe it possible that I retained for Cleveland one shadow of a sentiment that might justify *him* in doubting whether the heart of his wife was entirely his? I stifled the fearful whisper in its birth. Stracey could not imagine so much evil of the wife of his bosom.

"I was in my boudoir when Sir Greville and Lady Sophia arrived. My husband himself came to warn me that they were in the house, probably because he did not choose that the eyes of a servant should witness the agitation that could not be entirely suppressed. I knew that I turned pale; and I regretted it the more, because I dreaded that Stracey might misinterpret the emotion which produced it. It lasted, however, but a few seconds. A moment's thought put me in possession of myself; and, with a composure that almost surprised me, I entered the drawingroom.

"The usual salutations were reciprocated; and I do not believe that a stranger's eye would have detected anything from which he might infer that we had once stood in so peculiar a relation to each other. We discussed ordinary topics with much apparent ease, and I felt every minute more assured. At length I inquired of Lady Sophia after her two children.

"'Sir Greville is much more able to give you the bulletin of the nursery than I am,' was her remarkable reply. 'I consider that I have done my duty to the little monkeys, by placing proper people about them; and I do not think myself obliged to sacrifice all my personal enjoyments, for the sake of acting police over their attendants.'

"'The indulgence of maternal affection is generally a great *personal enjoyment* to your sex,' said Stracey, of whom Lady Sophia evidently stands in awe, and whose courtesy, as you know, never leads him to suppress a wholesome truth. 'You, who study effect so much, Sophia, might at least think it *graceful* to be surrounded by your children.'

"'They derange my drapery,' said her ladyship, coolly, 'and they spoil my temper. Moreover, they confuse my understanding. The cry of a child is so distressing, that my nerves do not recover their tone for a month, if they accidentally happen to be assailed by it.'

"'Pray let us beg them sometimes,' said I; 'for I confess I am so hard hearted as to be able to endure the cry of a child, for the sake of the smile which succeeds it.'

"'They are quite at your disposal; you will take Cleveland's heart by storm, if you are good enough to patronise his children.'

"Stracey looked as I have never seen him look since our marriage; as I would not that he should look on me, for worlds. I believe I coloured a little; but Sir Greville was more discomposed than any of us. Lady Sophia smiled maliciously, evidently enjoying the *sensation* she had produced.

"'I trust I shall appreciate the kindness of Mrs. Hamilton,' said Sir Greville; 'it will, indeed, be something to have my children put in the way of resembling her. The earliest impressions are sometimes the most durable.'

"'Precisely,' said Lady Sophia, with a point that could not fail to be intelligible: but before we had time to feel it, she adroitly changed the subject, and was profuse in her civilities to myself, offering a thousand services which I did not know I required, and alluding to innumerable wants, where I suspected I possessed all that was needful. It is hardly possible to resist the fascination of her manner; and I think she chose, as the time of her departure, the precise moment when she perceived the favourable impression she was making had arrived at its highest point.

"Three years have elapsed since I saw them, and I think double that time could hardly have effected so striking a change as appears in both. The mental excitement attendant on a life of extreme fashion, may explain much of the haggard look in *her*—the *blasé* expression in him. But I imagine there are evidences of the existence of a deeper cause than this. In the midst of their vivacity there is no appearance of happiness. Their smiles are from the *head*, not the heart—a mask worn only in society. From what we hear, both from themselves and others, I suspect they are never alone; and there is an indefinable something about them, which seems to me to indicate plainly, that solitude for them would have an awfulness before the presence of which they would shrink.

"Love has left them long since. There is an air of mutual indifference about them not to be mistaken by the most superficial observer. You feel that they are incapable of comprehending the blessedness of domestic happiness, and that far from enjoying, they do not even covet it. They exist *in* and *for* the world—the world in its most conventional, most exclusive sense. Stracey sometimes hints at reports which occasionally reach him, of Cleveland's inclination to retire from the prominent position he has so long occupied in the arena of fashion; but Lady Sophia tenaciously holds a sovereignty, which none are hardy enough to dispute with her. The children I *do* long to see. It is impossible to avoid pitying their helpless, deserted condition; and Stracey is anxious that we should, as far as may be, supply the cares their heartless mother withholds. How *can* a mother thus neglect the first, the dearest of her duties? What a contrast to the devoted mother whom I so lately saw in the midst of her family—I mean my cousin Rachel! Can that religion be too rigid which thus causes to bud forth the holiest charities of life. Unfortunate as some of her domestic circumstances are, the fragile blossoms of happiness still bloom around her, for her heart is filled with the purest affections. Do not fail to see her occasionally; and report to me whether Mr. Fulton's fanaticism becomes, as I fear it will, more gloomy. Oh, that God's best blessing to man, the revelation of himself, should be thus perverted!

"We dine on Monday at Cleveland House: which may be considered our *début* on the theatre of gay life. How often shall I long for our dear Highland home, before I am again permitted to enjoy its sweets!

"CATHARINE HAMILTON."

CHAPTER V.

THE dinner at Cleveland House was not a stately, magnificent, and consequently dull banquet, at which the guests assembled to be dignified and disagreeable. *Ease*—that great charm of society when everybody is conscious of enjoyment without effort—the ease of elegant people, who are not, even accidentally, capable of a vulgarity or a rudeness—pervaded the whole entertainment. There were none present who, having a character for wit to support, were silent from the fear of falling beneath themselves. Even Mr. Stark was absent. They were persons of distinction, but not lions; unless Lord Vere had pretensions in that line.

Lord Vere was young, rich, handsome, and had achieved for himself a celebrity which more than sufficiently rewarded the pains its attainment had cost him. He had been in Greece; had been the familiar associate of Lord ——; had narrowly escaped death by shipwreck in the Archipelago; had the *reputation* of having invaded the harem of a Turk of distinction at Constantinople; and finally he had been the *compagnon de voyage* and friend, *par excellence*, of one of the most enchanting singers who ever quitted Italy to become hoarse in these foggy isles. Lord Vere, therefore, was *the fashion*, and it must be confessed, that he had substantial claims to the distinction. If not quite the supreme dictator which Sir Greville had been, *in his day*, he was, perhaps, more caressed; and as there was an alliance offensive and defensive between him and Lady Sophia, each shone not only with personal but reflected lustre. Sir Greville rather disliked Lord Vere, but that might perhaps originate in the same spirit that produces, in certain monarchs, dislike of the heir apparent. He dreaded that the throne he had been compelled to abdicate should be ascended by another, who might possibly wield the sceptre with more grace.

Chance placed Lord Vere, at dinner, next to Mrs. Hamilton, of whose person he took a very minute survey as soon as he ascertained he was in her immediate neighbourhood. The result probably was satisfactory, for he deemed her worthy of being honoured with a few consecutive sentences, spoken *sotto voce*, and with that peculiar air which seems to indicate not only that their purport is of great interest, but that there exists a mutual confidence between the speaker and listener. Considering that no more important communication was made than a remark on the unusual fineness of the weather and the fulness of London, Catharine may be forgiven if she was considerably amused at the inconsistency, and mistook her companion for a simpleton, whereas he was only a coxcomb.

Colonel Hamilton was, in society, what is called a quiet, gentlemanly fellow; that is, he went through all the *convenances* incumbent on him, conversed only by accident when he happened to meet with a neighbour suited to him, or to hear some topic discussed which particularly interested him; and had, consequently, leisure to observe the proceedings of anybody whom he thought worth the trouble of observing. There was much to attract his attention under present circumstances. He fancied that Lady Sophia found abundant leisure, in the intervals of a conversation she was sustaining with the Duke of ——, at her right hand, to scrutinize the proceedings of Catharine and Lord Vere, and he was quite sure that occasionally her cheek was flushed with a deeper carnation than any woman of taste would choose to acquire at her toilette. Moreover, conversant as he was with her countenance, and with the varying expressions that indicated emotion, slight as these indications were under the calmness of fashion—as the ripple of the water beneath the ice—he perceived that her feelings were really excited; that she was wounded, irritated, restless. Why? This was not quite so easy of solution, but Colonel Hamilton remembered something of the past, and feared for the possibilities of the future.

In the character of host, Sir Greville lost much of that air of constraint of which he could not divest himself, when compelled to come into more immediate contact with Catharine in a narrower circle. There were so many demands on his attention, and he could avoid addressing her, except in the necessary courtesies of the table, without betraying any particular embarrassment, or subjecting himself to remark. He could also please himself with looking at her occasionally without the fear of being observed. He could admire the pure glow on her cheek, the healthy radiance of her eye—healthy both in mind and in body—the perfection of her features, the mingling of sweetness, dignity, and intellect, which rendered her countenance one of the finest in the world, and he could wonder at his own infatuation that had "cast a pearl away richer than all its tribe," even while he affected to be occupied with a prosing old dowager whom he had been condemned to lead to table. But there was one eye which penetrated much that he desired to conceal; and that was Colonel Hamilton's. Catharine herself was too evidently and sincerely amused by the discrepancy between her companion's manner and matter, to afford a shadow of suspicion even to the most jealous scrutiny; and Stracey Hamilton was *not* jealous of her sentiments for others, even if it were his misery to doubt her love for himself. A sigh did occasionally escape him as he admitted the vain wish that *his* acquaintance with her had preceded Sir Greville's, that she had never known a warmer attachment than that perfect esteem, that trusting friendship, she felt for him. But he appreciated Catharine too highly, too truly, to believe that she, the wedded wife of a man she so justly honoured, was capable of indulging a lingering thought of tenderness for one whose whole conduct towards herself had been pervaded by the most unredeemed selfishness. Colonel Hamilton's reason again and again suggested that he ought to be satisfied with the knowledge that he was now preferred by his wife to all the world; but feelings not within the control of reason painfully reminded him that this did not suffice to the burning, consuming passion, which asked for devoted, undivided love, in return for its own idolatry.

"Do you think Cleveland altered since I have had the kindness to take charge of him?" asked Lady Sophia of Catharine in the course of the evening, as they sat together in a convenient niche which rather screened them from the rest, occupied, too, as all were with their own peculiar pursuit of pleasure.

Catharine felt one moment's embarrassment, but rapidly recovering her self-possession, replied by a quiet affirmation.

"Not for the better, I fear," said Lady Sophia, who was really amused by the novelty of an answer made in the naked simplicity of truth. "Time and fashion are such terrible destroyers of good looks! It is but just that one of the enemies should teach us the art of repairing their united ravages."

Catharine looked at the bloom which certainly "Nature's own sweet and cunning hand had *not* laid on."

"Sir Greville's appearance is—*faded*," said Catharine, hesitating for a word.

"Oh, my dear Mrs. Hamilton," said Lady Sophia, laughing, "that would perfectly destroy him! *Faded!* gracious Heaven, he would expire if he thought the veriest dowdy in existence but ventured to dream such a thing! And from *you!—you* for whom he entertains so profound a respect, so entire a—a—friendship—'that was the most unkind cut of all.' I really must make him aware of it: he will die beneath the infliction."

"As you please," said Catharine; "it was an unfortunate word, but I could find none better to express what I felt."

"Surely we must be in the palace of Truth!" said Lady Sophia, who scarcely knew whether she was more amused or chagrined. "If I appear to say anything particularly strange or disagreeable, pray attribute it to the irresistible influence of the place, and do not believe that my will is in fault."

"If I have said anything disagreeable, I have only to regret it," replied Catharine, unable to avoid the inference. "Do not forget that I have been a whole year learning to be savage in the Highlands. One cannot resist the effects of the wilderness."

"Oh, the novelty of the thing, like charity, will cover a multitude of sins, with *me*, at least. Cleveland is another person, and as we never happen to agree on any one point, it is hardly to be expected that we shall fall into an impossible unanimity now. I assure you I never make a quarrel with any person living for his beauty. That is his own affair. At forty a man must be *passé*. Cleveland always looks worst where Vere is. Apropos of Vere—did you ever happen to meet him before?"

"Never."

"Then I have had the pleasure of being the cause of your making a very distinguished acquaintance; decidedly the man of the day."

"And what invisible qualities have led Lord Vere to notoriety?" asked Catharine.

"If that were not Mrs. Hamilton's, I should think that it savoured of affectation. Lord Vere has been perfectly devoted to you during the whole dinner, and you really have not discovered his claims to the admiration he receives from women of all parties and denominations?"

"Sincerely and positively, no."

"Then I will not be his *proneuse*. I fear Stracey has inoculated you with some of his opinions."

"Not regarding Lord Vere; for until to-day I was not aware of his existence."

"You will not be so candid shortly; you will find that 'not to know him argues yourself unknown.' I have a suspicion that Stracey's report of *me*, not *now* his favourite sister, has not prepared you to think very favourably of me. I am resolved, nevertheless, that you shall like me. I assure you, when I choose, I am quite irresistible."

And Lady Sophia turned her beautiful eyes full upon Catharine, her whole countenance beaming with a smile so fascinating, that her companion began to feel she *was* almost irresistible, and that Cleveland was *not* inexcusable.

"I was resolved on saying a few words to you *tête-à-tête*, notwithstanding the disagreeable circle assembled here tonight," said Lady Sophia. "Excepting Vere—yourselves, of course—there is not an endurable creature here; all high and mighty people by birth and privilege, but bores by nature, which is the most anti-aristocratic of divinities. I must go and make the agreeable to them nevertheless; I must have them at my house, and I must be seen at theirs, because all the world does the same. If I can steal five minutes more *commerage* with you I shall; but I charge you, do your best to like me, and *au revoir.*"

While conversing with Lady Sophia, Catharine felt that there *was* danger of liking her, but reflection was always an enemy to her ladyship. The most devoted of her admirers were not only loudest but most sincere in their homage in her presence. Memory lent no embellishments either to her mind or person, for the images of memory are best defined in solitude, and solitude gives leisure for thought.

On the whole it was a pleasant evening to Catharine. She saw hardly anything of Cleveland, for he purposely avoided her, and she conversed with two or three people whom she could not agree with Lady Sophia in classing with the vast community of bores. Moreover, Stracey was near her—spoke to her often, and she felt that, in *his* presence, she never could be discontented or unhappy. How often she sought his eye! and if he could but have divested himself of the unfortunate prejudice that those glances indicated only sympathy of thought and mind, none of feeling and heart, what pure and devoted affection ought he to have read there! He was miserable, because he suffered from the disease of a perverted vision, a malady of the imagination, and, like tens of thousands besides, he was writhing under his torments, because false delicacy or false pride prevented him from making that unreserved communication of his feelings, which would have placed the power of relief in the hands of her who alone could relieve him.

How many patients have perished, because they confided only half their symptoms to their physician!

CHAPTER VI.

The talents of Colonel Hamilton were so highly appreciated by both parties, the *ins* and the *outs*, ministers and the opposition, that each was animated with a desire of attaching him to itself—of transforming him, in short, from an independent member, into a mere partisan. But the firmness of Hamilton's temper was his safeguard, his integrity was his security. Free from debt, unexpensive in taste, moderate in his wishes, and with an ample and unencumbered estate, *place* had no attraction for his avarice, and his ambition, a more vulnerable point, nevertheless was not strong enough to tempt him to sacrifice his principles on its shrine.

Perhaps, also—for where is the man inaccessible to the homage of his fellows?—he was flattered to find himself thus courted, thus solicited; and it may be doubted whether he did not find as much satisfaction in rejecting the offers of ministers, as the most inveterate and needy placehunter ever derived from the sudden gift of a sinecure he has long solicited in vain.

Politics possessed for him that fascination which they exercise over all who once admit their influence. Deeply impressed with the vast changes in the human mind evolved by every successive year, he watched, with an anxious eye, the march of events which his sagacity assured him were prophetic of some mighty result. An extensive acquaintance with the past, and an unshrinking examination of the elements whose struggles were felt in the present, opened to him glimpses of the future most consolatory to a man ardently desirous of the improvement and well-being of his species. Political power, that draught which intoxicates the wisest, had its charms for him also. He felt that, should the day ever arrive when those with whom, on every great question, he agreed, should preside in the councils of their country, to be one of them might supply a balm for the disappointments of his domestic life. And yet, when he owned to himself that he *had* been disappointed, his conscience smote him as if he were committing an injustice. What legitimate ground of complaint had he? He wedded Catharine in the conviction that her entire esteem, her sincere affection were his; and what right had he to seek for sympathy in that impassioned love which formed the scourge, as it ought to have been the blessing of his existence?

It is not wonderful that Colonel Hamilton hailed, with a sensation of relief, a pursuit which offered him the means of escape from a state of mind produced by such conflicting feelings. Neither is it surprising that sometimes the presence of her who was the source of these feelings should be painful, for it necessarily forced them again on his consciousness. And yet even at this period—painful as it was to both of them—perhaps the admiration of each for the other was greater than during all their preceding intercourse.

The society of a man, courted by all parties, was necessarily sought by all. His house was the rendezvous of leaders of the most opposite political sects, and it was impossible that any of them could arrive at an intimate acquaintance with Catharine without being aware of her extraordinary attainments, or of the influence she exerted—perhaps imperceptibly to himself—over her husband. It became, therefore, an aim with all to endeavour to direct that influence in favour of their own peculiar views, and Catharine found a sphere opened to her ambition, to the charms of which women of the finest talents are proverbially alive—political influence.

Catharine felt the full force of the temptation—and she resisted it.

It soon came to be pretty generally understood by the hangers-on of all parties, that dead weight which has retarded the progress of so many government movements, that Colonel Hamilton had the means of serving any man whom he might be willing to assist—that hardly a minister would reject a request from him, be the individual in whose behalf it was urged what he might. Consequently his house was besieged by as many applicants as the office of a secretary of state, and more memorials, petitions, &c., &c., lay every morning on the table of his study than he could have read, if he had devoted the whole twenty-four hours to their perusal.

Even Lady Sophia Cleveland was aware that her brother might do much for people if he chose it, and as it was not her habit to allow her friends' power of obliging to lie useless, she too attempted to storm a fortress hitherto found impregnable. Her visits to Portland Place had been so perseveringly frequent, that she had established herself on a footing of intimacy, the claims of which were not very easily disallowed. Then the charms of her manner were, *if she chose*, almost irresistible, and even Catharine, with reasons of dislike founded on circumstances so painful to herself, could hardly persevere in maintaining that coldness and formality of deportment by which she intended to intimate, "Hitherto shalt thou come and no farther."

"Alone, at last!" said Lady Sophia one morning—"an hour's waiting for the departure of a dozen stupid people is a tolerable trial of human patience. I give you credit for saying *no* very civilly, Mrs. Hamilton; to the petition I have to prefer, I hope to receive a very gracious *yes*."

"I do not possess the power those persons imagine," said Catharine. "Stracey is not quite so pliant in my hands as they seem to infer."

"Not pliant! Surely by this time you have tamed him into the domestic animal Heaven and nature ordained to be the destiny of husbands! It must be confessed, indeed, that there is not quite so much of the turtle about him of late; but London, you know, is the grave of sentiment, and conjugal fondness always seems to me like the ghost of romance. You are more rational now you practically demonstrate to the world that you are both capable of an independent existence."

"You do us too much honour in supposing we have arrived at that high point of reason," said Catharine, becoming, nevertheless, rather paler—a change which the keen eye of Lady Sophia did not fail to discern.

"You wrong yourself," she replied, with one of those inexplicable laughs which sound like mirth, but wound the heart like a sarcasm. "Stracey spends the morning at his club, the evening at the house; rides in the Park by way of relaxation, and sleeps at home by way of amusement. I trust, my dear, you console yourself during these absences with rather more rational recreations—see agreeable people—pluck the roses of life—and do not feel it essentially necessary to your felicity to resemble 'Patience on a monument, smiling at grief.' Constancy is not the masculine virtue of the age. *Apropos des bottes*—poor Stark! his admiration of my fair self is an exception, always unvarying. You will be sorry to hear he is in great distress, for he boasts of an alliance between you ages ago, on the strength of which he fancies he has a claim on your compassion."

"The claim common to all human nature, *only*," said Catharine. "I believe the alliance between us consisted in my laughing occasionally at his satire, and in his making me elsewhere the object of it. Thus each derived amusement from the other, but beyond this tacit compact, I know of no alliance with Mr. Stark."

"How unkind to disclaim that of which he boasts so loudly and so often! Then you positively do not feel particularly inclined to do a service to poor Stark, which will rescue him from great difficulty, and to prevent that most intolerable of all things, to a man who actually lives by public opinion, degradation."

"Not *particularly* inclined, but *generally*," said Catharine, with a smile, "which ensures to Mr. Stark my good offices, so far as they do not compromise my rule of action; yet in what manner I can possibly benefit *him*, is really beyond my comprehension."

"You do not pretend to deny that a great many influential people, the most influential, are not only ready and willing, but absolutely anxious to oblige you. A word from you in the proper quarter would do everything, and is all Stark requires."

"Pray explain."

"Of course you know that Stark lives by literature; the most uncertain and painful of all modes of existence, he says. Being so much among *us* as he is, he is necessarily obliged to support a certain appearance, and as there is but a dead market in the evil days on which we are fallen, for literary traffic, as well as for traffic of every kind, Stark has been compelled to incur debts to an inconvenient amount, which embarrass him greatly at present, and may prove much more troublesome if not liquidated. Now it happens that a snug sinecure has fallen in at this moment, and a word from you to your friend —— will secure it to Stark, who will thus be rescued from much actual distress and more possible, and will, moreover, greatly oblige me, who really *am* interested in his welfare. He is the most amusing creature in the world."

"Mr. Stark and you are in error," said Catharine, coldly; "I have no interest whatever with ——, and may truly say that, in his political character, I have positively no knowledge of him."

"That is really being rather too mysterious," said Lady Sophia, pettishly. "All the world knows that men of every party are absolutely fighting for Stracey, and do you think so thoroughgoing a politician as —— would consider the paltry office I want you to ask of him too large a bribe for the exertion of your influence with your husband?"

"And will your ladyship be good enough to state the precise nature of the object for which I shall be expected to use my influence with Colonel Hamilton?" asked Catharine, with a proud coldness very unusual to her, and so extremely disagreeable to Lady Sophia as almost to deter her from prosecuting the unwelcome subject, important as success was to her; for she had pledged herself to Stark that the appointment should be his, and she felt that to offend him would be not only inconvenient but dangerous.

"You need *not* exert any; you need only allow it to appear to —— that you will do so; that you will contrive, in fact, to attach Hamilton to his party," replied Lady Sophia, resolved to do courageously and thoroughly that which she felt it necessary to do.

"Act a falsehood, and allow it to be supposed that my husband is weak enough to be persuaded into wrong by his wife!" said Catharine, almost sternly, her beautiful eyes and mouth expressing ineffable disdain. "No, Lady Sophia; I have neither the will nor the courage to do this."

"I never can understand the heroics of your superlatively excellent people," said Lady Sophia, concealing her real chagrin by an affectation of coolness. "Just as if all men had not, as Horace Walpole says, 'their price,' and as if Stracey would not be bought, at last, like the rest."

"His wife, at least, will not sell him," said Catharine. "And as long as human nature is able to conceive the idea of immutable truth, I shall, notwithstanding Horace Walpole, continue to have faith in Colonel Hamilton's independence."

"Ah, my dear," said Lady Sophia, changing her ground, "I do really believe now, that there is some truth in the whisper that you and Stracey have outlived the honey year. You are absolutely afraid of him, for I cannot believe you would be so unkind as to refuse me this slight favour, if you did not dread that it might transpire, and be, like the equinox, a signal for violent storms and contentions."

"I *do* fear the loss of Colonel Hamilton's esteem; I could not survive the possibility of being degraded in his eyes, and to secure myself against so fearful a result, I shall take care not to be degraded in my own," said Catharine, decisively.

"Politics have been debateable ground between husband and wife from the days of the first diplomatists," returned Lady Sophia, carelessly; "Stracey is not the first married man who has disapproved of female interference in that lordly line."

"As I have carefully avoided the slightest attempt at an intrusion into the sacred ground, I have not experienced the mortification of a repulse."

"Then, my petition is absolutely rejected, and poor Stark is ruined!" said Lady Sophia, rising.

"I can but wish him success in another quarter; whenever I *can* be of use to your ladyship, I shall be only too happy to prove my desire of being so."

"If it should not happen to be particularly disagreeable," said Lady Sophia, ironically, and she returned to Cleveland House to communicate to Mr. Stark the failure of her application; and to enjoy with him a manuscript satire of Catharine, circulated among a few very particular persons, so extremely delighted with an attack on an individual who, by refusing to be one of them, seemed to place herself above them, that they entirely overlooked the incongruity of ridiculing, as a *nuovelle Corinne*, one of the most unpretending and most natural characters in the world.

CHAPTER VII.

But although Catharine was able to parry Lady Sophia's insinuations that there was less affection between herself and Colonel Hamilton, they left their sting behind. The consciousness that half the charge was untrue—that on *her* part there was an increase instead of a diminution of affection—did not tend to weaken the conviction that Hamilton was, from some secret cause, estranged from her of late. When present his manner was constrained; instead of the easy chitchat into which they used to fall when alone, there were long intervals of silence, during which she occasionally met his piercing eye fixed on her with an expression she found it impossible to define. He was never unkind. On the contrary, when with her his attention was all that her peculiar situation demanded, and his consideration for her comfort—

his evident anxiety for her safety in the trying hour which awaited her, were such as might have satisfied the most exacting affection. But her expressions of gratitude seemed to be so distasteful to him, that she soon ceased to utter them, and her wounded feelings, shrinking as she did from complaint, added to the coldness of her manner, and strengthened Hamilton's already too firm assurance that he had never been the object of her love.

If Catharine ever, even in the secrecy of her own heart, charged Hamilton with unkindness, it was at this period. With no friend near her to whom she could seek for soothing and support in the awful moment of woman's trial, she had naturally clung with double tenderness to the fondness of her husband, and expected to hear from him that cheering encouragement to hope, which so much lightens the apprehension of an inevitable suffering. That was precisely what Stracey, with his present sentiments, could not offer. He dreaded lest the overflowing of his heart should pour forth those declarations of passion and love, which appear always extravagant to people who do not share the sentiment, and which, with fastidious delicacy, he dreaded that Catharine might deem ridiculous. She could not penetrate the anxiety with which he watched the slightest change in her countenance; she had not heard the injunctions again and again impressed on her medical attendants, to care, at every risk, for *her* safety. She did not know that often when she felt his sudden departure most unkind, he had quitted her presence only because he felt it impossible longer to restrain the expression of his doubts, hopes, fears, and because he dreaded the danger of the least agitation, the slightest excitement for *her* in such a state. A mistaken refinement kept both silent, and rendered both miserable, adding one other instance to the many on record, that the concealment of the truth is, in many cases, as mischievous in its results as the falsifying of it, and that the moment we ascertain that feeling and reason are at variance, we may be confident the former does not flow in a pure and legitimate channel.

Catharine longed for the comfort of Mrs. Warren's presence, a comfort dependant on the health of her friend, and she may be pardoned the natural selfishness which awaited with even more anxiety than usual, reports of the progress of her complaint. Lady Darley, also, had been constantly fixing and deferring a journey to town, anxious once more to revisit her former haunts, yet shrinking from the prospect of the change which awaited her there. Deprived, by a frightful accident, of a limb, she had shut herself up in rigorous seclusion, cheered only by the presence of her niece, who flew to her in her hour of distress, and by her forbearance, her judicious kindness, her gentle temper, her affectionate attention, repaid a thousand fold the ecuivocal interest Lady Darley had once manifested in her welfare. Perhaps Lady Darley best demonstrated her own gratitude by offering little opposition to the marriage of Catharine with Stracey Hamilton, by which she lost a companion absolutely necessary to her happiness, and consented to her niece's alliance with a man who, notwithstanding his high personal recommendations, was, after all, but a younger brother.

The society of Lady Darley was not always particularly acceptable to Catharine, but now, in her almost restless craving for female companionship, she read with feelings of bitter disappointment the following characteristic letter :—

"My Dear Catharine,

"I have great reason to complain of your writing to me so seldom. Now that a letter containing intelligence of the movements of a world in which I have ceased to exist is really not only an enjoyment, but almost a necessary of life, it is inconceivable how seldom my pretended friends favour me with a line of their correspondence. People were ready enough to fill up sheet after sheet for my amusement, when I was able not only to amuse myself but them also. Human nature generally is a mass of ingratitude; a person who has no longer the power of obliging, in vain appeals to the past, and derives from thence his claims to consideration. His place is already filled by others to whom that homage is paid which once belonged to him, and who will in turn be forgotten when no longer able to sustain a part in the pageant.

"You see I am at the cottage. Mrs. Warren is one of the few very good people whose society I cannot only tolerate, but really consider a source of pleasure. There is no religious pretension about her. She is content to practise all the cardinal and Christian virtues without lecturing about them. She does not consider it a sin to be agreeable, and thinks it no waste of time to minister to the amusement of an unfortunate like myself, who, from the habits of my previous life, naturally depend very much on others for my recreations. My own thoughts are quite sufficiently painful to render me sensible of the relief of escaping from them, and grateful to any one who affords me the means. Your marrying was a very serious evil to me. I must do you the justice of saying, Catharine, that you always seemed to recollect what you owed me for my good intentions, to say the least of them, in times past. That they were not realized was your fault, not mine, and even at this distant period, though you are fortunately settled in life, I cannot help complaining that you carried your resentment or refinement, or whatever you may call it, much too far by relinquishing so brilliant a *parti* as Cleveland, for no earthly end or cause that I can perceive, except that he might marry that detestable Lady Sophia Barron.

"Apropos of whom. I had a letter from Mr. Stark a week or two since, rather an addition to the annual sheet with which he has vouchsafed to favour me, since my retirement from the world. His writing on such an occasion, I consider very impertinent, especially as he has thought fit to refuse all my invitations to come to Darley House—he who, before my unlucky accident, would have given one of his hands for admission within its portals. I only repent I ever asked him—it is so mortifying to be refused by such an animal! What do you think procured me the honour of his letter to which I am alluding? Want of money. He solicits a loan, supposing that, as I am unable now to spend my income myself, it matters not how worthless the channel through which I allow it to be diffused for the public benefit. A man who really has not the shadow of a claim on me; whom I honoured only too much by classing him among my acquaintance! He complains of literary disappointments: what are they to me? I do not see why I should pay him for the chance of being exhibited to public view in his next farce. People who subsist on literature must be content, like other adventurers and speculators, to endure the rise or fall in the market. I wonder Mr. Stark was not brought up to a profession, or trade, or something. I remember Lord Edmund Gresham once said of him that he was half qualified to become a surgeon already, for he was perfectly accomplished in the art of *cutting up*. I did not think this so good at the time; but now many things which happened in former days recur to my mind, and I fancy memory embellishes them.

"Stark's letter says much of you—your beauty, your success. I always predicted *that*, and it is something to know that Cleveland has lost the only woman capable of adorning his superb residences. He—Stark I mean—conceives, I suppose, that being myself *hors du combat*, I am accessible to flattery through you. He may find himself deceived, for although I do rejoice in the happiness and éclat of my niece, when I hire a reporter to communicate it to me, my choice will not fall on *him*. His letter, independent of his impudent request, is amusing enough—a complete chronicle of court news. I was really glad to hear of the admiration you excited in the highest quarter; if you would only condescend to a little management, I have not a doubt that you would completely eclipse Lady Sophia, who has hitherto, I understand, been in certain eyes, 'the glass of fashion and the mould of form.' If her ladyship's discretion were equal to her beauty, it would be well for Cleveland. Stark hints and insinuates—not asserts—that there is a very dangerous flirtation between herself and Lord Vere, a young man come out, it seems, since I retired from the bustle of life. I have seen his name occasionally in print, as the companion of Lord ——— n Greece and elsewhere, so that altogether, I had pictured him to myself as a half-wild kind of creature like some of Byron's heroes, half pirate, half madman. I can find nothing in Stark's description of him which explains how he came to attain the fashionable eminence which he seems to occupy. I am sure he would not suit *me*, but Lady Sophia's taste appears to differ marvellously from mine. Her fickleness does not surprise me; the whole of her affair with Cleveland, from beginning to end, prepared me for it. Nor do I at all wonder that coldness and disunion have arisen between *them*—Cleveland and Lady Sophia, I mean. Nor do I pretend to regret it. If ever man had claims to be utterly and essentially miserable, he has. His behaviour to you was quite unpardonable; and to *me* also, for whose kinswoman, considering the long and intimate acquaintance which had existed between us, he ought, to say the least of it, to have shown more consideration. They have two children, I hear, with whose persons anybody and everybody is better acquainted than their mother. Poor little wretches! though I never mean to advocate the system of maternal slavery, I do think we have a right to give a small portion of our time and attention to the helpless beings we have brought into the world.

"As I have a frank *post dated*, and am not obliged to despatch this until to-morrow, and am, moreover, in a scribbling vein, I shall write on, for I do believe you will not be wearied by reading my volume, tinged as its contents may be by that bitterness which so surely indicates unhappiness.

"I cannot make up my mind to go to you in Portland Place; far less to reoccupy the house in Grosvenor Square. I have not nerve enough, in my crippled state, to encounter the crowd who will throng around me, to see how I bear the melancholy change, and perhaps to exult in it. As I get more accustomed to my cork leg I find it more useful, and perhaps, in another season, I may, with Mrs. Warren's assistance, overcome my repugnance to emerge from my present *almost* solitude. Having relinquished the plan of visiting you, I found Darley very dull; the excitement of suspense was at an end. I had at length arrived at a decision: I thought of Mrs. Warren, and wrote to beg the alleviation of her society, but I heard from her that she was too complete an invalid to venture from home just then, and was moreover anxious to nurse herself, to be able to fly to you when you most needed her. 'If the mountain would not go to Mohammed, Mohammed must go to the mountain.' I gave her a few days' notice of my intentions, received an assurance of welcome, and am here.

"Your cousin Rachel, Mrs. Fulton, had been, I found, in attendance on the invalid, but flew away the day preceding my arrival, fearful, probably, of encountering one laden as I am with all the faults and frailties of this unrighteous world

She did not like to incur the danger of touching pitch and being defiled. She was accompanied by her two children, lovely little creatures they were, Mrs. Warren said, but the frolicksome gayety of infancy was checked by the mistaken system of an austere education. The result will be that the body, having been neglected for the sake of the mind, will prematurely perish. There will not be sufficient corporeal strength to sustain the spirit when it begins to put forth its energies. Rachel herself, according to Mrs. Warren, is much altered. There is a look of anxiety and restraint about her, quite incompatible with the idea of happiness. Her gentleness is tinged with a melancholy nearly allied to gloom, and the smiles of her poor children, which so rejoice the hearts of other mothers, seem but to inflict pain on hers. Mr. Fulton appears to have adopted a strange system of doctrines, to say the least of them. When on the death of Mr. Revely he succeeded to the living of Saint Andrew's, it seems that his desire of keeping the congregation together, as those people call it, led him not only to adopt all the severe, and, I think, startling, opinions of his predecessor, but even to go beyond him. It is very strange that one cannot long affect to view things in a certain light without really coming to do so at last. I dare say this Mr. Fulton had no idea to what extraordinary lengths he should in time be carried. I drove over last Sunday to Golden Magna—to satisfy my curiosity, I confess, though I do not class myself exactly with those who 'go to scoff.' I doubt whether Mr. Fulton's preaching will ever induce any to 'remain to pray.' He was quite beyond *my* comprehension; all I could discover was that the plain precepts—the beautiful doctrines of Christianity—were entirly overlooked for the sake of an attempt—in my apprehension an impious attempt, to penetrate the mysterious counsels of the Divinity, and to read his secret decrees! He looked wretchedly thin, and his eyes emitted a fearful brightness indicative either of comsumption or insanity, a pitiable spectacle, but not *so* pitiable as that of his poor, pale wife, in whose pew I sat, and in whose anxious apprehensive countenance I read the confirmation of suspicions which had previously suggested themselves to my own mind. As to the unhappy children—severally three and two years old, they sat in their prescribed places, motionless as a statue in a niche, hardly venturing to move a limb or an eye. Imagine the discipline which could so subdue the overflowing joyousness, the restless motion of infancy. Well may their poor mother look pale and sorrow-worn; the severity, whatever may be its degree, has no existence in *her* gentle heart. Altogether the scene presented so melancholy a spectacle of the bad uses to which the best things may be perverted, that I returned to the cottage too depressed by the exhibition to hazard a repetition of it, and resolved to be content with the homely benevolence by which *your* vicar contrives to benefit a whole parish, persuading them into piety, not more by the purity and simplicity of his doctrines, than by the excellence of his example. Nothing can be so unprofitable as hunting after *popularity preachers*, except, perhaps, *popularity preaching*.

"I am disinterested enough to hope Mrs. Warren will be sufficiently recovered to show herself in Portland Place at the expected time. By-the-way, I cannot yet reconcile myself to your being north of Oxford-street; except in honour of an ambassador, my horses' heads were never turned in that direction. But Colonel Hamilton, with all his excellences, has the bad habit of being unpersuadable. I am really so comparatively comfortable and cheerful here, that I look forward to returning to the solitude of Darley as a thing *à faire frémir*. It is astonishing how much good this woman, with her small income, contrives to do! I shall certainly try her plan of happiness, the enjoyment of the consciousness of being useful. My past existence does not afford a very satisfactory retrospect. I shall only postpone my reform until you are safe; the birth of my heir will be a fine era to date from. For Heaven's sake take care of yourself."

CHAPTER VIII.

Lady Sophia Cleveland's carriage was to be seen more frequently than ever at the door of Colonel Hamilton. Her visits were so constant as to encroach considerably on Catharine's leisure, and they brought with them two disagreeable consequences, the presence of Lord Vere and Mr. Stark.

If Catharine had a prejudice against any person in the world, this particular pair were decidedly the objects of it. Neither coldness nor silence could check the impertinence, or awe the familiarity of Stark. He had the constant habit of remarking the absence of Colonel Hamilton, whom he had always the luck to meet accidentally an hour or two before he paid his devoirs to Mrs. Hamilton; sometimes at one of the clubs—sometimes in the park with a party of equestrians; and he never failed to relate some anecdote descriptive of Hamilton's gayety and high spirits, founded perhaps on the merest trifle, but so dressed up in his hands that the original actors would not have recognised the scenes in which they had been performing. Then he assumed the abominable freedom of rallying Mrs. Hamilton on her conjugal devotedness, assuring her that she was the Griselda of the era, that the men lauded her to the skies, while the women made common cause against her, as a deserter from the party to which nature had decreed she should belong. Others in her situation would put forth their hand to pluck those flowers of life, which only required to be plucked, whereas *she* chose to imprison herself in her cage; sure to be found whenever the truant sought her. Lady Sophia never failed to bring her wit in aid of his, laughing at Catharine's assertions, that her mode of life was the result merely of her own taste, and, which was true, that she herself, by her persuasions and entreaties, had induced Colonel Hamilton to seek for those recreations which offered so necessary a relaxation to the ordinary tension of his mind. They affected to consider these declarations as further proofs of her exemplary, but *unexampled* patience and submissiveness, ever ready to find apologies for the offender, until Catharine was compelled to take refuge in silence, as the only means left of terminating a theme so impertinent on *their* part, so irksome on hers.

If possible, Lord Vere was even more disagreeable. In Lady Sophia's presence his devotion to *her* was too palpable to escape the notice of the most indifferent observer; but he contrived often to remain after her ladyship's departure, and sometimes to precede her arrival. There was a lover like tone in his manner to every female—the most repugnant possible to a woman of good taste, and infinitely more so to one whose heart happened to be entirely occupied by her husband. Lord Vere had been spoiled by the homage of the other sex. A fine person had added to the effect produced by his somewhat singular adventures, and these, in their turn, had embellished his person. It was new to him to meet with a repulse—the very circumstance probably which rendered his intercourse with Catharine more piquant. To do his lordship justice, he possessed no inconsiderable share of that kind of moral courage, which some *anti-periphrastic* persons *will* call impudence. His perseverance was not diminished because he saw that his attentions were a source of considerable annoyance: Catharine perceived that in his society she had but one means of escape from his distasteful homage, and that was the presence of Lady Sophia.

"I am truly glad to see you," said Mrs. Hamilton one morning, welcoming her sister-in-law with unusual warmth; "Lord Vere has been so good as to sit out all my visiters for the express purpose of making me some of the prettiest compliments you can imagine! I fancy it was a sort of rehearsal of a tribute he means to pay to you, for I find your arrival is always the signal for a cessation of his artillery. I am most delighted you are come."

"Excellent!" said Stark, who had entered with Lady Sophia, and who, notwithstanding the office he actually filled between Lord Vere and her ladyship, was unable to repress his satisfaction at anything that savoured of sarcasm. "Very good faith! After all nothing is so severe as truth."

"And yet your wit is thought tolerably pungent, Stark," said Lord Vere.

"A capital hit!" said Stark, affecting to laugh; "I am fortunate in being not only witty myself, but the cause of it in others."

"*Trève!*" said Lady Sophia; "I do detest a hailstorm of *bon-môts:* keep your good things for your next book, Mr. Stark; it is a pity to waste them on us who do not value them. So Vere has really bored you to death, has he, Mrs. Hamilton, with his 'honeyed sweetness?'"

"Precisely."

"A rehearsal merely, my dear Lady Sophia," said Lord Vere, piqued; "Mrs. Hamilton's penetration, you see, discovered it."

"And Mrs. Hamilton's candour revealed it, which was rather more *mal-à-propos*," said Lady Sophia, with an appearance of jealous anger that could not escape even the *unwilling* eye of Catharine. "A scene for your next comedy, Mr. Stark."

"My muse essays a bolder flight when she next takes wing; I mean to gratify my bloodthirsty propensities by achieving a tragedy."

"A tolerably safe feat of heroism," returned Lord Vere, with his quiet and scarcely perceptible sneer, the most opposed imaginable to Mr. Stark's sardonic expression of sarcasm.

"I fear there is a bloodthirsty principle inherent in all the nature of mankind," resumed Stark, with the air of a man beginning an essay; "if not, farewell the epopeia! Homer, the grand wholesale dealer in battle, and murder, and sudden death, must have sunk in the depths of oblivion long ago. We speak of the infinite variety of his modes of committing murder with as much *nonchalance* as if we were discussing Mrs. Glass's most approved method of trussing geese. Yes; we certainly admire; all ages have admired; a grand murderer on a truly magnificent scale, an Achilles or an Alexander. It is from this very principle that tragedy lives, and moves, and has a being. To produce a perfect tragedy, it is absolutely necessary to cultivate it; *ergo*, I shall offer myself as second in the very next affair of honour in which I can contrive to be a party."

"Why not get up a duel on your own account?" said Lady Sophia. "That would be a sure means of interesting your feelings more forcibly."

"For use, one must contemplate such things *en philosophe;* quite impossible, I imagine, under the circumstances which you suggest," said Mr. Stark, quickly.

"Steam has smoked away the bloodthirsty principle of which you speak," said Lord Vere. "*Utility*, not *heroism*, is the virtue of this age, and depend upon it we shall live to see the opera converted into a mechanics' lectureroom, and the two great theatres into experiment shops for the improvement of the sciences."

"China and Great Britain united by canals and railways; a chain bridge thrown across the North Pole, linking Europe and America; and a balloon caravan traversing the globe on a tour of observation!" said Lady Sophia. "Really, Mrs. Hamilton, the wit of your visiters is at a low ebb, since it can produce no worthier matter for our entertainment. With your permission, therefore, we shall entertain each other, and dismiss them."

"Too cruel!" said Lord Vere, rising; "we must really vanish; we dare not add to our other enormities the sin of disobedience."

And, to Catharine's unspeakable relief, the peer and the poet departed.

"Is it really true," said Lady Sophia, "as report says, that Stracey is *éperdument amoureux* of the *nouvelle danseuse?*"

"It is *not* true," said Catharine, calmly; "and if it were, I am the last person of whom you should have asked the question."

"*Mille scuse*," replied her dauntless ladyship. "You and he seem to have arrived at so comfortable an understanding of mutual independence, that I had not the least idea of your being annoyed by my frankness. The fact is, my curiosity was excited for the sake of a theory of my own; that, after the first love, association makes the second. Now, there is something so oriental in the character of this creature's beauty, that when the thing was first spoken of, I really fancied it not improbable that Stracey might choose to indulge in a repetition of his Indian dream. In your early matrimonial days, of course you heard his Eastern romance from the best possible authority—himself. When people are 'all for love,' they are supposed to have every thought, past, present, and future, in common."

"I *have* heard occasional allusions to his Indian career, from Colonel Hamilton," replied Catharine; "but nothing that approached to romance; except, perhaps, a picturesque description of a Hindoo prince's court, or a Mohammedan festival. If he has thought fit to have a concealment, I acquiesce in its propriety, and would not even attempt to penetrate it."

"You are too perfect, my dear, for the world in its present stage," said Lady Sophia, affecting playfulness; "your disinterestedness, however, will not entail on you a great sacrifice in this instance; for the affair was nothing after all; nothing in the world. The first young passion, you know—

violent as all young passions are—some suffering—some mystery. I myself heard it at second hand. Stracey never chooses to speak of it. I would not, for worlds, have breathed a hint of it; but how could I suspect him of reserve with *you*—during the honey year at least? Do not look so very miserable, my dear Mrs. Hamilton. *You* surely owe Stracey impunity on the score of past loves. As to jealousy of the *danseuse*, I have no doubt the report was altogether a quiz; and, besides, every man commits an infidelity."

"You altogether misunderstand my feelings," said Catharine, calmly; and by inquiring after Sir Greville, she contrived to give Lady Sophia's versatile thoughts another direction.

"Oh that it were with me as in times past!" thought Catharine, when, to her great relief, she was alone, freed from the companionship of the woman who never quitted her presence without leaving a sting. And as she breathed this wish —this half prayer—her heart asked the questions, "Why is it not so? why should there be disunion and doubt, or even coldness, between me and the husband of my choice? Wherein has either sinned against the other? In what has either offended? What word of bitterness has ever passed between us? Why are we thus? Why am I unhappy?" And it appeared inexplicable to Catharine, that she should be so. "If Stracey were less with her than had been his wont, had not his public duties large claims on his attention? would not *her* voice urge him to the due fulfilment of them, rather than allure him to the indolent enjoyment of ease? Did she really believe the mischievous insinuations of such a reptile as Stark, evidently made with the intention of annoying her; or the yet viler assertions of Lady Sophia, who, under the garb of the most overwhelming friendship, was daily torturing her with the repetition of reports, gross and abominable as the one she had *now* ventured? Should she take courage, and explain to Stracey the uncomfortable circumstances which surrounded her? Would not that imply a doubt of him? might he not construe it into a tacit reproach? And he, so fastidiously *true*—loathing the slightest appearance of *insinuations*, and requiring, on all occasions, the broad and open truth—would not he, so misunderstanding her, despise her mind for its want of candour? That, at least, should not—must not be." And again erring by feminine want of resolution, Catharine retired to her sleepless pillow that night, to regret the estrangement of her husband, and to indulge a secret conjecture on the nature of that Indian romance to which Lady Sophia had alluded.

CHAPTER IX.

It was a dinner given by one of the leaders of the *then* opposition. Colonel Hamilton was among the guests, and was discussing warmly the merits of a question of vital importance to the public interest. So animated was he, and so entire was his accordance on this particular point with the views of those around him, that they conceived hopes, little short of confidence, that they should shortly enrol him in their ranks, and fetter his independence by the trammels of party. If the homage of the powerful and the talented could infatuate him, he enjoyed the plenitude of that tribute, and he felt that there were moments when the intoxication of public success might entirely banish the consciousness of domestic disappointments.

It was precisely at the instant when the fire of his eye sparkled brightest, when the eloquence of his tongue was most powerful, when the triumph of his spirit was highest, as if to prove to him how impotent is man's effort to escape by means of factitious excitement from the influence of feelings deeply implanted in his nature, that the few following words, written hastily by Mrs. Warren, were put into his hands:—

"Dear Colonel,

"Catharine is so extremely ill, that although she has desired you may not be disturbed, I have thought it advisable to send for you.

"M. Warren."

A double pang; she was ill; Catharine, his own wife, and she craved not *his* presence, expecting neither comfort nor support, hardly sympathy, from *him!* But although this thought, the whisper of the evil spirit he had admitted into his bosom, shot through his brain as a flash of lightning, he hesitated not to obey the mandate immediately, breaking from the society of his companions, despite their importunate entreaties, and returning instantly to his house.

The knocker was muffled; and slight as the circumstance was, it smote on the heart of Colonel Hamilton as a reproach. Her hour of suffering had come upon her, and *he* was away, revelling in pleasures in which *she* had no share; leaving her to the comfortlessness, the desolation of solitude in the very midst of the most populous haunts of man, that most formidable of all solitudes. Had she deserved no better of him—she whose heart was so pure, whose friendship so sincere, whose whole character so full of truth? Was it a crime that she had been unable to return the burning passion which consumed *him?* Could he charge upon her, even in his darkest thought, that she cherished a guilty preference for another—even a lingering tenderness for the memories of the past? Oh, no, no! Such esteem, yea, such affection, as she had to bestow, were his: and what had been, was no mystery to him; he had known all; and so knowing, had loved and wedded her still. And how had he fulfilled the vows he had solemnly pledged to her? How had he realized the promises by which he had induced her once more to intrust the bark of her happiness to the pilotage of man? As, in the moment preceding death, the whole of its past actions are said to be brought before the view of the passing soul, so the certainty that Catharine was really ill, when it had come far within the verge of possibility that he might be compelled to surrender her to relentless *death*, placed in array before him all the claims upon his love and care, all his wayward neglect of those claims, for which he had no better excuse to offer, than the moody fancies of a distempered brain, the insatiable cravings of a disordered fancy.

The door was opened. Colonel Hamilton passed the servant without daring to make an inquiry. With a noiseless but hasty step he entered the drawingroom. Mrs. Warren awaited him.

"All is over!" she said; and before he had time to feel the pang words so equivocal might have inflicted, a glance at the bright and happy face of his kind friend reassured him. "She has suffered greatly, but all is well, and we have only to be happy."

"God be thanked!" said Hamilton, sinking on a chair, and for a few seconds covering his agitated countenance with his hands.

"And have you not a word of inquiry after the stranger?" asked Mrs. Warren, reproachfully.

"I thought only of its mother," said he, with animation; "but *now* I am alive to all the bliss of being the father of *her* child. Can I see them?"

"Oh, you most unfeeling of men, not to ask me one question of the circumstances I am dying to communicate!" said Mrs. Warren, with that cheerfulness which security succeeding to anxiety is sure to produce. "Have you no curiosity to know whether you have a son or daughter?"

"Forgive me, I have been too happy to think of details. Whichever it may be, a father's best blessing welcomes it."

"You have a daughter; and Catharine, if she is capable of one feeling apart from joy, fears you may be disappointed."

"How she wrongs me! I have not permitted myself even to indulge a wish on the matter. But now that it has happened, I can see a thousand reasons for rejoicing that it is so. As Catharine recedes from youth, shall I not see her child advancing towards it? Delightful! to feel that her graces will not perish, but be treasured up in her daughter."

"You rave!" said Mrs. Warren; but she smiled, one of those tearful smiles which spring most immediately from the heart, as Stracey's love for his wife thus manifested itself. "Catharine is hardly more sane than yourself! The poor little creature is like nothing, at present, in the shape of man or woman; yet she protests again and again, that it is its father's 'softened image,' and obliges me and the unfortunate nurses to vouch for the truth of her romance. One never contradicts a newly made mother."

"And when—when, my dear madam, may I see my treasures?"

"Now—this instant, to be sure," said Mrs. Warren; "but I warn you, do not smother the wee thing; and don't be frightened if it is not quite a Venus. Let mothers say what they will, children of an hour old are not so beautiful as Cupid."

Despite this warning, Colonel Hamilton entered Catharine's apartment, like all new-made fathers, a proud and happy man—with a heart palpitating with emotions as sweet as they were novel, and indulging a secret certainty that the babe must be beautiful. And when he held its tiny form in his arms, and imprinted a first kiss on its soft and downy skin, he felt that it was a miniature model of perfection.

"Are you satisfied, Stracey?" asked the sweet but enfeebled voice of Catharine, as he bent over her to whisper his love and gratitude.

"Satisfied, and with *your* child—oh Heaven!"

But Mrs. Warren, who was absolute in this season of female despotism, interposed, and the happy father was compelled, with reluctant steps, to quit the spot which was now his world.

Oh, what a new vision of delight had opened upon Catharine! What a fountain of delicious feeling had gushed forth in her heart! In vain they bade her sleep; she could not shut out from her soul the joyful certainties that surrounded her. There was a music in the breathing of her child, sweeter than a seraph's choir, and how could she endure that her senses should become deadened to it?—at least, not yet,—not until she had realized her dream of ecstasy. Never had Catharine been so unmanageable—so irrational, Mrs. Warren thought. But alas, Mrs. Warren, though one of the best of human beings, irreproachable in all the relations of life, had never been a mother; and Catharine felt that she was not competent to sit in judgment upon her.

When happiness seems entire, let man ever apprehend a change It needed the calamity which occurred to sober the mind of Colonel Hamilton down to its ordinary level. It needed that he should feel that "the desire of his eyes" was about to be "taken away by a stroke" that he might be sensible he was mortal—that dependance was only to be placed on Him who is "higher than the highest."

Whether from the extraordinary excitement of her feelings, or from one of those thousand maladies incidental to her situation, Catharine, on the third day after the birth of her child, was pronounced in imminent danger.

Who shall paint the agonies of the adoring but not irreproachable husband! Day after day Colonel Hamilton sat by that couch of suffering, contemplating the change pain and disease were working in the beautiful face of his wife, and absorbed by feelings, of which, perhaps, remorse was the most painful. He had not been unjust to the excellences of Catharine. Her patience, her piety, necessarily appeared more admirable now, as they were developed by more striking circumstances; but he had previously been aware of their existence, and had loved them as constituent parts of a character realizing all he had ever imagined of human perfection. It was when her brightening eye and feeble smile welcomed his return to her side, after the short absences the preservation of his own health required, that he suspected how much suffering his late estrangement must have caused her, and felt the pang of self-reproach for his own wayward and exacting passion, which not being content with her pure and simple-minded affection, had manifested its selfishness by withdrawing from her the entire confidence, the perfect friendship, resulting from sympathy of taste, feeling, and pursuit, which had constituted the happiness of the early period of his union, before his too "absolute contentment" had left him leisure to crave from her that species of attachment which, perhaps, she could not feel. How often did he mentally record a solemn vow, that should Heaven spare her, his whole existence should testify his repentance of the errors of the past—his anxious care for the happiness of the present! In those dark hours of suspense, all interests independent of Catharine ceased to occupy his mind. Compared with *her* life, the fate of nations seemed but as feathers in the balance. Public occupation was forgotten in the intensity of private suffering. Even his child assumed a very subordinate place in his anxieties. He looked, indeed, on its little face with a thrill of delight, but not unaccompanied by a pang; for he sighed as he thought the existence of the babe all too dearly purchased by the sacrifice of the mother's life, and could have prayed in sincerity, "If one must be taken, oh let it be thy last gift!"

A fortnight of intense, unmitigated suspense and anxiety passed away, and Catharine was pronounced out of danger. Who shall venture to paint the gratitude to the Supreme, which then bowed the heart of the man of lofty thoughts and vast designs, even as the heart of a little child! Sacred be the communion between man and his Maker!

All was happiness and congratulation. Catharine was permitted to fulfil the dearest of a mother's duties, and to nurse her child. As to Colonel Hamilton, he felt that it was sufficient bliss to gaze upon her with *his* infant in her arms; and he almost unconsciously fell into a question—perhaps never yet satisfactorily solved—whether the enjoyment conferred by the affections be not greater than that conferred by the intellect. The philosopher who decided against the affections was, be it remembered, a solitary man, unblessed by the dearest of the social relations.

"How perfect it is!" said Catharine, ensconced in all the ease of a *fauteuil* in her drawingroom, her babe smiling in her arms; "one cannot imagine anything more lovely! If the mind of an infant be a *rasa tabula*, what gives so much expression to its face? And if countenance indicate character, how is it that our child has so much the look of you, when yet it *can* have no character?"

"Do not let us dive into the 'bottomless pit of meta physics,'" said Colonel Hamilton, smiling: "and depend on it, Catharine, you are wrong regarding the likeness. Is that delicate skin inherited from me? No," he continued, viewing himself in an opposite mirror; "my weatherworn and clime-stained complexion has nothing in common with the morsel of animated waxwork which so delights you."

"Because it *is* weatherworn," persisted Catharine. "But —*apropos*—Stracey, do tell me what romantic adventures occurred to you during the two years you spent in India."

"*Salaming* a nuwab, and performing the *ko-to* to Runjeet Sing, both picturesque ceremonies enough, if that be the meaning you attach to romantic."

"No, it is not," said Catharine, rather more gravely.

"Seated on the back of an elephant I have slain a tiger. I have hunted an elk, shot a bear, some scores of wild boars, lost my way in a jungle, been robbed in my tent, assisted in quelling a mutiny, and once performed the marriage ceremony in favour of a sergeant, by virtue of my being the senior officer on the spot. I cannot remember anything more at present; and surely I have made out a very sufficient list."

"*No* concealment, upon honour?" said Catharine, playfully, but with a heightened colour.

"None," returned Hamilton, with a thoughtful air, "unless that unfortunate affair of poor Devereux."

"What was that, if it be not a secret?"

"A brave and gallant man was Devereux," he said, gravely, "unfortunately mated to one of that class technically called in India half castes. I cannot pretend to describe the origin and progress of his infatuation—he a fine, sensible, well-educated, noble-hearted fellow, she one of the worst specimens of a bad class; *made* bad, Catharine, by education and political injustice, involving social degradation. A miserable marriage while it lasted, dissolved by her infidelity, which preceded and caused his death."

Catharine turned pale for a moment, and looked anxiously into the face of her husband; but it expressed no deeper gloom than the natural regret a man must feel for a friend so lost.

"The woman married her seducer," he continued, "and disappeared from society. This, Catharine, is the most painful of my Indian reminiscences, and one from which I always endeavour to escape as quickly as possible. And now tell me, to what was the question '*apropos*' which led to this subject, for I confess I am at a loss to discover."

"We were talking, you know, about our child resembling you; and I was fancying that there was surely something a *very* little like Lady Sophia Cleveland in the curve of its mouth."

"Very natural that it should be so; but your explanation is like many marginal notes, rather more mystifying than the text."

"And I thought of Lady Sophia's oriental style of beauty, as I have heard it called; and frankly, Stracey, I remembered her quizzing me about your *liaison* with a *danseuse*."

"Absurd!"

"But capable of being mischievous; *nearly* rendered so, in this instance, by its being explained as a recurrence of feelings you once felt for some eastern beauty, with whom you wrought out a romance so painful, that you never speak of it, but the whole of which was hinted, or insinuated, or related, to Lady Sophia, by a third person."

"Of course, you immediately convicted her of falsehood, by the fact, that *you* were ignorant of any such circumstance in my past career."

"Had I a right to expect perfect openness from you on the subject of past attachments?"

"If they were capable of influencing present feelings, which Sophia meant you to believe, because otherwise her report would bear no sting."

"At least, I am satisfied *now*, dear Stracey. But jealousy, you know, feels and suffers without reason."

"*Jealousy!*" said Colonel Hamilton, his countenance shining, as if with sudden light; "is it possible that *you* could be jealous?"

"It is a weakness common to all who love," replied Catharine, with a deep blush.

"But not to that kind of love—esteem—affection—what shall we call it? which you bear to me."

"Great Heaven! and what do you suppose to be the nature of my love for you?"

"Do not agitate yourself, dearest; let the past bear its own faults. Our child will win you to love me more warmly for the future."

"Have I yet that lesson to learn?" said Catharine, with tearful eyes and trembling lip. "Dear, dear Stracey, how you have wronged both of us!"

The arms of her husband were clasped round her, and for some minutes neither spoke, but their emotion penetrated the heart of each.

"Is it possible, Catharine," said Colonel Hamilton, at length, "that you have loved me—that you *do* love me, with a love as warm, as tender, yea, as passionate, as you *once* felt for another, and an often envied man?"

"Unjust to me—to yourself!" said Catharine, with a voice and look of affectionate reproach. "If all my past conduct has failed to convince you, how will you now believe my words! What a self-flatterer have I been! I rejoiced when I married you, that my choice of you afforded the best testimony of my recovery from past delusions; of my entertaining a new, a fervent, a disinterested affection. None could suppose me influenced by mercenary or ambitious motives; if you had possessed great wealth or exalted rank, my consent to be yours would have been won with far greater difficulty. I should have feared the calumnies of the world; I should have dreaded your doubts—unjust they would have been, but too natural to our imperfect nature. But as it is, Stracey, surely you owe me large amends."

"Let my life testify to my truth, when I swear to you that, at this moment, the whole earth contains not a being so truly blessed as myself."

And again and again Colonel Hamilton poured forth his bitter regrets for his past blindness, the waywardness that had driven him from the society of her in whose presence alone his existence was blessed, to the agitations, the fever, the tumult, of the struggling world of political strife.

"And yet you must not forsake your duty, dearest Stracey," said Catharine; "with your talents, your influence, your country has large demands on you. Let the Highlands be our home, but let us be found here whenever those interests which are intrusted to you demand your presence."

"Anywhere with you!" said Hamilton, fondly. "And with this little herald of future happiness."

"One of Lady Sophia's three-cornered notes, *couleur de rose*," said Catharine, taking it from the servant, who at that moment entered. "An affectionate inquiry after us—me and the child, that is. Pity that all which pleases should be only on the surface!"

"I have a great inclination to forbid her the house," said

Colonel Hamilton. "It is dreadful to feel, that no enemy could have striven more strenuously than my own sister, for the ruin of my happiness. She cannot forgive your having driven her to the necessity of wooing back the love of Cleveland; and her revenge craves the gratification of seeing you as miserable as herself, for, despite her splendour and her apparent vivacity, she *is* wretched beyond doubt."

"Can it be otherwise, when the frivolity of her existence is unredeemed by the performance of one duty?"

"And deepened by positive crimes. Ay, Catharine, you may start and turn pale at so fearful a charge, but is it not a just one? As a mother! you press your babe more closely to you, and so furnish a reply; you feel that *hers* have been abandoned to hirelings. As a wife! extravagant, cold, indifferent, *defying;* evincing, as caprice prompts, the most marked preference for other men, which, if it be no more than a means of annoyance to her husband, is criminal—if more, damnable! As a sister! the would-be destroyer of her brother's happiness. As a member of society, envious, slanderous; by turns the tyrant and the slave of a wretch such as Stark, whose influence over her is apparent through all the affected disdain with which she treats him. And wherefore? alas! the constant attendance of Lord Vere sufficiently explains why these things are, but does *not* explain the blindness of Cleveland."

"It is not for us to cast the first stone," said Catharine kindly. "How many would gladly use our example as a pretext for degrading from her proud eminence the object of their envy! Our happiness is now above her influence; let us not attempt to build it up on the ruins of her reputation."

"You are Charity's sweet self; but be it as you will."

"Lady Sophia wishes to be admitted to a sight of the child. When shall it be?"

"Let her see her own!" said Hamilton, sternly. "What interest can an indifferent, a careless mother, feel for the child of another? None that has not its root in a bad feeling. Sophia hopes to find your babe less lovely than its nurses report it; and, for the gratification of such a hope, she would have travelled in search of us even to the Highlands."

"We do not fear her criticisms," said Catharine, with a smile of maternal complacency; "and we are satisfied with our child as she is, without presuming to court for it beauty, or wit, or any gift but goodness; for *that* we have a right to pray; for the possession also of its natural faculties, the free use of its limbs, its freedom from absolute deformity, but for no more; *if* more is given, we have but to 'rejoice with trembling,' and to bestow additional labour in fortifying a citadel which contains unusual treasures. It is a fearful, if a delightful thing, to look on the face of a newborn infant, and feel that sorrow *must* mark those innocent lineaments. Well has it been said, that 'to be born is more awful than to die!'"

CHAPTER X.

"Home!—quick!" said Lady Sophia Cleveland, stepping into her carriage at the door of Colonel Hamilton's house.

Obedient to her command, the wheels rolled rapidly along. In an inconceivably short time she was at home, and with a haste quite unusual to her, she ascended the magnificent staircase of Cleveland House, entered her dressingroom, and desired her own woman to accompany her instantly to the nursery.

The attendant obeyed, and as Lady Sophia paced the long corridors with a speed that rendered her almost breathless, she thought, *for the first time*, that the apartment appropriated to her children might possibly be too remote from her own.

"Where is Miss Cleveland?" said Lady Sophia to the astonished authorities of the nursery, who, in their surprise and dismay, almost forgot to pay their lady the necessary respect of rising to receive her.

"Really, my lady," said the elder and more practised of the mercenaries, "miss is so unmanageable, that we should have no peace if I were not to shut her up now and then by way of punishment. Since Sir Greville has interfered with us, miss is almost spoiled."

"Silence, woman!" said Lady Sophia, sternly, for she had too much worldly tact to be ignorant that her child was suffering from the tyranny of the wretches to whom her own culpable neglect had permitted an undue power. "Show me my child immediately."

The reluctant nurse opened a large press and released the prisoner, pale with confinement, and obstinate in wrong from that keen perception of injustice which renders severity so dangerous a system with a high-spirited child.

"Go to your mamma, miss," said the nurse, but the child did not stir, and Lady Sophia intercepted a glance from her to her victim, which it was impossible to misconstrue; it conveyed an evident threat of future vengeance.

"Come to me, my love," said Lady Sophia, in one of her blandest tones, extending her hand, and looking at her neglected child with those irresistible glances of persuasion which few had been able to withstand.

The child obeyed, and gazed in the face of her mother with an expression of mingled delight and curiosity.

Lady Sophia looked at the lovely eyes fixed on her with so intelligent an expression, with a delight not unmingled with affection, for the maternal instinct, though stifled, did exist. For the first time in her life she seated the child on her knee, and caressed her with a fondness that reached the heart of the babe immediately: she burst into tears.

"Why do you cry, dear?" asked Lady Sophia, redoubling her caresses. "You are not sorry to see mamma, are you? Would you not like to leave the nasty nursery, and see me every day?"

"Oh, yes, yes, yes!" said the child, throwing her arms closely round her mother's neck, "go with mamma, and send nurse away. Naughty nurse, go, and never come back."

"Oh, fy! Miss Augusta," interposed the alarmed attendant; but Lady Sophia's imperious "silence!" terrified her into becoming a passive auditor.

"Is nurse cross to you?" asked Lady Sophia.

"Yes," said the child, boldly, for she felt that she was in the arms of a powerful ally. "When papa's gone, she shuts me up, and takes away my playthings, and shakes me, mamma. And sometimes I have no supper, and if I cry, she says the black man come take me. Ah, mamma, don't let black man come to poor Augusta."

"Where is my boy?" asked Lady Sophia, restraining the passion which almost convulsed her.

"Out with Sir Greville, my lady; Doctor K. has ordered him to be in the fresh air as much as possible, my lady."

"Browne," said Lady Sophia to her own maid, "carry Miss Cleveland to my boudoir, and desire the steward to send these women from the house within the hour. Not a word, wretches!" stamping with a passion that might have terrified less guilty spirits than these. "Be thankful that the law cannot reach your crime. You have no mercy to expect from me."

Crime! Yes—*theirs* was a crime, but of how much deeper die was the guilt of the unnatural mother, who, by abandoning her children to the tender mercies of hireling ignorance, rendered them the victims of a tyranny the miserable effects of which might tinge the whole of their future lives; the prey of the darkest superstition, ere yet their tender years permitted them to understand what superstition was!

Once seated on the cushion at her mother's feet, the wonderful beauty of the child shone out with a splendour that animated the heart of Lady Sophia with a thrill of intense delight. The more she gazed on the infant face sparkling with unrepressed glee, the more she felt convinced that time would improve instead of marring its perfection. The glorious eyes—the transcendent complexion—the softened Roman outline of the profile—the cloud of glossy dark ringlets hanging over a brow, already a well defined arch—the fairy form of exquisite symmetry—the small and delicately rounded limbs, were but as the dawning of the light which is to increase to noontide splendour. Lady Sophia was "insatiate of gazing," and in *her* instance, maternal vanity awakened a feeling akin to maternal affection. She did not belong to the class of fond mothers who, in the little claimants on their affection, find beauty even in deformity. The keenness of her judgment was not blunted by previous affection; the severity of her criticism was not softened by the interference of her heart. She appreciated with all the acumen, the accuracy of a connoisseur, and her thoughts had penetrated far into the future, when Mr. Stark was announced.

"Without a word, look at this creature," said Lady Sophia, parting the ringlets from the fair forehead of her child.

"Beautiful!" said Stark, with unaffected admiration. "Fifteen years hence she will have ripened into the perfection of beauty."

"The child is mine. Now, fifteen years hence, unpleasant as the fact may be, I shall be more than *un peu-passée*—fallen 'into the sear and yellow leaf;' valued not for myself, but for my power of gratifying the taste and vanity of others. It is pleasant to perpetuate my empire in my daughter. Before she is old enough to contest the sovereignty with me, I shall depose myself, to deprive others the pleasure of pulling me down; and who should ascend my vacant throne but my child?"

"Such a declaration does credit to your sense and judgment. And Lord Vere—"

"Will doubtless then have married, and have children of his own almost ready to be produced. Our romance will have found its termination in a sentimental friendship. Henceforward the great object of my existence will be to educate my child. Do not sneer—I have no design of turning schoolmistress, or of abandoning the world at present. Augusta is emancipated from nursery jurisdiction. *This* is her abode, and I shall see for a proper person to lay a solid foundation for the superstructure of elegance and accomplishments I mean to erect. To render study agreeable to her, I shall take care not to shut her up in a dark and dismal schoolroom, with a host of ill-looking books bound in calf, clumsy inkstands, and all the horrors of which my memory can summon a crowd of apparitions. No, no—her path shall be strewn with roses. Elegance shall be the handmaid of instruction; knowledge shall be acquired, not as a toil, but as a means of delight. Existence seems to me invested with new charms since I have looked on the face of this small miniature of humanity. I owe something to my excellent brother and his pattern wife. I have been so wearied this morning with their parental ecstasies, that I was absolutely driven to see whether *my* child was not of as fair promise as the poor little wretch in which they see a beauty unparalleled."

"Infinite are the mortifications of female motives!" said Stark. "Since your daughter is to engross all your ladyship's care and affection, who is to patronise the heir of the house of Cleveland?"

"I am sensible of the difficulty. The barbarous nurses are, by this time, out of the house; by-the-way, I should really like to behold Cleveland's surprise when he finds that their dynasty is so completely and so speedily overthrown. The monsters would shortly have destroyed the beauty of the child by their system of tyranny, starving, beating, all manner of atrocities. As to the boy, it is necessary to have an heir, especially when a dowager may be in the case; a great misfortune to depend, for the slightest accommodation, on a distant kinsman, who takes possession of one's houses and estates as heir-at-law—a man who has been looking out for the death of the late possessor for these dozen years, and wonders, at last, how it happens that the property is saddled with so large a jointure for a widow whom *he* deprives of her own home. Besides, Cleveland particularly dislikes *his* heir-at-law—some horrid creature with eleven children, and one thousand a year—poor, proud, and expecting the exertion of family interest even to the tenth generation. We must not lose the boy. *His* looks, you know, are of secondary importance. I rather think he struck me as a remarkably sickly, pale, plain little thing. He must be attended to, however. I shall have a room fitted up for him near me, and see him often. This will put Cleveland in good humour, and it will also be policy for the sake of Augusta, that her childhood should be spent as much as possible, without sacrificing higher considerations, with her brother."

"This is a wonderful metamorphosis!" said Stark. "I have heard that violent changes are seldom permanent."

"If the offspring of mere caprice," said Lady Sophia; "but mine is the result of a process of reasoning commenced, in the first instance, I grant, by accident, but not the less permanent. Who would sink into the insignificance of age, when they may preserve the importance of youth—almost *more* than its importance—in the persons of their children!"

"Your wisdom is indisputable, and there is besides the hope of future successful rivalry of Mrs. Hamilton on a new arena," said Stark, with one of his most sardonic smiles.

"You illustrate always the Frenchman's axiom—'show me the most benevolent action, and I will engage to furnish for it a hundred bad and probable motives,'" said Lady Sophia, whose calmness was quite beyond the reach of Mr Stark's satire, except when in public circulation, and from an attack of that kind she knew herself secure.

* * *

"Is not Colonel Hamilton disappointed in the sex of his child?" said Stark. "The confirmed celibacy of his elder brother seems to promise an earldom to him and his line."

"*Confirmed* celibacy! There is no such thing until a man is declared incompetent by a statute of lunacy," said Lady Sophia, pettishly. "It is the absolute duty of elder sons to marry, and I hope yet to make acquaintance with a Viscountess Ampton."

Stark looked incredulous.

"Stracey, I am sure, by no means relies on Ampton's not marrying. I shall invite Ampton to Cleveland House. I have no idea of a man of his prospects burrying himself in the obscurity of his family seat; but my father has so inoculated poor Ampton with his own taste for study, and retirement, and that kind of thing. With their everlasting experiments, the castle is become one vast laboratory, and I heard by accident, from somebody who had been hovering about their neighbourhood during the last grouse season, that Lord Edinburgh's pursuit of chymistry amounted to absolute infatuation."

"And with similar tastes, you persist in thinking Lord Ampton a marrying man!"

"Why not? Management has achieved as great improbabilities. The difficulty lies at the outset—how to bring him within the reach of temptation. I will get Cleveland to ask him to be his son's godfather—a compliment he can hardly refuse, and I shall take care to decline receiving the honour by proxy. Besides, it will be an act of real charity in me to rescue Ampton from the visionary solitude of his present existence."

"I admire your ladyship's disinterested benevolence," returned Stark. "Meanwhile, what line of policy do you adopt towards the *ultima Thulienses* of Portland Place?"

"Leave them to their own devices," replied Lady Sophia, with a shrug. "A new honeymoon has risen for them, and there is something in their manner which puts it out of doubt, that they have taken the benefit of one of those full and perfect explanations, which place them beyond the power of direct or indirect attacks."

"And Colonel Hamilton is really content with a daughter?"

"In the seventh heaven of beatitude! Stracey's wife is a happy woman!"

In the midst of all the splendour which surrounded her, the brilliant Lady Sophia Cleveland envied the woman whom *she* had deprived of that very magnificence, the tranquil happiness of the unostentatious existence in which the bounty of Heaven had secured her felicity.

And the wedded life of Catharine was henceforth hardly sullied by a cloud; her happiness was permanent, because it was built on the immutable foundation of *truth*.

PART THE THIRD.

CHAPTER I.

Eighteen years have passed away, and the world dates from a new era.

And was Catharine changed?

Changed! Yes. Eighteen years ought to work a change in a human heart, or man is dull indeed. What fearful lessons time inculcates! How much that was once mysterious, becomes plain—how much that, in the presumption of youth, we believed we grasped, now soars above our ken in the sublime darkness of "excessive light!" The opinions of the sternest philosophers even are tinged by their feelings—they are tainted by the crucible through which they pass; and can those of a woman hardly arrived at maturity be founded solely on the rock of eternal truth? Is the wife and mother of *forty* likely to be swayed by the same prejudices as the loving girl of twenty? Are we to wander over the surface of the globe, too see human beings under an infinite variety of aspects, and to retain all the narrow exclusiveness of our days of mental babyhood? Oh, no! Experience should effect changes; must, with all rational beings, produce innovations—they are the result of its lessons. It should implant enlarged charity where bigotry lurked before; should exchange presumption for humility, rashness for caution, precipitance for habits of investigation, passion for reason.

Still was Catharine beautiful. The soft light hair yet retained its glossy profusion. The figure was somewhat more luxuriant, and its grace was that of dignity rather than the airy elegance which had been its distinguishing charm in youth. Her complexion had hardly lost a tint of its peculiar delicacy; a pure life, a pure mind, pure air, are staunch friends to beauty—its sure preservers from premature decay. Who could believe, that the suns of forty summers had shone upon that smooth fair brow? The fact required all the unanswerable evidence afforded by the appearance of the blooming girl of eighteen who stood by her side, and called her *mother*.

Mrs. Hamilton and her daughter stood on an elevated terrace commanding a landscape possessing almost every variety of beauty. To the north the horizon was skirted by a long line of blue hills, and the intervening country was rugged and uneven. Looking to the south and west, the eye was gratified by a view of the perfection of a highly cultivated valley, teeming with the promise of all the riches of husbandry, having the appearance of a vast succession of gardens. A broad river might be traced as far as the vision could reach, from the west to the east, where it joined the "father of waters." *There* in all its grandeur foamed the most magnificent of sensible objects—the sublime, the glorious ocean; and on *this* the two were gazing with rapt attention.

"Can anything on earth equal this?" asked the youthful beauty, her starry eyes glittering with emotion. "Why, why, dear mamma, do we leave a home where we are so happy?"

"To secure our happiness by performing our duty. Your father's presence in London is necessary to the well-being of hundreds, and it is fitting that you, dearest Helen, should be acquainted with that world which you are to inhabit. *Here* you have too much the habit of depending on us, and mental strength, like physical, degenerates if not exercised. We must treat our minds much as we do our bodies, if we would preserve their strength and their activity."

"And after all, I certainly have some curiosity to see a place of which one hears so much, and to know people whose names are in the history of our country. Only it is painful to look round and think, that one is forsaking a place so very beautiful for dismal streets, for which it is impossible one can ever feel anything like an attachment."

"You are mistaken. Men who possess vast wealth, have been known to prefer the dark and dingy houses in which they have acquired it to spacious mansions in the midst of the finest country in the world. Man is altogether a creature of habit."

"Mamma," said Helen, after a pause of a few minutes, "I am curious to know whether—whether—recent circumstances have not made it more desirable, in your opinion, that I should be presented this season, than you might have thought it if—if—those circumstances had not occurred?"

"Decidedly. At present you yourself are not able to decide on the reality of your attachment to Sir Alfred Maitland, far less to rely on its permanence. In the opinion of your father and myself, your union with a man so every way excellent, is calculated to secure you as fair a share of happiness as falls to the lot of humanity, but it would be a fatal error to marry on a preference—a fancy, which, after all, may be but the result of ignorance and inexperience. You would indeed, have reason to condemn your parents, dear Helen, if they allowed you to form an indissoluble engagement, without affording you the means of comparison. Moreover, you possess that which all men desire, *wealth*. Being introduced into life, to speak conventionally, as an heiress, shoals of admirers will flock round you as moths round a torch. The ordeal which is to try you is a severe one, but necessary—both for Sir Alfred's sake and your own."

"He need fear nothing," said Helen, her colour deepening with the excitement of her feelings. "How I should despise myself if greater wealth, greater splendour, or more distinguished qualities even, were capable of rendering me inconstant! Such as Maitland is, I have loved him with an affection beyond the power either of time or circumstances. In the whole range of temptation, I am persuaded that none exists which could alienate my heart from him."

"Suppose that *he* were to desire the separation!" said Mrs. Hamilton. "Are you quite sure that you can rely on his firmness—his constancy? You must be prepared not only for the change in yourself, but in him."

"And I can answer for one equally as for the other," replied Helen, with a glow of indignation.

Mrs. Hamilton sighed.

"It is wiser, my child," she said, "though a hard lesson for youth, to doubt the permanence of any earthly feeling—any human affection."

"Dreadful!" said Helen, with unaffected horror. "Can I not rely on *your* unchanging love, mamma, on the steadfast affection of papa?"

"They are the holiest instincts implanted by nature, parts of ourselves. They are hardly subject to the same possibilities as attachments which, after all, are but the effect of accident, and consequently more dependant on the will or on circumstances."

The silence was for some minutes unbroken. The thoughts of both lay too deep for words; the one was somewhat melancholy from *experience*, the other from anticipation.

Presently Colonel Hamilton joined his wife and daughter. Both looked an inquiry, and the cheeks of the latter were pale with anxiety.

"Maitland is all that might be expected of him, dearest Helen," he said, answering those speaking glances; "quite sure of his own constancy, relying, with as much firmness as could be required from a lover, on your fidelity, but nevertheless satisfied, that the meditated probation is necessary to the future happiness of both. He will shortly follow us to town, and he is to be received as an intimate friend ought to be, but your conditional engagement is not to become matter of publicity, nor is he to enjoy any of those privileges which will naturally be consequent upon its avowal. You are satisfied, I hope, Helen, that all has been done with a view to your ultimate happiness; and surely mine is involved in that of my children."

"I *am* satisfied," said Helen, "and Maitland does me justice. He shall never have cause to repent his reliance on me."

"Be not too sure, my child. However, Maitland is now on the bridge with your brother, and I have told him I shall not forbid your walking in that direction."

Helen smiled gratefully, and, with a heightened colour, glided away.

"I think we may hope that our wishes will be realized," said Colonel Hamilton, watching the retreating figure of his child.

"With me doubt predominates," said Catharine. "With her brilliant advantages, such success must attend her in society, as is likely to be too captivating to her lively imagination; men of qualities much more dazzling than Maitland's will hover round her, and offer their homage; and how will her inexperienced mind be able to decide how much is paid to her wealth, how much to herself? Besides, she will rarely meet Maitland but in the world, and his excellences are most apparent in retirement. His somewhat reserved character necessarily obscures his higher qualities among strangers, and his modest appreciation of himself will be no advantage, when he is surrounded by people who view their own endowments on an exaggerated scale, and are never impeded by any diffidence from impressing strangers with the same opinion."

"*Memory* will be in Maitland's favour, and the very imagination of which you speak will lead her to dwell upon the past."

"May it be so! My own desire for their union renders me doubly cautious of promoting it by any undue influence. If it occured now, and she were thrown into society afterward, wretched indeed would she be, if she *then* first perceived and regretted the absence of those more showy qualities in him which the world so overvalues! What would be our remorse, if, by injudicious precipitation, we had hurried on a marriage which, in such a case, could be productive only of misery? I could not justify myself to use persuasion to forward a measure which appears to me desirable. My influence would, doubtless, be exerted to prevent an imprudent connection, but never to promote one, how much soever even my judgment might be in its favour; it is dangerous to play with the hearts of our children."

"Nevertheless, Helen cannot but be sensible of *our* wishes, and a child so affectionate must be influenced by them, venerating as she does, as she ought, the intellect, the principles, the excellence of her mother."

"And the noble disdain of falsehood, in all its forms, of her father, I should add, if we were bandying compliments," said Catharine, with a smile. "It is right that we should possess that degree of influence of which you speak, and, in accordance with that perfect truth and candour which have marked our conduct to our children from their earliest infancy, I have told Helen the precise nature of our present feelings, and why it is that we have objected to any decided engagement between her and Maitland. What people call *management* I have generally found to be bad policy, to say nothing of the base perversion of truth which it generally implies."

"Helen's wealth exposes her to great temptations; Lady Darley would have been a wiser friend to her godchild if she had equally divided her large fortune among our children."

"All my entreaties, and they were urgent, could not, as you know, prevent this unequal distribution. My poor aunt desired thus to testify her exceeding fondness for our first-born, and she silenced my hints at the injustice of such a proceeding, by reminding me, that Stracey would ultimately inherit the title and estates of your family, and that your present property would form a provision for Catharine not much inferior to the dower *she* gave to Helen. The necessary consequences of her wealth our child is, I think, prepared for, and she has sense enough to estimate, as it deserves, the adulation with which the world will honour the *heiress*. We have not followed the unwise plan of educating our children in ignorance on any point that concerns them. I have good hope that we shall reap the advantage of fencing their understanding against danger, instead of blinding them to its existence. Helen knows well all her advantages of person, mind, position; and, instead of being vain and arrogant, she is humble and grateful, for she has the habit of asking that question which lays the axe to the root of all pride, 'What hast thou that thou didst not receive?'"

CHAPTER II.

"LET me tell you, Greville," said Lady Sophia Cleveland, "that your country cousin, as you call her, would be an admirable *partie* even for you."

"When I approach the end of my career, possibly," said the premature man of fashion, who had not yet numbered twenty summers. "The wealth of all the Rothschilds would not tempt me to bestow myself on a hoyden from the Highlands. I really think it would be adviseable to cut the Hamiltons altogether. It is paying too dear for family connections to surround one's self with Goths whom no decent man could patronise."

"And pray, Mr. Greville Cleveland, if I may presume to ask a gentleman of your elegance the question, how comes it that your superlative wisdom has arrived at the conclusion that these people are Goths?"

"Partly from your ladyship's hints," returned Mr. Cleveland, carelessly: "partly from Stark's more explicit declarations, that the mamma was always a pattern woman, even in her best days, and that is a class for which, I am proud to say, I inherit your abhorrence."

"I wish you inherited my dislike of quoting people so questionable as Mr. Stark. I very much disapprove of your intimacy with that man."

Mr. Greville Cleveland favoured Lady Sophia with a stare of the most unequivocal surprise.

"I really imagined myself a model of filial propriety," said he, "by choosing as my 'fidus Achates,' a person so decidedly patronised by my mother."

"Patronised!" said Lady Sophia, angrily. "Yes, as one patronises anything that contributes to one's amusement, or that is positively useful. Mr. Stark is admitted *here* as a *mime* or a messenger."

"And *I* patronise him because he is both decidedly useful and agreeable to me; again I defend myself on your principles."

"At your age your father's wishes might be supposed to influence your choice of companions."

"*Pardonnez*—that is quite new doctrine," interrupted the youth, flippantly.

"And Mr. Stark is his aversion," pursued Lady Sophia. "So long as Stark was a mere litérateur he was not so objectionable, but since he has found *rouge et noir* more profitable than satire, I doubt whether you will ultimately have much reason to congratulate yourself on his acquaintance"

The young man rose, and affected to be occupied with the *bijouterie* that crowded a mother-of-pearl table near him.

"As an only son," resumed Lady Sophia, "you may possibly overvalue your advantages. Ample as Sir Greville's income may appear, it has never yet covered his expenses; consequently the estates are encumbered, and *my* property, as you know, belongs to younger children, represented by Augusta."

"Thrice happy Augusta—*ter quaterque beata!*"

"Abominable!" said Lady Sophia, indignantly. "If my wishes have no weight with you, at least pay sufficient deference to my experience to leave off a habit that must condemn you among any people worth knowing. If you wish to be detected immediately as a novice, with all the rust of academic life about you, quote your detestable Greek and Latin: otherwise, forget that you have ever learned them."

"I wish I could," said her son, with ludicrous solemnity; "but alas, my Eton discipline is all too recent."

And with a yawn intended to express at once carelessness, independence, and the precise quantity of ennui a well-bred man ought to feel in the society of his mother and sister, the heir of the house of Cleveland sauntered from the apartment.

"The most impracticable of human beings!" said Lady Sophia, with a sigh that was at least sincere. "His intimacy with Stark is a real misfortune."

"I must confess your objection to that person appears as inexplicable to me as to Greville," said Augusta Cleveland, coldly. "It is strange that you should deem a man evidently so greatly in your confidence an improper associate for your son."

Lady Sophia's countenance changed, and she subdued, with difficulty, the rising pang inflicted by an insinuated reproach from the child from whom, in one sense, she assuredly had not deserved it.

"Do not," she said after a short pause, "allow Greville's absurd opinion to influence yours. The Hamiltons are not Goths, rely on it; nor will you find the new heiress a rival to be despised."

"I always make it a point to forget Greville's opinions. One needs not burden one's memory with nonsense."

"Very true," replied Lady Sophia, with one of her blandest smiles. "And really, my love, Mrs. Hamilton, pattern woman as she doubtless was and is, has certainly claims to consideration which are not likely to be disallowed in society. In her young days, there were many who thought her positively beautiful, and I have heard she is in excellent preservation. Consider the advantage to beauty of a life of repose, exempt from all anxiety! Then, you know, she is bringing out her daughter—reputed a beauty—known to be an heiress. Lady Darley had an immense fortune to bequeath, of the whole of which this girl is the independent possessor, unencumbered by any condition except that of bearing the name and arms of Darley, time-honoured as they are."

"She is fortunate," said Augusta, with the air of a person *gêné* by a narrative of facts quite uninteresting to her.

"And *dangerous*," returned Lady Sophia, with a look the significance of which was not to be mistaken. "Men are proverbially fickle, and he who is conscious that he may roam through the parterre of beauty and fashion, and cull what flower he will, may too possibly deem that fairest which is newest."

A slight increase of colour was perceptible on the elegant cheek of her ladyship's exquisitely beautiful daughter.

"I perceive you understand me," resumed Lady Sophia. "Lord Lawton is not yet committed by any proposal. At present everything promises well, but how often, dearest Augusta, does hope fall short of fruition!"

A gentle inclination of the head marked the listener's acquiescence.

"Lord Lawton is decidedly *the parti*. There is not a mother but strives to entangle him—not a daughter but to the utmost of her ability aids those efforts. Your delicacy has adopted the wiser policy of indifference, which, whether real or assumed, has nearly been rewarded with success. It would be hard, indeed, if a novice were to snatch the wreath from your brow!"

Augusta's smile expressed her conviction that the thing was impossible.

"Be not too secure," said Lady Sophia, replying to that mute eloquence. "You are beautiful, well born, wealthy—and Lady Darley's heiress is all these. You are the fashion—she is not, at present—but she is *new*, a more than equal advantage when the object is a man almost *blasé*. I confess I have great curiosity to see Mrs. Stracey Hamilton's daughter."

"Which I cannot be expected to share, not being acquainted with Mrs. Stracey Hamilton," said Augusta, with her ordinary *glacè* polish of manner.

"There is Lord Vere; appeal to him whether Miss Darley—beautiful by nature, and fashioned by Mrs. Hamilton—be not in danger of *un grand succès* in society," said Lady Sophia, as Lord Vere entered with the familiarity of established intimacy.

Although eighteen years had brought with them their customary changes, Lord Vere still played a distinguished rôle in the drama of fashionable life. Still unmarried, his position and *presumed* fortune rendered him a desirable object to all matrimonial speculators—that large class consisting of mothers who have daughters to dispose of, and daughters who desire to *be* disposed of. At forty, if his person had lost some of those graces which belong to youth, it had, *en revanche*, acquired a dignity and an elegance, the effect of constant intercourse with the élite of the highest circles. Always pre-eminently handsome, he was still the Magus Apollo of the Pantheon; his eccentricities were just sufficient to remind the world of the genius which rendered them pardonable, and to separate him from the mass. The whole of his establishment was in the best possible taste, affecting simplicity rather than ostentation. The plainness of his liveries, his carriages, his toilette, just stopped short of affectation. As Sir Greville Cleveland in his day had achieved empire by a magnificence without parallel, so Lord Vere had arrived at a not less agreeable autocracy by the unimpeachably simple taste which was *his* great rule of right.

"Doubtless," he said, answering Lady Sophia's remark, "if she *be* beautiful, at least among those who deem her so. One hears of beauty so perfect as to please the universal taste, but I confess it never was my good fortune to find it. I heard a man complain that the Medicean Venus was too short, and another that her countenance wanted expression. After that, I despair of ever sunning myself in the beams of a loveliness which all agree to commend."

Miss Cleveland smiled—a smile which showed that the statue *could* be warmed by the Promethean fire.

"Well, well," said Lady Sophia, with some petulance, "but *un grand succès* exists without being universal. I have ascertained the fact of her being handsome, and her enormous wealth is bruited about already. The Hamiltons have given up the house in Portland Place, and have taken possession of Lady Darley's splendid mansion—part of their daughter's vast inheritance. After all, wills so partial as hers are extremely unjust: and *she* turned Methodist, I heard, before her death—converted by the efforts of the old woman with whom Mrs. Hamilton was living when she married—*my* ci-devant governess—Warren, I recollect, was her name. I always distrust excessive religion, and consider an act of injustice as inconsistent with real piety."

How easy it is to *talk* rightly!

Lord Vere *rather* opened his eyes—just as much as a man of his good breeding might venture to do.

"I always thought Mrs. Hamilton's manners too *brusque*," said he. "Her understanding also was of that masculine kind which, for my own poor part, I consider, to speak gently, misplaced in her sex. The perfection of female manner is, in my opinion, perfect repose, which is unattainable by a person who expresses herself so strongly as Mrs. Hamilton. People talk of her dignified composure—I call it the austerity of a stoic. Her daughter is, I have heard, her pupil—and Mrs. Hamilton at second hand would, I fancy, be rather too much for my nerves."

"I would certainly rather not encounter either mother or daughter," said Lady Sophia. "But what can we do? That dreadful evil called family connection imperatively prescribes a certain mode of conduct, and one must swallow the disagreeable like a dose of medicine, only without the satisfaction of making a wry face. Sir Greville, you know, always was remarkable for his adherence to *les convenances de societé*, and that is about the last vestige of his youth which remains to him."

"*Heu, quantum mutatus ab illo*! Sir Greville is indeed but the ruin of the past—arrived at the lees of the cup of life—to *him* a rich draught, but quaffed all too quickly—mingled with the poison that exhilarates and destroys," said Lord Vere, with an air meant to be melancholy. "How I could moralize, if I dared inflict my tediousness on you!"

"Pray endeavour to be amusing," said the beautiful Augusta; "I have been wearied to death with these eternal Hamiltons the whole morning."

"One would really imagine you dreaded a rival near the throne, Augusta," said Lady Sophia.

"Forbid it, heaven!—the heaven of love and fashion!" said Lord Vere, with mock emphasis. "A rustic from the Highlands would bring her rural graces in vain among *us*, I fancy, but that the pebble is set in gold—and the world, in this age of political economy, has grown more than ever mercenary. *Apropos des bottes*—have you seen Lawton this morning?"

"Not this week," said Lady Sophia, "which may be explained by the fact that we saw him every day for the previous fortnight, and he would tire of the same faces even in Elysium."

"True; *change* is to him the vital principle, and he literally goes about, like the Athenians, inquiring for some new thing! Somebody has given him a glowing description of the new heiress, and as his imagination has sufficient food to occupy itself withal, he is almost in love through expectation. He would have been a worshipper of Mokanna, if the veiled prophet had been among the cheats of our days, for so long as mystery kept him in a state of excitement, he would have been the most devout of adorers."

"Nevertheless, when the fever of youth has subsided, I have no doubt he will settle down into a state of contentment with the world as he finds it," said Lady Sophia.

"I am quite willing to agree with you in anything favourable to Lawton, for I absolutely perceive in myself very friendly dispositions towards that young man," said Lord Vere, with one of his most peculiar inflections of voice; "and really, if I can in any way promote your ladyship's views, that is, if I can put things in a more desirable train—supply a *momentum* to Lawton's uncertain impulses—I don't know whether I make myself intelligible—but, plainly, you are aware that in this, as in everything, I shall in all my best obey you, madam."

"Pray do not trouble yourself, Lord Vere," said Miss Cleveland, with greater animation than her perfect features had hitherto seemed capable of expressing. "You are pleased to be very incomprehensible, but as regards Lord Lawton, neither Lady Sophia nor myself desires the slightest restraint to be placed on his inclinations, be they as changeable as the moon. I do not fancy myself likely to suffer an eclipse during this present anno Domini, and until I am in despair, I beg to decline all friendly interference."

"What's Hecuba to him or he to Hecuba?" said Lord Vere, with the air of a man *distrait;* and opening a *souvenir*, he seated himself by Miss Cleveland, affecting to be occupied by its contents—occasionally reading aloud a line that particularly pleased him; and, whatever might be the taste displayed in his quotations, they certainly had the effect of propitiating the divinity he had offended, and of bringing to her cheek a deeper bloom than even its own rich carnation.

Meanwhile Lady Sophia, absorbed in her own plans for the future, had no eyes for the present; like a man who, calculating on the sunshine of harvest, disregards the clouds that threaten to deluge the earth, ere yet it has received the seed from which all is to spring up.

CHAPTER III.

WHILE one half of the world was conjecturing *when* Cecil, Marquis Lawton, *would* propose to the beautiful and brilliant Augusta Cleveland, and the other half wondering whether he *had* proposed, he, the said Right Honourable Cecil, was debating on the wisdom or necessity of taking that step at all.

"Beautiful!" thus his thoughts shaped themselves; "as Byron says, 'nothing earthly can surpass her!' Graceful, fashionable; not too witty, not *gênant* everybody with a parade of accomplishments, the showy coin which imbecility forces on the world for the sterling ore of sense—of intellect—what more can man desire? What would one have that there is not? what would one wish away that there *is*? Ay, there's the rub! Brilliant she is, and lovely withal—and gentle too, or at least so polished as to pass excellently well for gentle; but *cui bono!* For this hotbed called the world, out of the atmosphere of which all her graces must necessarily perish, for they owed their existence to it—have been reared, nurtured in it, and could no more withstand the ruder gales of a more wholesome temperature, than an exotic from the tropics, the summit of Ben Nevis. And has *my* vocation the same direction? Laying my hand on my heart, I answer my own question in all truth and soberness—assuredly not. Are these the scenes among which I mean to trifle away the precious boon—existence? Heaven forbid! May I perish rather *now*, and be preserved from the augmented guilt of such a career! Wherefore, then, am I seeking my wife amid such? Where but here shall I find the females of my order, and can I venture to marry out of the aristocratic pale? Fettered, circumscribed by convention, how dare I venture to break the hidden but cumbrous chains that bind me? And I *must* marry. Cheerless indeed is the vista of life to me, unblessed by female companionship! And the companionship of the class of 'tapestry-workers!'* After all, it will be through the error of making our women such as they are, that all our privileges will finally crumble into the dust. Such wives—such mothers—exerting their sure influence on us and our successors! After all, and for the nine thousandth time, would that I had belonged to the *just milieu!*"

And as the revery of Lord Lawton arrived at this point, he drew up his cab at the door of Cleveland House.

"*Not at home.*"

"Not at home!" repeated his lordship, giving his card, and glancing at the equipages evidently in attendance on visiters.

Somewhat piqued, he had re-entered his carriage, when he recognised Mr. Stark on the pavé.

"Are you going to Cleveland House?" said he, rather more familiarly than was his wont with this person, whom he did not patronise very warmly. "I wish you better success than I have had, for I have been turned away with 'Not at home.'"

"Then my attempting the entreé is useless," said Mr. Stark. "How annoying! Cleveland promised to drive me to Richmond, and I must be there at three. I have lost an hour."

"Cleveland's movements do not depend on Lady Sophia's, I fancy, and my visit was to her," said Lord Lawton, coldly. Then, after a moment's thought, he added, "I have no objection to drive to Richmond myself; therefore if you will accept of a seat, get in;" an offer of which Stark availed himself with alacrity, and in an instant was by the side of his lordship.

* See Lady Morgan's dramatic sketch, "The Recess"

The cab rolled on, smoothly as aristocratic cabs do. Mr. Stark had tried the first drawingroom of the season, and its usual host of *parvenu*—presentations—the first night at Almack's—still the marquis was taciturn, and his companion had the mortification of feeling he had made no impression, the more bitter because, to do him justice, he did not often experience a similar failure.

"Did you see the carriage at the door of Cleveland House?" inquired Lord Lawton, after an inauspicious silence, the misery of which, Stark thought, greatly counterbalanced the honour of his present position. He revived, however, at this question, and answered in the affirmative.

"I did not remember the liveries, and there were no arms," observed Lord Lawton, who felt that uneasiness natural to a man on finding himself unpleasantly convinced that that which he has been accustomed to consider his own, whenever he would take the trouble of appropriating it, may probably fall into the hands of another.

"The Hamilton liveries," said Stark, with the pride of giving information to the ignorant. "I heard of the arrival of Colonel Hamilton's family in Grosvenor Square, some days since."

"Ah! Lady Sophia's brother. I recollect hearing he was expected. Not particularly intimate at Cleveland House, I believe?"

"No," said Stark, with a smile intended to excite curiosity, and hardly ever failing of its effect. "It was rather a *mal-apropos* arrangement, the marriage of Miss Vernon, the present Mrs. Stracey Hamilton, with Lady Sophia's brother."

"It took place before my day. I was abroad, or at college, or at school, or in the nursery. How was it?"

"Sir Greville was engaged to Miss Vernon when Lady Sophia appeared in the scene, and regained the fickle heart of the baronet to whom she had been betrothed previous to her marriage with Mr. Barron. You know, *on revient toujours a ses premiers amours*."

"Often quoted, never believed," said Lord Lawton, dryly. "However, Lady Sophia had the charity to provide for the lady on whom she bestowed the willow. In such cases a brother is useful enough."

"Nevertheless, it never was in the power of Lady Sophia, or any other human being, to make use of Colonel Hamilton, unless his own will did most seriously incline that way. And in marrying Miss Vernon, *soi dit en passant*, he committed, in the opinion of her ladyship, an unpardonable sin, for he wedded neither fortune nor high family connection."

"Beautiful?"

"As usual, opinions differ. Regular features, splendid complexion, but the expression rather intellectual than tender, the indication of a mind that had more of the man than the woman in its composition."

"I have sometimes met Colonel Hamilton; but I don't recollect his wife."

"His visits to London have been few and far between of late; he lost his seat during the last parliament, and came in again the other day on the liberal interest, as they call it—that is, the levelling. He is a thoroughgoing reformer."

"Ah!" said Lord Lawton, thoughtfully: but the intonation was so equivocal, that even the acute and practised Mr. Stark could not penetrate the mystery of his lordship's politics—a mystery deemed worthy of being known by many more distinguished than himself, and a knowledge which *he* felt might be made profitable.

"A very eccentric person, Mrs. Hamilton," he resumed: "I confess I have some curiosity to see her daughter, whose education, I hear, has been the entire work of her mother. When I detected the Hamilton carriage at Cleveland House, I made quite sure that they were going through the ceremonial of returning Lady Sophia's visit. It astonishes me that Lady Sophia received them—almost as much as that your lordship was not admitted."

"There will be no end to your astonishments, Mr. Stark, if the caprice of a woman of fashion has the power of exciting them."

"In such a case Lady Sophia is too systematic to be capricious," returned Stark, whose good humour was imperturbable whenever his interest required it to be so. "I rather apprehend she did not choose to be the first to exhibit this importation from the Highlands to the *élite*. No person is more shrinkingly susceptible of the possibility of being compromised by the *gaucherie* of her friends than Lady Sophia."

"There may be some reason in your conjecture," said Lord Lawton, who felt that it was at least a balm to his wounded vanity.

"Lady Sophia is not always correct in her calculations. Mrs. Hamilton's daughter, as the heiress of Lady Darley's large fortune, will be sufficiently *répandue*, let her be as plain or as blue as she may."

"I have rather a curiosity to see the heiress," said Lord Lawton. "A young woman educated in profound retirement by her mother, is a novelty among *us*. We trust our children to hirelings—which, perhaps, it is our wisdom to do, until their mothers have educated themselves."

"You are too severe. Blue is becoming a prevalent colour among the aristocracy. I heard a remark the other day of a different tinge—that more women now write than read. Regarding Miss Darley—for Mrs. Hamilton's eldest daughter bears that style and title—Lady Sophia could arrange an introduction for your lordship with the greatest ease. Possibly, however, that may not be within the limits of her ladyship's politics," continued Mr. Stark, with a sagacious shrug. "The splendid Augusta must reign alone, and it is within the compass of probability that *la cousine* may be *too* beautiful. The amiable infirmities of the sex will find their best apology in your lordship's known gallantry."

A cab at this instant passed them rapidly, and was as instantly pulled up. "Who is there?" said the voice of Mr. Cleveland. "Anybody with you, Lawton?"

"Mr. Stark."

"The fellows at Cleveland House gave me reason to expect as much, but I did not. You were denied, I learned, but suspected a mistake."

"True, nevertheless."

"*Ah, je devine!* Where are you going?"

"To redeem your pledge of setting down Mr. Stark at Richmond."

"If that be all, Stark may have my cab, and I will take the vacant seat in yours. I want to initiate you into a secret of diplomacy."

The arrangement was made, Mr. Stark being the only dissatisfied party, and the person whose sentiments were least important, and least regarded, in all *strifes of selfishness* between him and his companions, *but not his fellows.*

"You generally shun that double of mine, as if plague, pestilence, and famine were in his train," said Mr. Cleveland, as they rolled along one of the finest roads in England. "I suspect you wanted to pick his brains, and you would have found nothing there worth your labour."

"He is such a court chronicle of the last twenty years, that one may pick up occasionally an anecdote of the past."

"Not often worth preserving," said Cleveland, with a laugh that savoured strongly of *the boy.* "*We* are the men of the new era."

"*To be,*" said Lord Lawton, with emphasis. "Meanwhile, for your piece of diplomacy."

"I hope it struck you as sufficiently extraordinary that *you—cher et cheri*—should bear the brunt of the ominous *no* of my lady mother's porter."

"Brightness belongs to the sun—coolness to the air—heat to the fire—transparency to the water—and caprice to woman. *Que voulez vous?*"

"But Lady Sophia's caprices are never *inconséquent,*" returned Mr. Cleveland, who affected French commonplaces, to prove that he belonged to the mob that had just left Paris. "What will you give me for the reason?—with which Stark *could* not favour you if he *would.*"

"Just what it is worth—nothing."

You wrong me and disappoint yourself—or you might

if I were not resolute on telling. Lady Sophia and I are ever playing against each other, you know, and let us see who has the game. Augusta always *was* the favourite, but *tenez, ma mére, je vous en rendrai compte.*"

"Dreadful!" said Lord Lawton, rather to himself than his companion.

"Is it not written that people shall reap as they sow?" said Cleveland, with more energy and deeper feeling than was usually apparent in his manner. "But I will not be young enough to have a *scéne.* Lawton, do you mean to marry Lady Sophia's daughter? I ask the question *en ami* not *en frére.*"

"Marriage to my contemplation is always in the *paulo post futurum* tense," returned Lord Lawton, carelessly.

"Lady Sophia flatters herself it is approaching to the present. And, to unmystify the mystery, the new heiress, Miss Darley, *la belle cousine*, was at Cleveland House this morning, and you were paid the compliment of being excluded; under the circumstances, a compliment of the first magnitude."

"Mrs. Hamilton's daughter?" inquired Lord Lawton, with an air of interest. "And she is not very plain or gauche, is she?"

"*Gauche!*" repeated Cleveland, laughing—"a very grace! Beautiful as her mother, always celebrated as a beauty, *vide* my father's history *ætatis* thirty-five, and to my taste, more attractive, because she is less *prononçée.* Natural, but not simple, *naïve*, not ignorant; in England, I confess, I never saw so charming a person, and I honour Lady Sophia's policy which put it out of your power to make invidious comparisons between truth and artificiality. Trust to my knowledge of the *carte du pays.* The whole world was admitted at Cleveland House but *you*, because, a reason to gratify any man's vanity, you only were formidable. If *you* had shown signs of defection, *la belle sœur* could not have survived."

Lord Lawton's spirit admitted a new light, as a glimpse of a sudden revelation. But he made not Cleveland the partner of his thoughts. He glided into the *nonsenses* of the day, and by sinking to the level of his companion, effectually concealed the deeper thoughts that were struggling within him.

CHAPTER IV.

It is the easiest thing in the world for two persons moving in the same sphere to become intimate, especially when that intimacy happens to be ardently desired by one of the parties. Lord Lawton, in a very short time, was received in the house of Colonel Hamilton as a familiar acquaintance—almost a friend: and even Helen Darley, with all her blushing *naïveté*, had learned not to shrink from his approaches, and had ventured once or twice to argue a point of taste with him—a courageous effort in a girl who had, all her life, been accustomed to lean on her mother's judgment, and who was now learning independence of thought and action as a task. And even to the most prosperous, the most courted, the world is a stern taskmaster. With all her endowments, natural, acquired, accidental, Helen did not escape her share of the minor miseries of human life. Sometimes in society she committed a *gaucherie* not very unpardonable in a tyro, but sufficient to excite the impertinent and not always inaudible remarks of the more practised, among whom were the envious, the plain, the poor, the *passées*. Helen was made to feel that the rich gifts of Heaven are like the honey carried by the bee—accompanied by a sting. With the affectionate enthusiasm of extreme youth, her heart yearned for female friendship, and met, for the gold it coveted, the dross of flattery and meanness, yea, even from the scions of the proudest of the aristocracy. There were those who found that the way to the wealthy Miss Darley's purse was through her feelings, and that professions of extreme attachment were paid for by very solid presents, which her ample allowance enabled her to make at will. It must not be supposed that Mrs. Hamilton—anxious mother as she was—was blind to all this, but she desired that her daughter should gather wisdom from her own experience, that most impressive of instructers. She left her, as far as prudence permitted, to her own guidance, and to that correction of errors which time, the infallible asserter of right, inevitably effects in his progress, with all rational beings.

But there was a point to which Catharine's attention was intensely directed; the gradually deepening interest with which her daughter received the evident admiration of Lord Lawton. When bent on pleasing, it was hardly possible to resist the influence of his manners, and feeling her own increasing pleasure in his society, she trembled for Helen's constancy, and sighed as she contemplated the probable disappointment of the sometime wish of her heart—the union of her child with Arthur Maitland. The time of his prescribed separation from his *almost* betrothed had not yet elapsed, and Catharine would not permit herself, by hint either seriously or in *persiflage*, to recall to Helen's memory all she had so lately promised—the self-reliance with which she had derided the bare possibility of change in herself. In the forming of that most important of human connections, where the happiness of a moral and intellectual being is at stake, she shrank from expressing a wish that might warp the judgment or even bias the inclination. She had watched Maitland from youth to maturity; knew all the strength, all the weakness of his character; felt that the proportion to be loved and admired so greatly exceeded that which was to be regretted—*the only perfection to which mortal man can attain*—that all her reason was satisfied, as well as that affection which a long intercourse between honourable and indulgent maturity and candid ingenuous youth is almost sure to generate. But there were points on which even she doubted, and fearful of allowing her wishes to influence her judgment, her repugnance to offer even an opinion, to hazard a caution, approached to fastidiousness; and it was in the very point that the dearest interests of her child were at stake, that the ordinary confidence existing between that mother and daughter was violated. Not a look warned Helen that her constancy was in danger; and she indulged in the agreeable excitement of Lord Lawton's society with the greater delight, because, unsuspicious of the possible meaning of his attentions, she felt no necessity for defending herself against them.

"After all, the tact of woman is worth all the boasted superiority of man's reason," said Colonel Hamilton one day, after Lord Lawton had trifled away his morning at Helen's side. "I begin to fancy that your doubt of our girl's constancy was better grounded than my implicit belief in it."

"Woman knows woman," said Catharine, smiling, "and we are a mystery even to those among you who pique themselves on understanding us best. There is so much to attract a novice in Lord Lawton!"

"*Only* a novice?"

"Your inquiry implies a question which I admit. To *more* than novices; to me, practised woman of the world as I have been. What can exceed the fascination of his manner—that air of *empressement*, contrasting, too, so forcibly with the somewhat cold seriousness of poor Maitland?"

"*Poor* Maitland!" interrupted Colonel Hamilton. "It is very bad with a man when he sinks into *poor* A. or B."

"He *is* to be pitied, should my fears be realized, for the loss of Helen's heart, even if *so* lost, if not 'false she should be fickle,' is a thing to be regretted. Of Maitland's worth we are assured, and it is my conviction that the happiness of woman's life is more dependant on the worth of her husband than his talents; which made me, in this instance, hail with delight the dawning attachment between him and Helen. And yet there have been moments when I have doubted the result," she added, thoughtfully, and in a somewhat subdued voice.

"How could that be, dearest? We can but judge of particular contingencies by applying general principles."

"I have never attempted to bias my child," resumed Catharine, with energy; "I have been her friend, her counsellor, never the attempted despot over her feelings. How could I venture to decide for her; I, who am not absolutely sure of my own wishes, of the correctness of my own views? How dare I venture to press the springs of her heart; I, who am so ignorant of all its fearful machinery? But I have occasionally asked myself the question, whether Maitland's deficiency in the more brilliant qualities of the intellect would not be a fatal defect in her eyes, when her own enlarged experience should render it more glaring. The tone of her mind may vibrate to loftier aspirations than his—not incompatible with that perfect conjugal happiness, but yet offering a valid reason for her possible change of sentiment now. If we could have ensured her continuing in the Highlands for ever, there would have been no doubt of her happiness; with him among his tenantry her life would have glided on in tranquil usefulness and content. But that *could* not be. She must have entered a more gladiatorial arena for masculine intellect, and wretched for her if she, who had not suspected the inferiority of the lover, were first awakened to that of her husband! Remember he has not that knowledge which must always give your sex a conventional superiority to ours—knowledge of the world, of human nature. In short, I can hardly discern my own wishes."

"And you have made out a very sufficient case against the approved suitor of your child," said Colonel Hamilton. "If you had been special pleading in extenuation of Helen's inconstancy, you could not have seized on stronger points."

"I have occasionally suspected that neither of them has a perfect knowledge of the species of affection each entertains for the other. The heart of an isolated being like Maitland—an orphan without brother or sister—naturally yearned for the love of some human creature, and Helen fell in his way, a beautiful child—and I certainly *did* originally rely on their habits of intimacy giving them a similar affection to that between brother and sister, and I am not always sure that my calculations were erroneous. Perhaps, if exposed to temptation, his constancy may not exceed hers."

"You are convinced, then, that hers *is* in danger."

'I fear so. Foolish phrase! Why should I fear that which I am not sure is not positively desirable? There is danger. She is more embarrassed in the society of Lord Lawton, occasionally; there is an evident trepidation of manner when he appears; a change of complexion at the accidental utterance of his name; a restlessness if he does not immediately address her; a wandering of the eye in a crowded assembly until he is perceived."

"Alas, poor Yorick! Infallible symptoms! But are there not rumours of Lord Lawton's engagement to Miss Cleveland? when shall I learn to call her my niece Augusta?"

"I have heard such, but in such a state of society who credits a rumour? One cannot arrive at our degree of intimacy with Lord Lawton without being convinced that he is incapable of the very shadow of dishonour. Moreover, it might be dangerous to trifle with the daughter of Sir Greville Cleveland."

"Might *have been*," said Colonel Hamilton, significantly. "Twenty years have made a wondrous change in the hero of the circles—the courtly favourite of George the Fourth—the arbiter of all that was most graceful and most elegant—the worthless lover of Catharine Vernon! Nay, dearest, spare me that unkind glance—unkind even in its playfulness. The one redeeming action of Greville's career, in *my* apprehension, is that which gave *me* such a wife; my children such a mother."

"But after what *we* have seen of the exquisitely polished Miss Cleveland, do you believe that she has a heart to be wounded? Do you deem her capable of a feeling beyond the intense selfishness of her caste? Amid all that frostwork of artificiality, can you think her susceptible of one natural emotion? An alliance with Lord Lawton might possibly gratify the ambition of Augusta or her mother; just as the votaries of an ancient superstition evinced their veneration for their deity, by the costliness of the sacrifice they were able to offer on his shrine."

"But her impassiveness does by no means extenuate his fickleness, if, indeed, 'he hath so offended,'" said Colonel Hamilton. "An excellent rule of action, the old song—

'Tis good to be merry and wise,
'Tis good to be honest and true,
'Tis good to be off with the old love,
Before you be on with the new.'"

"Time alone can set us right," said Catharine, with a sigh. "There is, however, one subject for congratulation; that Stracey is not exposed to an intimacy with that strange, wild young man, Greville Cleveland. And yet there is much that is attaching in the poor youth. There is a frankness about him which throws a halo even round his follies, but this would not render him the less dangerous to an inexperienced boy like ours, and I can only repeat my satisfaction that he is away."

"The most dangerous of Greville's propensities is for Stark's society; a man of whom I hear from all of whom I make inquiries, that he is a confirmed gamester; a person, considering that he is still among *the admissibles*, in the worst possible odour. Lady Sophia, it appears, is hardly civil to him, her scanty notice being probably the guerdon of past services."

"Notwithstanding the pre-eminent beauty, the brilliant success of his daughter, I cannot help feeling how unfortunate Sir Greville Cleveland is in his children! And there appears such a sad want of paternal care on his part, especially in the headlong career of his son."

"A want which commenced when he selected Sophia as their future mother," said Colonel Hamilton, with that severity of manner which, in him, always indicated deep feeling of the most painful nature. "In the first era of her life, the character of woman influences principally her own happiness, for even that of parents, for the most part, is affected by childern *in the aggregate*, not by one child in particular. In her second era, its effects reach a more extended point—a point still—the happiness of that other human, moral, responsible agent, her husband. But in the third, the great era of woman's destiny—*her age* of empire—when the duties of maternity demand her exertions—then, indeed, her rôle becomes the most important which an accountable being can sustain; affecting, by the manner in which it is sustained, not only the mortal but the immortal interests of those on whose minds she makes the first impressions; the *rasæ tabulæ* on which she traces characters permanent often beyond the reach of time or circumstance. The destinies of the world are more in the hands of woman than we in our masculine pride are always willing to admit. *She* moulds the wax when it is most ductile; *she* prepares our successors, the future controllers of the earth. It is as a mother that woman must always appear to philosophers and politicians most interesting, most important."

"Reflection only can make us comprehend how awful a thing it is to hold the deposite of the happiness of a fellow-creature," said Catharine, pale from the strong emotion with which she had listened to her husband; "even the *temporal* happiness; and carrying one's ideas forward to those other infinitely more sublime interests—*eternal* interests—one can but shrink from the perception of one's own weakness, and feel the immeasurable comfort of a reliance on Him 'who is higher than the highest.' How miserable, how unsustained, must a thinking, irreligious mother feel, even in the plenitude of her love for her children!"

"*Are* there any *thinking* irreligious mothers?" said Colonel Hamilton. After a moment's pause he added, "It is an extraordinary thing, that one never meets with, hears of, reads of genius in your sex unaccompanied by religion; I do not mean *Christianity* always, but aspirations after the immortal, the invisible, far more earnest, more influential, more actuating, than in us. Perhaps the very delicacy of your perceptions, your conscious need of protection, makes you cling more tenaciously to the Divine aid. A female atheist seems .o me not only a monster, but an anomaly."

"There are none," said Catharine, "none among mothers. No woman ever closely watched the progress of infant life, and infant intellect, without believing in a special providence, without also being convinced of two great scriptural truths, that evil is born with us, but there is *not* an absolute and necessary and total incapacity of good. Watch closely the workings of a child's spirit, and you will gather a deeper insight into some of the elements of religion, than are unfolded in whole folios of homilies."

"Happy those mothers who *do* so watch, happy those children blessed with such," said Colonel Hamilton, seriously. "Meanwhile, dear Catharine, we will trust our girl to—"

"Her own heart, her own principles; they cannot lead her far astray."

CHAPTER V.

Mrs. Hamilton was alone when Sir Alfred Maitland was announced, so early that Helen, who had spent the preceding night in the fatigue of pleasure, was recruiting her exhausted energies by a protracted repose.

"*You* here!" said Catharine, extending her hand. "Fully three days sooner than you were expected! People suffering under your malady never are punctual; always too soon or too late."

A deeper tint suffused the countenance of Maitland, but that was so àpropos to the allusion as not to be remarkable. "I found the Highlands so dull after you had left my neighbourhood," said he, "that I remembered with pleasure an invitation given me by Mrs. Warren ages ago, and have been for nearly the last month at the cottage."

"A month!" said Catharine, with unaffected surprise "Frankly, that was rather an exorbitant visitation; and how *did* you contrive to dispose of your time?"

"Mrs. Warren found me useful," replied Maitland, seriously. "Painful even.s have occurred within that period, my dear

Mrs. Hamilton, events of which you were not previously apprized, because it was deemed useless to afflict you with the knowledge of what was inevitable, which you could neither prevent nor alleviate."

"My cousin Rachel, Mrs. Fulton?" said Catharine, turning very pale.

"Her sufferings have ceased," said Maitland, in a tremulous and subdued voice.

"I will see you again in half an hour," said Catharine, in strong emotion, and she retired to her own apartment.

We cannot but weep for the dead. Even when every feeling, when our reason, warns us that the transition to them from life to immortality is full of happiness, that they have welcomed the voice of the angel of death as the harbinger of peace, the herald of joy. We weep over the grave, even when we know it is the bed of rest for which the weary sufferer longed, as the wayworn traveller for his home. When compelled to look as it were from the chambers of rejoicing upon the dismal dark abode of the dead, our hearts are chilled as it stands in relation to ourselves, the happy, the rich, the loved; we forget to contemplate it in relation to the wretched, the poor, the desolate, who are gone to occupy it. Even in our sorrow for the dead, our tears are stained by the selfishness that makes half our mortality; the shadow of death falls upon ourselves, and after the first bitter pang, the conviction that something we loved is gone beyond the voice of our affection, we begin to sorrow, partly, for that we too must die!

Catharine knew full well that the happiness of Rachel had been shipwrecked; that her marriage with Fulton had been the *curse of a granted prayer*. In the first hour of her widowhood, Catharine had stood forth the friend, the protector, of her hapless kinswoman and her orphan child, but her society had evidently so great a tendency to depress the weakened mind of the mourner, that their intercourse had gradually been confined almost exclusively to occasional letters. Not that the welfare of Rachel had ever ceased to be a matter of the liveliest interest to her happier friend; but it was from Mrs. Warren that she was constantly assured of the tranquillity of her relative, and from her she had learned to regard the early death of Rachel as a probability for which all who loved her ought to be prepared. And now that it had occurred, it was soothing to Catharine to feel that she had secured to the last years of her life the consolation of a friend; that the excellent, the pious Mrs. Warren had been to her as a mother—had been present to support her in the last trying hour of existence. If ever the recollection of a duty, of a kindness, can give us a foretaste of the charity that may be felt in heaven, it is when the object on whom it has been conferred has passed the precincts of the tomb. To be conscious that *we* have cheered the heart that has ceased to beat, is one of the first best consolations that softens our grief for "the dead we have buried out of our sight."

As Catharine sat in the silence of her chamber, Rachel, as she had known her in her days of innocent and blooming girlhood, filled with the tenderness of that love which had spread its darkness over the whole of her future life; when *she*, the unwilling rival, had inflicted the first sharp pain on her guileless heart, rose up before her spirit like the phantom of her own youth. And then, by one of those inexplicable acts of the mind, which in a moment pictures an existence, the career of the three then so materially influencing the destiny of each other, appeared as if traced on a map before her—how variously coloured—how strikingly contrasted! Human life is indeed a wondrous spectacle, and never perhaps is its moral so forcibly illustrated, as when contemplated from such a point of sight as that whence it was now pictured forth to Catharine.

When she returned to Sir Alfred Maitland, though her cheek was pale and her eye saddened, she was "calmly in possession of her spirit." *His* emotion was more apparent than hers, but he was yet in the very dawn of youth, when feeling lies nearest the surface.

"I need not ask you if her last hour was tranquil," said Catharine; "after a life of faith and charity such as hers, how could it be otherwise?"

"It was all peace," said Maitland. "I looked on her soon after the last struggle was over, and it is hardly too much to say, that 'her face was as the face of an angel.' I would not but have witnessed the last moments of that dying martyr to woman's love, for the most rapturous of worldly pleasures. It was a lesson to make its effects felt during the whole of my future existence."

"The loss must be a grievous one to Mrs. Warren. She had become warmly attached to my afflicted cousin; the more so, perhaps, because she felt how necessary her friendship was to the sufferer."

"I have a letter from her," said Maitland, in some confusion. "Pardon me, that in the excitement of first feelings I was a forgetful messenger."

With the deepest emotion, Catharine read the letter:—

"Sir Arthur Maitland will have prepared you in some degree, my dearest Catharine, for the melancholy details I am to have the pain of communicating; mourn, I am sure you will, for the untimely death of the friend of your youth, but you will not be insensible to the consolation derived from her sincere piety, her willingness to resign this life for a better, her conviction that, while overflowing joy awaited her in the kingdom of her heavenly Father, *this* world could offer her nothing but gloom and darkness; the memory of a past too terrible to reflect upon, the prospect of a future to which the grave only afforded one single ray of hope.

"While we look back on the trials with which a mysterious Providence rendered the blameless existence of our departed friend a series of chastenings, let us humbly feel that this last stroke of a comparatively early death, has been a remembering of mercy. For the last six years, what has been her daily employment? To watch the desolation of the mind she had revered—to behold how shattered was the intellect she had venerated—to listen to the gloomiest ravings from lips on which she had been accustomed to hang for lessons of the wisdom that is from above! Oh, ye delicate Sybarites of this world! look upon *such* sorrow, and hush the impious murmurings breathed by your insatiate luxury! Look around at your chambers 'painted with gold and vermilion,' and contrast them with the narrow cell in which this martyr to woman's love watched, with unwearying patience, the maniac wanderings of the idolized husband of her heart! Oh, Catharine! mysterious indeed is the course of this world, and but for the hope of the revelations of that future world in which mystery is swallowed up by the full light of knowledge, who, that feels and thinks, but must despair? What has been the life of this creature, who to the learning of a schoolman, united the patience of a saint, the fortitude of a martyr, the beauty of a seraph, the love of a *woman?* Our hearts die within us as we ask the question, and *I* cannot but inquire of myself, why have I been permitted to heap content upon content, to add year to year; I, whose existence, compared to hers, has been but a succession of vanities? Alas! all that we know is, nothing can be known!

"Direct reference to the past always pained the dear unhappy sufferer so much, that I have carefully abstained from asking any questions that might revive the violent anguish of former afflictions. Yet in our intimate intercourse much has incidentally fallen from her, that cannot but awaken compassion in all who are alive to the sorrows of human nature. As the religious views of Mr. Fulton deepened into sterner and yet sterner gloom, his manner to those most nearly connected with him became gradually harsher and more petulant. In proportion as his religion ceased to be a religion of love, so his benevolence to man decreased. Promulgating the inevitable decrees of a justly incensed Sovereign, he had no compassion for rebels predoomed to punishment; he recognised not the bond of universal love which unites erring children to a merciful parent; with an austere righteousness, he 'came out from among them, and was separate,' forgetting to repeat the words of him who spake as never man spake, and cried 'Whoever *will*, let him take of the waters of life and drink *freely*.' The peculiar doctrines of that sect lately sprung up in the Christian world—

Millenarians, who venture 'to fix the times and the seasons which the Father hath put in his own power;' believers and preachers of unknown tongues, regardless that, against the apostolic injunction, none 'are there who can interpret;' attracted his already diseased mind with an influence too strong, at last, for the frail tenure by which man holds his distinguishing blessing, reason. His unhappy wife did occasionally venture a whisper of remonstrance, did humbly attempt to counsel, but checked by the consciousness of her sex's inferiority, so laboriously, so indelibly impressed on her by education and habit, she feared that she was overstepping the boundaries of *her* natural sphere, and in meek silence continued to watch and endure. The death of two of her unhappy children were trials that wrung her heart, 'but that,' she said, 'was a selfish sorrow—a mourning over herself, her own bereavement, for *them*, from the moment when their young eyes closed in this world to waken in another and a more glorious, she felt that she had abundant cause of rejoicing.' Catharine, do you believe that the mother of a dead child, a *little* child, ever was, could be, in heart, a predestinarian?

"What love is like the love of woman! Even to the last the unhappy widow breathed not a whisper that might savour of irreverence to her husband's memory. She never alluded to his malady; shrinking, with the delicacy of her undying affection, from exhibiting him to less pitying eyes in his state of prostated reason. It is from her daughter—the sole remaining tie for which, she said, she would have been contented to endure earth a little longer—that I have arrived at the details of her misfortunes. In character, as in person, Rachel greatly resembles her mother, whom she loved with all the devoted affection natural to a warm young heart, that had but that one outlet for its love. Of her father she speaks with pity, with respect, with grief, but in a manner which, spite of herself, warns us, that when life has passed the age of instincts, human affection must be preserved by other means than a mere reliance on natural ties. His character, his manner, his sternness, even his terrific doctrines, how repulsive, how terrible must they have been to the youthful heart of a tender girl, craving acquaintance with all that is gentlest and kindest in humanity, unable to reconcile what she is taught with what she feels; and in youth *one* feeling outweighs a hundred dogmas, *that* only to them is the infallible test of truth. Can we love by command? Can we love that which has not the qualities requisite to inspire love? Can we condemn this timid girl, if she substitutes respect for tenderness, as the means of cherishing her father's memory? Describing him in the last afflicting stage of his life, her voice trembles and softens; but in recurring to him as the teacher of her childhood, she is calm and subdued. What an index is the voice of the unsophisticated!

"The mortal sickness of Mrs. Fulton wore a mild, a flattering aspect. Hardly any of us but herself suspected her imminent danger; but she warned us, her child particularly, that we were hoping against hope, that the fiat had gone forth, and that but a few more suns separated her from the chamber of death. Her parting moment was apparently without pain of body, and with an evident fervour of piety that amounted almost to triumph. She, the meekest of the meek, in that dread moment was more than conqueror. It was an hour of solemn comfort to all who witnessed it, an hour pregnant with an awful lesson to those who are yet to pass through those solemn portals which have for ever closed upon *her*.

"The grief of Rachel is the more touching from its stillness. The pale cheek, the sickly smile, the tearful eye, the suppressed sob, are its indications. *Here* everything reminds her of her mother; and it is not difficult to perceive that the image of the dead is brought vividly before her by all those familiar objects which must be inseparably associated with her idea. This is the food which nourishes her sorrow, and which, I fear, will inflict a severe shock on, if not actually undermine, a constitution of hereditary delicacy. Were you in any place but London, I should ask you to receive my charge for the present. Your society—the companionship of Helen, would necessarily wean her thoughts from that perpetual recurrence to the past which now entirely occupies them. But situated as you are, I scarcely know how to suggest it. Your time is of course occupied; and Helen—a *débutante* heiress—is surrounded by the homage of half the world. Rachel's recent loss renders seclusion incumbent on her for some time; and even were this not the case, in her circumstances, an introduction into the society of *your monde* would neither be advantageous nor desirable. If my increasing infirmities would permit me to chaperone her to any place beyond this immediate neighbourhood, I would borrow Helen's Darley House, and hope for good effects even from such a change. But why talk of 'probable circumstances in impossible situations?' Why, but that one outlives all the beauty of life, without losing its weaknesses!"

"Rachel *must* be our guest, nevertheless," said Catharine. "If she remains at the cottage, the poor child will perish; and on this earth she has not another friend to receive her—none on whom affinity might give her claims, in the widest sense of the word, an orphan. And I too have been an orphan; and in *my* dark hour, *her* mother's gentleness was the single star of my dismal night, and I will pay back my debt."

"I was sure of it," said Maitland, earnestly; *so* earnestly that Catharine gazed at him, for a brief moment, as if to penetrate what had surprised him out of his habitual composure. "I represented to Mrs. Warren, that the retirement proper to Miss Fulton's situation, under her afflicting circumstances, was quite as attainable here as elsewhere; while she would, at the same time, enjoy all the excitement of novelty, by being in the way of hearing, at least, of the gayeties in which all around her were partaking."

"Not generally a very satisfactory position for a girl so young as my poor little kinswoman," said Catharine. "However, it is the best that *can* be done for her as things are; her immediate removal from the cottage is a matter of the first necessity. And we ourselves can shut our door for a week or two; the death of my poor cousin will be a valid reason: there is nothing to prevent our giving to Rachel such comfort as our constant society may be able to afford. Colonel Hamilton will be here almost immediately, for he has an appointment with Helen."

"And where *is* Helen?" asked Sir Alfred, with a deepened complexion.

In the excitement caused by Mrs. Warren's letter, it had not before occurred to Catharine, that this was the first inquiry the *all but* engaged lover had made after his mistress.

"Helen is not yet risen. She had a fatiguing duty of dissipation to perform last night. Fashion has its penalties, and that is one." A short pause. "I fear her unfortunate bereavement will sadly alter poor Rachel. Her excessive delicacy of beauty hardly promises to last—it seems almost too pure to stand the wear and tear of life."

"It is the beauty one imagines of a seraph," said Maitland, unconsciously. "How dreadful, that the fairest of created things bear, in their very loveliness, the seal and sign of their decay!"

"Mrs. Fulton had that same almost spiritual beauty; yet I question whether, if the circumstances of her life had been less unfortunate—if she had been cherished by fostering love in the retirement for which she was adapted, we should now have to mourn her premature death. We will permit ourselves to hope that, in inheriting her mother's beauty, Rachel will escape her misfortunes. *She* has not been an only and fondly beloved child; her mind has not been softened by over-much tenderness; if she has not encountered the rough discipline of the world, she has been, in some measure prepared to meet it by the severity in which her unfortunate father believed it his duty to nurture his children. Let us at least have the consolation of hoping that Rachel may be happy."

Sir Alfred spoke not, but his eyes expressed that a more earnest prayer for the orphan was breathed from the depths of his heart than words could have pronounced.

Catharine saw that he felt deeply, and even amid her first grief for the dead she began, with human interest, to question concerning the future, and with a shuddering uneasiness to ask herself whether human affections, in their purest and least earthly form, were not as evanescent as human existence. And if there be one view of ourselves and the things around us more touched with melancholy than another, it is when the irresistible conviction is borne upon us of the mutability which is a condition of our being.

CHAPTER VI.

"AND they allow this Sir Alfred Maitland actually to run tame about the house!" said Lady Sophia Cleveland. "Well, your extraordinarily clever women do the strangest things!"

"He is harmless," said Lord Vere. "Moreover, I rather fancy I heard a whisper of some attachment, as people call it, between him and the fair lady of Darley."

"Which, if eyes are interpreters in such cases, has been transferred to that piece of still life, who occupies a niche in their circle, and who is called by the very appropriate name of Rachel."

"I wish she were visible to profane eyes. She must be new, which, in these days, is rare as in those of Solomon."

"A most absurd thing, Mrs. Hamilton's having the girl here—just as if she could not have cried her eyes red just as well with Mrs. Warren in the country, as in Grosvenor Square. There are people in the world who affect to indulge their superfine feelings, at the expense of violating every dictate of common sense."

"Not the least absurd thing was their shutting their doors against all the world. Even the privileged marquis was not an exception."

"I fancy he was not displeased with the opportunity of withdrawing. Lord Lawton exerts, to its full extent, the masculine prerogative of inconstancy."

Lord Vere smiled—a smile that might mean everything or nothing, accordingly as he found it convenient to explain it.

"With all her advantages," said Lady Sophia, "for her beauty is as indisputable as her wealth, Helen Darley has not had that universal success which might have been anticipated."

"Simply because she is not *of us;* she has not been educated after our prescribed fashion, and we feel that we neither understand nor are understood. It is impossible that any degree of beauty or talent can ever entirely overcome this disadvantage."

"Talent!" repeated Lady Sophia, contemptuously. "It is in itself an obstacle; is it not in its very nature the antithesis to that mental inanity which is the perfection of a woman of fashion? To men belonging to *us*, talent in our sex is only a bore, for it obliges them to think instead of yawning; who would voluntarily encounter such an infliction?"

"It is impossible always to distinguish whether you mean praise or sarcasm, Lady Sophia. Mrs. Hamilton and her daughter have, at least, the advantage of being intelligible."

"Do you think they are *understood?*" asked Lady Sophia, quickly.

"By the most noble and puissant prince, the Marquis of Lawton," said Lord Vere, carelessly; "at least *he* thinks so, which will answer their purpose quite as well."

"Rely on it you are mistaken," said Lady Sophia, more seriously and earnestly. "I who—there is no mystery between us—I who have so deep an interest in ascertaining the real *carte du pays*, do you think *I* can be deceived? It is impossible!"

"That very interest blinds you," said Lord Vere, somewhat *en philosophe*. "Moreover, you are under another great error. Except on the point of vanity—where all women are susceptible—Augusta cares not if Lawton wed mother, daughter—all the Hamiltons. At her age the heart now and then will be half awake, notwithstanding the torpedizing influence of education."

"*Heart!* Do you suppose any girl with one atom of sense could resist such an establishment—the man too so *distingué?*"

"Augusta has resisted them, or I mistake it greatly—impenetrable to the combined charms of houses, equipages, rent rolls, titles, and distinctions of every kind and degree."

"You rave—or which is less tolerable, because more voluntary, you mystify," said Lady Sophia, petulantly. "Can she be insensible to the triumph of fixing a man whom the whole female world has been striving for these four years? Nothing could render such a folly explicable, but some entanglement on her part—a piece of insanity, thanks to my vigilant but not oppressive guardianship, quite and utterly impossible."

"There is nothing like the comfort of being satisfied on such points," said Lord Vere, and he made his *adieu* in the satisfactory conviction, that he left Lady Sophia at the climax of discomfort.

Augusta Cleveland entered almost immediately, and as

Lady Sophia gazed on the perfect beauty of her daughter, all her doubts and fears dissolved into thin air.

"Have you breakfasted, love? You look divinely. Nothing is such a beautifier as sleep. I hope you rested well, dear?"

"A little disturbed by the echoes of Lady Adelaide Willoughby's concertos. Her musical *soirées* are a positive affliction. Those interminable pianoforte concertos, people talked about fifty years ago, are the most wearisome things in nature. Never desire me to bring such a misery on myself again, mamma."

"But you are really such a passion of Lady Adelaide's, dear! And it is so amiable in you to go to her occasionally —so graceful a charity—a thing everybody talks of and admires; and then she is Lawton's aunt, and people tell the most astonishing facts of her influence over him. Kind to him in his orphan boyhood, she retains her hold on the affections of the man, and many have been wooed and won through the relations they loved, or were accustomed to fancy they did, which produces just the same effects."

"Lord Lawton did not speak more than three sentences to me last night; a poor payment for the *ennui* to which I had doomed myself. He was quite an *attaché* to the Hamilton party; and really, mamma, I find that Mrs. Stracey Hamilton a most disagreeable personage. Her eyes are quite overpowering. One shrinks as if they were asking impertinent questions which, in spite of one's self, one was compelled to answer *au pied de la lettre*. Can you conceive anything more oppressive?"

"I fear, my sweet love, your coldness has put Lawton in despair, and obliged him to seek consolation in warmer regions."

The polished cheek of Augusta acquired so deep a tint, that a less practised eye than Lady Sophia's might have mistaken it for the index of wounded affection or outraged feeling, instead of placing it, as her acute ladyship did, to the account of mortified vanity.

"Lord Lawton has a new caprice every week," said Miss Cleveland. "The Hamiltons will reign during their short hour, to make way for successors. To attract him, neither beauty nor wit is requisite. It suffices to be *new*."

"And you, dearest, possess inexhaustible powers of novelty, that might fix a lover versatile as the winds and waves, if you would but take the trouble to exert them. After all, Lawton is a most unexceptionable *parti*, and one would really feel regret at seeing him irremediably in the power of those Hamiltons. One can fancy how much the Darley heiress would triumph in detaching such a lover from Augusta Cleveland."

"Her want of general success will at least lower its tone"

replied Augusta, after a short pause. " A host of the *desirables* pronounce her *mauvais ton*, and declare, that in making acquaintance with all the sciences and all the virtues, she has forgotten to cultivate one of the graces."

" That is from Mr. Stark's mint, let who will be the utterer," said Lady Sophia, " and as usual, it is base coin. Helen Darley is anything but a *précieuse;* and I must do her the justice to declare, that I have rarely seen a young woman so perfectly natural."

" Really it is so difficult to understand you, mamma," said Augusta, with a petulance unlike her usual well-bred *rétenue*.

" It is not difficult to understand, that it is the worst possible policy in one beauty to depreciate the claims of another; and should that other, in any ascertained point of view, appear as a rival, I can imagine no line of conduct so likely to make her ridiculous, and ridicule is always fatal."

" A rival!" said Augusta, with as near an approach to a sneer as her gracefulness would permit.

" Most decidedly—in person, in youth, as an heiress, as a relation. See how many points in which you touch. Above all, the evident admiration of Lord Lawton would suffice to place you in that position, were all other subjects of competition impossible."

" It is a comfort to remember, that Lord Lawton is not precisely the last man," said Augusta, with irrepressible ill humour."

" But the *best*, which it would be as unsatisfactory to lose as the last."

" At any rate, I shall not go into mourning for his lordship's desertion."

" Anger can make the most elegant *vulgar*, it appears," said Lady Sophia, coolly. " It may be some satisfaction to you, however, to feel that the loss of Lord Lawton must be attributed to your own want of tact. The least possible management would have fixed him irrevocably."

" I am not ambitious of the honour," said Augusta, now thoroughly provoked.

At that moment, Lady Sophia recollected Lord Vere's insinuation.

" If, Augusta," she said, angrily, " if, forgetting what is due to me, to yourself, ungrateful for the watchfulness with which I have endeavoured to make your education perfect as regards the sphere in which you were born to move, if you have been guilty of the imprudence of falling into any unworthy entanglement—but why admit the suspicion? the thing is impossible."

" Perfectly," said Augusta, quietly, and fixing her lovely eyes full on the face of Lady Sophia. " In learning my lesson from your ladyship's vocabulary, I have found constantly *selfishness* substituted for *love*. I cannot accuse you of having darkened my mind by a single allusion to the unprofitable romance of the affections."

Lady Sophia felt—how bitterly!—the sting that is "sharper than a serpent's tooth." If, in the cloud of worldliness which hung over her mind, one ray of the light of love penetrated, it was for this daughter, in whom all her ambitious hopes were bound up. During the last eighteen years of her existence, the establishment of Augusta had been "her being's end and aim;" to qualify her for effecting it the cause of ceaseless toil and thought. But as the spirit of the world had been *her* inspiration, so she gathered of the tree she had planted, and her sigh did but express "I should have known what fruit would spring from such a seed."

In all her occasional *demêllées* with her daughter, Lady Sophia was the first to smooth her brow, and harbour thoughts of peace. "After all, dear," she began, "we are wrong in considering Lord Lawton is irretrievably lost. It requires, I am persuaded, but a little address to recall him, and if Greville were not so utterly unmanageable, he might be of the greatest use."

"I do not exactly see *how*, but I think you might purchase his services at this moment, if you came up to his price," said Augusta, coldly. "He is in dreadful distress for money."

"Scandalous—with such an allowance! But who told you this, dear?"

"Himself. He wanted to borrow, but you know, after my quarter day, I never have a farthing in the world. *Rouge et noir* makes the honour of Mr. Stark's acquaintance expensive to poor Greville."

"Mr. Stark is quite a monster, and it has been in direct opposition to my wishes and counsel, that he formed and continued that degrading intimacy. There is not a more detestable—a more mischievous person in the world than that man."

"Greville's is a debt of honour, and of course must be paid. He told me unless I could persuade you to assist him, he he must, though unwillingly, raise money on—bonds of some kind—I forget the horrid name—but he would have to pay enormously for the loan, he said." . .

"Post obit bonds—Sir Greville would never forgive a transaction of the kind."

"But he *must* have the money—and if papa will not give it—and you know how ill-natured he is—it is really quite distressing to encounter his frown—and *this* fit, Doctor W. told me, promises to be very severe."

"Gout improves no man's temper, and to one of your father's disposition—he who was 'the glass of fashion and the mould of form,' now compelled to swathe his limbs in hundreds of yards of flannel—it *is* trying."

"But really one would hardly suppose papa had been so very distinguished a personage in his youth—when one sees him in his easy chair, his legs on cushions, so petulant, so gloomy, who could fancy that he had ever sustained the rôle of a gallant, gay Lothario? Fashion is very well while one is young and in health, but of what use is it in age and sickness? *Now* what does it matter to papa, that he is not one of the *canaille?* Time and gout are as great radicals as Mr. Cobbet."

"You are quite philosophical; one would think you had taken a lesson from Mrs. Hamilton. However, as I certainly have not, we will, if you please, talk of lighter matters, and see if anything can be done for this silly boy. I wonder if he is distressed for a large sum."

"A thousand pounds would do, he said."

"I will speak to Stark. If *he* is chief creditor, it will not be difficult to silence him. That man certainly is my nightmare."

CHAPTER VII.

Young, rich, lovely, innocent—Helen Darley afforded yet another illustration, how much human happiness is under the dominion of circumstances.

Attached to Sir Alfred Maitland by the ties of long companionship—of habitual affection—his avowal of a warmer love had awakened in her inexperienced heart such emotions as dictated her frank acceptance of his suit. If she did not murmur at the trial to which the wisdom of her parents desired to subject her constancy, she had yet been indignant at the possibility that she could change; self-relying she had entered the arena of trial, and—she had failed.

It came upon her at first as the glimmer of dawning day to the slumberer—faint and indistinct—to startle for a moment, but from which he turns away to renewed repose. Then, when the suspicion became stronger, her reason suggested a thousand arguments to repel it as a thing impossible. It was perfectly unnatural, she thought, that she could, under any species of infatuation, prefer the acquaintance of a day—a stranger—to the friend of her youth, the associate in all the joys and sorrows that had thrown their light and shadow on her short career. It was not wrong—Alfred himself would approve it—that she should find pleasure in the society of one so amiable, so intellectual as Lord Lawton; one, too, who, her father had said, was making for himself a name that would belong to the annals of his country

It was impossible not to be sensible of the friendship with which he honoured her—not to feel flattered that he deemed one so young, so simple, not unworthy of his attention. There was no treachery to Alfred in her gratitude; surely she had not one thought—one wish—to violate her conditional engagement with him!

But when Maitland appeared again, when in the presence of both she was made to feel how differently her heart beat as they approached her; how often, in conversing with Lord Lawton, she absolutely forgot the existence of Alfred, and he so near her; while on the other hand, if Lawton suddenly approached when she was addressing Alfred, how embarrassed and bewildered—she was obliged to pause, conscious of a confusion which increased by thinking on—*then*, even the unhackneyed heart of Helen suspected that all was not right within her.

Yet she yielded not to her inconstancy without a struggle. Full of remorse, she compelled herself to a minute recollection of the various claims which Maitland had to her fondest love. How many kindnesses he had lavished on her during the long years of his affection! Could she possibly repay him by an ingratitude so base? Was it in nature, that she could even indulge a dream of abandoning him for a stranger of yesterday? Would not the image of his wretchedness haunt her even if—how improbable a supposition!—she could have courage to confess the change in herself, and ensure, as a necessary consequence, their separation?

And oh, the indelicacy of indulging such visions as *had* sometimes occupied her fancy! That she should have allowed her heart thus to escape from her! What presumption to imagine that Lord Lawton's kindness—courtesy—meant more than the complimentary intercourse, into which men of the world fall daily with females with whose families they happen to be in habits of intimacy! How could she reveal even to her mother—her constant friend—the *possible* wandering of her heart, without at the same time confessing, as the only assignable cause, that her vanity had fancied! Oh the folly, the presumption of which she had been guilty! It was too much to endure with composure! Her shame—her self-reproaches—were incessant, and the only consolation she found, was in the conviction that her error was unknown, unsuspected, by any other human being!

How little deemed she of the watchfulness of her mother's love, when she believed that *she* could suffer, and that anxious eye fail to perceive the restless manner—the changed complexion—the altered voice—the less elastic step—the uncertain temper! Talk of the sixth sense of a lover! What is that to a mother's instinct?

It was just when her distress of mind was most poignant,

that Lady Sophia made unusual demonstrations of kindness. It was impossible one so new to the world as Helen Darley should suspect that what was so specious might possibly be hollow, and it had not entered into the plan of education so consistently pursued by her parents, to darken the brightness of her youth by inculcating the lesson of distrust. Time teaches that fatal necessity all too early, and distrustful youth is one of the most unnatural, as it is one of the most ungraceful characters, which this world of moral anomalies can furnish as matter of painful speculation.

Mrs. Hamilton, however, did not permit the intimacy which Lady Sophia was evidently courting, to deprive her of much of her daughter's society. She knew that selfishness was the fundamental principle of Lady Sophia's character, and she was not, for an instant, the dupe of her prodigal expressions of good will. She did not indeed wholly keep Helen under the shelter of her own fostering wing, for she felt that her acquaintance with Lady Sophia would at least be a step in her progress towards knowledge of the world—that knowledge which is to maturity the compensation—how inadequate!—for the loss of the glow of young imaginations. But she took care that her solitary visits to Cleveland House should be as infrequent as possible consistently with the preservation of those amicable relations which she knew it was *respectable* to maintain with so near a branch of her husband's family.

Lady Sophia, therefore, enjoyed and used abundant opportunities of insinuating into the mind of Helen a most painful impression of the attachment of Lord Lawton to Augusta Cleveland, if not of their actual engagement. Not that Lady Sophia committed herself by a single positive assertion which, supposing the failure of her plans, could, by its repetition, render her ridiculous. Her half confidences had all the effect on which she calculated. They made Helen not only unhappy, but indignant at herself that she had permitted her heart to be affected by an affianced man, whose tenderness had evidently been assumed as a means probably of amusing himself with her delusion. How many bitter tears, in her solitary hours—and now she was beginning to affect solitude—this mortifying conviction cost her! Her memory increased her suffering, for it seemed but a treasury in which were deposited all Lord Lawton's "whispered words," all the sweet hopes that had almost unconsciously been garnered up in her heart! How often she returned from Cleveland House, burning with desire to be able but to say to the mother whose tenderness had never failed—never wounded—"Let me see Lady Sophia no more!" and as often the prayer died away on her lips when she remembered the questioning maternal love would prompt, and the confession of inconstancy of a too forward appropriation of the mere compliments of a stranger, which must necessarily follow. To conceal was difficult, but to distort the *truth* by evasion or self-pity, impossible!

Helen's manner to Lord Lawton was naturally affected by the painful trials to which her feelings were exposed. To one so *true*, so candid, it was a grievous task to assume calmness when all within was agitation; and as she perpetually constrained herself, she of necessity appeared cold, formal—as unlike the *naïve*, sportive, but always graceful Helen, who had charmed his fancy and his heart, as could well be imagined. The change startled and alarmed him. *He* had by no means steered beyond the range of Lady Sophia's artillery. She had played off a battery on him also, but with less success. Lord Lawton knew Lady Sophia by reputation, by observation, by experience. It was in vain that she first hinted—then broadly asserted—the fact of Helen's engagement to Sir Alfred Maitland; he smiled at so palpable a manœuvre, too practised in the wiles with which matchmaking mothers seek to detach a coveted *parti* from a new aspirant to be the dupe of it. But *now* that Helen herself evidently repelled his assiduities with an air of apprehension and coldness, so unlike the interest with which she had *once* listened to him—that interest so dear to a lover's hopes, the fosterer of incipient attachment into passion—he could not but doubt, could not but follow her averted eye, and watch with all the vigilance of jealousy whether it rested on Maitland. But it did not. It was nevertheless painful to perceive that her manner to Sir Alfred had not the ease of indifference. There was a consciousness, a trepidation in it, which, though not perhaps resembling the embarrassment of love, indicated some peculiarity in her position towards him that filled the mind of Lord Lawton with a thousand alarms. Often he resolved to dare the worst by an avowal that would at least terminate uncertainty, and as often he was deterred by the unwillingness common to his sex—the *practised* part of it—to expose himself to the possibility of a refusal. One look—such a look as he had once dwelt on with rapture—would have decided him. But it was not there, and he, mistaking reserve for self-command, unconsciously confirmed all the suspicions Lady Sophia had laboured to infuse into her mind, and raised Helen's sufferings to their climax.

CHAPTER VIII.

THERE was one eye watching the progress of feelings and events with no small vigilance and anxiety, and who, at the precise point when, as in the Greek tragedy, the descent of a god cuts the knot that cannot otherwise be untied, became an actor on the scene, which the other dramatis personæ were, it must be confessed, carrying on in pantomime.

"Rachel improves very much," said Mrs. Hamilton to Sir Alfred Maitland; "her sorrow is more rational, more gentle, indicating her progress in the acquirement of that strength of character on which human happiness so greatly depends. The beneficial effects of this change of mind extend to her person. She is acquiring that intelligence of expression which was all that was wanting to render her beauty perfect."

Sir Alfred appeared to be absorbed in the columns of the Times, and uttered a faint affirmative, as if the act of mind, by which he indicated his acquiescence, were but a parenthesis in his more important speculations.

"I am glad I decided on having her here," resumed Mrs. Hamilton: "complete change of scene has done much for her: and the necessity of exertion in a house to the habits of which she feels it, at least, a graceful propriety to conform, has done the rest. It would not be indecorous now if she were to appear occasionally in society, in small circles, I mean; not that she

> 'Should bear about the mockery of wo,
> To midnight dances and the public show,'

but she might enjoy the recreation of seeing a few people worth knowing. Yet how could I answer it to myself, to open to her the vista of a style of life so far removed from her probable sphere, and which might have the bad effect of rendering her discontented with the lot apparently appointed for her."

"Rachel—Miss Fulton—would adorn *any* sphere," said Sir Alfred, colouring deeply the instant after he had spoken.

"Possibly," said Catharine, calmly; "but as

> 'Full many a flower is born to blush unseen,
> And waste its sweetness on the desert air,'

we must not therefore calculate on her being elevated to the higher grades of society, because she is endowed with all that might embellish such a life Considering her birth, fortune, connections, it is proper for us to look on Rachel as one born to fulfil the duties of a comparatively humble station; and it would be both imprudent and unkind in her friends to awaken in her tastes for a higher sphere, which, while they slumber, are as if they did not exist."

Sir Alfred laid aside the paper, and commenced a rapid march up and down the drawingroom. Catharine calmly allowed his mind leisure for the examination of itself.

"Why is it so absolutely a matter of necessity that Rachel—that Miss Fulton—should be doomed to the misery of drawing an humble lot in life?—why—"

"You are arriving at conclusions which I never anticipated," interrupted Catharine; "suffer me to set you right. There is no misery in the *juste milieu* of existence to which Rachel properly belongs, in which I myself was born and nurtured. It is fruitful in knowledge, virtue—consequently happiness. There is nothing in the higher places of the earth to render a rational and thinking being covetous of ascending them; and it is as true as trite, that safety is in the vale, not on the summit of the mountain."

Sir Alfred's paces became rather more irregular, and there was again a pause.

"Perhaps you have reason to think that her tastes, that she herself has some predilection," he said at length; "a preference—a—in short, one of those attachments which invest with a thousand charms the particular grade in society to which the object of them belongs."

"Considering that we are discussing the probable lot of a woman in whom your interest is of very recent date, I do not exactly recognise your right to ask such a question," said Catharine. "However, as matters stand—as Rachel's delicacy will not be compromised—I need not scruple to say, I have not the slightest ground for supposing that any preference of the kind to which you allude influences her to a choice of the cottage style of life."

"Oh, Mrs. Hamilton! if I dared—" said Maitland, and he paused, with the air of a man who, having suddenly "screwed up his courage to the sticking pitch," finds, just at the moment necessary for exertion, that a string is loosened.

"I am all attention," said Catharine, composedly, cruel enough to enjoy the embarrassment suffered by the inconstant lover of her child: for the wisest of us have our weak points, and alas, Catharine was human—a woman and a mother!

"You who have always been my friend, my adviser, my counsellor," said Maitland, with a degree of passion seldom apparent in him; "you who, if I err not, predicted, suspected, that what has happened would happen; you who have so long borne with me, as a mother with her most cherished son; you whom I have so venerated, so *obeyed*—yes, even now, now, when I am about to outrage your dearest feelings, I will venture to say to you, pity, forgive me; vouchsafe to learn all the weakness of my feeble heart, to know the extent of my fault, and pronounce my sentence."

"*Much* at least I have not to learn, Maitland," said Catharine, gravely, but kindly; "perhaps what is most to be condemned, is want of candour. You will yet discover how much misery is escaped by those who venture to be true."

"Accuse me not of deceit," said Maitland, earnestly, seating himself opposite to Catharine, and meeting her eye with that *uprightness* which is one of the most infallible indications of integrity. "Weak, wavering, fickle I have been—I acknowledge all my fault—but not *false*, not voluntarily false, not playing the hypocritical farce of making protestations of love to *one*, while my heart yearned after another; not concealing a change which was perfectly known to myself! I have not been base, my dear Mrs. Hamilton; I can yet venture to ask for your pity and forgiveness. I cannot charge myself with the consciousness of the extent of my—my wandering, until even now it has been revealed to me. And even while I speak, my heart is torn with a thousand conflicting feelings. How can I do this great wrong to the companion of my childhood, the beloved of my youth? How can I inflict on that true and innocent heart one pang? Could I endure to listen to one sigh from Helen, and to think that my weakness had called it forth? In my case, weakness is wickedness; no—no—my dear Mrs. Hamilton, heed not my ravings, my folly; whom have I ever loved, whom can I ever love—as I have loved Helen?"

"Rachel," said Mrs. Hamilton. "Meantime, listen to me as calmly as you can, and do not dread reproaches for a weakness which, after all, was involuntary. *Your* error was in the commencement—an error of inexperience; in the rashness with which, but for the interposition of Colonel Hamilton, you would have rushed into an engagement which would have entailed on you that great crime in the eyes of all honourable men, in the eyes of society—*breach of faith*. Why was it that he was unyielding to *all* your entreaties for the immediate ratification of your engagement? that he, that I resisted the yet more pleading eloquence of Helen's looks? To subject you to probation, to try whether you knew yourselves; not to allow you to fetter yourselves by the most indissoluble of all ties, and then dignify the unhappiness resulting from ignorance, by calling it *destiny*. As if man's conduct were not man's destiny! The affection of each of you has been put to the test, and *both* have failed."

Sir Alfred gave a start of surprise, and—so inexplicable is the human heart—not of pleasurable surprise. A few minutes since, he would have purchased, at considerable expense, the knowledge that his inconstancy would not effect the happiness of Helen; but now, when it was hinted that *her* love had been as fleeting as his, perhaps had even preceded his in its inconstancy, his self-love felt a momentary pang. He bowed thus to the infirmity of nature, but in another instant reason, its strength, was heard, and he could say with truth, "You restore me to new life. To secure the happiness of Helen it would have been little to sacrifice my own."

"I trust that Helen's happiness could *not* have been so secured," said Mrs. Hamilton, with the dignity of a justly proud mother. "Of *her*, her parents and herself must think, not *you;* and do me, do her the justice to believe, that the moment it was suspected by either of us you indulged the slightest wish, the merest dream, of change, we should, I *did*, afford you every facility of explanation—of honourable dealing. You owe myself and Colonel Hamilton gratitude for the hardness of heart of which, a few months since, you complained; a tribute I am very careful to bring to your remembrance, that the past may not be without its moral. If I have allowed you to suffer the pain of conflicting feelings without immediately hastening to relieve them, it was that the transient pain might have its use, and now, in all friendship, you may kiss the hand that smote."

And Maitland did gratefully, and with filial tenderness kiss that fair hand; and he felt, in his perfect restoration to the favour of Mrs. Hamilton, as if a mountain's weight were removed from his breast.

"If I *might* venture to ask," he said at length, "who is the happy, enviable man for whom Helen—"

"Pause," said Mrs. Hamilton; "do no task a question unworthy of you, and which you cannot expect me to answer. It is absolutely necessary that Helen should prefer another, before she could contemplate the probability of her union with yourself with feelings of pain? Might she not, in her enlarged intercourse with society, be aware of deficiencies or failings in you not hitherto perceptible; just as in ascending a mountain we see new beauties rising gradually in the more enlarged horizon, and are sensible of the pigmy proportions of the landscape that had first charmed our view? Is it quite out of the compass of possibility, that some such intellectual or moral process may have been at work with Helen?"

Maitland was silent, but his flushed brow told Mrs. Hamilton he was somewhat uneasy beneath the keenness of her probe.

"Meanwhile," she resumed, "are you quite sure that you shall be able to animate the gentle nature of Rachel to return your love?"

"Hitherto I have not dared to essay the experiment. But if an occasional blush—the sudden kindling of her eye, generally, you know, downcast—the sweetest smile to welcome me—"

"Oh, if you come to the freemasonry of love I have done. We have contrived to be intelligible to each other so far, and now you shall tell me as much of the plain story of your *new* love as pleases you."

"It will not please me at all," said Maitland. "I am ashamed to reflect how soon I ceased to regret our separation, after my arrival at Mrs. Warren's. But then let me justify myself so far as to remind you of my temptations. Rachel so young, so lovely, so distressed, so helpless—and I thrown into her society always to cheer and sooth her, when, by Mrs. Warren's absolute commands, she occasionally left the bedside of her dying mother. It was so new—so delightful—to be confided in by such a creature—to be looked up to—"

"Ah!" said Catharine, as the change became more and more intelligible.

"Pity, too, possessed my whole soul before another wish arose," resumed Sir Alfred, hardly conscious of the interruption; "and pity, you know—"

"Oh, no, no—*do* spare me that commonplace."

"In short, it *was* a mingling of pity, admiration, the consciousness of being useful, of being necessary—"

"And of being agreeable."

"Perhaps so, and a desire, hardly understood, of transplanting so fair a flower to a more genial soil, to save it from the chilling winds of sordid cares—from contact with a hard world. That is the whole of the romance; but do me the justice, my dear Mrs. Hamilton, to believe—to allow—that since her arrival here—since my precise position became more realized to my mind, I have honourably endeavoured to avoid her, severe as was the struggle! I have not the consciousness of one dishonourable feeling."

"*If* this avowal had been perfectly voluntary!"

"*Always* intended, believe me, but the feelings which delayed it—what painful feelings!—are not, surely, unnatural or unpardonable! and you will at least be my friend with Rachel?"

"Be your own; true to yourself, you will need no other advocate."

CHAPTER IX.

"Cleveland," said Lord Lawton, as the young heir of that ancient name was listlessly teazing the three beautiful spaniels that were suffered to luxuriate round the splendid breakfast table of the marquis, "you are the most tristful man of your years it ever was my fortune to be troubled with at this unconscionable hour. I doubt you are possessed by that demon whose name is Legion."

"What demon is that?" inquired Cleveland, affecting indifference.

"*Gambling*," returned Lord Lawton, so suddenly as to startle his companion into a blush his premature manhood would else have scorned, "which brings in its train a myriad of carking cares, bad passions, mental prostration, irretrievable moral debasement, to say nothing of poverty, which some—all the luxurious—have deemed that worst of ills which flesh is heir to."

"I cannot stand a lecture," said Cleveland, affecting that dogged firmness by which man intrenches himself more firmly in wrong.

"And lecturing is not my vocation, unless I see certain indications that it will not be labour in vain."

"Let us change the subject then," said Cleveland, with increasing petulance.

"No," said Lord Lawton, with that firmness which gives a superior intellect an instantaneous ascendency over an inferior, "not until you have told me the amount of your losses, and consent to accept such assistance as I am able to offer."

"By Jove, you are the most generous fellow in existence!" said Cleveland, with all the animation of extreme youth when it sees the possibility of escaping an evil hitherto deemed irretrievable. "But," he added, with a sudden change of tone, "I fear you have little suspicion of the amount for which my honour is pledged."

"In a word, how much?"

Cleveland named it.

"A large sum, doubtless, but not ill spent, if it be for the *cure* of a malady the most fatal which can seize upon man," said Lord Lawton. "Do not suspect me of the folly of designing to throw away a portion of wealth, which might be a means of placing hundreds in the way of being useful, and consequently happy. I lend it to you for causes which I am going to explain, and on conditions which I would not have you accept without reflection."

"If to forswear cards and dice for ever, gladly will I bind myself anew, for I have already 'an oath in heaven,'" returned Cleveland, with fervour. "Bind me as you will; and for repayment demand what security you choose."

"For the loan I will take your bond, because it is a duty I owe to my heir, and because you will be able to pay it; and for your future abstinence from a detestable vice, I will receive the past as a pledge. I have not been an unobservant witness, Cleveland, of your sufferings these many days, and if I have not sooner extended a helping hand, believe me it has been, that the warning might sink deep, and the impression be indelible. I have seen your struggles, and notwithstanding you have trifled away existence, hitherto, on things to be despised or condemned, I am persuaded there is material for better things in you. For my conditions, I will not ask you to discard your evil genius, Mr. Stark, that will be a matter of necessity. A man who lives by gambling cannot possibly long maintain a respectable position; and Mr. Stark, having been suspected of divers mal-practices, will speedily be blackballed at the clubs, to which he ought never to have been admitted, and will merge into that obscurity from which nothing but sheer impudence originally elevated him."

"I rejoice that I quarrelled with him yesterday," said Cleveland, with the glee of a boy; "it is not pleasant to cut one's particular friend merely because others do; and I hardly think I could have brought myself to it."

"If your friend is convicted of a base action, you have no alternative. You must either obey the conventional laws of society, in such an instance, or share his ignominy, which is not only a weakness, but a crime, a violation of your duty to yourself, and an injury to society, in the precise degree by which you countenance vice by your *supposed* example."

"But your conditions?" asked Cleveland, looking rather bored, and considerably impatient.

"That you cultivate the acquaintance of your relations the Hamiltons, who are full of kind and friendly dispositions towards you. In the parental tie, of which, however, let us still speak with reverence, I know that you have been singularly unfortunate. The splendid Sir Greville Cleveland, sunk into the morose invalid, regarding you only as the perpetuator of his family name and distinctions, neither seeks your affection nor desires your confidence. Always an egotist, he murmurs that you do not voluntarily tender that filial regard which, like all other human sentiments of kindliness, must, after the age of instincts, be excited by the qualities which inspire it, but which Sir Greville believes to consist in his having done you the favour to contribute to your being placed among 'the Corinthian capitals of polished society.' Of Lady Sophia, it is sufficient to say that, engrossed by her daughter, she considers herself a paragon of maternal duty, in that she vouchsafes to endure occasionally the presence of a son, whom she has not been able to render useful. Your heart is void of the natural affections of our kind, so affluent of happiness, such securities likewise of our respectability—a thing sneered at by the fashionable, but venerated still by the wise and good. As your friend, therefore, I counsel you to accept the substitute which offers in your nearest relatives, the family of Colonel Hamilton."

"Would you have me marry my cousin Helen?" asked

Cleveland, with an air of meaning, for he was young enough to possess, in its full perfection, that happy elasticity of mind which rebounds to its proper dimensions as soon as the pressure is removed.

"Why not precisely," replied Lord Lawton, *without* em phasis. "Having heard my conditions at large, are they ac cepted?"

"Fully, freely, joyfully! But are your quite sure Colonel Hamilton will receive with cordiality the advances of my father's son? There is something very awful, too, about Mrs. Hamilton. I assure you I am rather puzzled how to set about it. I feel so unpleasantly young in the presence of a woman of her class."

"Have the courage to confess as much to them, and you will find large amends for your temporary embarrassment," returned Lord Lawton. "Be encouraged by knowing that they are already interested for you in no ordinary degree, for they place sufficient faith in my penetration to believe my assertion that, beneath all the frivolity, the folly, the affectation of the age, in which you have chosen to ensconce yourself, there is much of the sterling ore which, when coined and stamped with the lawful impress, will make the mental wealth of an honourable and honoured man. Respect *yourself*, Cleveland, and believe that there are friends in the world as indulgent as Stark, without being tainted either by his meanness, his vices, or his crimes."

CHAPTER X.

No young woman ever was more rejoiced at listening to the declaration which secured her lover, than Helen at being freed from one; and he too the lover of her own free choice. The origin of half the *first loves* of young hearts is *ignorance*, and their death blow, *experience*. And yet she discovered a thousand points of excellence, for which she could fairly pour into the willing ears of the grateful, gentle Rachel Fulton, his praises; now that she herself had honourably effected her escape from him, she discerned countless reasons why it was quite impossible that any woman should be unhappy as his wife.

"Well may love be painted blind," said Mrs. Hamilton; "but I question whether the inventor of the allegory ever intended to prove that the ceasing to love would open the eyes to the discovery of new excellences in a past object."

"I speak of Alfred precisely as I judge of him," said Helen. "Of late I seem to see all objects differently; and while I am sure that no woman *ought* to be otherwise than happy as his wife, and am equally certain that Rachel will be one of the most enviable of human beings, I am not the less convinced that marriage with him would have been the seal of *my* wretchedness. I have been accustomed to *look up* all my life, and I have of late asked myself the question, whether I could endure to *look down*, or whether it would be *safe* that I should be placed in such a situation. You have taught me to observe facts and to draw inferences, and I have done so."

"But Maitland's intellect is more than respectable; his acquirements far above mediocrity; these surely are not points for which you would look down on your husband."

"Assuredly not; but, mamma, I have lately thought it possible, that acquirements of *that* kind are not precisely the qualities for which woman venerates man, or *should* venerate him. I can imagine a wife possessing much more cultivated intellect than her husband; much more literature, and yet immeasurably inferior to him in those points in which—in short, in which one would *choose* to be inferior. Dignity of character now, such as all *must* respect; firmness too—the power to rule wisely and well; and all tempered by that manly kindness, which is tender of the feelings, and cares *for* the comforts of woman as naturally 'the weaker vessel;' this is the superiority proper to man. Of what use is a column, however graceful, if it has not strength enough to support that which it was intended to support? Now I should always have had courage to oppose Alfred's opinions, even on points of worldly knowledge, and I would rather not have that courage. I should, all my life, have ventured to find fault with him, as in our days of childhood. In fact, I think the real origin of my change of feeling is, he is too young for me; I feel myself his equal. Now Rachel will never do this, and it is infinitely better as it is—quite delightful; I do not think I ever felt so happy in my life."

"Yours does not seem quite a fancy sketch, Helen," said Mrs. Hamilton, "Tell me, dear, the original of your picture."

"Papa and yourself, of course," said Helen, after a moment's hesitation, and with a cheek glowing at her conscious and unaccustomed evasion, for though reflection told her the portrait did resemble her parents, it was not they who had occupied her mind while she drew it.

Catharine was silent, for she respected the maiden modesty of her daughter, and would not tempt to disingenuousness a mind generally as transparent as the crystal stream.

Lord Lawton, meanwhile, with all the keen-sightedness of anxiety, perceived that a change had occurred in the relative positions of Maitland and Helen. There was a greater cordiality between them than before, but it was the open and friendly intimacy that may exist between brother and sister;

no symptoms of that embarrassment which had lately cost him so much uneasiness. It was so different, so thrillingly different, from the timid blush with which she shrank from his own approaches; not repulsively, but as from too deep consciousness. Doubt there still was, for with sincere attachment there must be doubt; but he had arrived at the precise point when hope and fear so equally alternate, that an honourable man feels that, for the preservation of the peace of the woman he loves, it is incumbent on him to expose himself to the possibility of rejection.

"Give me five minutes," he said to Colonel Hamilton, whom he met in the Park; "I have a matter of some importance to discuss with you, and, as 'the mind is its own place,' it may be done as satisfactorily here as in your study, if you will allow your man to take your horse, and stroll with me towards the Serpentine."

"I am rather in haste; if your business will bear postponement—"

"No, it will not, indeed, my dear colonel. Ten minutes—I shall hold my watch—ten minutes shall limit our conference."

"Now what is it?" said Colonel Hamilton, as he passed his arm through Lord Lawton's.

"Frankly—for I am a man who, by nature and habit, must steer a direct course—is there any invincible obstacle to my attempting to win the heart of your daughter? or, which I *have* suspected—does Sir Alfred Maitland stand in such a relation to her as must compel me, for my own peace, to—to think of other occupations?"

"A month since I could hardly have answered you as explicitly as now—*no*. Thrown much together, they fell into the not unnatural fancy of mutual attachment, but Mrs. Hamilton, with the tender caution of a mother, doubted its stability, perhaps its character, and insisted on a test which it has not stood. I confess I desired the match. I have been accustomed to Maitland, and I have the predilection of Alphonso of Castile for old wood, old wine, old books, and old friends. Helen's mind is more timid than her mother's, and perhaps she regretted in him the absence of that—moral strength, shall I call it?—which renders man a wife's best protection. Or perhaps more enlarged acquaintance with society revealed to both that others might be as agreeable—better adapted to themselves, for you are to understand that not only Helen but Maitland has yielded to the influence of time or circumstances, or both. In short, *she* is 'free as air'—that is, to the best of my belief—while he has forged new chains for himself, and will, in due time, become the husband of our little kinswoman, Miss Fulton."

"Then my way is clear—*your* permission being understood."

"In emulation of your frankness and truth, let me say, if you can win her, wear her. I know not the man of whose alliance I should be prouder. But there have been rumours of your attachment to Miss Cleveland."

"To every new beauty who has risen above our horizon during the last seven years," said Lord Lawton. "I disclaim all. Let me confess to you, that the extreme loveliness, the exquisite elegance of Miss Cleveland *were* temptations, but who would unite himself to a mass of artificiality, beneath the smooth and frozen surface of which he knows not how turbulently the stream may run? Lady Sophia was the beacon that warned me from her daughter, for what man, seriously calculating the chances of his future happiness, would venture to intrust it to the guardianship of her pupil? Though no believer in hereditary virtue or hereditary intellect, I have an unshaken faith in the power of education, and I would give my children a mother whom I might proudly desire they should resemble."

"I honour your sentiments, but—the ten minutes are expired. *Au revoir!*"

CHAPTER XI.

Stark is expelled the clubs," said Lord Vere to Lady Sophia Cleveland; "in short, *cut*, cleaned out, and cleared out. Nothing could have been more *mal-àpropos*, and it is really a satisfaction to my conscience, that he is a confidant of your ladyship's selection, not of mine."

"It is a misfortune," said Lady Sophia, with a sigh of real feeling, for it resulted from pity for herself; "his mal-adroitness deserved the fate it has brought on him, if his sufferings were but confined to himself."

"The effects will reach even to us, it is to be apprehended. The price of Stark's silence will be high, for we are his last resource."

"Could you not provide for him in the colonies, or somewhere? That would be cheapest and safest."

"But having a character to lose, I shall be careful not to forfeit it by any such recommendation."

"What *is* to be done then?" said Lady Sophia, impatiently. "Those impracticable Hamiltons, who might do everything and will do nothing—"

"Or Lawton—your son-in-law elect—"

"Spare your sarcasms. All my influence, which you have so often termed omnipotent, suffices not to affect one thought, one feeling, in my own daughter—the person I really have most loved and cared for in the world!"

"Not quite," said Lord Vere. "And the fair Augusta absolutely will not attempt to avert the defection of her swain?"

"She is really the most impenetrable, the coldest, the most artificial *young* woman I ever had the misfortune of knowing!"

How much Lord Vere's sarcastic smile expressed! What a sentiment for a mother, whose whole object, during the childhood and youth of her daughter, had been to check every natural feeling, to subdue every natural impulse, to substitute calculation for affection. And now she reprobated the artificiality, the coldness, the *hardness*, she herself had so assiduously laboured to perfect! She expected from the being on whom she had daily, both by precept and example, impressed the lesson of courtly insincerity to all others, undeviating truth, consistent candour, and the gentlest pliancy towards herself. While she had laboured, with a zeal worthy of a better cause, to accomplish her in the worldly lore of subduing all appearance of emotion, she required, in their moments of private intercourse, that a ready sympathy with her own excitement should not only be felt but exhibited, forgetting her theory, that habit influences manner, even beyond the control of the agent.

"Lawton has been so spoiled by society—by women, particularly," resumed Lady Sophia, "that Augusta's coldness and indifference must be tenfold more repulsive to him. And she listens to all my representations, all my persuasions, as calmly, as tranquilly, with the same frosty smile, as if I were discussing the *trousseau* for her own bridal!"

"Therein evincing a sound discretion, for it falls to my unhappy fate to announce to you, that Lawton marries the little Darley."

"Impossible!" said Lady Sophia, in uncontrollable anger; "he cannot—he dares not—he shall not!"

"Excuse me, my dear Lady Sophia—this is really too amusing. Ask Sir Greville."

"Sir Greville!—my plague—my pest—my abhorrence! Yes—he does well to proclaim it; he who would prefer the elevation of that detested woman's daughter to his own! Would to Heaven he had married her! Would to Heaven my folly had not led me from the delicious clime, the happy liberty of Italy!"

"For once your feelings are in unison with his. What would not Sir Greville give to recall the unredeemable past—to recur to that precise point of time when your ladyship, by one of those happy accidents you so well know how to manage, met him at the chancellor's! There is no teacher like experience—no scourge of our faults comparable to the lash Time places in the hands of Repentance."

"At least, Augusta will be sufficiently punished," said Lady Sophia, unwounded by Lord Vere's impertinence. "That is some consolation. With all her impassiveness, she will shrink from seeing advantages that might have been her own pass into the hands of her rival; and she will have the gratification of knowing herself to be considered by all the world as *plantée*. What human being will believe she would have refused Lawton, if his *devouement* had been followed up, as it ought to have been, by a proposal?"

"I do," said Lord Vere, coolly. "Augusta would not have married Lawton."

"Once already you have insinuated an entanglement," said Lady Sophia, veiling her anger under the affectation of superciliousness, "and now decisively let me say, that a folly of that kind is quite beyond even the folly of Augusta Cleveland."

"*Nous verrons*," returned Lord Vere. "Suppose it were Stark himself now—your *protégé*—the whilome friend of your son—the convenient acquaintance admitted at all hours, with the privilege of making the agreeable in season, and out of season—recommended, too, by the implied approbation of one of her parents, whose confidence in him has been *demonstrated* boundless. Would this be so very much out of the regions of possibility?"

"There is but one thing more impossible,' said Lady Sophia, unable to suppress the sarcasm, even in the midst of her extreme mortification—"that she should descend to—Lord Vere."

"Between us, wit is not safe," said he, coolly. "However, to pass from words to actions, what are we to do with Stark?"

"I have no money," said Lady Sophia. "My expenses and Augusta's more than absorb my own income, and Sir Greville has undergone the natural transition from a youth of profusion to an old age of avarice. I could not obtain a hundred sovereigns from him, at this moment, to rescue me from ruin. We detest each other, as you know and he knows, because we understand each other, and *his* selfishness is perpetually at war with *my* selfishness. He takes no interest in Augusta, who most accurately returns the negative quantity, and except that Greville is his heir, I do not think he would care if we were all extinct to-morrow."

"Meanwhile your son is clear of Stark, *cum multis aliis*. In plain English, his debts are paid, and he has escaped their worst encumbrance, a dishonourable associate."

"Indebted, I suppose, to Colonel Hamilton for his deliverance, on the faith of a promise to sin no more! I wish Colonel Hamilton joy of the extent of his faith."

"Colonel Hamilton is not the man."

"Is it yourself?"

"I? No," said Lord Vere, with a shrug. "I protest I have not the wherewithal to purchase a cake to fling to that Cerberus, Stark, far less to throw away on the heir of Cleveland. The most noble the Marquis Lawton is the man."

"What has bribed him?" said Lady Sophia, from whose vocabulary the terms "disinterestedness" and "generosity" were expunged. "In these days man does not give something for nothing."

"I do not pretend to solve enigmas; however, not to lose time, something must be done to silence Stark."

"Could you not shoot him?" said Lady Sophia, quietly.

"With pleasure, if he were in a condition to be shot at. But being without the pale of *gentlemanhood*, he is not, I fancy, entitled to the privilege of the cartel. I could as soon go out with my tailor."

There was some serious deliberation on this point between Lady Sophia and Lord Vere; for beneath their affected carelessness there was a real anxiety that Stark should be satisfied, lest, exasperated by neglect, he should break the silence on which they knew more depended than either cared to avow to the other. A very businesslike examination of their separate resources terminated their conference, and permitted Lady Sophia to drive to Grosvenor Square, where she was fortunate enough to find Mrs. Hamilton alone.

"My dear creature," she began, with an air of *empressement* intended to be exceedingly affectionate, "I have just heard the strangest tidings, and hasten to ascertain their truth. People are so mischievous as to assert that our dear Helen has actually accepted that dreadful *roué*, Lord Lawton."

Mrs. Hamilton looked at Lady Sophia with all the surprise she actually felt at such a combination of epithets.

"I thought Lord Lawton had long enjoyed the honour of being one of your own particular friends, and assuredly the excellent friend of your only son."

"Possibly not the less *roué* for either of those circumstances," said Lady Sophia, with an air of nonchalance. "If he pays Greville's gambling debts, of which there are rumours, I should attribute it, *entre nous*, rather to an *engouement* for Greville's mistress than for Greville himself."

Catharine shuddered with irrepressible disgust.

"You have not the least idea of Lawton's bad reputation," resumed Lady Sophia. "With his advantages of person, rank, fortune. manner, he might have commanded any woman in the kingdom. It is inconceivable with how many distinguished female names his own has been united within the last few years; but, somehow, nothing ever came to a decided arrangement. During this year past, he has affected a passion for Augusta, which she has discouraged—in truth, much to my displeasure; for it is only lately that I have been put in possession of the fact of his enormities. I confess I harassed the poor child cruelly, for really Lawton's rank, fortune, and fashion were great temptations; and I knew little against his morals—nothing that placed him below the regulation standard in the present day."

"Nor I," said Mrs. Hamilton, quietly; "but much that places him above it."

"I hope I am not in error," said Lady Sophia, affecting an air of dignity; "that I am not offending where I meant to preserve. If everything is finally settled between Lawton and Helen, I feel silence would be wise, and that nothing remains but to offer a fervent, if a vain wish for their happiness."

"Since Colonel Hamilton is satisfied, I may venture to thank you for the fervency of your good wishes, and to console you by imparting my firm persuasion that they will not be vain."

Lady Sophia coloured through her rouge; and finding it impossible to injure, contented herself with the less sublime occupation of endeavouring to annoy.

"I really envy you your talents," she said. "It is confidently rumoured that you have managed to marry your little portionless kinswoman to the man you had secured for your daughter as a *pis-aller*. How few women could have done so much!"

"I am compelled to avow myself undeserving of your applause. The only management I have ventured, has been not to attempt to stem the tide of circumstances—a piece of diplomacy of which politicians of both sexes sometimes forget the value."

"Sir Alfred Maitland, I hear, has a very fair estate."

"Much improved by his long minority," added Catharine; "at present, I should think, ten thousand a year."

"Ha!" said Lady Sophia, with a sigh; and she indulged herself in a prolonged diatribe on the extravagance of Sir Greville, the follies of her son, the unfortunate insensibility of her daughter, and the perverseness of her own fate in general.

"In your son there are, at least, the elements of good," said Catharine, gravely. "Parents err in their conduct to their children, and then complain because they reap the natural and necessary results. Mr. Cleveland seems to possess a heart capable of warm affection; it is his misfortune if he imagines his mother has no desire to call it forth."

"He has ventured to complain of me?" said Lady Sophia, with a flushed brow.

"Indeed *no*," replied Catharine, earnestly. "Mr. Cleveland's own good taste and good feeling would have withholden him, even if he had not been restrained by the certainty that such complaints would be most unacceptable to *us*, whom he numbers among his sincere friends. It is from yourself that I have learned the fact of your partial fondness for your daughter—a fact to be deplored in proportion as it renders you unjust to your son."

"And what fruit has that partial fondness produced?" said Lady Sophia, with bitterness; real, honest feeling becoming too strong for convention, as in a conflict it always proves. "Would Augusta sacrifice the least of her prejudices—the most indifferent of her whims—to *me*, even if the sacrifice were to affect my permanent happiness? Does she permit my counsel to direct her, except just so far as her own policy warns her, that my experience must have an advantage over her inexperience? Affection! You and I, my dear Mrs. Hamilton, are too old to be juggled by mere names, and are perfectly aware that *love* hardly ever passes beyond the circle of *selfishness*."

What a sentiment from the heart of woman! and to Catharine Hamilton, enshrined as she was amid all the brightest and best charities of life, loving and beloved as wife, mother, friend! How she pitied the wretched being to whom all these blessings had been offered, and who had rejected them, or converted them into curses!

Lady Sophia departed, with the miserable conviction that she had striven to wound in vain; that not only had her arrow fallen harmless, but that the shaft had recoiled into her own bosom. If ever she had envied mortal woman, Catharine was that woman. If ever she felt the brightness of goodness, the excellence of unpolluted intellect, the power of unperverted principle, it was in her presence. She never quitted her without feeling humbled and self-abased—without being made to feel practically the impassable gulf that separates virtue from vice—without sighing over the wretched consciousness that, in the fulfilment of the duties of life, there is a reward beyond the bestowal of fashion, or splendour, or all the glittering baubles for which myriads are sacrificing their eternal hopes. What availed it, that, in the one great event of woman's life, she had borne away the costly prize from her to whom it rightfully belonged? How few were the roses that had bloomed on the wreath which crowned her brow, how countless the thorns! From the spring to the autumn of her life, what had existence been to her? A series of vanities, which had left behind them self-loathing—the aching, gnawing, incessant consciousness of utter worthlessness—of time wasted at the best, and too often employed in positive sin. *Sin!* what a word to a woman whose wit had ridiculed, whose skepticism had disbelieved, whose life had violated, every precept of that religion which *so* nominated almost every action that had marked her mortal career.

The carriage stopped as these unwonted thoughts reached

their climax. With the rapidity of one who strove to escape by bodily motion from the painful excitement of the mind, Lady Sophia flew up the ample staircase, and rushed into her splendid boudoir. Around her were all the appliances by which art stimulates luxury to sensation. Fragrance impregnated the atmosphere, and on every side elegant or magnificent objects delighted the eye. Taste could have detected nothing that was inappropriate or ungraceful. Each, individually perfect, blended into an harmonious whole, producing on the eye that was not palled by satiety, the same effect that a fine concert of accordant instruments produces on the ear. Sense and intellect might have contested the supremacy in such a temple; but how worse than tasteless were the splendour, and the pomp, and the grace, to her who had been wont to deem herself the fitting divinity of the shrine!

Ensconced in a silken *bergére*, her beautiful foot pressing a silken divan, the fair Augusta Cleveland reposed, in all the luxury of indolent revery. The air of tranquillity which pervaded the expression of her whole figure contrasting so forcibly with the turbulent emotions which struggled within the heart of Lady Sophia, chafed the angry spirit into yet stronger indignation.

"I am returned from a congratulatory visit to Mrs. Hamilton," she began, with that assumed calmness which, when the veil of passion, is more fearful than a whirlwind of violence; "pity that you were not with me, to add, by the sincerity of *your* good wishes, to the emphasis of mine."

"But I have no good wishes to bestow on any of the Hamilton tribe, whom I dislike in all their moods, tenses, numbers, and persons," returned Miss Cleveland, listlessly. "Greville is enraptured with the whole set, which explains them at once to be a congregation of complete bores."

"Lord Lawton, whose praise is fame, shares, or perhaps has directed, Greville's admiration. I had to congratulate Mrs. Hamilton this morning on the acquisition of her son-in-law elect," and Lady Sophia fixed on her daughter a glance of malignant exultation, certain that *vanity* would writhe beneath the blow.

"Then Lawton has actually proposed to Helen Darley!" said Augusta, a very slight flush staining her polished cheek. "Well—that is just the only person on whom I would rather that his choice had *not* fallen. He will live to regret it: for his fastidious taste will be dreadfully shocked by her constant violation of *les convenances de société*."

"Lay not that flattering unction to your soul," said Lady Sophia, with a bitter sneer. "A very brief exposure to the friction of the world will add to the natural grace and beauty of the Marchioness Lawton all the artificial polish they need to be perfection."

"Lady Sophia Cleveland the eulogist of Mrs. Hamilton's

daughter! Well, that is new, and in these days of monotony, therefore welcome."

"Ay, do preserve your coldness, your superciliousness, your perverseness!" said Lady Sophia, her assumed calmness thawing beneath her vehement indignation. "Pointed at by the world as the forsaken of Lord Lawton—the baffled, unsuccessful candidate for the honours of his marquisate, I recommend you to perfect your brilliant *rôle*, by selecting from the crowd of your adorers the man most notorious for profligacy, for extravagance, for poverty; the one, too, whose name will cast the blackest shadow on that of Cleveland; and then sink gracefully into the obscurity your ingratitude, your unfeelingness, your folly deserve."

"Why, really, mamma, I fear you could not spare Lord Vere for me," said Augusta, with a laugh that entered "like iron into the soul" of her stricken mother.

Lady Sophia could not speak. The *real* emotion nearly suffocated her. Even Augusta, accustomed as she was to appeal to hysterics when entreaty and violence had been employed in vain, saw that here was no artifice. She felt that she had said too much; and, with most unaccustomed emotion, she flew to the side of her mother.

But Lady Sophia, crushed, wounded, insulted, repulsed with violence the assiduities which repentance would have offered. She attempted to articulate; but a wild scream burst from her, and Miss Cleveland was compelled to summon assistance, glad to leave to the care of others the parent she could not respect, whose love for herself she believed to be so mingled with the alloy of selfishness, as to exonerate her from the necessity of returning it. She was careful to send, at proper intervals, the requisite messages of inquiry; and when at length informed that her ladyship had awakened refreshed by the deep sleep which had occurred on the subsiding of the attack, she sent the following note to her boudoir:—

"After the scene which took place this morning, it cannot surprise you, mamma, that I should desire to escape from a repetition of it. I know very well that, until you have recovered from the first effects of the intelligence of silly Lord Lawton's engagement to Helen Darley, there will be no peace for me; and I cannot submit to be again so dreadfully discomposed and agitated as I have been to-day already. I have an invitation from Lady K. to go to her at Richmond for a week or two, which I have accepted for to-morrow morning.

"I trust when I return all will be forgotten by both of us. It is rather too much to be annoyed about a man who was positively disagreeable to me, and whom I never would have married.

"AUGUSTA."

To which Lady Sophia immediately returned the following:—

"I insist on your remaining at home. I command you to decline Lady K.'s invitation. Lady K. is a most improper companion for you at all times and under all circumstances. *I* have sufficient respect for the opinion of the world to decline any intimacy with people of dubious reputation, unless their other claims chance to be sufficiently resplendent to dazzle away one's eyes from their delinquencies—which is *not* Lady K.'s good fortune. She is a most exceptionable chaperone for any young woman. Remember, I have always disapproved your intimacy with her. Recollect, too, that your retiring from the scene just now would but expose you to derision. The thousand tongues of the malicious would exult over such a demonstration of your disappointment. If you *must* go anywhere, let it be to Lady Adelaide Willoughby's. Your being seen with her will be a very con vincing proof that the entire arrangement is satisfactory.

"S. C."

"I cannot accept either of your alternatives. I will not remain at home; and to expect me to submit to the boredom of Lady Adelaide, is rather too much. There are a thousand people in the world whom one sees and caresses every day, much more exceptionable than Lady K., of whom I do not believe one half of the *on dits*, and do not care for the other. I shall positively go to-morrow morning, but wish to be at peace with you, if possible. Opposing each other never can be pleasant or convenient to either of us; but indeed, mamma, I cannot always be the person to yield. My own caprices must occasionally be attended to.

"Augusta."

"Attempt to go, and I shall call the authority of your father to my assistance.

"S. C."

"Indeed you will not, mamma. You have not spoken to Sir Greville this fortnight; and to do so under the circumstances, would not be favourable either to his gout or your comfort. I shall go to Lady K.

"Augusta."

In this last note was the subjoined enclosure:—

"Lord Vere recommends his fair friend to go out of the way for a little. To let a captive escape may be hardly vexatious; but to see him exhibited in the train of another may be rather annoying. Lady K. has a very agreeable *ré-union* at Richmond, to which she invites Miss Cleveland. The people who compose it all understand precisely how little Lawton ever had the power of interesting her, and are quite able to appreciate the extent of the attractions he found in the large estates of the Darley heiress. The involvements of the marquis are much talked of; and it has been whispered that Sir Greville's interference shut the doors of Cleveland House against him. It is unfortunate that Lady Sophia rather dislikes Lady K. Should she oppose the visit or the wishes of her lovely daughter, Lord Vere desires to throw himself at her feet; and, assuring her of his profound deference to the thousandth part of the very smallest of her caprices, to impress on her his conviction that Miss Cleveland's visit to Lady K. is inevitable at the present moment."

Alas!—Lady Sophia had not the habit of opposing Lord Vere's caprices, even if, by acquiescing in them, she was compelled to the difficult sacrifice of her own! Miss Cleveland went to Lady K.; and hardly had Lady Sophia recovered from the mortification of her cold adieu, when her son entered her presence with an agitation which effectually repressed her meditated reproof of his unwelcome intrusion.

The boyish carelessness of his countenance was gone. Strong emotion imparted to his air and gesture the strength, the power, which passion only can give to extreme youth. His face was pale; a stern experience had evidently comprised, in a brief interval, lessons that might have been for years the teaching of time. He stood before Lady Sophia, gazing on her so earnestly, so searchingly, that the mother stood awed before her child. No words passed between them; his was the silence of agitation—hers that of the shapeless fear which is the attendant demon of conscious guilt.

"Mother, is that *true?*" he said at length; and Lady Sophia started as at the voice of a stranger; for the passion which had worked so marvellous a change in his appearance had even more marvellously affected the voice, the subtlest indication of emotion. He flung a packet before her as he spoke.

Her recognition of the writing was instantaneous—it was Stark's; and now indeed Lady Sophia's innermost soul was shaken. For a few seconds the characters were indistinct. A mist was before her eyes—her hand trembled.

"Endeavour to be calm," said Cleveland; "give me but the power of rebutting the foul lie, and never had mother a more fearless defender than you shall find in your son."

Lady Sophia collected herself, and read the three following letters:

"My Dear Cleveland,

"My unjust and unmerited expulsion from the clubs compels me to collect around me the valued friends on which

I can most confidently rely, that their countenance, which I do not deserve to forfeit, may rescue me from the opprobrium and ignominy which I must otherwise incur. Our long intimacy naturally directs me to you as most willing to assist me, while your position and connections leave your power of doing so unquestionable. Not a single tangible charge can be brought against me; were any such attempt made, I should know how to defend myself. Nothing can be more offensive to a man of feeling than to know himself the victim of a conspiracy against which he has no power of redress. The continued acquaintance of yourself and your friend Lord Lawton will be a vuluable means of retrieving myself. Lady Sophia Cleveland will, I am confident, advise the measure, and it would be most presumptuous in me to doubt the influence of her ladyship either with her son or her son-in-law. I shall be happy to ride with you in the Park at three, when we can settle about you or Lord Lawton proposing my being re-elected at Crockford's.

"Ever, my dear Cleveland,

"Yours sincerely,

"P. Stark."

"Mr. Cleveland cannot adequately express the surprise and displeasure Mr. Stark's note has caused. Concurring, as Mr. Cleveland does, in the decision of the clubs, Mr. Stark must see the utter impossibility of the renewal of any intercourse with him. Mr. Cleveland has no such influence with Lord Lawton as Mr. Stark supposes, and if he had, he would be extremely cautious how he used it. Mr. Cleveland having declined the acquaintance of Mr. Stark *before* his expulsion from general society, cannot be supposed ambitious of it *after* that occurrence. Mr. Cleveland suggests to Mr. Stark the fruitlessness of persevering in a correspondence which can be only a source of mortification to himself, as of pain to Mr. Cleveland."

"My Dear Cleveland,

"Your letter must have been written under a delusion, and in that conviction I shall not take such notice of it as, under other circumstances, I should, however reluctantly, feel myself compelled to do. As the *intimate* and *confidential* friend of Lady Sophia Cleveland and Lord Vere, I have claims on you which you will hardly be able to evade, even were you, which I do not believe, inexperienced enough to attempt doing so. Ask her ladyship whether it will be prudent to irritate me. An angry and an injured man may be tempted beyond his powers of forbearance. I owe it to myself not to permit my services to be repaid by neglect and ingratitude. I have applied to Lord Vere for such assistance as would enable me to exist respectably on the Continent, and he has had the rashness to neglect my application. Something *must* be done. If replaced in society here—which with your numerous and respectable connections is a thing quite in your power—I shall continue to preserve an honourable silence. If enabled to go abroad, it would be equally satisfactory. But one alternative or the other must be brought within my reach, a conviction to which Lady Sophia, to whom I beg you to show this, must have arrived.

"In conclusion, allow me to suggest, that it cannot be a pleasant reflection to any man, that his own unjustifiable obstinacy has been the means of exposing his mother to much severe animadversion.

"*Still*, my dear Cleveland,
"Yours sincerely,
"P. Stark."

"Now," said Cleveland, having patiently waited until the eye of Lady Sophia had passed over the last line; "now speak one word, mother. False—false: is it not unutterably, basely, maliciously false?" and he flung himself suddenly on his knees before her.

"How dare you venture even to ask the question?" said Lady Sophia, sternly; for during her deliberate perusal of the letters she had decided on her plan of action. "Stark is a villain, which *you* knew long ago, and you are—a simple fool, of which I am most satisfactorily convinced."

"Anything—everything—if it be but false!" said Cleveland, still kneeling. "Mother, if you had but permitted me to love you, this never could have happened. I would have so clung to you, that no breath of calumny should ever have had the power of assailing you. Oh, mother, mother! why was my sister all to you, and I nothing? Has she loved you better than I might have done? Is your fair reputation dearer to her than it might have been to me?"

"No sentiment, if you please, Greville," said Lady Sophia, resolute to suppress every appearance of emotion. "You have assailed me with a violence which I am hardly strong enough to support. You have ventured to suppose me in the power of a wretch like Stark, with whom your own vices associated you, contrary to all my remonstrances—all my persuasions. He endeavours to terrify you into continuing your always unwise intimacy with him, and you bow before his threats, and treat me with a tragic scene that would disgrace a schoolboy."

"No sentiment, mother! no sentiment! But is there to be no affection?" and he clasped her hand in his.

"Rise, Greville, and let us talk like rational beings. The interests of my children have always been dear—*equally* dear—to me. If, hitherto, I have seemed to attach myself more zealously to the advancement of those of Augusta, it has been because she, as a woman, was the more helpless.

What has been my reward ! Lord Lawton is, as you know, the best alliance of the day, and she has lost him by her coldness and indifference. Never man was so captivated as he, and her invincible *insouciance* has driven him to the feet of my brother's daughter—a brilliant *dénouement*, is it not ?"

Cleveland gazed on his mother—half in surprise, half in fear.

"Then," resumed Lady Sophia, "as if she could not cause me otherwise sufficient annoyance, she flies to Lady K., a person with whom I have the slightest possible acquaintance, and against whom I have warned my daughter as importunately and as vainly as my son against this wretched man Stark. Well—don't interrupt me—just as I am on the eve of recovering from the effects of my daughter's perverseness, my son, with the impetuosity of a barbarian, rushes into my presence, shows me two or three vulgar and ridiculous letters, prostrates himself before me like a dying man in a tragedy, rants considerably, and expects me, forsooth, to love him all the better for his folly."

Cleveland, versed as he was in Lady Sophia's tactics, was even *speechlessly* astonished.

"To complete the scene," said Lady Sophia, "find Mr. Stark, and confront me—*me*—your father's wife—your mother—with that base, bad man. Then call in the whole tribe of the Hamiltons; assure them that I am not altogether unworthy of the honour of being named among their noble kindred ; tell them how warmly you admire your fair cousin Helen Darley, and assure them that you are perfectly and justifiably satisfied with Lawton's engagement with *her*—albeit it happens to have deprived your own and only sister of the best *parti* in the market. Meanwhile, allow me to say, *au revoir*."

"So be it, mother," said Cleveland, rising. "In anguish I came to you, in affection I remained, and in kindness would I have departed. Why will you not allow me to forget, for one short hour, how much you dislike the son of Sir Greville Cleveland ? By Heaven and earth, if it were not madness to think that way, I could—but no ! Mother, fare you well ; I will do you so much justice as to force his recantation from the miscreant Stark."

How unspeakably relieved was Lady Sophia when her son disappeared ! The exertion her interview with him cost her was too exhausting to have been much longer endured. Her grand support had been the certainty that Stark was, by this time, at a very safe distance, and that from him she had nothing more to fear.

The sale of part of her diamonds, effected by Lord Vere, —diamonds lavished on her by the profuse affection of her first husband and the lavish splendour of her second—had furnished a very sufficient bribe to induce Mr. Stark to quit

England for ever. When delay is to the interest of neither party, such transactions are rapidly effected. A few hours had sufficed for the disposal of the jewels, the money, and of Mr. Stark. Unwilling to divide with his creditors any part of the spoil, Mr. Stark had very quietly retreated from town, and with the least possible delay, had betaken himself to the shelter of a steam vessel proceeding to Boulogne. In the certainty that there he should meet with associates quite as distinguished and as honourable as himself, he resolved to enjoy to the utmost his pleasurable disreputability, not being particularly apprehensive of another revolution—the only inconvenience he thinks it possible that his sentence of outlawry could entail on him.

Never loving her son, nothing could have been more humiliating to Lady Sophia than the position which, though but for one short hour, they had assumed relative to each other. Exulting in the moral courage, as she called it, which had so disdainfully trampled on his suspicions and the accusations of Mr. Stark, she nevertheless found it impossible to pardon his momentary superiority. What had formerly been only indifference. was now positive dislike; and using as her plea the agitation and indisposition occasioned by his late violence, she refused to admit him within the privileged precincts of her own apartments.

Accustomed to occupy herself with the interests of her daughter, she endured with considerable impatience the estrangement which subsisted between them. A billet of the most conciliatory kind, sent by her to Lady K.'s, had been answered only by a line to say, Augusta was well, happy, and not about to return just at present, that the house was delightful, the guests united, and Lady K., the most charming person in existence, much wronged by the malice and envy of the world. All this irritated Lady Sophia into a state of feverish restlessness, not at all improved by her perception of the great satisfaction with which her dear five hundred friends congratulated her on the approaching marriage of Lord Lawton with her niece, Miss Darley. Lord Vere too had disappeared. She had seen nothing of him since Augusta went to Richmond, and habit had rendered him as necessary to her as even her daughter was. Weary of herself, but even more disgusted with a world on which —while she knew its heartlessness, its hollowness, its faithlessness—she depended for all the excitement of an existence *without consolations*, she did occasionally question herself whether this was fitly her "being's end and aim." Whether disgust and satiety were so agreeable as to deserve the toil and weariness of spirit with which she, and so many like her, strove to attain unto them. She detected herself deep in an inquiry whether the domestic affections were not really the best blessings of which human life is susceptible;

whether the household charities, homely as they are, were not as worthy of being cultivated by the peer as by the peasant; whether, in short, the grand distinction between herself and Catharine Hamilton did not consist in the fact, that to her the relations of wife and mother were merely conventional associations, while to Catharine they were moral ties comprising moral duties.

Discontented with herself—dissatisfied with the world—having paid a reluctant visit to the now world-forgotten Sir Greville Cleveland—she retreated to her *boudoir*.

She had given orders to be denied to all visiters; and yet as the morning wore away, and her mind became more and more imbittered by its meditations—more and more disgusted by the images presented by conscience, which, like a broken mirror, seemed to reflect not one picture of her distempered self, but a thousand—she felt that the relief of almost any companionship would be welcome. She had forgotten that solitude has no balm for such sorrows as hers—sorrows as depraved as their source—the product of dissipation—leavened with its leaven—existing only in its tainted atmosphere; wounds hopeless of mitigation, except from still deeper draughts of the poison which had inflamed them. Before the grief of the disappointed worldling can find relief in the wisdom which is born of solitude, it must be hallowed by repentance; and Lady Sophia Cleveland knew no holier penitence than the remorse produced by pain. She sighed and wept, not because she would be amended, but because she suffered.

In a mind so constituted—so perverted as hers, reflection rapidly advances to a point where discontent first changes into listlessness—where indignation subsides into ennui. Lady Sophia had reached that point, when an interruption occurred which concentrated all her feelings in one vast surprise. Sir Greville, almost before she was aware that the noiseless door had hastily been thrown open, was in her presence.

Had a phantom risen from the dead it could hardly have more astounded—more appalled her. A martyr to excruciating gout, the world for which he had lived had become one vast blank before him. Society was around him, but like the longed-for draught of Tantalus, it rose continually to his lips without permitting him to quaff it. Solitary within hearing of the echo of the multitude, he was like the prisoner condemned never to pass over the confines of his cell, while voices of joy and rejoicing sounded on all sides. Lady Sophia had that morning left him confined to a chair, from which cushions of the most elastic and elaborate construction could not chase the tyrant pain. He was slowly recovering from one of his severest grapples with his tormentor—just beginning to feel his limbs capable of carrying him across his own apartment—trembling beneath the summer breeze—shrinking from the pressure of the softest female hand; and yet, an hour had but passed, and lo! there he stood—unsupported—alone, with a countenance convulsed either by pain or passion; and for a few brief moments, Lady Sophia admitted the terrific belief that his bodily sufferings had at length affected his senses, and that he—the courtly, the refined, the intellectual, the aristocratic—stood before her, a monument of the ruin of all of Heaven's best gifts—a wretched maniac.

But Sir Greville was not the prey of that worst dread affliction which can assail human beings. He was yet capable of feeling to its full extent—according to the partial view *he* was able to take of the case, *beyond* its full extent—the calamity which had really, in the violence of his mental emotions, rendered him insensible to all corporeal pangs, placing him, during their access, beyond the reach of any agony that was not of the mind.

"Good God!" said Lady Sophia, gasping from terror, "what *has* happened?"

"Do you ask?—can you dare to ask?" said he, in a voice which sounded to the ears of Lady Sophia like the rolling thunder. "Wretched woman, where is my daughter?"

"At Richmond—at Lady K.'s," replied Lady Sophia, terrified into candour and humility.

"Answer me—to whom, and for what have you sold her?" said Sir Greville, leaning against the wall for support.

"Heaven and earth!" shrieked Lady Sophia. "Do not madden me! What of Augusta? What of my child?"

"Your child—my child is at this moment beyond the borders—and with Lord Vere," said Sir Greville, yet more sternly.

Lady Sophia's countenance became rigid. Every tint that was not artificial assumed the hue of death. Her eyes were distended—the veins of her neck swollen. Even Sir Greville was, for a moment, alarmed and softened by her evident agony.

"Did not you suspect—encourage this?" he inquired, in a milder voice. "A cold and estranged father Augusta may have deceived, but surely not the mother who had room in her heart for none besides."

"What was it?—repeat it; no, no—do not slay me!" gasped Lady Sophia, with a bewildered air, her eyes glaring fearfully.

"Our daughter, Augusta Cleveland, is in Scotland with Lord Vere," said Sir Greville, regaining his sternness as he repeated the assurance of the fact which so outraged at once all the pride, the worldliness, and every better feeling of his nature. "Thanks to your example—your tuition—

your counsel—your delusions—your daughter has turned even your own weapons against yourself. Instructed to deceive her father, she has ended by deceiving you, her instructress. Accustomed to regard all things and persons as instruments to be used whenever her selfishness deemed the use of them justifiable or necessary, she has employed even you as the convenient screen, under the shelter of which she has carried on an intercourse which thus finds its scandalous termination."

The eyes of Sophia glared horribly. Twice she essayed to speak, before, half inaudible, the self-convicting exclamation burst from her, the implied avowal of the justice of her punishment—"*Avenging God!*"

They were the last words that burst from a heart oppressed, even to bursting, with the depth of its own guilt—the awfulness of the retribution that had overtaken it. As one scathed by Heaven's lightning, she fell heavily; the blood gushed forth in torrents; it was evident a vessel had been ruptured.

The gay, the brilliant, the rich, the courted, the once beautiful Lady Sophia Cleveland spoke no more. Let us not venture to draw aside the curtains of a deathbed on which "no sign was made!"

There are events of peculiar solemnity occurring in human life, which make the most thoughtless pause, and perhaps are, for the instant, felt most keenly by the least reflecting. Even the cold and icy heart of Lady Vere was appalled by the awful circumstances attending the death of the misguided mother who had loved her beyond all other things; and under the first impression of emotions which partook, perhaps, more of terror than grief, she sought earnestly—almost humbly—a reconciliation with the father she had widowed; and she sought it in vain. The terrible present had revealed to Sir Greville a dim shadowing forth of the deeds of the past, so full of horror that he dared not contemplate them steadily —such as to render the very image of his daughter not only hateful but loathsome to him. Lady Vere, not conscious of the enormous reality of her crime, received his formal renunciation of her with an indignation that dissipated the more gloomy and more healthful terror of her spirit. And the world knew not that such terror had, even for a moment, subdued her; for with all the decency of wo—her countenance, her voice, her manner, just touched by the propriety of sadness—Lady Vere resumed her place in the world, enriched by the inheritance of her mother, and exhibited herself to the augmented admiration of society. As to Lord Vere, impenetrable equally to love and remorse, he used, without scruple, the wealth that so increased his means of luxury and pleasure, and tolerated, with the habitual politeness of an apathetic worldling, the instrument by whose means he had procured it.

In the hour of his double trial, it was the Hamiltons who supported and consoled the stricken Sir Greville; it was they who laboured to direct his mind to higher and worthier aspirations; to soften his memory of the dead into sorrow; his feelings for the living into pardon. But it was long before he could endure the kindness of the husband of Catharine—long before he could submit to the humiliation of accepting consolation from her whose very name had, for years, sounded to his senses as a knell of remorse and regret. And when he saw her surrounded by the husband whose honour she was; the children who revered her as the best blessing bestowed on their sunny lot—how could he avoid the painful self-reproach: "All this might have been mine, and I put it from me!" But he was not quite beyond the reach of better feelings. He was not inaccessible to a gratitude, approaching to veneration, for those by whose efforts his son had been saved from the perils of a course which threatens shipwreck to all who have the temerity to navigate it. He could venture to contemplate the future with something like hope, as he viewed it connected with his son. "And even this, this solitary blessing—I owe to her and hers!" he repeated often, but gradually with less bitterness; and Colonel Hamilton hailed it as a symptom that his mind was regaining a healthy tone, as he observed that the society of *his* family, instead of being endured painfully as at first, began to be sought as an indulgence, and afterward as an indispensable necessary of life.

But it was impossible that a man constituted like Sir Greville could avoid contrasting the different results produced by different principles of action, or cease to regret the self-indulgence which had been his destruction.

"Now," said he to Colonel Hamilton, "as we approach the decline of life, behold the vista which is to terminate our several careers. You—happy—honoured—surrounded by your children's children—recalling the past with satisfaction, rejoicing in the present, contemplating the future without fear—honouring God and useful to man; you will number your years only by augmented blessings. Even the indispensable trials which make an integral part of human life will be softened to you by the consciousness that, if they are afflictions, they are not punishments. It is the proudest wish of your son to resemble you; it is the best prayer you can offer for your daughters, that they may be worthy of their mother. While I—

"Reflect on my boundless advantages—the abused talents for which I have deserved *many stripes.* A youth of vice, a manhood of indolence and luxury, an autumn of asperity and misanthropy—what will, what ought age to be to me, but a perpetual repentance?

"Instead of being an example to my son, what am I but a beacon to warn him? Instead of being cheered by my daughter in my last hour, I dare not venture to look on her, lest the perfect charity befitting that dread moment should be broken. Mine was the crime of giving her such a mother—mine the neglect of leaving her to that mother's guidance. Verily, 'I have sown the wind, and reaped the whirlwind.'

"Is not that man to be pitied for whom his friends can implore no greater blessing than that he may never cease to repent?"

"Sir Greville Cleveland may still be useful," said Mrs. Hamilton, to whom her husband repeated the gloomy strain of thought into which the unfortunate man had fallen. "Happily for us, so long as we have active duties to perform, we cannot be miserable. Occupation—labour, if you will—brings content. Benevolence also brings its reward; and to be interested for others is the sure way of increasing our own measure of happiness. Roused from his incessant care for self, Sir Greville is beginning to feel pleasure in thinking on the means of being useful to Lawton and Helen—*useful* if only so far as lending them a house for the honeymoon. Then he insists on giving Rachel a splendid trousseau—an act at once kind and becoming; he will find satisfaction in reflecting that he is removing from a young and portionless bride, if a trifling, yet a natural subject of anxiety. Then I can percieve he is indulging sundry speculations on the probability of the marriage of his son with our little Catharine—visions, of the vanity of which you and I, who have had ample proof of the mutability of youth, are satisfied, but which do not the less delight him, and which, if not realized precisely as he wishes, will nevertheless not inflict any severe disappointment. Thinking of women as he does, and growing humbler and wiser, as he is, Greville will present such a daughter-in-law to his father as that father will be proud to acknowledge. *The past* will teach Sir Greville to walk humbly with his God, and *the present* will furnish him with daily experience of the happiness to be found by being useful to man."

"Do you think," said Colonel Hamilton, looking on Catharine with all the fondness of a lover, "that he will ever cease to regret having thrown 'a pearl away, richer than all its tribe?' Maid—wife—mother—oh, Catharine, may my children resemble thee!"

THE END.

CPSIA information can be obtained
at www.ICGtesting.com
Printed in the USA
LVHW101117120123
736978LV00003B/229

9 783375 130473